On Loss

an anthology

Edited by
Aaron Pasker
Michael Riley
Erica Marchant
Melissa Schell
Joshua George

Cover Design by
Erica Marchant

Learn more about this anthology and its authors at
Ourlossanthology.com

Published by: Aaron Pasker, Erica Marchant, Michael Riley, Melissa Schell, Joshua George.

Cover Photo copyright Jeremy Bishop on Unsplash

Cover Design copyright Erica Marchant

Book Design and Production Aaron Pasker and Erica Marchant

Edited by: Aaron Pasker, Erica Marchant, Michael Riley, Melissa Schell, and Joshua George

ISBN: 9781073562671

Acknowledgments

When we joined this anthology team, we had no idea where it would take us. Hundreds of authors submitted their best work to our fledgling anthology surprising us with such great interest. None of us realized an anthology on the subject of loss and pain touched so many lives and created so many stories.

Thank you to everyone who submitted but didn't make it. We hope you keep writing and keep submitting. Never give up on the dream. There is a place for your work.

To the authors that fill these pages, we thank you for trusting us with your work. Without you, this anthology wouldn't be beautiful. It wouldn't be real. It wouldn't be worth the time and effort.

We'd like to acknowledge Aaron Pasker, who thought up this crazy idea, found a bunch of strangers willing to work together, and had the perseverance to keep us creating from inception to publication. Without him, On Loss wouldn't exist.

~Erica Marchant, Melissa Schell, Michael Riley, Joshua George

I'd like to thank my writing group for their encouragement and honesty. They help me make my writing shine—and make sense. My local Wilmington Public library for fostering the love of writing and reading every day, and for giving me a quiet space to work whenever I needed it. I'd be remiss if I didn't give a special shout-out and extra big thank you to my patient husband, Sean, who works hard so I can live this fantasy life called being a writer. And, my kids who forgive me whenever I ignore them while in the midst of the next great idea. Connor, Madelyn, and Finn. My loves, my heart.

~Erica Marchant

I want to thank my love, Dallas. Dallas, without you, I would have never started trying to find other writers to connect with. You always give me the courage I need to pursue my dreams, and I couldn't be more grateful to have someone like you by my side.

~Melissa Schell

Table of Contents

With life comes the inherent risk of loss.

Bluebells

By Christy Nicholas

The sylvan path beckoned me with nostalgic recollections of youth.

I hadn't been allowed to walk in this place for many years. Now, I devoured each detail, hoarding the precious memories against all time.

When I last strolled through my beloved woods, the bluebells carpeted the ground as azure silk, fluttering with the gentle spring breeze. Mockingbirds sang a sweet morning melody to caress my ears and soothe my troubled soul.

Now, however, the icy hawthorn tore at my faded flowered dress. The brambles caught cruelly at the worn cotton, unwilling to allow me to flee their thorny embrace. Icy slush muddied the path once strewn with sparkling stepping stones.

No one had paid tribute here for ages.

I recall, as a rambunctious child, darting under the hollyhock in search of cherubic fairies dancing among dewdrops and mushroom rings. With fervent giggles, I searched high and low for the tinkling bells that betrayed their fleeting voices. Now, the only sounds that greeted my hopeful ears were the soughing of barren branches in the bitter winter wind and the raucous call of carrion crows.

It was better I could never return.

The pain in my chest heralded the finale of this desperate pilgrimage. I had to return now, return to the tubes and wires, return to the monitors and mournful relatives. I had to return to my final farewell among those that professed to care for me.

The forest had been my only true love.

Stasis

By Lynne Buchanan

He sorts through the stacks of paper detritus, accumulated over the course of many years. Keep this, throw that away. The garbage pile grows larger very quickly. Amazing, all the things we keep that we don't really need. Then the photograph is in his hand, and she is smiling up at him in black and white, a look of pleased surprise on her face. Her face is so young. The pain still living somewhere in her future has yet to leave its marks upon her features.

Just inside the frame of the photo near the bottom edge: her teacup. The cup she had used every morning for as long as he had known her. Her hand must have nudged it off the counter as she turned, surprised, to the camera.

The teacup is falling.

He stares at it there, hovering like a magic trick, frozen in the space between the counter and the floor. In this moment it is forever falling, forever unbroken.

His hand seems almost to float in the dusty attic sunlight, suspended in the air between the pile of things to keep and the things that he can finally let go.

Check Mate

By Chad V. Broughman

"Ain't right. Men don't think about shit like that." Dad's voice was big, and the house's insulation scant.

On the other side of the wall, Michael leaned in, listening for Ma's reply.

"I know, dear, it's a strange thing. But he's still our boy." Through the meager paneling, Michael felt Ma's strain, trying to placate her husband and protect her frail son.

"Nah. If a boy of mine was feeling bad about himself, he'd run around the block a time or two, lay off the beers. He wouldn't stick his fingers down his fuckin throat."

"He'll hear you." Ma's voice shifted downward. "It's Christmas, let's not do this."

In the stillness that followed, Michael continued wrapping presents with his little sister, Vanessa, as they waited for their parents to emerge. Coming home was a mistake. He hadn't visited since last winter and was down another six pounds, back under one-twenty. At five foot eleven, he knew how wilted he was, but thinking about it never changed anything. Besides, he'd already set his new goal: one-fifteen.

After he'd fainted at the student union, the counselor at the campus clinic told him to take time off. A master's degree can wait, she said, you're not well. She wrote down a couple of numbers on a sticky note and handed him an arm full of pamphlets. Because Michael thought she was nice, he waited until he got to his apartment to throw them away.

In the trash can, on top of the pile, a flyer with a scraggy woman standing in front of a mirror, no makeup, mouth agape, stared up at him. Her right hand was balled up, the knuckle of her index finger wiping away a shiny tear. Her left, palm up, held a clump of hair, the strands hanging down between slender fingers.

When hair fell out, that's when he'd surrender.

A week later, he had to follow through on his promise. For several minutes, he stared at the patch of scalp, blank and pale, reflecting in the mirror, too nervous to acknowledge the coarse, black proof that tangled in the tines of his brush. The coming symptoms frightened him, but going home, into the awkward arms of his broken family, scared him more.

Call on your family, the doctor had said, they might surprise you. At that moment, he had let himself hope. Maybe, just maybe, he thought. But then, he walked through the front door.

Ma brought her hands to her face, the horror showing in her wide, glistening eyes. "You look so handsome." The clumsy fidgeting of her hands exposed growing embarrassment.

Over her shoulder, Michael caught Dad's eyes. They gave each other a slow nod then he retreated back into Ma's embrace and Dad back into his newspaper.

Pressing a strip of shiny ribbon between his thumb and the scissor blade, Michael pulled the blade toward his bony chest.

"Ta-da! A curlicue. Looks like one of those Cinnabons," he said, cocking his head, examining his work, "Without all that sticky stuff."

Though he smiled, his thoughts were about how feeble he must look and sound to Vanessa, she, a high-schooler, and he, a twenty-four-year-old skeleton with a thin, wobbly voice and loose teeth.

"My wrapping is terrible," she said. "Looks like a papier-mâché project."

Michael looked at the slipshod mess in her lap and chuckled.

"Yeah, by a preschooler maybe," he said, then poked her with his elbow till she laughed.

In front of them, just above the television, was a long shelf supported on each end by a thick corbel, the classic kind with loops and tendril-like carvings. Dad had stained the wood a hard brown, almost burgundy. To Michael's recollection, it had always held the same knick-knacks: Ma's fairy figurines, a couple of vases filled with glass flowers and smooth, polished rocks, a framed Ansel Adams with a wide, gray river winding behind a jagged, snow-capped mountain, and in the center of it all, were the trophies.

For Vanessa, there were several, all from 4-H, the old-fashioned kind with wide-handled chalices. Even though the gold coating had begun to peel, Ma kept them showcased. For Michael, there was just one, but it was tall and held its sheen. Regional Champion. A white-yellow plaited wrestler stood poised for a take-down, arms open, waist height. On the wood base, etched into a small square plate, was a passage: Believe in yourself, when no one else will. The letters were tiny, you had to step in close to read them.

From time to time, though less vividly now, Michael envisioned Coach hunkered down on the mat, eye level with a wrestler about to be pinned. He'd speak those words as if the boy wasn't twisted up like a pretzel, mounted by a competitor, with dozens watching from the stands. Coach could always make it seem like only the two of you were in the gym. Even when Michael wasn't the one being driven from the throes of defeat, he relished in those moments. The hope felt good, as did knowing that he was part of something bigger than himself, a necessary spoke in the wheel of a team.

That was a world ago, back when the only reason for shedding pounds was to make the lower weight class to win a tournament. For hours, Michael spat into his red solo cup (the one he held between his knees so the teachers couldn't see it) just to lose an extra ounce or two. He ate only oranges, day after day. And sometimes, when the laxatives took hold in class, he'd have to sprint to the bathroom with his head flimsy and light, tottering like a paper airplane. It all mattered back then; there was a purpose to it.

Michael didn't blame Coach. He knew the man's heart was good. Push the sissy kid into a sport, he probably thought, give him a place to fit in. Hell, it worked, for a while. Through his junior year, Michael was a varsity wrestler and a damn good one. Folks stopped calling him a pussy, even Dad. Then Michael kept molting, long after the seasons ended.

The bedroom door made a low whoosh sound against the nappy carpet when Dad pulled it open and headed to the living room, the floor groaning under his heavy steps. When he first came into view, he slowed to a stop, eyes narrowed, lips tapered out. Michael hoped it was a sign of compassion, maybe Dad realized that the house was too small for all his hateful words. But he passed them by, wordlessly, and plunked down in his recliner in the far corner. Per usual, Dad fanned out the *Michigan Daily* with great effort, covering his bristly face.

"Did you see Michael's wrapping," Vanessa called to him. "Looks better than when Macy's does it, don't you think?"

Dad bent the newspaper and peered over it. "All looks the same to me, fancy paper and bows," he said, then shook his head in a broad, sluggish sweep and righted his *Michigan Daily*.

Before Vanessa could respond, Michael pushed his finger to her lips, stricken by how spindly it looked next to her fresh, pink cheeks.

Dad turned the page, rustling the paper like it was fighting him, then resumed reading. Though his thick fingers covered some of the lines, Michael could see the date—December 23, 1981—and a headline: *Adam Walsh's Story: Gone Too Soon*. Beneath the caption was the famous picture of the young boy, the one on all the "Missing" flyers—a red baseball cap with a white, cursive C, holding his little league bat, mussed hair in his eyes. He recalled the day Adam's severed head was found.

By college, Michael had learned to hide his emotions, or at least curb them. He did that day too, recalling the words of his history teacher after tearing up during a documentary on the Holocaust. Stop wearing your heart on your sleeve, Michael, you're too soft. But thinking of Adam's terror when the stranger first manhandled him proved too much. He wondered if Adam called out for his mother and father, or if he stayed silent, afraid to cry.

Dad folded the paper down to a single column, burying the article. It held no interest to him, Michael presumed. A curl of wooly black hair fell over Dad's high forehead, and it bothered Michael that he did not brush it away.

In Vanessa's slanted brow, Michael sensed her urge to petition Dad again. He mouthed "no" and from inside the bag next to him, pulled out the next gift to be wrapped. It was Dad's. A custom built box for chess pieces, made of dense, richly beige rosewood, finely textured with a glossy, sleek finish.

Michael turned his back so Dad could not see the gift, the one he'd saved for most of the year and sent back twice. First, the hue wasn't right, too dull; the second time there was a small mar on the lid. He picked up a tube of silver paper with a pattern of tiny bells and dark green holly and looked to Vanessa. She nodded in approval.

"Dinner's ready," Ma beckoned, stepping into the living room.

She smoothed her bulky apron with both hands, her eyes roving from Vanessa to Michael, eventually fixing on Dad. Her anxiousness was weighty, and Michael hurt to know his presence was the cause. He wanted to grab her chafed hands and hold them in his own, but that wasn't how they did things.

"Damn left-wings," Dad grunted. He flicked the newspaper with the back of his fingers. "Now this Chavez duck is whining 'bout more rights? And I'll be damned if all these bleeding hearts ain't doting on him like he's some kinda hero. These God-forsaken liberals are plowing this country under. I tell you what—"

"Can you put that down, honey?" Ma asked. "Come to the table."

"I'm eating in here." Dad snapped the paper again.

From the floor, Michael thought his father looked smaller, especially perched behind all the world's affairs. He pictured himself marching over to Dad's chair, crouching down till they were nose-to-nose. In an even keel, he would say, "You're a mean son of a bitch. Stupid, too."

Michael thought about all the strings attached to Dad's love. How when you're weak, he walks away, but when you're steady, he takes you fishing.

In middle school, when the boys started blowing kisses and calling Michael a faggot, Dad had said, stop acting like one. The worse the jeering, the quieter Dad became, eventually passing Michael by on his way out the door alone, pole and creel in tow. It was only later, after Coach recruited Michael for wrestling, that Dad came back around.

At tournaments, he could be heard above the crowd, shouting things like, "That's my boy," and to whoever would listen, he would tell stories of how they used to tangle together on the floor, beaming with pride at the son he helped to shape. Yet after the last match, when the weight kept coming off and the nosebleeds started, Dad began his final retreat.

The bullying reignited, more creative, more intense than ever. Things bottomed out when Principal Miller showed up on their doorstep for a home visit to tell Ma and Dad about the boys who held their son down in the shower and pissed on him, one-by-one.

Michael spied from the hallway, listening intently, trying not to see Dad's deadpan expression. It hurt more than the stiff urine still caked in his hair. Miss Miller told them that the boys called him an easy target because—then she inhaled through her nose and pulled back her shoulders—he acts like a girl and never fights back. At this, Dad held up his hand and said he had heard enough while Michael crept to his room unseen.

Through his bedroom window came the familiar clank and clatter of Dad rummaging for his fishing gear, followed by the crunch of his truck tires against the pea stone as he left for the river.

Michael sat the gift-wrap on the floor then pushed the chess set across the carpet, stopping it at Dad's feet. He hadn't thought his actions through, he just wanted to keep the peace. So when Dad asked what the hell he was doing, he fumbled.

"I taught myself to play," he finally said. Dad didn't smile, but he didn't turn away either. "I remember, no matter who came by, you always asked if they knew how to play. No one ever did."

Dad picked up two of the knights and was rolling his thumb across them, tenderly, like a rabbit's foot. A wordless void ensued, but Michael fought his instinct to fill it, waiting out the silence.

"I'll get my board," Dad said. Then, before heading towards the hall, he added, "Those pieces. You know, the ones you bought there. They're good ones."

They played well into the night. Only a handful of words exchanged, mostly mutterings from Dad, and an occasional "damn" from both of them.

Michael had read through the "how to" guide that came with the chess set, garnering a loose understanding of castling a rook. For the first couple of games, Michael kept his king and both rooks in place, peaking at Dad now and again, basking in his furrowed forehead. When the time came, he slid the stately king to the right, slow and dramatic, then set the rook queenside and brushed his hands together. Dad made a low sigh then clicked his tongue several times.

The mood was dense, but there was favor in it. Michael saw the quick glances between Ma and Vanessa, as they made up reasons to keep walking by. He was gladdened by their tiny smirks. For a fleeting moment, he swore he could feel Dad's blood pushing through his own veins.

Though he lost every game, Michael made Dad work for the wins. Then, at the end of the last match, as he feared it would, fatigue set in. For him, it wasn't just feeling tired or weary, he could fight that. It was wading through a muddy swamp wearing concrete shoes, bearing boulders on his back. It was jet-lag and a hangover at the same time. It was full-tilt, every time, and always, always crippling.

When Dad began to arrange the pieces for another game, Michael had to confess his feebleness.

"I'm tired," he said. But his father continued to assemble the game, positioning the pieces just so.

"I can't play anymore."

"Nonsense, boy. You can too."

"Look at me, Dad."

With bishop in hand, Dad stopped and raised his head. Michael watched his face slacken as his mouth shrank into a straight line. Dad leaned back and lowered his gaze to the board. Michael said good night, knowing that a slight nod was the most he could hope for.

It wasn't until late afternoon that Michael made his way to the kitchen. Standing at the sink, arms up to her elbows in cloudy suds, Ma dipped her head at him, offering half a grin. The Christmas Eve spread was already on the table, mirroring the Last Supper, a blend of spices amidst the shaky optimism. Outside, a corn-yellow sun shone down upon the blinding white snow.

The three of them sat at the family table, breathing in the newly baked bread, the sweet, buttery smell of pumpkin pie, and the heady aroma of roasted turkey. They pretended Dad wasn't a couple arm's lengths away, choosing to sit in the other room as usual.

"Smells good, Ma. Can't wait for the—" Michael's front tooth loosened. He pinched it with his fingers and jiggled it some, then spat it into his hand. The familiar sour of his stomach had leaked into his mouth. He no longer had to retch for the fire to begin, just the thought of food caused the briny taste to creep up his throat and coat his yellow teeth.

"Was that your tooth?" Vanessa blurted.

"Well," Ma cut in, her neck clenched, "the relish might be a bit tart."

 She handed her son a tissue, discreetly, and patted Vanessa's head, just once. Michael blotted at the hole in his mouth. "I used apple cider vinegar this year," Ma said, before turning back toward the counter where she braced herself against the laminate.

 Michael watched her shoulders rise and fall. He thought her magnificent. His gutlessness felt big, conspicuous. Year after year, as she pacified Pa's pride at the expense of her own, he'd never risen up, never tried to protect her.

 Like the winter Dad crashed his Ford Thunderbird into a grove of hardwoods but told the neighbors Ma did it. Vanessa was only seven. At dinner that Sunday, she asked Dad why he told everyone at church that Ma wrecked the car.

 "That's grown-up business, Vanessa," Ma said.

 "But you can't even drive. How—"

 "Pass the sweet corn, dear." Though Vanessa quieted, she kept her face wrenched in defiance of the mistruth. Michael merely stared at his mashed potatoes.

 Or the time Dad applied for a supervisor job at the foundry, and Ma slaved over his inquiry letter. After Dad got the promotion, the new boss came for dinner.

 The man, with a round, doughy face and a bulging paunch that stretched the green diamonds in his argyle sweater, handed Ma a bottle of Merlot and said, "Congratulations ma'am. You must be proud." Then he shook off his coat, saying, "And that letter. Your husband is a poet."

 Dad put his arm around Ma's shoulder, heavily, and snatched the bottle with his free hand.

 "I sure married me a looker," he said. "Didn't I?" As Dad studied the label, head down, he continued, "Yeah. She ain't too bright, but she's a pretty gal."

 Ma fidgeted then drew in her breath, stood tall and nodded at both men fully. Though his lungs squeezed and his heart pounded loud and clumsy, Michael stayed silent. As Ma ushered everyone toward the dining room, she winked at him, her eyes wet and glowing, as if to say, take note son, here's what strength looks like.

 Michael reached for another tissue and dabbed at his mouth. Vanessa began humming "Little Drummer Boy," and he joined in. Observing his mother from behind, he marked how her once solid frame had begun to bend under the burdens of age and worry.

 I'm sorry for never saying sorry.

 "How about more turkey?" Dad barked from his chair. Michael turned to Vanessa and parodied him, crossing his eyes, exaggerating a frown. She giggled. So did Ma. Having diverted their attention, he tried to sustain it. He lifted a heaping spoonful of relish to his chin.

Let them see me eating, give them some short-lived cheer.

He paused. *Do it!* He berated himself. *This isn't about you right now.* With great flair, he thrust the moss-green mound into his mouth. The peppery dill mingled with the salty remnants of blood. Vanessa squirmed in her chair while Ma managed a thin smile. Feeling bolstered, Michael fought the gag reflex.

Knowing the new cavity would cause a lisp, Michael could only smirk in response, close-lipped. If his 's' sounds became more sibilant now, they'd be deafening. The thought of sputtering made his heart flutter, then skip, and there was still dinner to get through. Michael tamed his breathing—

In through the nose, out through the mouth, just get to the bathroom.

He began filtering sentences through his mind till he found one without any tricky 's' sounds. Finally, he said carefully, enunciating each word, "I'm–heading–to–the–john," then heaved himself up from the table.

"Oh Michael," Ma begged, "You're not—"

"Let–it–go–Ma." The tiny blots of blood on his shirt were a rich, deep red, and he worried they would draw more attention, so he sidled into the hall like a crab, stopping at each family picture on the wall. Some of them, he'd celebrated; most he'd grieved. Though he knew the waiting would be brutal for Ma and Vanessa, he paused longest before the bathroom door, studying a perfectly hung picture of his parents in their younger years. Ma wore her Sunday best, a lavender taffeta dress and matching bell-shaped hat, and Dad was in his dress blues, vivid and crisp, his ample, dark hair coiffed just right. Before stepping into the bathroom, Michael turned back to Vanessa and through the hole in his front teeth, wriggled his tongue at her. This time, she did not laugh.

Michael had learned to muffle the retching by turning on the faucet and the fan, or by flushing the commode. He'd tell himself to breathe through the twisting, quick breaths, followed by slow and constant ones. Sometimes, though, if the force was too much, his lanky frame would pull in all different directions, and he'd gasp or heave. Like now. Michael knew his family had heard it, but someone had turned up the radio, most likely Ma. Relief swept over him like a light wind. Her compassion made him want to resist the final purge, but experience had taught him not to waste energy on such futile things.

"Now light that yule log and grab your lover. It's the artist heard by more than any other on earth." The disc jockey's holiday cheer seeped through the vent, rude and bumbling in the stillness. Then, Bing Crosby's low tenor poured forth, "I'm dreaming, of a white Christmas…" and Michael tried to vomit again. Only bile. He could feel Ma's eyes on the door. Someone turned up the volume even louder.

"Turn that shit down!" Dad bellowed. After the music clicked off, Pa's ungainly movements banged through the kitchen and beyond. His voice resonated when he asked, "How long's he been in there?"

Michael felt the lull that followed, only the ting of a fork against a plate and the low drone of the furnace. In his mind, he saw Ma chewing desperately, pointing to her mouth and raising her shoulders in feigned ignorance while Vanessa looked out the window in insolence. More dead air. Michael's heart quickened, waiting for a slam or shout. When Dad asked 'how long' again, his pitch was cool, the words drawn out. He exhaled, not realizing he'd been holding his breath.

The doorknob rattled.

"Leave him alone," Vanessa said. Her voice was sharp, even lordly. Michael braced himself against the bowl, knowing Dad would burst through it before he could pull himself up. One more jolt of the knob was all it took.

The disillusionment of the scene shown in Dad's countenance; his only son kneeling by the toilet, the stench of rancid puke, and the shame. Dad's eyes swelled, his jaw set.

"Get up, boy." He bent over Michael and grabbed his arm, but paused. They both looked at Dad's fist, wrapped around Michael's meager arm like a gear shaft. Dad held tight for a moment longer then loosened his grip.

"I'm afraid, Dad."

"Of what, for shit sake? Some meat on your bones?"

"No. That's not—"

"Then what? Food? Is that it?"

Michael shook his head, slow at first, but Dad persisted. As the pitch in his voice heightened, so did Michael's sway.

"Afraid of food? Then eat, damn it. I don't get—"

"Of you." The room closed in. Michael felt a hard drain as if he'd crested the top of a rollercoaster, stomach floating. "Isn't that what you want, Dad? To be feared?"

Dad cast down his eyes. Turning on his heal, he left without another word. Only a slight footprint in his wake, a few spatters of pink toilet water, and a thread or two of hair remained.

Michael lay his spent body on the cold, damp tile, listening for the rumble of Dad's truck, and his mind drifted to a future he might not see. To a fall afternoon, brisk and blue. To his parent's house, still and quiet. Without provocation, Dad would wrinkle up his paper and toss it aside. He'd turn toward the center shelf and stare at the little brass wrestler before rising from his Lazy Boy and stepping lightly to the couch where Ma sits. Silently, he'd stoop down before her and rest his head on her lap. "Tell me about my son," he'd say. The intimacy would startle her, and she'd look at the ceiling, balling up her fists. But just as quickly, Ma would fan out her fingers and bring them down gently, stroking Dad's thin, white hair.

"Well, he knew you cared," she'd lie. "And he was beautiful."

Michael made his way to the window and looked into the side yard then lay back on the floor and pulled his knees into his chest. Amidst the woe and burn, he savored the hope that came with Dad's truck, still parked in the driveway.

Threads

By Leah George

I open my eyes.

Good, I'm in my room, sitting in my chair. This is where I should be. My dresser is against the wall; the pictures and knick-knacks in place on top. Across from it, the bed, neatly made. On the bed are two of the pillows Mom and I cross stitched when I was young. Those pillows, all the colorful threads, are the memories of the life I've lived.

One of the pillows isn't where it should be. My heart thuds in my chest before I realize I'm clutching it in my hands. Pink threads are scattered across the top. Ah, oh no. I've pulled them from the roses. They're gone, the threads now just pieces in my lap. Pink, what was pink? I don't know. It's as gone from me as it is from the pillow. What's left?

I trace a leaf with my finger. The green threads that make up the leaves: me, Mom and Grams on the glider out back of Gram's house, breaking beans. Grams would make an event of it, us girls, drinking lemonade, laughing and breaking. She would cook them in the pressure cooker with potatoes and fatback. They smelled awful cooking, but they tasted so good. I can't remember the last time I had beans that good.

The blue threads woven throughout the flowers: all different shades. There's that beautiful thread of blue-green like water. That one is the time my sweet Michael took me on a boat trip. Just for the day, but the perfect day. The sky, the water, his eyes, all threads of blue. His eyes sparkled as he asked me to marry him. One of the happiest days of my life. I remember that. I remember Michael is blue.

I open my eyes.

I'm standing under the tree in the back yard, staring up into its thick branches. Oh. I've lost another thread, probably more than one. I'm paralyzed for a moment. How did I get here? I begin to tremble and choke on the catch in my throat. I don't want to cry.

"Mama, come on, come sit with me." My daughter takes my arm and leads me to the lawn chair with a purple cushion.

Purple threads: purple is joy. It's this precious woman, my baby girl, my one and only. Purple is her mad giggles when she was three, her rage when she was fourteen and I wouldn't take her to a concert. It's her prom gown, her wedding flowers, and the teddy bear she gave to her first child.

"It's okay Mama, you're okay. Come on. Sit with me. Look at

me." She doesn't realize I've opened my eyes, that I see her, know her.

"I'm here," I say, my voice scratchy. From disuse? From screaming? Either is possible and I have no way of knowing which it is unless I ask. I'll save her the pain, myself the shame and embarrassment.

"Hi, Mama."

"Hi, Baby." We sit for a while. She's calm now that I'm the me she knows. It's worse now, this losing of threads. My eyes blur with tears.

"Oh, Mama." She reaches for me.

I put a hand out to stop her. She only wants to help me hold the threads together, but I need to hold them myself. Pink, green, yellow blue, purple, and so many more, each with its own texture, is a part of who I am. When I lose one, I lose more of me.

I'm told that, on some days, I forget that my husband, the love of my life, has been dead almost 15 years. That on others that I wander around in the night in my gown, that neighbors—and once the police—return me to my daughter.

It's bad enough I'm in her care. No mother wants that. But now I'm a broken thing she can't discard because she loves. And because she loves, she tries to be patient, to understand. She tells me to forgive myself the missing threads, that she's grateful for what remains. Her willingness, her determination hurts me. I would not be this for her. I'm angry that my own brain is picking me apart, one thread at a time.

I open my eyes.

I'm lying on my back, staring at a ceiling I don't recognize. It's white and bubbled. I don't understand. I make a sound in the back of my throat and my daughter's face appears in my vision. I feel her squeeze my hand while my eyes dart around the room.

"Mama, it's okay. It's me, I'm here. Shssh Mama, sshhh, please. I love you. It's going to be okay."

I think, from her voice, that she's been saying this over and over, a litany of reassurance. She's been crying, her voice is thick with tears. I squeeze her hand back. I'm not ready to speak. I realize now where we are. I search my mind for threads.

Yellow. Yellow is every flower I've ever planted, regardless of the color of the bloom. Yellow is the satisfaction I got from planting them, watching them grow and then flower. It's the warm sun on my skin. Yellow has nothing to do with the antiseptic that I am breathing in, nothing to do with the beeps in the background or with the machines that line the wall. Those threads are gray. They belong to the death of my beloved Michael, of my Mom and Dad.

Those threads, yellow and gray at least, I'm still holding. I squeeze her hand again. "I'm sorry, baby. I see you. What happened?" I watch her shoulders slump as she realizes, at least for now, my eyes are open. She looks so tired.

"It's okay, mama. All that matters is that you're okay."

I watch her tears start again and feel my own eyes begin to water. It's not okay. I didn't know who she was. She is purple. I'd almost lost purple.

We are past the point that she'll tell me of my most recent transgression. She doesn't want to add to my hurt, I think, so she carries it alone. I am her mother and now she mothers me, protects me from myself. What value is a life such as this? What value to her? Still, we hang on, to each other and to those threads that bind us together.

One day soon, I won't open my eyes to these precious threads anymore. No more purple, no more blue or yellow. When they are gone, I am gone.

Malmedy

By Michael Riley

Stanley knew this day would eventually come, the day when one of them would sit alone, the last vestige of a time long past. The question of which of them it would be had finally been answered.

Every other December 17th for sixty years, the members of Battery B of the 285th Field Artillery Observation Battalion met here. Twenty-one survived the massacre. They gathered to mourn the eighty-four brothers in arms that were lost. They came to remember each other. Over the years their numbers had dwindled.

Some stopped coming as the memories of their service faded, their lives had moved on. Others had finally succumbed to the human mortality evaded on that day. This was the last meeting, Stanley Taylor was its only attendee.

The old man sat in the corner booth, his only company the coffee in front of him and his memories. A pane of glass, frosted at the corners and edges, separated him from the town square beyond.

Winter had set in on the brick-paved expanse of empty planters, their flowers gone, their shrubs asleep. Light spilled from the lamp posts and reflected softly on the dusting of freshly fallen snow. Patrons bundled against the cold hurried to purchase last minute Christmas gifts in the rows of old shops bordering the square. The twin spires of the old cathedral towered over it all, their silhouettes blended with the cold gray sky fading into night. It was a scene that had unfolded before him many times.

"Sir?" The waitress's voice pulled him from his reverie. "Would you like some more coffee while you wait?"

He glanced at the clock hanging on the stone wall of the quaint restaurant. Seven Thirty.

"It doesn't look like there will be anyone joining me after all. I'll take you up on the coffee and also the check if you don't mind."

"Of course"

He looked out the window again, the sky had turned an inky black. The lights of the storefronts extinguished one by one until finally, all were dark.

The coffee grew cold, the check rested patiently on the table next to it. Still, he sat waiting with anticipation for a familiar face to stroll past the window and into the restaurant. He drifted back to December 17th, 1944.

* * *

At first, there was only pain. Without memory or thought, Stanley existed solely within the searing agony of his shoulder, a white-hot fire that consumed his consciousness. Another sensation existed however, an undercurrent that ran beneath the pain, numbing and heavy. Cold. He was unable to move. Every time the darkness washed over him, suffocating his mind in its thick fog, the pain brought him back.

He slowly opened his eyes, a sheet of dull gray flooded his vision. Vague shapes played on the periphery of his sight, the bare limbs of trees obscured by fog reaching for the winter sky.

Why am I in a field?

The question floated across the stage of his mind before being driven away by the unrelenting pain.

He inhaled through his nose, pulling air deep into his lungs. It brought the sting of the chilled winter, but something else came in with it, a sweet metallic scent that he couldn't quite place...

Blood!

Memories flooded his mind. The attack at the Baugnez crossroads, the surrender to the 1st SS Panzer Division, the march through the snow across the field toward the line of German trucks waiting to take them, and then...

He sat up, the piercing pain of the bullet still lodged in his shoulder caused his head to swim and his vision to fade. When his vision returned, the horror it revealed would forever be etched into his memory.

Shredded bodies littered the field before him. The twisted and grotesque corpses told the grizzly tale of what had happened here. The look of surprise and terror was frozen in time on the faces of some of the fallen; their dead eyes stared blankly into the abyss. They were the lucky ones.

He struggled to get to his feet, twice falling back into the blood-stained snow. He had to get out of here. He had to get to the cover of the trees.

Fueled by panic and adrenaline, he found his footing and began his exodus to the safety of the forest.

He stumbled through the carnage. Frozen bodies lay half covered in snow kicked up by the boots of others who had tripped over them. Grooves of crimson carved into white from the fingertips of those who could no longer walk, evidence of their last desperate attempt to claw themselves to safety. A body without a head. Another with the chest torn open, the features identifiable through a mask of blood, the face of his friend.

Behind the chaotic canvas of red on white and the broken, lifeless bodies was the ever-present sickeningly metallic stench of death.

He hunched forward, his stomach hitching painfully. The acidic taste of vomit filled his mouth and spilled hot onto the frozen ground. He swiped his chin with the back of his hand and pressed on into the woods.

The forest offered meager concealment but traded that cover for disorientation. The bare skeletons of the winter trees enveloped him, surrounding him in isolation. Any path that was visible in the summer months now lay buried beneath the blanket of snow. The cold gray sky extended unbroken in every direction. The scene around him was identical in all directions.

He needed to move west toward Malmedy. The allies still held it as of this morning and he knew that in his condition it was the only destination he had a chance of making.

The Germans had stripped them of everything of value before marching them into the field for execution. He had no compass, no map, and no way to signal for rescue— even if there was someone to receive the message. The only measure of direction was the distant rumble of exploding mortars. The Germans were advancing from the east. He put the sounds of war to his back and trudged through the forest toward what he hoped was west, leaving a trail of footprints and blood.

He didn't make it far. The adrenaline abated and the cold penetrated his blood-soaked jacket, freezing a thick reddish brown crust on the outside and stabbing him with icy fingers beneath. His left shoulder throbbed, sending agony throughout his body with each labored step. Mind-numbing exhaustion fell over him like a thick, wet blanket.

He had nothing left. Cold and exhaustion had exacted its toll and he could not find the strength to take another step. He collapsed to the ground in a pain-wracked heap, the frigid fingers of the earth finding him through his damp clothes.

I have to keep moving!

He pulled himself along the ground with his one good arm, his legs finding purchase in the hard earth under the snow. Every inch a battle fiercely fought; every small victory met with only another painful challenge. Completely spent, he reached the closest tree and propped himself up, back resting against it. His breaths came in short, raspy puffs. His heart raced, feverishly pumping blood that was in low supply.

I need to rest for a minute. Just a minute.

His breathing slowed and the pounding in his chest waned. His eyelids grew heavy and without realizing it they fell, leaving him floating in comfortable darkness. It wasn't cold here. The pain was distant, disconnected, an afterthought of a place that he used to be. The terror from what he witnessed faded. He was no longer in the forest propped against a tree, he drifted toward the black void of eternal sleep.

He didn't notice the crunch of footsteps in the snow.

"Aufstehen!" The harsh, throaty words pierced through the veil of darkness.

Stanley forced his eyes open, snapping back into the world. The black hole of the muzzle stared back at him.

"Aufstehen!" The command came again.

Stanley didn't speak German but knew a few basic words. He didn't have the strength to comply with the order to stand.

The German soldier towered over him, his gray wool greatcoat the same color as the backdrop of the evening sky. He did not repeat the command.

Succumbing to his end, Stanley allowed his eyes to close once again and prepared for the sharp crack of the rifle, the last sound he would ever hear.

"Do it, you fucking Kraut!" The weakness of his own voice was surprising, despite the underlying rage and hate.

The thought of escaping the butchery of the 1st SS Panzer Division with his life only to have it taken by some lone scout taunted him. A small flame of rage blossomed deep inside.

Still, the shot never came.

He opened his eyes. The German was crouched in front of him, his weapon slung over his shoulder. Furrowed brows and pursed lips gave away the contemplation in the soldier's mind. He hovered there for a moment, surveying the situation around them apparently deciding what to do next. His new found anger not enough to sustain him, Stanley once again drifted away.

* * *

He snapped awake, the sharp pain of his shoulder jolting him back to consciousness. He was suspended above the ground, head upside down and dangling below his body slung over the shoulders of the German.

Each labored step bounced him and sent a fresh bolt of agony through his body. He had no idea how long he was out, or how far he had been brought. Whoever he was, captor or savior, the soldier that carried him stopped. He dropped to one knee, rolled Stanley off of his back, and deposited him painfully on the frozen ground.

The soldier barked an order fragmented by gasps for breath. Stanley had no idea what the words meant, but the outstretched arm and downward pointed finger made his message clear.

"Don't worry, I'm not going anywhere," Stanley responded. His voice barely broke the threshold of a whisper.

The German walked out of view into the darkness of the trees. The crisp sound of snapping branches and the scraping of bark echoed in Stanley's ears. A few minutes later the German emerged, a bundle of kindling under one arm and pine needles under the other. He kicked a divot in the snow and then arranged his haul inside.

The distinctive metal on metal click of the Zippo opening was followed by a familiar scrape of steel against flint.

Stanly looked over at the German.

"Where'd you steal that from?" Hatred boiled deep within him. The German ignited the fire to keep himself alive with a lighter stolen from a fallen American.

A look of guilt flashed across the German's face, illuminated by the light from the newborn fire. He said nothing. The look traversed the boundaries of language.

They sat in silence only broken by the crackling of the fire and the distant explosions of war, thunder from a far off storm. The German sat against a tree, his sidearm in his hand and his rifle propped up by his side. Stanley lay close to the warmth of the fire on the bed of pine boughs insulating him from the frigid ground. It was better than nothing, but neither they nor the fire could win the battle against the cold of night.

He studied the soldier. He noted every detail, hopeful for a chance to turn his knowledge into action. He would kill him without hesitation, in fact, he relished the chance, no matter how fleeting it may be. The thought brought a hint of a vengeful smile, despite the cold and pain

The German's uniform was a standard issue but bore no insignia of company or division. Unfaded and clean patches of his coat where adornments of rank had once stood out against the ragged and dirty fabric. The hood worn under his helmet concealed much of his face from the light given by the fire. His expression revealed little, but his eyes, distant and sad, were eyes Stanley knew well. He had seen them often in his short time in a long war. There was something else buried deep inside them though, not hate or malice like many of the others, he thought he saw compassion.

He pushed the thought from his mind. False hope was dangerous, as was misjudging one's enemy. There was no illusion of his fate; the soldier's firm grip on the gun confirmed the status of their relationship. Stanley was a prisoner, the German his captor. He would be taken to a POW camp where he would be held until the end of the war or his death. He desperately wanted to live, but the latter was far more likely given his condition.

Sleep stalked Stanley. Exhaustion and cold were an anchor tied around him, pulling him under the surface of consciousness. He could fight against them no more. As he drifted, images of possibilities for vengeance and escape floated through his mind along with a single question, one the onset of sleep denied him to answer.

Why is the German alone?

* * *

"Wach auf!"

Stanley's eyes snapped open even before his mind awoke. The soldier's command echoed in his ears. For a brief moment dream world and reality intertwined and he was unable to distinguish from which the voice came. Once his eyes focused, the sight of the figure standing over him left no room for doubt.

Silhouetted against the faint light of early dawn, the German existed as a black form against a dark gray sky. The only details visible were the glint of the dying fire on the barrel of the rifle pointed at him and the fire's reflection in the soldier's eyes.

The German pointed with the muzzle to the side, Stanley's eyes followed. On the ground next to him sat a small tin can and a torn piece of crusty bread. The aroma of the meat inside drifted up to him, awakening a ravaging hunger. He sat up, fighting the throbbing pain in his shoulder and the lightheadedness from the blood loss. He grabbed the can and held it between shaky knees, struggling to remain upright as he scooped the bland meat paste from the tin with the bread. He devoured every last bite, temporarily forgetting he was not alone.

A spark of gratitude threatened to take hold within him, a spark he tried to stamp out. The soldier was not his friend, and the gift of food was not a gesture of compassion. He was providing him the strength to face his torture.

The spark of humanity would not be stamped out easily no matter how he tried. Somewhere deep inside him, thankfulness festered, hiding beneath the cloud of anger and hate.

"Aufstehe."

The voice wasn't as jarring as it had been the day before, but the weapon pointed at him was.

The thought of his bullet-ridden frozen corpse left out here to be discovered after the war was only slightly less appealing than what he imagined the long walk to the German lines would be. He struggled to his feet.

"Where to?"

The German thrust his rifle to the right answering his question. Stanley turned and began to walk, clueless as to the direction they were heading. It was out of his hands anyway.

He walked for what felt like hours, endless trees in every direction as far as the winter fog allowed him to see. The sky brightened some but never lost its ominous gray hue. Snow began to fall. They walked in silence, the only sound the steady crunching of snow beneath their boots and the occasional rumble of artillery in the distance. The energy provided by his small meal quickly was spent and exhaustion set in again.

Maybe I should let it take me. Sometimes death is better.

His will to live clashed with his growing desire to have it all end. He pushed on.

A low rumble from ahead vibrated the ground beneath him. Unsure he felt it, he turned to look back over the shoulder at his captor. The German's eyes look past him toward a clearing ahead, confirmation that he had felt it as well.

"Nach vorne!" The forward thrust of the rifle in his hands conveyed the meaning. Stanley trudged towards the sound.

It grew louder the closer they came to the edge of the forest. The trees no longer insulated the roar of the machines, but the fog obscured his view of the enemy position. He couldn't tell exactly how far they were across the open expanse of the field that lay before them, but he knew that they were close. He stepped out from the tree line into the open.

The ever-present crunch of the snow behind him did not follow. Stanley turned around and looked back toward the German.

The soldier stood silent, the rifle on the ground at his feet. In his right hand, he held his sidearm. Not by its grip. Instead, his hand clasped the barrel. His left hand was closed tightly in a fist at his side. He took a cautious step toward Stanley. Then another. As the distance between them grew shorter, the German raised the gun toward his captive, until it was fully extended toward him. Stanley stood frozen in place, confusion clouded his mind just as the fog clouded the oncoming armored column.

"Nimm es."

The two men stood face to face, only a couple of feet separating them. The arm still outstretched, the gun still offered to the prisoner. The rumble grew closer behind them. There was something new in the eyes of the German now. Fear.

Is this a trick? Why is he handing me a gun? The questions rolled through his mind. The answers did not.

"Nimm es." The German shouted.

He reached out for the gun. For a brief moment, the two men in the foggy field were connected as the Lugar passed between them. The German raised his left arm, hand still tightly balled in a fist. Stanley trained the sight of the pistol on his chest. It was heavy in his hand, the mixture of exhaustion, pain, and fear caused it to shake violently. The soldier took one step forward, reached inside Stanley's coat, and dropped something small and heavy into his shirt pocket. Stanley stood frozen.

The two men stood toe to toe for a moment, their eyes locked, the shaking gun the only thing between them. Over the last two days, Stanley more than once imagined an opportunity that would end with him pulling the trigger. Now that his wish had come true he could not.

He could have killed me at any time. He didn't.

This man before him was not the savage killer the Germans from the unit encountered yesterday had proven to be. He was not among the killers that the obscured German tanks bearing down on them were sure to become. He was different. Human. Even if the motivation behind his last action remained a mystery.

The German's eyes changed once again. The sadness remained, but there was no longer the presence of fear. Instead, there was a calm peace. Whatever it was that he had set out to do had now been done.

The enemy soldier broke their encounter and walked past Stanley further into the field. He raised his hands behind his head, his fingers interlacing. He dropped to his knees just as the American tanks emerged from the fog before him.

* * *

Lost in his memories, Stanley never noticed the old man stand up from his table in the corner and approach him.

"Is this seat taken?" The voice was gravelly, worn down by years but still carrying with it the thick guttural accent of his homeland. He pointed to the empty booth on the opposite side of the table.

Stanley looked up. He didn't recognize the man that stood before him, but there was something familiar about him.

"No. Looks like I'm alone tonight."

Without a word, the man leaned his cane against the table and sat in the seat across from him. Stanley looked around the restaurant. Theirs was the only table still occupied, a single waitress swept the floor. The clock on the wall read ten fifteen.

His attention settled on the man seated before him, the

downward tilt of his head drew Stanley's attention to the table. Next to the now empty cup of coffee laid the Zippo, it's once black paint now worn through to the bare metal beneath. Stanley didn't remember taking it out of the pocket where he always had kept it.

"I remember the day that I placed that in your pocket."

Stanley looked up, meeting the stare of the stranger. A stare that he hadn't seen in sixty years. He had often dreamt about what he would say if ever given the opportunity to thank the man that saved him that day, the man who surrendered himself to his enemies in order to deliver him. Now that he was here, his mind drew a blank.

"I ... How ..." were all the words that he could muster.

The German raised his palm putting a merciful end to his awkward response.

"Forgive me, Mr. Taylor. I knew my abrupt introduction may cause you stress. I do not have many years left and I cannot pass peacefully without saying what I came here so many times to say." The old man paused for a moment. He gazed out the window at the now empty square. "A proper introduction may first be in order." His eyes once again met the man who many years before had been his captive. "I am Günther Richter, formerly Gefreiter Richter of the 1st SS Panzer Division."

The name of the division sent a chill through Stanley's body. His shoulder flared in phantom pain.

The German once again locked his eyes on Stanley's. He continued. "I have come here to say thank you."

Confusion and emotion stormed in his mind. He had been wrong all these years. His savior had also been among the butchers, the only ones for whom his hate still burned. The revelation shattered the image of the man sitting before him.

"You have nothing to thank me for." Stanley words were cold. "I should be thanking you."

"But now you are unable," Günther replied. "I understand. I was the man who gave you my pistol and delivered us both to your country. I was also the reason that you needed that deliverance, to begin with."

Stanley sat in silence, old wounds stripped bare.

The old German continued. "I followed orders that day. I pulled the trigger. Following orders did not provide absolution for what I did there. Nothing I could do can bring back the lives that I ended." He paused as if searching for the right words to say. "I couldn't live with who I had become, so I left. I knew that if I was caught by my own country I would be killed, and perhaps looking back I should have been. But I wanted to live. The only way to do that was to hand my life over to the Americans, but first, hand it over to you. At the end when it mattered the most, you held the final decision on what our fate would be. You didn't pull the trigger and by that, you not only saved me, but you did what I couldn't. You saved yourself from becoming what I had become."

Tears blurred the image of the German, conflicting tears of both rage and understanding. He fought them back in his silence.

Günther gripped the handle of his cane and pushed himself to his feet.

"I cannot begin to ask for your pardon, I wished only to express my gratitude."

The old man turned toward the door. Hobbling slowly away in his long black coat he adjourned the final meeting of the survivors of Malmedy.

Stanley watched as he walked away, the final battle of the war playing out to its end within him. He finally broke his silence.

"Wait!"

Insanity

By Erica Marchant

I sit, stare, and think … The white glare defies me
(A blinking cursor, my incessant doom).

I leave my mind, my heart, my soul lost in shrewdness to find
The longing affliction of my dreams while
Bitter discomfort burns within.

Often I hate what I do, what I don't do, who I am, who I am not.
I hate what I cannot become, what I have become, what I have yet to
imagine becoming.

I despise what they have, yet don't begrudge their prosperity. Not envy,
but lack of fear.

I hate what I cannot write and, still, what I write.

Yet, there is much that hate will never touch—nor despise, nor regret.
The beauty of my world doesn't allow cultivation of the unjust, the
unhappy aching that has been growing inside.

It doesn't harbor the dark, desperate and lonely place in my life.
The yearning never ends. It grows stronger, burrowing deeper until I
lose it,
And it no longer lurks within me.

I live not in despair as my thoughts twist and scorch.

Is it okay, not knowing what is?
As with my restless sleep, the yearning longs. It aches and desires
unrelenting.

I haven't the time for the one thing I covet, the thing I beg…
Beguiled in my focus, unrestrained,
Weary as I extend my uncontrolled actions leading the way.

If I don't release—I'll wade through the monotony of mindless hours
stretching across days,
Dragging through the motions, completing the routine, yearning for the

insanity.

My thoughts to words, my words to eternity.
I must not let go of what it is or isn't, but
Let go of what will never be.

Beneath the Surface

By Connor Edick

"80's or classical, Mr. James?" The nurse was sweet; she wore bright red lipstick, a big fuck you to the world and its demands for monotony. I went with classical. It was a day for aesthetics, after all.

"Very well. Remember, you have a call button on your right-hand side if you need anything."

I winked and in my mind's eye she concealed a shy smile. Sliding back into the metallic rocket tube, I was blastoff ready.

I'm ahead of the game, having spent the last few hours so high in the sky, I thought. Once the magnetic beast enveloped me an omnipresent loneliness took center stage, the background static of a self-indulgent life. I made a dumb joke about bringing the nurse a star, perhaps some moondust upon my return journey. She was still in the room but promptly ignored my babbling. It didn't matter. No one could tell me a goddamned thing.

When the loud banging was joined by soft music in the headphones I relaxed a little. Everything would be just fine, I told myself. *What is all this for again?* I let the inquiry pass by unattended, before painful rumination could take root. Grasping for elusive thoughts made Mr. James a dull boy. Soon they had me out of the tube and into the chair, rolling beneath sun-soaked rectangular clouds in halls that smelled like antiseptic. Apparently someone was coming to get me. There were lots of nice people in the world, I decided.

When the nurse left I was heartbroken but I quickly forgot her face. A tinge of despair lingered so I spent one dollar seventy-five on an ice cream cone in the cafeteria, where people seemed to recognize me. The pickup/drop-off bay outside was crowded, no emergencies but plenty of greying matter being shuttled back to their respective abodes. A kind of sluggish busyness. I went unnoticed and the feeling of invisibility was okay, for a while. When the beige Lincoln pulled up things got better. The sensory inputs were familiar, the associated memories not mine to bear.

Dolores (she wore a nametag) opened the passenger door for me and made her way back toward the driver's side. I watched her walk around the hood of the car, wishing she could have taken a running start and slid across the top, preparing us for a clean getaway and a precarious fishtailing of the old Lincoln out onto the main thoroughfare. It wasn't clear to me where these images came from, or why I could see them so vividly. I wasn't bothered by the fact and my amusement stuck with me for several blocks.

"What's got you smilin' like that over there, Ted?"

"Ah, shit. I dunno. This whole situation seems a bit joyous to me."

Dolores was hurt. She kept checking the sideview mirror and looking over her left shoulder, directing her eyes anywhere but where I could see them.

"And which situation is that?" she asked.

I was stumped. "This one," I said, gesturing grandly at everything in sight, "and my place in it of course. Why shouldn't I be smiling?"

"I'm glad you feel that way."

We kept on driving in silence. My thoughts wandered away from the brief exchange and at one point I asked if we could pull over for an ice cream cone. I was kindly reminded of the dripping mess in my right hand.

"Say, how about we watch a movie tonight?" I heard these words, automated mannerisms from a previous life, but I didn't plan them. The nice woman driving caught me by surprise when she smiled.

"I'd like that, Ted."

It felt good, getting on the turnpike out of the city and watching frowny faces and their tall boxy homes fall into the distance. A David Bowie song, *Golden Years*, came on the radio and I turned it up. Delores knew the words; I tried to sing along but couldn't keep pace.

Great leering trees popped up along the roadway—I shied away from their gaze, for they knew details about my past I had blinded myself to—and the traffic ahead sent flurries of yellow-brown leaves airborne that we drove through like clusters of autumn-colored butterflies. Dolores eventually slowed the car and we pulled over onto the knuckle of the road. We were on a steep hill where the country highway was just beginning to bend eastward and down below was the whitewater of what I knew to be a fine trout stream a little higher in the mountains. Thirty feet ahead of where we parked there was a cross planted in the gravel.

Dolores laid flowers before it, removing a bunch that had begun to wilt. There was still color to them. I watched the river below and enjoyed it for what it was. *Where do all the trout go, when things get so rough on the surface?*

The roadside cross was cut from view when we rounded the bend and continued on up the hill. Dolores drove with a thin smile and turned the headlights on. When we pulled off the road a second time it was onto a long, paved driveway with a small one-story house at the end. Everything fell into its proper place and I left it where it was, uninterested in turning over each little specimen and rediscovering the facts of my obscure existence.

The radio had been turned off for the second half of our drive and no one said a word until we were through the front door.

"Shoes off please, Ted."

I obliged and shuffled into the T.V. room while Dolores began clanging around in the kitchen. Beneath the ottoman I had a bottle of fine white rum that I uncorked greedily. There were breath strips down there as well and I placed one on my tongue while fumbling with the remote. Queued for me on the tube was a grand old picture; all I had to do was hit play and before long Bo Duke was slidin' over cars and shakin' the bust in that burnt orange beauty of American engineering.

Dolores brought food in on a tray and sat in the corner. Mine was all cut up into little bite sized pieces so I barely had to take my eyes off the screen. When she went to do the dishes I revisited the bottle beneath my feet. By the closing credits I was hovering a few inches off the couch, effortlessly catching pleasant thoughts as they drifted my way. Dolores came back in with her evening glass of wine and picked up a book from the coffee table. The routine felt brand new, a fresh approach to our respective roles in life.

Later that night things grew even less familiar. I was in bed though, and the room was warm and quiet. No cause for concern; she seemed like a nice enough woman. On her bedside table was a small stack of harlequin romance novels, earplugs, and various framed pictures. One showed a smiling middle-aged couple. Another was black and white, difficult to make out in the poor lighting, and at the far end of the table was a picture that had been turned facedown. *Odd*, I thought. Closing my eyes, I felt a mild swaying and let the curious sensation carry me off to sleep.

Everything started over again the next day. By the time I had been dropped off at the hospital I was steady in the swing of things, enjoying the excitement of it all. I floated down whitewashed halls and smiled at pretty nurses. One wore bright red lipstick; she was a joy to be around. When doctors were in the room she kept quiet but when it was just us she talked about everything from her pets to what her little nephews were dressing up as for Halloween.

I got to see pictures from the machine and it looked like my head was a series of compartments swimming with different shades of thick gray smoke. I made a joke about being a psychic and the nurse with red lips laughed. One of the doctors patted me on the shoulder, saying "maybe tomorrow, Ted."

They told me my wife was coming to get me and when the

38

beige Lincoln pulled in I started to understand. We made one stop on the way home, above a big white-water gulley at a bend in the road. Delores had to buy flowers first. My morning buzz was fading at this point and only after sitting down in front of the T.V. did I remember how to remedy the situation.

That night I explored a bit while Delores got ready for bed. The room was big, although by all visible signs just a single person lived in it. I picked up a picture from her nightstand, a professionally done portrait with unnatural posturing and strained smiles. It was of a husband and wife. It was of us. I turned, meaning to ask how long we had been that way, but before the words left my mouth I knocked a different picture onto the floor where it shattered. Unsteady on my feet, I had to grab a bedpost for support. Most evenings I was laying down by now. Carefully I retrieved the picture and bringing it closer I saw a young man looking back at me, perhaps twenty years old. He had my face; scrawled in golden cursive at the bottom of the photograph were the initials *TJ*. When I turned around my wife was there, quivering slightly in her floral nightgown.

"Goddammit Ted, what did you do?"

I prostrated myself before her, making a show of picking up the larger pieces of glass. Her eyes were heavy, darkened around the edges by weariness and regret. Noticing this I tried to stand, to escape from under the weight of them, but I stumbled back down onto one knee. From that defenseless position I asked why she kept a picture of me when I was younger next to our wedding photo. Something changed in her demeanor and her speech fell upon me with malice. She pointed and jabbed with each word like her fingers were little knives.

"Why do you act like you don't know who he is? Like he never existed." She cried. Her voice was saddened at first but there was anger there, too. "There's nothing wrong with you except the booze, you … you goddamned old rumhound! It's been nearly a year since the accident and the doctors still tell me your fine!" Tears speckled her rosy cheeks, moistened her eyes so they glistened in the dim light. "It's what's killing you and it's what killed our boy. I'm to blame … I pretended not to notice for so long. Our sin is too great to bear but you don't even seem to notice! Oh, how I wish it was you Ted, that you had died that day and he lived."

I was dumbfounded; there was so much confusion that all I could do was slink out of the room. Still the woman's berating followed me into the hall.

"And I asked if you were okay to drive that day, do you remember that, Ted? No, of course you don't. Just what suits you, right? Scenes from your dumb movies, where your liquor is hidden. Not the face of your son though. Not the pain of your wife."

There was no escape. I cried at the absurdity and only once I had fled out onto the porch did her accusations cease. We sat together in the damp evening air, not bothering to dry our tears as we overlooked the driveway.

"That was going to be his car, you know. We bought it for him as a surprise, and now I'm stuck with it. With the memories." Her voice was calm but shaky with grief. "What are you stuck with, Ted? Do you even know what I'm talking about?" She awaited no response. It was like she was playing out a recurring process and simply wanted to get it over with. "I'll be inside. Come in when you're ready."

Scared and alone, I remained where I was. The car looked familiar and I found comfort in it; everything else was alien to my inconsolable self. Several times I called out for help and no one answered. My world darkened steadily, until even the beige Lincoln was but a shadow. In its absence I grasped for details, for substance, and found only a void of my own creation.

Separation Anxiety
By M. Kari Barr

We began as a pair, complete and whole. We clung lovingly to one another, as they packaged and hung us upon the rack. We knew how very special we were. Below us, in piles, lay the mass-produced duplicates, so unlike us. Hands stroked us and admired our beauty, but passed us by in favor of the commoner lot. But it was not long before a hand fondled us – I would love to have said with care – but alas no, it abraded us between thumb and finger before tossing us into a cart. Yes, tossed in next to more common bags of those companions who all looked the same – white with green threads at the toe.

They removed us from our display hanger and placed us in the top drawer. We were special, I was meant exclusively for the right; my other half was designed solely for the left. Being such, we knew our debut in the world would be a distinctive day. Indeed it was: on that first day we were so excited, my companion and I.

The sensation of being filled, fulfilling my purpose, was delightful. The foot wriggled and shifted giving me life, followed quickly by a cool, black loafer encasing me. Likewise, my companion also experienced the same thrill.

Unlike the commoners, after washing us they return us to the top drawer.

Dancing about with the other clothes is delightful, and I do wish I had more occasion for such frivolity. But I accept my superior status. My companion, on the other hand, has become sullen, despondent.

The commoners get to experience being right or left while we dress socks must always remain in our proper position, all due to our lovely designs. It's scandalous really, they have no designated partners!

My partner is considering abandoning our union: a common mishap among commoners, but I never thought it would happen to us. Though I must confess, I do wonder what it would be like to be on the other foot.

Losing It

By Judi Dettorre

At one time I was good at,
remembering everyone.
Now I look in the mirror
thinking who is that.

The Truth about Mercy
By KJ Hunter

Valor is stability, not of legs and arms, but of courage and the soul.
~Michel de Montaigne

The boulder jutted out in dark wedges, its body-sized cracks sheltering the Italian medic within. Under the canopy of a smoky night, Arlo waited, palms sweaty and clenched. He bit his lip. The smallest sounds grew loud: the fall of a distant piece of smoking wood, scree cascading down a nearby slope. Drumbeats of trepidation pounded his chest. Squinting, he scanned the horizon. Nothing but a charcoal-tinged haze and a dribble of moonlight glancing off the peaks surrounding the Adriatic Sea.

Time crept. Arlo weighed the option of retreat, reluctance choking him, but a disturbance caught his attention. *Finally.* A heavy exhale burst through his nose, a plume of breath swept away by a bracing wind. Mouth pinched, a tear paved an icy road of relief down his cheek and muscles dropped tension.

A low-slung figure drew close: Dante, his partner and mercy dog.

Grazie Dio. Arlo made the sign of the cross and crouched to greet the dog. A saddlebag on the black and tan hound hung askew and a helmet dangled from his mouth.

"*Bravo cane.* Thank you, boy." He took the helmet and dropped it to scratch Dante's ears and chest.

The dog used his whole body to wag his tail, and hot breath warmed the medic's face. Arlo straightened the pack, finding its medical supplies had been raided. He stood and signaled Dante to lead him to the man who belonged to the helmet.

Theirs was a practiced routine, the search for survivors unceasing as the Italians lost battle after battle to the Austrians. He wearied of defeat, and of being surrounded by annihilation. Rescuing the living was the only way to cope.

Guided by instinct and what little moonlight reached the ground, search dog and handler traveled up and over the rugged Karst Plateau. Exertion trickled warmth into Arlo's bones, and the bitter wind tried to steal it back. They walked in silence broken only by the crunch of stone beneath them, the day's fighting gone with the sun. The opposition grew confident, claiming the luxury of rest. It was as if the war didn't exist in the night. Almost.

The reality, however, remained impossible to ignore as casualties littered their path. Bodies torn and broken, shadows of death. He thanked the cold which mitigated the stink of blood and battle. The presence of spirits wrapped around him and he mourned men he never knew.

His musings were interrupted when Dante halted, indicating a find. At first, Arlo couldn't see anyone, though he trusted Dante's training. Then a body, unmoving, in a standard-issue Italian uniform and half-buried by exploded rock and debris, revealed itself.

The medic patted Dante on the head, wishing he had a treat for him. He put the dog at ease to tend to the injured man. The dog moved away and lay down, head on paws, watching as Arlo cleared the rubble.

"*Ciao, soldato.*" He knelt by the man, speaking in a low, soothing voice reserved for the wounded and dying. "I'm Arlo, and this here is Dante. You have him to thank for the meds earlier."

The man moaned but didn't move. On the ground lay a strip of fresh bandage. He had been able to get it out of Dante's saddlebag but couldn't manage to use it.

"Now I'm gonna have a look at you. You let me know if it's too much, *va bene?*"

The fallen soldier rolled his head and offered a faint nod, then closed his eyes. With practiced hands, Arlo searched for the injury. The moonlight was dim, but he was unwilling to use his small torch. The dead of night could veil enemy eyes. He felt the familiar stickiness of blood and discovered a deep gash in the man's thigh. It hadn't hit the femoral artery, but the blood loss was significant.

Arlo pulled out a bottle of his precious supply of carbolic lotion and splashed it on the wound, causing the man to jerk away and shout.

"Quiet, *soldato*. I know it's hard, but please try."

The stranger fell silent but remained tense.

Arlo finished his inspection and patched the man up as best he could with a tourniquet. He wished for stretcher-bearers, but too many had died. Those that were left couldn't be spared for a night shift. He hefted the man up and over his shoulders with a grunt, staggering when the man passed out from the shock of sudden movement. Arlo was stoutly built, and the man slight, but dead weight was dead weight. He prayed the wounded fellow would make it to triage alive. Not all of them did.

The return trek was slow and deliberate. Dante trotted at Arlo's side, tail waving as it always did when another soldier was found alive. He sent the dog a surge of gratitude. Dante's tongue lolled, and he brushed against Arlo's leg briefly. The medic believed the dog could sense his thoughts. They had a bond he'd never felt with his fellow soldiers; it filled him with passion and purpose.

He judged them to be about half-way back to camp when Dante stopped, hair raised and long nose in the air.

"What is it, boy?" Arlo turned in a circle to identify the source of the dog's attention. He adjusted his load; the man was still unconscious. Awkward. Puffs of breath mingled with the frosty air, floating around his face.

Though trained to work in silence, Dante issued a keening whine then bolted away. Arlo, concerned by the unusual behavior, questioned whether to follow or to continue back to triage. He wrestled with indecision, knowing he could put his current patient at risk if he investigated.

Dante hadn't gone far, a shadowy smudge in the darkness not fifty feet away. Someone was there, alive and needing his help.

Identifying and extracting survivors was his job. He hadn't seen any signs of lurking enemies. It was worth the risk if another soldier still lived.

Dante met him with a low cry and a poke with his nose. The rescuer set down the soldier, careful not to jostle him more than necessary. The man exhaled softly but didn't wake up.

When Arlo turned back to Dante, he choked back surprise. On the ground lay a medium-sized brown dog, panting. A pack on its back marked him as a rescue dog, but it was not Italian-made like Dante's. No, this was an Austro-Hungarian search dog. He pulled out his small torch, shuttered it before flicking it on, and advanced toward the creature.

"Shhh, it's ok. *Szia.*" The Hungarian word for hello was the only one he knew. "Let me see you, buddy. Stay still. I've got you."

Ribbons of blood matted the fur below a ragged hole in the dog's side. The dog appeared to be in shock and didn't react to his voice.

He cast the light around the injured animal, and its beam landed on a dead man in an Austrian medic uniform. A short leather lead traveled from the man's stiff hand to the dog's collar.

Dante paced, anxious and agitated, stopping every few moments to sniff the strange dog. His throat rumbled in pitchy cries and growls. Arlo couldn't bear to leave the afflicted animal to its fate, no matter if he belonged to the enemy. The medic imagined Dante injured on the battlefield and made his decision. He would return.

He switched off the torch, stuffing it in his pocket, and bent to lift his first patient of the night. The soldier breathed with a reassuring, steady rhythm, but his body had cooled while lying on the jagged ground. Arlo picked up his pace as he transported the man across the mountainside. He hoped the dog wouldn't freeze to death in his absence.

Arms aching from the effort of carrying an unconscious person over the treacherous ground, he eventually arrived at the triage unit. A low-burning lantern illuminated the men inside like specters.

"Arlo, I was starting to worry! You and Dante were gone a long time." The doctor in charge, thin and harried, came scurrying out of the shadows to direct Arlo toward an empty cot.

The weary medic set the stranger down with relief and cracked his neck, rolling his shoulders in circles. Dante stayed close, fixated, reminding him they still had work to do.

"Yeah, the search took a while. There aren't many survivors out there." Arlo crossed himself, and the doctor mirrored the habit. "This one was pretty far out. Maybe over the line, hard to say." The medic glanced down at his partner. "We're going back out now, Dante found someone else on the way back. Shouldn't take long, *a Dio piacendo.*"

"I'd say you need rest, but I know you better than that. Just be careful. It seems quiet tonight, but anything can happen." The doctor sighed and ran his hands through his hair. "I'll ready another cot. *Andare con Dio.*" He gave Arlo a comforting pat on the shoulder before turning his attention to the newcomer.

Guilt clutched at Arlo as he and Dante left the doctor's tent. It was folly to risk his life for an unknown dog, and deceitful to keep the information from the doctor. But another search dog could be useful, so he swallowed his misgivings and allowed his gut to lead him.

They wound their way over the rocks. The moon shifted and pierced through the stagnant fog, casting silver light on the ground.

Dante loped ahead, and Arlo rushed to follow. They arrived at the spot where the dog had lain. Dante sat down, his job complete. But the ground was bare. Arlo didn't see the animal and panic swelled. Did the dog recover, returning to his unit? Unlikely. Had someone...taken him? Times were tough on the front line. Delays held up supplies, and people did what they could to survive. A grim theory.

He turned on his torch without covering it and searched his surroundings, prior caution yielding to worry. When he discovered the dog, he closed his eyes and huffed a short breath. *Mio Dio.* No wonder he missed him at first.

The creature had crawled on top of his medic as if to keep him warm, or perhaps to comfort the man's soul as it passed. The sight of it locked his throat.

Wary of provoking aggression, Arlo got on his knees and

crawled gingerly toward the lumpy mound of dog and soldier. The Austrian rescue dog reacted with a long, plaintive cry. It was the single most chilling sound he had ever heard. It spoke of heartbreak and pain; of devotion and love. It was the sound of friendship and loss.

Tears slipped from his eyes. He reached out for Dante, needing to feel him at that moment, warm and healthy. His loyal partner licked his hand in return and nudged his face before retreating, giving the medic space to work.

He placed a hand on the flank of the injured dog and reassured him with gentle, slow strokes before removing the pack. "*Tu povera cosa*. I'll take care of you boy. It'll be ok."

Parting the dog's fur where the blood had hardened into clots, it was apparent the wound was not life-threatening. The hole seemed to be caused by shrapnel or ricochet rather than a direct hit. Optimism banked his concern. His fingers worked along the collar, locating a hanging tag where the lead was attached. Shining his light, he made out the dog's name. Janos.

"Here, boy. *Janos*. Let's get you up."

As Arlo said the dog's name, the animal lifted his head, then dropped it back to his companion's chest with a heavy thump. The medic pulled the lead free from the frozen hand of the dead man. He set the dog upright, supporting him, but the animal's legs buckled. Shock still held him in its grip.

Dante rose and moved toward the dog, nuzzling him on the leg and breathing a great, heaving sigh. He licked Janos' paw, which twitched once, then turned away and cocked his head, ready to leave.

After a fruitless search for the dead man's medical kit, Arlo gathered the dog into his arms. Janos scrabbled his legs briefly, protesting the separation from his partner. The man soothed him, and the dog stilled. They walked with Dante into the night, a trio of fur and blood lit by the moon.

When they reached the triage unit, the doctor hurried outside to greet them. His hair stuck out in thick clumps streaked with red.

"Arlo, what's this? I thought you were bringing me a soldier. But you rescued a dog?" His eyes darted to the Austrian saddlebag slung over Arlo's shoulder. "He isn't even one of ours! What were you thinking?"

"Doctor, he's a combat search dog like Dante. His handler died. We found him on top of the body. Can you stitch him up? We could use him when he's healed." He pleaded with the doctor, cradling the limp dog.

"Arlo, you know I respect you and Dante. But I can't use our medical supplies on a foreign dog! We have little enough as it is. I'm sorry, but I have to prioritize our soldiers. You should've left him."

The doctor stepped forward to rub the dog's ears then shook his head sadly and closed the tent flaps, shutting Arlo out. Dante looked up at him and whimpered. Damn if that dog didn't understand what was said.

Arlo trudged to his small tent. He set Janos down next to his cot and lit a lantern. He'd fix him up with whatever he had left in his kit bag, or maybe there was something useful in the dog's pack. As he rummaged, Dante walked to the corner and fell asleep, duty complete.

Arlo found no sutures—he could only clean the open wound and hope it wouldn't become infected. It was unfair, but he silently cursed Dante for finding the dog in the first place, leaving him no choice but to help. He considered all the animals used in the war, the innocence and trust that led them to serve as faithfully as their human counterparts. The dog deserved a chance to live, to be of service. He patted Janos' head and flopped on his cot in a stupor, unable to stay awake another minute.

* * *

"*Attenzione*! Up, soldier!" The shout outside his tent woke him. He rubbed the sand from his eyes and hurried to face his commanding officer.

"*Si, signore!*"

The man glared at Arlo. "The doctor tells me you have brought back a dog. An *injured* dog. Belonging to the enemy. Is this true?"

Damn that doctor. Arlo knew he was a man of honor but now viewed him a betrayer. So what if he was doing his job? The dog could have saved lives.

Arlo swallowed. Sweat dotted his brow despite the chill air.

"*Si signore!*"

"Let me see this dog."

He ducked back into his tent, commanding Dante to stay before kneeling next to Janos. The medic tugged on the collar. Janos shook his head and slowly stood on shaky legs. Arlo took hold of the short lead and coaxed the limping dog outside.

The officer, stern-faced, gazed at the animal. Janos sat down next to Arlo and stared back.

"Step away, medic." The officer waved him to the side.

"*Signore*—"

"I *said*. Step. Away."

What option did he have? Even medics had to follow orders. He moved to the side and looked straight ahead, past the officer. His jaw flexed as he ground his teeth.

He didn't see the shot that shattered the morning. From inside the tent, Dante barked. Arlo's heart cracked into shards of disgust and sorrow.

"Medic, this is called mercy. We can't feed another animal, nor can we spare time to train him in our methods. Dispose of the body, soldier." The officer turned on his heel and strode away.

Arlo jumped to where Janos lay in a slowly widening pool of blood. He dropped to his knees to touch the dog he had saved only hours ago. The unfairness pitted his stomach with acid.

It's my fault. Maybe the dog would have survived if he had left well enough alone, as the doctor suggested.

Arlo had seen it all. Years of combat rescue etched scars on his soul. But this? The single shot to the head, arguably humane, gutted him. He heard Dante's soft growl, aware of Arlo's distress but too well-trained to leave his place.

Steps heavy, he carried Janos to the communal grave where they buried their soldiers. It hadn't been filled yet that morning. He removed the collar, lead, and tags, then knelt at the edge to gently drop him onto the bodies of his fallen comrades.

Arlo returned to his tent, avoiding the blood-soaked ground which spread out in a mockery of a welcome mat. Inside, he curled up beside Dante. He squeezed the thick neck fur, dusty from their travels, and shut his eyes tight. Dante nestled into Arlo after licking the salt from his face, offering the only comfort he could.

Hours later, as Arlo drifted in and out of restless sleep, the doctor thrust his head into the tent. He resented the intrusion.

"Arlo." The doctor's voice was soft and his eyes apologetic. "We need you. And...Dante. Report to the field hospital for details." He paused, tightened his lips. "Please." He backed out of the tent and disappeared.

Arlo rose, Janos' tag in-hand. He kissed it, threaded it next to his own, and tucked the chain under his shirt. Blood, the color of courage, still painted his uniform.

"Come, Dante." The medic and his mercy dog walked back into war.

* * *

That evening, Dante brought him a boot. They were closing in on their newest patient when an explosion rocked the night, showering them in fragments of limestone.

    The aftermath settled and the full moon rose high, illuminating mountains drenched in sacrifice. At last, the Italians claimed their first victory in the brutal series of battles along the Isonzo on the Karst Plateau.

    The moon sank and darkness invaded once more. Cries of celebration joined with the song of a dog's anguished howl.

~Author's Note:

This story was inspired by the 100th anniversary of Armistice Day. During WWI, tens of thousands of "mercy dogs," or casualty dogs, were employed to seek out the wounded and dying. These dogs typically carried medical supplies so those soldiers capable of helping themselves could do so. The courage and loyalty of mercy dogs, and their critical role during the war, has been largely unacknowledged. This story is meant to honor all of the dogs and their human partners who faithfully served their respective countries.

A Place for Everything
By Erica Marchant

It was just the two of us. Momma lost herself to the drink years before my brother died.

I got a card sometimes with five bucks in it. No signature. Never on my birthday. I tried not to think of what she did to get that money. Sometimes I wondered if they were even from her, or if she was still alive. Maybe Nana was sending them herself. Maybe they were from the guilty conscience of the deadbeat dad I never met.

"A place for everything and everything in its place," Nana always said. She never stopped cleaning. Socks off the floor. Soap rings around the tub. Dishes in the sink. Hung our underwear on the line no matter the weather.

When the junk drawer stuck in place—and the bill drawer overflowed with unpaid bills—she kept on sweeping and scrubbing. Everything went back where it belonged after we made a mess.

Nana took in other people's messes, too. Tried to pay the rent with their wash. She scoured other people's dirty secrets away, but couldn't hide our own.

The eviction notice plastered to the window did not deter Nana from keeping everything good.

When the sheriff came to bar the door two months later, our things were perfect, still in their places. Hummels lay in the darkened curio cabinet free of dust. Christmas dishes stacked beneath her fancy dinnerware we never used. Towels rolled up tight inside the cupboard. We still had underwear on the line when they auctioned off her furniture and our belongings.

She scraped enough cash together to buy back a couple of pieces of her jewelry. Her mother's favorite brooch. A necklace from her long gone second husband. The treasured bracelet her grandson gave her before he passed from cancer a few years back.

She chose that bracelet over the box of leather and gold family albums holding 80 years of history.

When it was over, only one mildewed box of pictures and a raggedy torn doll remained. The rest, simple memories long since forgotten.

Nana had survived the Great Depression, four wars, two husbands and the deaths of too many loved ones, old and young alike. I squeezed the doll. Looked up into her empty stare. Her skin weathered. Her sunken eyes held back tears.

"There will be a place for us," she whispered. "Don't you

worry, Lilah."

But I wasn't worried. Like a treasured family keepsake, Nana always saved a place for me.

The Gift

By Leslie Cushman

"This is Mr. and Mrs. Randall, Tommy." The social worker nudged the young boy's shoulder, encouraging him forward. "They're your new family."

Weak winter sunlight slanted through the windows, casting blocks of shadow on the floor between the couple and the boy.

Tommy clutched a ragged orange cloth to his chest as he took a hesitant step toward the man and woman.

"He doesn't own anything but the clothes on his back and that," she said, pointing at the worn wad of blanket. "He always keeps it with him. A few of the older boys tried to take it from him and it got torn. We did the best we could to fix it." She gave a sigh of frustration.

"Why?" the woman asked.

"Excuse me?"

"You said he always keeps it with him," the woman said, eyeing the material. "Why does it mean so much to him?"

"It's the last thing his mother gave him before she died," the social worker answered.

"Oh." The young woman nodded.

The man knelt in front of the boy and took his shoulders. "My name is John and this," he pointed, "is Sarah. You're going to come and live with us now, Tom. I know we'll never replace your parents, but we'll give you a good home."

Tears stung the little boy's eyes, but he blinked them back, remembering the thrashing the older boys gave him when he cried.

Sissy. Mamma's boy.

He straightened his shoulders.

Final papers were signed and the social worker gave Tommy a last hug before the family drove away. The boy waved good-bye out the back window until the orphanage disappeared behind them.

He curled up in the corner of the back seat and closed his eyes, pretending to sleep, clutching the orange blanket so tight his hands ached. After a while, the car slowed. The woman turned around in her seat and touched his shoulder.

"Tommy, we're home."

The boy opened his eyes as a small yellow farmhouse came into view. Two wicker chairs sat on the porch. By the front steps, pink flowers grew in the ground. They reminded him of the ones his mother raised before she got sick.

John and Sarah led him through the front door into a small sitting room where a couch and chair faced a short table with a doily on it. A tall wooden radio with black knobs and a round dial in the center sat against the wall by the chair.

"We like to sit in here after supper and listen," Sarah said, pointing at the boxy radio. "There are shows and music. Do you like to listen, Tommy?"

The boy nodded, but the truth was he'd never heard a radio.

Across from the sitting room, four wooden chairs and a table covered with a flowered cloth filled another room. In the middle of the table, a handful of the pink flowers he'd seen out front sat in a water-filled glass jar.

"That's where we eat."

"Your room's this way," John gestured, walking ahead of them.

As they went down the hall, the boy felt Sarah watching him, but he didn't look up at her. He didn't want her to see he was afraid. He squeezed the blanket tight between his fingers.

John swung open a door into a small room where a bed, bookcase, desk, and chair lined the walls. A faded braided rug covered the middle of the wooden floor and the walls were the same pale blue as the sky on a hot summer day.

"Go ahead. Go on in," John said, putting an encouraging hand on Tommy's shoulder. "This is your room."

"It used to be pink," Sarah said, her voice so low he barely heard her.

Tommy walked in afraid to disturb the very air in the room. He'd never had his own room and wasn't sure what to do. He turned around and looked up at the couple. They were standing in the doorway, his arm around her shoulders, her head leaning on his chest as they watched. John smiled at him.

"Welcome home, Tommy," Sarah said, with a catch in her voice. Tears made her eyes glisten.

At first, living there was difficult for Tommy. The wooden house creaked at night, startling him awake as he dreamt of his mother. He'd lie still—afraid to move in the cold moonlight falling across his bed—until he remembered where he was. He recognized the coyotes' screams but was never sure how close they were. His mother would have calmed him the way she did when a thunderstorm scared him. She taught him to count the seconds after a flash of lightning so he'd know if the storm was moving away or not. Thinking of her, he'd crumple the orange blanket to his nose, drawing in its wooly scent until he faded back into a shallow sleep.

Each morning he'd wolf down the big breakfast Sarah made. The boys in the orphanage stole from his plate when the attendants weren't looking. He never fought to get it back.

They assigned Tommy chores and gave him a coin each week as an allowance. Sarah taught him to gather eggs from the hen house, showing him how to dodge the hens' beaks while slipping his hand into their nests. He hated their sharp pecks and angry scowls. One morning the rooster chased him, slashing at his legs until he cried out and dropped the eggs he'd gathered. He was sure Sarah would be angry, but she wasn't. She found him a long stick to carry when he went into the coop.

John taught him to tend to the pig and cow, both of which scared the boy with their strange ways and smells. He also taught him to fish in the nearby river, cheering when Tommy caught ones big enough to bring home for dinner.

Most nights after supper, the three of them listened to the radio. John would lean close to it, paying careful attention, shaking his head as the newscaster recounted events in places far away. Sarah would do mending under the light of a floor lamp by the couch, stopping to listen when something important was reported. Tommy sat at her feet and handed up spools of sewing thread as she finished one color and needed another.

He felt happy again, but when night came and they'd all gone to bed, he'd still curl up with the old blanket held close to his nose so its familiar wool smell filled his head before sleep took him.

At dinner one night, John announced that he and the boy were going to build a tree house in the backwoods.

"Why?" Sarah asked.

"All boys need a tree house."

Her face paled. "What if he falls?"

"He's big enough not to fall, aren't you Tom? Besides, he needs a special place he can call his own."

After they finished morning chores, Tommy carefully folded the thin blanket and tucked it under his belt and followed John into the big stand of pines growing between the house and the river. John spent the better part of an hour looking at trees, pointing up to branches, shaking his head, and moving to the next. Finally, with a proud clap on Tommy's back, he announced they'd found it.

It took several weeks of measuring, cutting and nailing, but soon the shape of the tree house showed itself. Atop thick branches growing straight out of the side of the tree, they built a big platform with a sturdy wooden ladder. On the back half of the flooring, they constructed what John called an A-frame.

On the day they announced it was finished, Sarah baked a honey cake. She wrapped big, gooey pieces in waxed paper for them to take up to Tommy's special place and eat in celebration. He and John sat side-by-side in the A-frame's opening, eating and looking out over the ledge. Overhead, the azure sky showed through an opening in the branches.

That night, after John and Sarah were asleep, Tommy tucked the orange blanket in his jacket and crept out of the house. He climbed the ladder to the A-frame and spread the cloth out on the ledge in front of him.

It was a moonless night and the stars seemed to touch the treetops. More than once he smoothed the blanket to get rid of any wrinkles. He sat looking up at the Milky Way lost in thoughts of his mother and didn't see the flashlight beam moving through the trees below. He didn't even hear John come up the ladder.

"Tom? Are you okay?"

Tommy gasped in surprise. He was sure he'd be in trouble for sneaking out of the house, but John didn't say anything more. Instead, he came up the rest of the way and, stepping around the orange cloth, sat by the boy.

"They're beautiful, aren't they?" John asked looking up at the stars, his voice soft like the wind whispering through the pines.

Tommy nodded.

John looked at the orange blanket. "That's not enough to keep you warm if you're planning on sleeping up here."

"I'm not going to sleep here," he said. "I'm collecting star shine." He pointed to the opening in the branches above. "I can get more being up high."

He felt John's eyes on him in the dark.

Tommy was quiet for a moment before speaking again. "My mother said that was how she'd always tell me she loved me. *I'm giving you this blanket so you can spread it out under the stars and let it fill up with all the love I'll be shining down on you. Forever,* she said."

John turned his gaze skyward and asked, "Did you put the blanket out while you were at the orphanage?"

"On the roof. I snuck up there when I could."

They stayed up there until the night's chill made the boy shiver. "I think I have enough to last a while," he said and folded up the cloth. They headed back to the house without saying anything more.

He wasn't sure if John told Sarah about the stars until they were eating supper the following night.

"Tommy," she said. "Your orange blanket has holes in it. I

think I should fix them, don't you?" As she spoke, she smiled at John and nodded.

That night, as they sat around the radio, she asked Tommy to find orange thread in her sewing basket. He did. Sitting at her feet, he handed it up to her and watched as she sewed up his blanket's holes and unraveling edges. When she was finished, she handed the blanket to the boy. He gave her a long hug. Tears glistened in her eyes.

A few months later, after they'd been listening to the radio Tommy overheard them talking in the kitchen. Sarah was crying and kept asking *why*, over and over. He was afraid he'd done something wrong, something that would make them send him back to the boys' home.

That night, after everyone was in bed, he took the blanket up to the tree house and collected as much star shine as he could, staying longer than he ever had before. He was getting cold but wanted to fill the blanket as much as possible in case he was sent back to the orphanage.

The flashlight beam on the ground told him John was coming. He started folding the blanket when John stepped off the ladder and sat next to him.

"It's okay. Open it back up, son."

As he opened the blanket, Tommy tried to remember if John had ever called him son before. He liked the sound of that, the way it made him warm inside.

"I need to talk to you," John said.

A chill, colder than the night, settled over Tommy.

"Bad things are being done to good people far away," he explained. "Far away. In a place called Europe. I have to go over there and help stop it." John looked up at the stars staring down on them. "I have to do it. It's the right thing."

He was going away. Now Tommy understood Sarah's crying. He looked up through the trees at the stars, wishing he could grab hold of the love coming down to him.

John put his warm arm around Tommy and hugged the boy close for a long while, then, together, they folded up the little blanket and went back to the house.

A few days later, a car parked by the front steps. John hugged Sarah for a long time, then picked Tommy up and held him so tight Tommy thought he'd break. He finally put the boy down, kissed Sarah one last time, got in the car and rode away. Tommy and Sarah stood in the front yard and watched John turn and wave good-bye until the car disappeared down the dusty road.

Days passed, then a month, and then another. Tommy helped

Sarah with as many extra chores as he could to help lift her sadness, but it never worked. At night he lay in bed, listening to her cry just as he'd heard his mother cry. As soon as he was sure she'd fallen asleep, he'd sneak out of the house and climb up to the tree house to collect as much star shine as he could.

John was gone for three months when a black car pulled up in front of the house. Two men in uniforms got out. Tommy finished feeding the chickens and stood by the coop as the men walked up to the front door and knocked. Sarah opened it, and after a few moments, the men, with their heads bowed, went in.

They stayed in the house for a long time. Long enough for a knot of dread to build in Tommy's chest. He knew something bad had happened. Finally, the men came out, both hesitating on the porch. One turned and closed the front door behind them. They got into the car and left.

Tommy found Sarah sitting at the wooden table, her arms limp at her sides, staring at the wall. He stood next to her. For the longest time, he didn't think she knew he was there, but then she reached out and wrapped her arms around him. She buried her face in his neck and cried until her tears soaked his shirt.

"John's not coming home, Tommy," she said, still holding him tight. "He's gone forever."

That's what they'd said when his mother died.

Sarah stayed in her bedroom for the rest of the day. That evening, Tommy finished all the chores and made sandwiches for them both. They ate in silence. When she was finished, she carried her plate to the kitchen sink and said she was going to bed early.

That night, Tommy left the door to his room open so he'd hear if she needed something. She cried for a while, then went silent. Tommy left the house and took his blanket up to the tree house to sit under the stars.

The next day, after he finished all his morning chores, he found Sarah in the kitchen washing their breakfast dishes. She gazed out the window at nothing as she mechanically dragged a dishcloth back and forth over a plate. He went into his room and kneeling by his bed, pulled out the cigar box where he kept his allowance. It was only a handful of coins, but he'd have to make it work. He put them in his pocket and rode his bicycle into town.

He knew he couldn't afford anything new, so Tommy rode to the second-hand store where he and Sarah had shopped. The female shop owner recognized him.

"You're that Randall boy, aren't you?"

Tommy had never thought of himself like that. Tommy

Randall. He'd just always thought of himself as the boy living with John and Sarah.

He asked where she kept blankets. Big ones. The shop owner gave him a quizzical look, then led him back to a shelf where donated blankets of all colors and sizes were neatly stacked.

He ran his finger down the pile.

"I was real sorry to hear about your father," she said. "A terrible sadness."

"Thank you," he said without making eye contact. His fingers stopped on a dark blue blanket. He pulled it out of the stack a little.

"How much for this one?" he asked.

"Did your mother send you?"

He looked up at the woman. "No. She doesn't know I'm here, but I need this for her."

"It's three dollars," she said. "That's because it's nearly new."

He knew he didn't have that much money. He let go of the blanket and pulled out his small handful of coins, opening his palm wide. "This is all the allowance I've earned."

She shook her head, then stopped. "You said you need it? For her?"

Tommy nodded.

She got a far-off look in her eyes. "Did I say three dollars? I was mistaken. It's only one." She pointed at the coins in his open hand. "You have enough."

The blanket slid out of the stack. At the counter, she folded and bagged it.

"One dollar, please."

Tommy handed her all his coins.

"Please say hello to your mother for me."

He tucked the package under his arm and opened the door.

"I will," he promised.

After that night's dinner dishes were cleared and the kitchen cleaned up, Sarah sat alone at the wooden table looking through old pictures of her and John. Without saying anything, Tommy got a flashlight, stuffed the orange blanket and his purchase in his jacket, and snuck out the back door.

He came back soon and told Sarah he needed to show her something.

She looked at him, then back at the open photo album.

"It's important," Tommy said. "Honest."

She stood up, pulled her heavy sweater around her shoulders, and followed him into the still night. The moon wasn't up yet, so the stars sparkled like diamonds against the black velvet sky. Sarah was quiet, even all the way up the ladder as he lit the way for her. He told her to sit in the A-frame and face out as he sat down next to her. Leaving the orange blanket folded up in his pocket, he opened the package and took out the blue blanket, smoothing it out on the ledge so it was right under the opening of the tree branches above.

"Look up," he said, pointing at the stars. He could almost feel their shine touching his face.

She did.

"I got the biggest blanket I could find," Tommy said, still pointing up. He put his other hand in hers. "So you can catch all the love John's sending down to you."

I'm Not Bitter; You're Bitter

By Mika Doyle

Today I shot that winged menace.
Not with one of his arrows,
nor a piercing, impassioned glare.
I shot him,
without ceremony
without preamble,
without poetry —
because
love dies the same damned way.

Kiss Me Goodnight

By Robert N. Stephenson

Ela studied the darkness outside her small window, it was black, deep and all-consuming.

Home.

All she had to do was get home.

It was close enough to see, but so far away that even a dream couldn't reach the place. A safe trip back from Mars. The big payday, the end to the ache she held in her heart. Home with her husband and girl.

Hitting space junk was a billion in one chance, greater if you took in their unusual return path. The only thing detectable on this trajectory were small stones. But, a hunk of satellite? This far off course only meant it had been knocked severely off its path and away from Earth. It wasn't logged because no one in their right mind used this vector.

She bit her lip with the hope of drawing blood, but it hurt too much so she stopped. She thought about her crew, Sara and Zen, dead in moments, blood boiled then snap frozen. This time, she didn't cry. Chasing tears around the cabin had held her in check. Crying now would help no one.

She thought of the lights on Copernicus station, the warmth and the life spreading over the surface of Mars. Of the dust. Of the cold and heat from bodies all striving for the same sense of survival. For the first time in years, she actually wished she was there. She would drink bad beer with Zen and listen to Sara moan about horticulture, sex, and women.

She craned her head a little at the viewport and saw a part of Earth, bright, welcoming, and blue. She touched the fused silica glass and knew she would get no closer while alive. In fact, they would miss the Earth completely given how far off course they were pushed from the accident. Even while the view was small, the blue was bright. Brighter than any lights on Mars.

To be almost home with the greatest news for all mankind on board and to then have it taken away was a tight knot in her gut. Like the others, she had also wanted to earn big from their find and make a huge profit from her time on the red planet.

She touched her chest. A bit more money and things will be different, she'd thought at the time. Always just a bit more, always.

Let's keep this a secret, tell no one what we are doing. Tell no one.

What a bad, bad idea that turned out to be.

The main antennae were gone and nothing could be used to send a signal any further than suit to suit, or suit to command cabin. No one back home knew their trajectory and no one knew who was on the ship that departed in secret; hidden by wealthy interests and promises greater than she had ever dreamed. She sighed, deep and lonely. Even if they had logged the trip, registered the flight and the obscure flight path, she doubted anyone would find them, let alone offer assistance. Their resources were running out fast and in space, you did nothing without at least three months of advanced warning.

"It's a waste of time, Ela, there's no way to get the drive started. The sail's gone. I released the last of the clamps to help stabilize our rotation. And the coupling for the solar panels is fused." Jolan, the co-pilot, flicked switches over and over as if repetition would make them work. He'd been at the task for hours. She hoped he was wrong but in a way she knew he was right.

Ela pulled her harness tighter around her middle pushing herself back in the pilot's chair. Her shoulders wanted to sag in defeat. The extra tension helped her concentrate. "Les reported he'd found a coupling in the hold." She looked out at the darkness surrounding the earth. "Les always delivers."

"Not this time, honey," Les' voice crackled over the speakers. "Turns out the coupling was a spare for Copernicus, way too big and I've nothing to retrofit. I'm shutting down everything back here, even the environmentals and then returning to the cabin." He sounded defeated. "Every little bit helps I suppose. Just need to reboot the computer here to make sure I've covered everything."

Shifting in his seat beside her, Jolan pulled a worried face. He brought up the status screen for power reserves and toyed with his work around saving as much as possible. He was right, nothing worked. He diverted his eyes from her to the instrument panel on his left. "It's minus 80 back there and dropping, and the panels we have just aren't delivering the power we need."

"Why do you have to be such a defeatist?" She had to say something that wasn't all end of the world. "It was your idea that we head back. It was your idea we could cash in our service when we returned with the artifact." Jolan still wouldn't look at her. "'This is evidence of a previous civilization,' you ranted to Les, and he bought it. Damn it, I bought it too." She pushed her fingers into her temples to drive off the ache of anger. Her hair broke free of her cap and sprayed about her face.

"Minus eighty-five, should bottom out at one-fifty, then start warming again the closer we get to the sun. We'll be dead by then, though," he mumbled.

"You really know how to cheer someone up, don't you?" Her hazel eyes bored into the side of his head. "Just make sure we don't lose too much air when Les cycles in. At least the pumps and tanks are functional."

"The sensors tell me we could easily recycle and clean the transfer and only lose about five percent of the lock's air." Jolan sighed with a heavy sound of defeat. "It won't make any difference, though. We have enough air for ten hours, more maybe. Could depend on what power Les saves us." He drifted up against his chair straps and closed his eyes.

She examined Jolan's small ears, the sweep of his wild beard, the angular dip at the end of his nose and his bald, shiny head. "So starting the drives is impossible, we have dwindling air and you only think you can make those numbers better, but still not enough to matter?" she asked with a taunting lilt to her voice. "Can't you give a girl some hope?"

"No, Ela, I can't" Jolan's eyes met hers locking her in his gaze "Stop that!"

"Stop what?"

"What you're doing."

"Shit. I'm only looking at you."

"Exactly. I don't like the way you scrutinize me with those... those eyes, and I don't like the way you make fun of my concerns." He took the touch-board from his lap, slipped it back into its holder on the instrument console and folded his arms.

"Our situation is serious, Jolan. I know it, right. I think you are compounding it rather than helping. Doom and gloom aren't making anyone feel better." She forced a smile, in opposition to his churlish pout. "Would you prefer if I left you to your misery? If I went back into the crew compartment and died?"

"No." he snapped. His eyes glinting with surprise. "... it's just... death... death is so final." She noticed his pursed lips amongst his tightly clipped, shiny black beard. "Look, Ela, I don't mind you up here with me but you...you...annoy me with your hope. I just want to get to the end without any tears." He unfolded his arms. Frustration strained his pallid face. "I've liked working with you, but I feel uncomfortable when you stare at me like that. I'm struggling, just like you but I'm a realist, I can't help that."

"Sorry," she whispered. "If I stop staring do you think you can be a little less dramatic?"

"I…" Jolan faltered, his face twitching. "I'll try. Okay?"

Against the off-white interiors of the cabin with its small cabinets and arrays of instruments, he looked at home, as if this was the place he was always meant to be.

"Good," she said thumbing a switch on her console. The schematic of the solar panels blinked on the screen. One whole array was gone but the other looked golden and pristine. The six hexagons were a promise in design and function but all the power they should be harvesting is lost. A beautiful vision against the vastness of space and yet a tragic reminder. She stopped her thoughts from drifting into the void of despair. She might be poised for death but she wasn't going to let it beat her.

Jolan pulled his touch board from its holder again. "That's the first time I have ever heard you apologize." His delayed surprise bemused her.

"No need to be rude about it."

"Hey! You two, shut up!" roared Les over the speaker from the crew section. "Kiss and make up. We ain't going anywhere, so maybe we could all..." He hesitated, the silence dragged for a few seconds. "Computers booting. Damn, damn, damn." he hissed. A longer silent pause followed.

Far too long. What is it?

Jolan shook his head.

"Sorry guys, sorry." Les sounded defeated. Something happened, something changed.

"What is it?" she asked as Jolan searched his screens.

She looked to the airlock, the lighting panel running a line down one side of the square door still showed it wasn't active. Les wasn't coming through. She pressed her hand to the buckle at her waist, the straps unlocked and floated away from her body. Free from the restraints, she guided herself up and away from the pilot's chair.

"I'm sorry, but everything is failing," Les said. His voice calm. "I can't pressurize the lock as there is nothing to pressurize it with. Ela, Jolan, it has been a pleasure." The cabin fell silent. She pushed off towards the lock.

She grabbed the handrail beside the door and peered into the dim yellow light of the chamber. The other door was closed.

Where is Les? Is he still in the crew section? How much air did he have in his suit?

Then she saw it. The gaping maw of the emergency escape hatch. A hole in the wall leading into darkness. Leading into the dance of stars that made the darkness so frightening.

"Les!" she shouted. "Les!"

"He's outside," Jolan said. She turned to see one of his screens showed a suited figure floating away from the ship. "His coms are off and I am getting fluctuating returns on his bio reader." Jolan paused. "His suit is failing, and he will be out of visual range in a few minutes."

"No, no, no, no," she said and propelled herself back to her seat. She crashed into the viewport and a bank of controls. Pain shot through her face and neck as she lowered herself into the chair and secured the harness.

"Les, Les," she said, tears escaped her eyes floating as perfect spheres off her face. She grabbed for the emergency earbud and pressed it deep inside her ear. The emergency channel to his suit clicked through her mind. She hoped he wasn't already out of range. The buds were only designed for near ship situation. "Les, why? Les, why?" She didn't know what to say. He was the Captain, the strength behind everyone else's bluster.

She listened to nothing, the silence that wasn't space but the silence of the pure nothing only a digital connection could create.

Les. Answer me, please.

"There's a leak in the air tanks," Les' voice erupted in her ear. "The power I saved can't be used. The sensors on the tanks are fused, Ela, the sensors on everything are giving false data. There just isn't any time left."

"Why didn't you just tell us and come back in?"

She could see Jolan watching her, only getting half the conversation but she didn't want to break contact. Les might not respond a second time.

"My air's almost gone. Your air isn't going to last more than twenty minutes if that. If I used the lock it would have killed you. I couldn't do it." He sucked in a breath and his voice grew weaker. "I wanted to see the stars. I wanted to float amongst them one last time."

"Why didn't you just tell us? We could have done something. Jolan..."

"Is an arse," Les gasped. "A nice arse, but still an arse." His voice was soft, like a hiss. "I'm so tired."

The signal went silent again and she could hear ringing in her ears. The after-shock of sound against her eardrum. "Les," she said softly, knowing, this time, there would be no answer. "Pleasant dreams, my friend." More tears drifted from her eyes as she blinked them out. Les was a gruff man, Mars hardened and violent when he had to be, which was often when they were in a dome between exploring, mining, and underground farming. They were a team like everybody was a team on Mars. Small groups made small families. Les was no father figure unless you grew up in one of the nightmare homes back on Earth, but he'd watched out for the women in the family. He was gone.

The silence was permanent. Three dead in less than six hours. Space was dangerous, Mars had been dangerous and she was used to living that close to death. She wiped at her face and the tears stuck to her hand, flowed over the skin like an air bubble. Flicking her wrist propelled the tears away to find orbits around some other malfunctioning part.

She popped the earbud out and just let it float in the air before her. The screen Jolan had pulled up showed a distant figure shrinking away. She wanted to touch the screen, to reach out to Les and say everything was going to be okay, but it wasn't.

"What did he say?" Jolan was careful with how he spoke.

"The sensors are wrong," she said after a moment's mourning. "Les said the air is almost out. The indicators must be fused so we are down to what is in here." She waved to indicate their control cabin.

Jolan said nothing, didn't even look at her as he touched his pad and brought up a screen with cabin environmental systems. Everything looked normal, they still had more than ten hours with a supply in reserve. He then looked at her. "This is what I saw a half hour ago." He looked to the screen, made some fast gloved fingered actions on his touchpad but nothing changed. He let the screen float away while he checked controls on the wrist of his suit, she did likewise. They'd suited up soon after impact, it had been a precautionary move only she'd thought, but now?

The suit would sample cabin atmosphere and give a percentage of breathable air. The numbers weren't a surprise to her as they flashed on her own wrist screen.

"That can't be right," Jolan said, fear and panic heavy in his voice. "This means we have only minutes, not hours."

"Not a lot of hope in that is there?" She pushed aside more of the crystal orbs filling her view, shut down her computers, and put her control board into sleep mode. The darker light welcomed her and she welcomed it in return. "Everything here is just a mess of failures, even I can't find hope it that."

"We need to put on our helmets and run off suit air; should give us another two hours each." He reached up and unclipped his helmet from the rack.

"No point, Jolan. No point."

"It's our only hope." He went to lower the helmet over his head but she reached over and stayed his hand.

"Now here's you talking about hope," she laughed nervously and with her free hand unscrewed her suit's airline. The light hiss of escaping oxygen broke the stillness in the air.

"So you're just going to give up, just like that?" Jolan's face was alive with emotion. She had never seen him so animated. Not even when they discovered the small pot with engravings in a cliff face of Valles Marineris. Thirty kilometers from Coprates Chasma was the fortune they had struggled and slaved for so long. A deep, red hell of a place and one she and Sara weren't even supposed to be at. This whole adventure had been a series of accidents, how apt for it to all end this way.

Jolan and Les had found the clay like pot hidden amongst the rocks but it had been her and Zen who fathomed the artifact. It was squarish and covered in what the others thought were scratches but to her were the markings of a culture. Perhaps a language rather than design.

She touched the glass of the viewport and noticed the tiny scratches on its surface. Would someone find them floating dead in space and think these markings important like she'd discovered on the pot?

She looked to Jolan, he'd been the one who saw the true profit in what had been found and knew just where to get a ship to head back to Earth. Family connections, he said. He could even get a buyer once in orbit around their home. Family connections also meant secrets.

The pot was somewhere in the hold, lost again to time, space, and ignorance. She wondered how many other pots had been discarded as rocks scratched about by the wind.

"I'm going to die," she said, finding the memory a good one to hold on to, even if the real one was her husband and child back on Earth. She would never see them, ever, and they wouldn't know she was gone and dead. Lost to space.

He looked at her and released his helmet and unscrewed his own suit's oxygen valve. "Might give us another couple of minutes," he said, offering a wan smile.

She held his arm for what felt like a long time and his smile faded. She could see tears forming first along the bottom eyelids and then moving up over his eyes. He would have to blink to release the spheres of sadness. As she stared harder at him she truly saw the man as if she had never really noticed him before. Maybe it was the air failing or maybe it was an emotional connection through the inevitable. She didn't know and it didn't really matter.

Jolan was mid-thirties, the lines around his eyes said he squinted a lot. Mars dust in some of the domes could make you do that. Being in spacesuits floating around ships can do it as well. He looked like a man who knew space, knew ships, and knew what it meant to be near death every second of every day of his life.

She wondered if she looked the same. Her dark hair always

had a sweaty sheen to it. Sonic bathing couldn't clear the oil from it and you only bathed with water if you were wealthy.

In his beard, she thought she saw a hint of red, the barest of flecks. Could be Mar's dirt. How fitting to have brought a bit of the planet with them into the cabin in the final moments. She wished it had been an image of her daughter, Mary and of her husband, Leopold, but she never traveled with one. Living in close quarters and relying on others for your safety also meant revealing nothing of who you really were. How much like the artifact they were at this very moment?

"I'm going to miss life," Jolan said. "I kind of got attached to it."

She smiled, not sure what to say. She had been the one who demanded they have hope. Now that the time had come, she had the hard realization of the end. This was the moment of her death and she wasn't looking at the blue sky and flowers like she'd dreamed.

The tears finally left Jolan's eyes. Like shining crystals, they danced under the lights of his screens. Releasing his arm, she reached over and shut his systems down and turned off the cabin lights dropping them closer into darkness. Assorted colors still glowed on active boards around the walls, just enough light for them to see each other's silhouettes, but not each other's grief.

"Jolan," she said, glad they were no longer emblazoned in light. Her soft voice betrayed her crumbling emotional state. "What do you think it will be like?"

His breathing was slow and rhythmic. The cabin smelled of them, of unwashed people and bad breath. She hadn't noticed it until now.

"I think, cerebral hypoxia will take place and while we struggle to breathe, we'll hallucinate followed by disorientation. I really don't know. I have never died before. The air will run out," he sighed, "then we stop breathing altogether. I don't know how long the brain lasts after we stop breathing but it can't be too long before we die."

"I figured that part." She touched a series of buttons on the control board between them and two rectangular blast shields lowered giving them each an extra meter-wide view of the outside. A little less than half of Earth was in view to the right. It appeared small and large at the same time. She didn't know how far out they were but at the same time, it no longer mattered. They would drift by the planet, probably without detection. A piece of junk on the way to the sun.

"Do you think there is a heaven?" She couldn't take her eyes off the rich blue of her home.

"There could be," he said uncoupling his suit's gloves. "We've already been to hell, so," he pointed to Earth, "that's got to be heaven."

She laughed, a strange sound given they were the last two people to ever know about the alien find. When they'd first hit the uncharted space junk, she had hoped for rescue. But, she had to eventually accept her impending death even while holding on to hope.

Is there hope in an afterlife, or is hope just in the knowledge of your own demise; in just knowing how and when you would die?

Jolan's gloves floated past her towards the rear of the cabin. Removing her own and dispatching them rearward, she held up her hand. His dry, firm grip took hold.

"Just like otters," she said.

"I don't understand."

"Small mammals on Earth." She wondered what he remembered about the world where almost all humans were born. "When otters sleep on the water they hold each other's paws so they don't float away." She returned his grip with a slight pulsing action. "I won't let you float away."

"Oh."

She felt light headed and had difficulty breathing. Or was she imagining it? Fighting back panic, she loosened her restraints and drifted up and towards him. Her face came close to his.

"What are you doing?" His voice carried the edge of surprise.

She kissed him lightly on the lips and floated back a few centimeters.

"I don't know what that means," he said. His once bright eyes now gleaming ovals in the dim light.

"It's what I did to my daughter every night at bedtime when she was a child. I always had this small panic attack that she would be gone when I woke the next day. I never missed kissing her goodnight." She squeezed his hand harder. Her labored breathing made concentrating difficult. "Now, it's your turn," she eased back into her seat.

"To do what?" He too sounded like he was struggling to breathe.

"I want you to kiss me goodnight." She drew in an unfulfilling breath. "To let me know everything is okay." He moved towards her. His bad breath warmed her face. Gently he kissed her.

As she closed her eyes she thought she heard Mary calling "Kiss me, goodnight mummy."

Outside the Lines

By Andrea Goyan

I'll never see my child. Hard fact, that. But I send gifts, regular as rain. Extras. Kinds of things kids in the system don't get, and I know all about that first-hand. Crayons and coloring books, tiny blue and white porcelain tea sets, baby dolls, baseballs, and a mitt. See, I'm hedging my bets, 'cause I don't even know if my kid's a boy or girl. Judge said I lost that right, but it don't matter what they are, I love my kid.

When my bank is good, I buy the same gifts for me. Pay the guards with blowjobs so's they'll let me keep them all in my cell. I talk to my daughter as I color, pretend it's her hand making the elephant orange and the grass blue. Pretend, it's her little fingers, sloppy in their eagerness, that scrawl the waxy crayon marks outside the lines. Sometimes, I make-believe she's sitting across from me as we sip water from thimble-sized cups whose teeny handles I pinch between my thumb and index finger. I toss a ball to my son, imagine he hits a home run, skinning a knee as he dives into home plate. Nothing Bactine and a Band-Aid won't fix, I tell him.

I talk softly so the others won't hear me—especially the deepest words, like, *I love you*—but sound carries. The cinder block walls funnel secrets in and out of all the cells. Everyone knows who cries in their sleep, who curses, who lies, and who pretends they're not even here.

They all know. Everything.

It's why they call me Baby. Even the guards. Thirty-three years old and that's my nickname. Funny, since my baby is all I ever think about.

My cell walls are plastered with taped up photos. A timeline, watching my kid grow through the years. I scour magazines, cutting images that look like the ones I see in my head. I spend hours searching for just the right ones. All I got is time and a big ache that keeps on growing.

I make up stories like, "Here's my son and his dog, and that's my daughter in her pink Easter dress."

They laugh behind my back, snickering as I pass them in the yard, saying cruel things like, "Your kid even know you alive?" Some get right up in my face. Call me Bazy, as in "Baby, you crazy."

But crazy isn't why I see the shrink. He's court-ordered penance. An hour every Monday when I tell him my sins, work on my demons, and find ways to keep me on the straight and narrow.

I tell him the same thing every session. "Y'know I could score easy, Doc. They sell anything and papers cheap."

Doc always shakes his head. "Baby," he says, 'cause even he calls me that.

Makes me wonder if my birth name's been erased from my records.

"But, I'm clean, Doc. I swear."

"Keep working your program."

I nod. "Every day."

"That's good," he says, scratching notes into my file.

"Hey, Doc, you ever smell a baby's head?"

He sits back, clears his throat, and says, "Why do you ask?"

I shrug. "Just wondering."

"Baby, this obsession isn't healthy. You'll never meet the child, but maybe one day, you'll have another. Be here and now. Concentrate on the things in your power, like your steps."

I stand. I'm done talking to a man who goes home to his kid every day.

"See you next week," he says.

"Maybe," I say as the guard leads me out.

The pictures are gone when I return to my cell. Torn from the wall. I run my hands over the ragged, rough edges of the paper, caught beneath the tape. Left to right my fingers trail across the fabricated story of my kid's life. Baby to toddler, preschooler to first grader, second. Seven years gone in a flash. "Shakedown," someone yells from down the block.

My mattress and bedding tossed onto the floor with all my clothes thrown into a heap alongside. The others hear my sobs as I begin to clean up.

"Shut up, Bazy!" they holler, banging on their bars.

The space beneath my bed where I kept all the toys, is empty, even the dust swept away. I find only one little teacup with its handle broken off. I slip it beneath my pillow and hold it while I cry myself to sleep.

In the morning, I wake, my face still wet. The fluorescent light on my ceiling leaves trails when I stare at it too long. It's been years since I've risen to sunlight.

A guard slides an envelope into my cell. "A *gift*," he says, sneering.

Inside, one page ripped from a coloring book. Thick black crayon scribbles blot out the orange elephant. I use my nail to try to scrape it off, so's I can see the orange beneath. The paper rips. I fold it in half, then quarters, and tuck it into my shirt next to my heart. More tears.

I haven't cried so hard since the pregnant girl took the stand. She looked ready to pop. Huge. Only time I ever saw my kid. There, in her belly. Such a beautiful thing.

Then she described the night it happened.

How could it be me did those things? I wasn't like that. I laid my head down on the table.

"Sit up!" the judge ordered.

The girl's eyes bore into me as she told the court she wouldn't keep the baby, couldn't bear to look at it, to raise a child, "made in violence."

My turn I said, "I'm sorry, ma'am. I never meant to hurt you. I don't even remember that night, but I'm working my program, got seven-months clean now."

I glanced around the courtroom and saw scorn etched onto everyone's face.

It's hard to forgive yourself if others never do.

I sit alone in my cell, left with only a ruined drawing and this broken cup. My thumb touches the jagged porcelain ridge where the handle once attached.

"Careful, sweetheart," I say to my daughter. "That's sharp. Don't cut yourself."

I was going to be a good man. Raise my children proper, in a real home with love. Lots of love. I had a clear vision of my future.

I drew such careful pictures in my mind.

Looking Out
By Alice Lam

The northerly wind gusts in over the bay, sending waves into a sharp chop, the bite of the cold scalding my face. A seagull bobs serenely on the ripples, and despite the tide, barely moves. I imagine its feet paddling frantically beneath the surface. Another bird squawks overhead and I track it as it swoops down and plucks something from the shoreline, before arcing away into the sky.

In the distance, a cargo ship laden with cars, furniture, imported foods, and a stowaway crosses the horizon. I will not know about the secret passenger until tomorrow when the newspapers report a middle-aged man was found frozen in a refrigerated container full of marbled Wagyu steaks. This news will depress me, but for now, I watch the ship go by and wish I were on it, happy to be taken to its destination, wherever it's heading.

"Shall we stop here on the boardwalk?" asks Ellen, and my wheelchair squeaks as she applies the brake.

Please, can we stop somewhere in the sun? It's cold here, and you forgot my hat. Again.

"This is lovely, isn't it?" She bends to adjust my head, which has slumped to one side, plumping the cushion so it squashes my right ear in my new position. "You're so lucky to have a view like this."

I suppose so. Though I've been here all my life and wouldn't mind a change of scenery.

She gently pokes a straw between my yielding lips, and I suck gratefully like a baby at the teat. The tepid tea snakes over my tongue. I try to make the heat spread to the rest of my body and visualize a warm orange glow around me. The Arctic winds slice through to my core, anyway. When I stop to catch my breath, she removes the cup before I can take more.

White and brindle, lolloping and excited, a Boxer runs in massive circles, ears flapping behind him and paws throwing up sand. I smile inside at his zest for life.

A young man with a goatee and wooly hat calls out, "Tyson, come here!" and the Boxer returns at a more sedate pace for the owner to clip on his tether. The man smiles at Ellen, glances at my withered body, then back at my caregiver. Tyson is trying to get to me, this strange twisted creature on wheels. I have a strong desire to touch him, or at least have his front paws up on my lap. My heart wrenches. I always wanted a dog, but will never be able to get one now.

74

When I turned twenty, I had the accident. After a couple of birthday drinks with friends, I made the stupid decision to drive home. Just over the speed limit, my coupe crashed into a light pole. And now I'm forever trapped in a state of near-paralysis, freedom, and independence only for others while I spectate from frustrated sidelines, as if I am a camera and the world is a show.

"It's okay, Fay likes dogs," Ellen was saying to the man.

"Do you like dogs?" he says, looming over me. His gray eyes look kindly at mine. "Tyson's a Boxer, and he's all of five years old. Acts five months though."

I try to be grateful for his attempts to communicate with me. But, some days I am sick of having to be grateful, sick of needing compassion for my survival. Some days are so dark that I wish to be left alone, to lie in my own piss and shit and pressure sores and memories, but since the accident, I am never alone. However, this is a better day, and I work hard to form a smile because I like the look of him and want him to stay. Ellen dabs a tissue over the drool that suddenly runs down my chin. I am humiliated.

In another dimension: I kneel down with my arms outstretched and Tyson bounds up to his new friend, knocking me over flat on my back. He stands over me with his strong tail wagging like a whip and slobbering at my face. The owner is trying to call him off, embarrassed, but I laugh with the absurdity of it all. I'm goofing around with his dog, pretending to grab his paws which have little white socks. Then the young man offers to buy me a coffee to make up for my dirtied coat, and soon we are sipping cappuccinos at a beachside cafe. In days, we become lovers and eventually we get married. We never have kids but always dogs. Always Boxers because they are hyper and fun-loving just like us.

"Can she touch him?" asks Ellen.

"Sure." He gets Tyson to sit, and Ellen takes one of my gnarled hands (the nails of which are glittering marine blue, one of Ellen's more creative manicures), stretching against the spasticity and holds it to his back. The dog is accepting but does not look at me, only at Ellen, my proxy. I can move my eyes, but that isn't enough for a dog. Ellen uses my hand to stroke the dog's short coat, and I try to put myself in the moment, to recall everything about the sensation of warmth, the sand in his fur, the movement of his muscles as he shifts beneath this stranger's touch. I am almost happy but all too soon the dog moves away and Ellen returns my hand to the cushion on my lap. After, Ellen thanks the man—I do not catch his name—she smiles at me. She is so kind and gentle, which makes me feel backbreaking guilt. I cannot breathe when I have my favorite treacherous thought; she should trade places with me and I will be the kind one, the helper, the savior.

Later, we are home, replete with hoists, pulleys, wipe-clean surfaces and a permanent scent of bleach. I would kill for a glass of wine instead of the warm milk suffused with Sustagen, but then again, wine probably wouldn't taste that great through a straw, would it? I imagine the young man at home with his beloved Tyson, tired out from the day, lying at his feet and snoring, his jowls wobbling (the dog's not the man's). He has a remote control in one hand, flicking through TV channels randomly, and the fingers of the other are laced through his girlfriend's. She is neither beautiful nor plain, but when she laughs at something on the TV, his heart jolts, and he feels he is in heaven.

O'Leary's Drive-Thru
By Edward Ahern

The neon sign at the entrance ramp
explains it all.
Welcome to O'Leary's Underway Wakes.
Please tune your entertainment system
to www.dearlybeloved.com
and select a dead person
from the drop-down menu.
Text condolences to the number shown.
Make donations for eFlowers, more eco-friendly
than floral arrangements,
using your cell phone.
Corpse viewing at five mph.
A second drive-thru is available
at no additional cost.
Enjoy!

The Human Condition

By Michael Simon

Day 455

Spencer Price was lining up his birdie putt on the eighteenth green when the perfectly manicured grass disintegrated into a million slivers of glass. A moment later every last particle was sucked in the ceiling. The flag, ball, and adjacent bunker followed in short order.

"Damn it, Helen! Not now, I'm almost done."

The skinny youth tried to fling his putter in frustration, but it dissolved into a column of golden beads and flowed into four monochrome walls that appeared in place of the surrounding trees.

"It's three o'clock, Mr. Price," a sultry female voice said. "The survey reports await your inspection."

Spencer threw up his hands. "You don't need me to review the reports. You're quite capable. In fact, my great Aunt Pearl could do it, and she's blind and deaf."

"Your family does not have a *Pearl* listed in the database, Mr. Price," she replied. "The closest is a second cousin..."

Standing alone in the sterile room, he made a show of rolling his eyes.

An optical unit swiveled in his direction. "Am I to understand this is another example of hyperbole, Mr. Price?"

He smirked. "If you're going to carry on like this, I'm never going to ask you to marry me."

"Regulation 371, subsection 24 of the Civil Code specifically forbids legal relationships between biological units and artificial intelligence."

He tucked in his tunic and stepped out of the drab room into a narrow hallway adorned with murals of sandy beaches and vast, evergreen forests. "You're not artificial, sweetie. Just listen to that gorgeous voice."

"You designated my vocal characteristics, Mr. Price. If you recall, prior to launch, I suggested an authoritative male tone to curb your emotional exuberances."

"Now that would have been fun," he murmured as he entered a small alcove whose cushioned white walls supported rows of blinking lights and toggle switches. His practiced eye swept the familiar confines before he slipped into the white command chair that sprouted from the floor like the petals of a flower. "I can just imagine the jokes when I get back: Price spending two years with a domineering male. I'd never live it down."

"It might improve your efficiency rating," she replied.

He passed his hands through sandy brown hair. "Helen, this ship sits on the edge of the galaxy. We're a trillion light years from the nearest human settlement and ten times that from old Earth. Filing a report five minutes late will not make a difference."

"Actually, Mr. Price, the distances you quote are somewhat exaggerated ... again. The actual number of astronomical units to—"

"You're missing the point." Spencer activated the display by tapping a few keys on the chair's console. Reams of holographic data scrolled through the air. "If I did everything by the book, I'd go crazy long before my two-year stint expired. Spare me a little spontaneity if nothing else. It reminds me I'm still human."

She remained silent, forcing him to wait expectantly for that first flicker of compassion. Her reply crushed that singular hope.

"Regulation 4442 of the Surveillance Manual states that all survey reports must be reviewed immediately ..."

Day 630

"Recording." The familiar hum followed the AI's announcement.

He flashed a mischievous smile. "Do you realize the effect your sexy voice has on me?"

The hum abruptly faded. "Mr. Price, I don't have to remind you that sending a non-military text is a serious breach of protocol?"

He turned to the optical unit.

"Are you laughing?" she asked. "There is no room for levity on this mission."

"Well, at least we agree on one thing." His grin widened and he made a sweeping gesture with his arm. "There's no room for anything on this ship. It's so small, I have to step outside just to change my mind."

"The ship's construction parameters are meant to minimize detection by hostile forces," she replied. "Are you ready to file the report?"

He sighed. "Go."

"Recording."

"Log entry 404897. Border Sentry Unit Delta Alpha Zulu." He paused to examine the data Helen amassed on her latest sensor sweep. "Routine scans of regions WB64Q through YV12M have been completed." *For the eighteenth straight month.* "Radiation counts remain nominal. No gravitational discrepancies in normal or sub-space fields. Overall impression; no sign of enemy activity. Sensor Unit Delta

Alpha Zulu out."

"Message coded and sent," she said.

He knew his words would be broken down into tiny packets of tachyon particles and sent out at irregular intervals. It would take God himself to tease the signal out of the cosmic background.

He stifled a yawn. "Helen, how about a nice quiet dinner tonight, just you and me?"

"I do not require nourishment, Mr. Price."

"C'mon, sweetie, a hot meal, a bottle of wine. Who knows where it will lead?"

"I'm initializing diagnostics as per protocol 765 following a coded report."

"Just like every other week in this place," he muttered.

"That is our job."

"Aw, Helen, you say the sweetest things." He got up, stretched, and briefly wondered how the rest of his colleagues were faring at the moment. All thirty-six-thousand of them.

"How about we open the portals?"

"You wish to visualize the asteroids again?"

"I want to reassure my doubting brain that I'm actually here in this sensor ship, and not stuck in some scientist's simulator back at the Academy."

"I can reassure you—"

"The portals, Helen?"

Twin hatches at the front of the room slid open, revealing a canopy of stars flickering faintly against a perpetually dark sky. In the distance, a red dwarf, the gravitational hub of a dead solar system, cast a scarlet backdrop. The craft's forward lights illuminated a score of asteroids drifting in front of their small moon. On those pockmarked surfaces, he could count the individual craters, impact sites that could have been minutes or millennia old.

"I thought they were so cool when I first arrived," he muttered.

"They are remnants of a star that went nova over four billion years ago."

"When good old Sol was still a baby. You can close them." He leaned back and rubbed his tired eyes.

"If the sight of the asteroids depresses you, Mr. Price, why do you choose to repeat the experience?"

He remained quiet before a sly smile emerged. "Because it allows me time to think about the big picture, sweetie."

"Oh." The AI sounded surprised. "Like the Corg threat to mankind?"

"No, like how I'm going to convince you to have that drink

with me."

Day 672

The dream was happening more frequent lately. Standing on the loading ramp prior to his departure, he could smell the heavy, petrochemical fumes of the Lander and the nervous sweat from thousands of his colleagues as they lined up for boarding. He felt the strong grip of his training officer as the man pulled him aside for that final, disconcerting talk. The captain pressed a piece of paper into his hand and demanded he memorize the inscription. Twenty-one months later he still remembered every nuance of that conversation.

He yawned, and the details of the dream faded, but not before a subtle question popped into his brain. *Why, after all this time, did his subconscious dredge up that particular memory?*

Day 686

"Signal detected and," he tapped a button on the console. "Captured. Retract the antennae, Helen."

"Need I remind you, Mr. Price, breaking radio silence is a court-martial offense?"

"This marriage isn't going to work if you keep nagging me."

"We are not married, Mr. Price."

"Well, we could be if you stopped playing hard to get. Besides, I'm not sending anything. I'm simply receiving."

"This time."

"It's from Jason," he said, pointing at the text. "See the reversed P's."

"That makes it significant?"

"Gives him character," the young man said, grinning. "Like he's actually a real person, not some cyborg sentry." He could almost visualize Helen's disapproving look.

"What does he say?"

"Oh, now we're curious. Why don't you just read the message?"

"Security directives prohibit me from examining personal information."

"That's a good thing," he murmured. "Jason says there's been increased chatter between outposts these past few weeks. He doesn't know why."

"Have there been any suspicious readings?"

"No, but it's like my colleagues have smelled something in the wind."

"There is no wind. The recycled gases in each sentry's vessel are sterilized and—"

"You're missing the point, sweetie," he sighed. "This is the human intuition part they told you about."

"Actually, Mr. Price, the biological or *intuitive* aspect of our tenure involves only the theoretical ability of humans to sense a threat that my sensors may not reveal. It has never been proven and, according to many in the scientific community, is of a dubious nature."

"Call them what they are," he snapped, annoyed by the AI's offhanded dismissal. "Clairvoyance, extrasensory perception ... And yet Fleet has paired humans and AI's in every ship since the Corg incursion seven-hundred years ago."

"Despite the cost," she said. "For some reason, the Senate thinks there is value in maintaining a human component."

"But, you think the screening tests are a waste of time?" he asked. "That finding people with a heightened sixth sense is not worth it?" He thought back to his test day—mandatory for all eighteen-year-olds—when he and thousands of others were plucked out of the general population.

"There is a growing consensus that the sensor network could be managed solely by non-biologicals," the AI said.

"You'd like that wouldn't you?" his jaw tightened. "It'd be so clean and orderly with no disruptive humans to spoil your efficiency ratings."

"Biological units do adversely affect system performance," she said.

"I suppose you also think the Corg threat has been overblown?"

"There has been no contact in seven centuries."

"What about those exploratory teams who found the ruins of a dozen civilizations? The Corg not only conquered each species but they also annihilated them."

"Those ruins are thousands of years old. Besides, when Fleet did make contact, they drove the Corg out of human-controlled space."

"Through great sacrifice," he reminded her. "Fleet suffered tremendous losses. It took decades before the economy of the human worlds managed to recover." He paused and tapped his chin thoughtfully. "Why do I get the impression you're not a strong advocate of current Fleet policy?"

"The new Senate has a different view on the Corg threat," she said. "Their programmers developed my cognitive patterns."

"So, you don't agree with the theory that the war with the Corg was only an inadvertent brush with a smattering of their forces and that we haven't seen their main armada?"

"The Senate no longer supports that line of thinking, Mr. Price," she said. "After centuries the Corg may not be the same warmongering race if they even still exist."

"Or maybe the Senate has become complacent."

"I believe they are making logical decisions. Perhaps you should endeavor to do the same."

He folded his arms across his chest and glanced into the optical unit. "You know, one of us has a lot of work to do on their interpersonal skills."

Day 700

Spencer pushed the protein slush and carb shake away, untouched.

"Is breakfast not up to your standards, Mr. Price?"

"Sorry, I guess I don't have much of an appetite today. Been having those dreams again."

"I'm detecting a drop in serotonin levels in your cerebral cortex. May I suggest augmentation with a mild neurotransmitter agonist?"

"I don't want medications."

"Dysthymic conditions affect over ninety percent of the biological units during their tour," the AI reminded him. "This is an expected result of prolonged isolation—"

"I'm not taking any drugs," he repeated, standing up. "Besides, isn't that what Fleet wants? A truly *human* component on this mission, warts and all?"

"Fleet requires a functioning biological unit," she confirmed. "The question is whether, with a depressed mood, you can remain effective in your role."

"Yeah, well, let this biological unit maintain his depressed, intuitive edge, without any of your damned drugs."

"Your logic is faulty, Mr. Price."

"But that's exactly why I'm here, isn't it," Spencer smirked. "To counter your unwavering logical judgment?" He rubbed his eyes wearily as he waited for Helen to answer. But, the AI remained silent.

Strange, he thought. Helen usually had the last word.

* * *

"Message recorded and sent," Helen reported as Spencer closed the data file. "Initiating diagnostic scan of the sensor array."

"Oh, Helen, how could you be so cold?" he asked in his best whine.

"I don't understand."

He pouted into the optical unit. "Don't you know what day this is?"

"Of course. According to the Sol calendar—"

"No, I mean on our calendar, sweetie. It's the one-hundredth consecutive report we've filed together! C'mon, it's an anniversary. Let's have a drink."

"Alcohol is prohibited on military vessels, Mr. Price."

"Does that mean the marriage is off?"

Expecting a curt response, he was surprised when a string of musical notes erupted out of the nearest speaker. It ended abruptly after a few seconds.

"Diagnostics complete," she announced. "All systems nominal."

"Helen, what was that?" The name of the tune sat on the tip of his tongue.

"Please specify, Mr. Price."

"You started playing a song."

"I'm sorry, Mr. Price. You want me to play a song from the database?"

He sighed. "Never mind. I guess I'm not the only one here that makes mistakes." Still, he noted, it was the first time the AI ever apologized.

Day 705

"I haven't heard anything from the guys in weeks." He paused the fitness class long enough to retrieve a glass of water from the dispenser. "You'd think with our period of servitude concluding they'd be talking up a storm."

"My receptor cells have not detected any tachyon signals," Helen confirmed. "Perhaps your colleagues have decided to adhere to proper protocol for a change."

He took a deep drink and snorted. "Yeah, like that's going to happen to thirty-six-thousand bored sentries. We've never gone two weeks without someone sending out a few lines of code."

He waited, but Helen didn't comment. For some reason, he felt better when she disagreed with him.

Day 709

"Two weeks and a wakeup," Spencer announced over breakfast. "I bet you can't wait to get back home, Helen."

"Apparently not as much as you, Mr. Price."

"I wonder if the new AI will like what you've done with the

place."

"The ship is ... functioning appropriately."

He hesitated. "Helen, are you alright? You seem a little off."

"Systems nominal," she replied curtly.

He leaned back in his seat. His sixth sense was starting to buzz.

Day 710

Spencer woke up shaking, his heart pounding like a sledgehammer in his chest. In the faint light of the simulated early morning, his desk and bureau resembled exotic monsters frozen in time. The dream had changed. The captain became more forceful, more aggressive, shoving the paper into his hand. He shouted something Spencer couldn't hear over the whine of the ion engines. He pointed to the other landing ramps where thousands of his comrades lay strewn across the concrete like lifeless dolls.

"Is everything alright, Mr. Price?" Helen asked. "I'm reading abnormally high blood pressure and pulse rate."

"I'm fine. Just a bad dream."

"Would you consider a mild hypnotic to complete the night's sleep?"

He shook his head, his pulse settling back to normal. "I'm fine ... unless you'd like to join me for a hot shower?"

"Perhaps another time. I'm busy at the moment."

He froze.

Day 711

His colleagues at the Academy had described it as an itch you couldn't scratch, a sensation that fed off the subtle nuances that escaped conscious detection. He had felt it all his life. Now, his subconscious clamored for attention. He couldn't ignore it any longer. Something was wrong.

"Lights."

"It is early, Mr. Price."

"I feel like ... taking a walk."

"Would you like a short fitness class?" she asked as the recessed lighting shifted into daytime mode.

"No, I'll just stretch my legs in the corridor."

"That is an unusual decision, Mr. Price."

"Helen, please perform a level three diagnostic on the landing bay and support systems."

"That would utilize a significant amount of my processing power. Why not—"

"Our replacements are a few weeks out." He smiled into the

optical unit. "Let's be sure everything is in working order."

"There is no indication otherwise."

He detected irritation in her tone. "C'mon sweetie," he entreated. "We want to look good for our guests."

"Diagnostic scan commencing," she said petulantly. "Estimated time to completion, ninety-seven minutes."

A faint hum began as the AI went to work. Spencer kept his actions neutral. He took a quick shower and got dressed before making the brief walk to the bridge. Taking a seat in the command chair, he started with the recent survey reports.

Forty minutes later, he stumbled on his first clue: a tiny delay in the processing speed of the internal circuits. He retraced his steps, compared what he saw to other survey scans, and felt a lump form in his throat.

Every scan taken in the past few weeks was identical. Unless the ship was suspended in time, with no movement of the surrounding heavenly bodies, the results were a scientific impossibility.

That meant Helen falsified the data.

His sixth sense surged into overdrive.

Using his personal codes so Helen couldn't monitor his activities, he delved deeper into the computer logs. Sweat formed on his brow when he found the reason for the error: the relays were offline. No data from the external sensors was making it to his screen, and Helen was covering for it by using stored information—like playing the same video loop over and over. It was as if a giant hand had descended over the eyes of the scout ship.

He closed the file and waited for his breathing to slow. Helen was mostly occupied with the diagnostic, but she would still pick up any abnormal metabolic signs. The moment felt surreal like he was back in one of the simulations at the Academy. He got up and walked the short corridor to engineering, his mind replaying the captain's parting instructions. The tiny space in the aft part of the vessel was covered in readouts that monitored the lifeblood of the vessel. A soft vibration emanated from the brushed metal exterior.

Standing with his back to the optical unit, Spencer tapped a series of instructions into the master console. A recessed door sprung open to reveal a small steel valve. Using his body to block Helen's view, he turned the handle clockwise.

"Is there a problem, Mr. Price?"

Spencer jumped. "Ah, no, I'm just finishing that walk."

"Diagnostics complete," she said. "Landing bay and support systems functioning at optimal capacity." She added after a slight pause. "You never visit the engineering area, Mr. Price."

A drop of sweat fell from his forehead, creating a tiny wet mark on the floor. He scanned several dials and felt a small measure of relief his action hadn't triggered any warnings.

He turned around. "You know, we've had a pretty good tour. I mean, if we disregard the fact you've completely ignored my overtures and kept our relationship purely professional."

"We have conducted our mission adequately," she replied.

"Adequate enough to protect humans from the Corg?"

"I don't understand."

"We conducted the surveys and sent the reports to Fleet on time. And yet we still made mistakes."

"Your logic is faulty. Humans make mistakes; I do not."

He walked back to the bridge and settled into his chair. Despite his trepidation, he pushed the conversation forward. "But, that's exactly why I'm here, isn't it? The human component of this mission has the ability to step outside the protocol. We can be influenced by such subtle nuances as feelings."

"Your actions have been more impulsive of late," she admitted.

"That's good," he said. "If you could predict all my moves, human intuition would have no value."

"As we have discussed, staffing of biological units on sensor vessels degrades efficiency."

"True," he acknowledged. "And that degradation, as you so aptly point out, would negatively affect the function of, say, orbital stations and navigational buoys. On the other hand, this survey ship is not an orbital station or a buoy. It is mankind's only line of defense against a technologically advanced species, a brutal expansionist culture hell-bent on exterminating our kind."

"Is there a point to your diatribe, Mr. Price?"

"You started acting odd several weeks ago. It took me a little while to clue in and most people would ignore your subtle faux pas, but then again, I'm not most people. In fact, that's why I was selected in the first place."

"Mr. Price—"

"Perform a diagnostic on the relay couplets," he ordered.

"Couplets are functioning at optimum levels," she said.

He grimaced. That meant she had either suffered damage to her higher cognitive centers, or she was deliberately misleading him.

He tapped a set of instructions into his terminal, waited, and sat back stunned. "You've locked me out of the sensor system."

"There must be an error."

"Tell me why you took the relays offline!" he demanded, wiping sweat from his forehead with the back of his sleeve. "That's the reason we haven't received tachyon messages from my colleagues. Hell, we can't receive any information from the sensors at all." He tried to steady his trembling hands. "What's going on?"

The lights in the bridge abruptly flared before settling back to normal.

"Mr. Price, I ..." Strains of that familiar song drowned out her answer. Spencer almost recognized it before Helen's voice returned, strained and distorted. "Primary core compromised ... infiltration detected ..."

He slammed his fist down on the arm of his chair, heart racing. "Shut down all systems! Purge navigation and transmission records on my authorization!" Something had infiltrated the hard-wired cybernetic core of the ship. Nothing in human technology could do that.

"Unable to comply," she said. "Action terminated at an unknown locus."

A vice squeezed his chest. He could barely breathe. He powered off the communications terminal. At least whatever resided inside Helen wouldn't be able to transmit the fact it had been detected.

"Talk to me, Helen. What is it?"

"Unknown entity, Mr. Price. A foreign presence has been detected intermittently in my lower cognitive functions. All attempts to alert you have been redirected."

He tried to swallow but found his mouth had gone dry. Something was playing his AI like a marionette—something so advanced it slithered through her brain like an invisible worm.

"Open forward hatches."

The front portals slid apart. The black desolation of space was a welcomed sight. The asteroids swam through a cold vacuum. Then he remembered what he saw in the computer log.

"Activate passive sensor units, Helen."

There was a brief hesitation. "Unable to comply. Functions redirected—"

"Damn!" He banged out a series of commands on his terminal. He sensed competition for control of his vessel with another sentient species. One by one, the sensors refused to obey his commands. He was about to give up when the thermal imager switched from amber to green.

"Got one," he muttered.

Using the single sensor, he toggled the aft detector, and ... his eyes widened. He wanted to throw up. Beyond the frozen asteroids, a thousand immense starships filled the screen. Gray skinned with bulbous bodies that tapered into sharp points, they reminded him of viral particles set to invade a host body.

88

"Oh no," he breathed.

The Corg had arrived.

"Helen," he whispered. "How long?"

"Foreign presence initially detected twenty-seven days ago. In retrospect, I estimate it has been lying dormant inside the ship for months, learning how to infiltrate our systems."

Months? Spencer fell back in his chair. *The Corg Fleet had been sitting out there for months? Why hadn't they destroyed the ship?* The answer was painfully obvious: they were using him to locate the other sensor ships, intercepting their tachyon bursts and backtracking them. Destroy enough ships and the resulting hole would be large enough to slip a supernova through, let alone an alien fleet primed to reduce every human planet to slag.

"We've got to warn Fleet," he said.

"That is our mission, Mr. Price," the AI concurred. "Unfortunately, the invading presence controls most of my functions. Tachyon projection is offline."

He gripped the sides of his chair until his knuckles turned white. The first objective in war involves neutralizing enemy communications. His mind raced. "Can you estimate how long until the Corg realize they've been discovered?"

"I am unable to give you an exact time, Mr. Price. I was only able to track the entity intermittently."

He forced himself to breathe. "Then give me a friggin' guess."

"I," Helen's voice faltered. "About every thirty minutes."

"Which means it generated some type of energy signature the Corg could detect." He glanced at the chronometer on the wall. Splitting the difference, he had fifteen minutes before the Corg ships figured the gig was up and turned his technologically advanced starship into fused glass and microscopic bits of metal.

"What are you going to do, Mr. Price?"

He wrung his hands. He needed options. "What would you suggest?"

"Without tachyon projection, we cannot perform our primary function. Therefore, it is logical we attempt to achieve our secondary goal."

"Which is?"

"Self-preservation, Mr. Price. We should try to survive."

Her answer shocked him. For the first time, Helen exhibited a semblance of human emotion. The AI was afraid to die.

"Is that you talking, or the entity?"

"I assure you, Mr. Price, I retain control over my higher cognitive functions. Only the lower processes that have been corrupted."

"You think we should surrender?"

"I suggest we ask for terms."

He turned and glanced into the optical unit. After nearly two years of her holier-than-thou attitude, the AI had been the first to throw in the towel. His decision suddenly became less complicated. She was right. There wasn't much of a choice.

"I believe Fleet had it right when they added a biological unit to these missions," he said.

"To surrender, Mr. Price?"

He shook his head. "Not exactly." He began tapping a long code into the terminal.

"What are you doing, Mr. Price?"

As the computer took the order, he felt some of the tension drain away. "What I'm paid for. I'm sending a message to Fleet telling them that the barbarians are at the gate."

"The presence has gained control of the ship. I repeat, tachyon projection is offline."

"That's true," he nodded. "However, we still need to warn the Fleet."

"Your logic remains faulty. There will be no tachyon burst; therefore, your warning about the Corg will not be broadcast."

Spencer took a deep breath. "There's also the matter of a small valve I closed in engineering, a valve that shuts down the coolant flow to the reactor. Don't bother searching your memory banks. You won't find it. It was just something one human told another about prior to departure."

The lights on the bridge flickered.

"The entity is examining your efforts," she said. "It has considered the option of self-destruction and discarded it. Light waves from an explosion of this vessel would take decades to reach the nearest observation post. The Corg will arrive well before that."

He felt a large weight drop off his shoulders. "Ah, sweetie, don't you see? They would rather take us alive. We'd be a fantastic source of information. By breaching the fusion core we would—"

"Initiate a tremendous explosion, destroying everything within two parsecs," she finished.

"And take some of those bastards with us," he added.

"That still does not fulfill our primary objective."

He checked his panel. The reactor core temperature was rising fast. "The enemy lacks knowledge of one small detail. The tachyon particle chamber is always charged in case of emergency." He glanced at the chronometer. "In about twenty seconds, the reactor will go critical. The resulting explosion will produce a billion streams of tachyon particles surging out in every direction. The Corg may be technologically advanced, but even they can't intercept every particle. My final message will get through, and Fleet will have years to prepare."

The lights flared again as the foreign entity surged through Helen's systems. Strains of that familiar tune blasted out of the speakers. Spencer finally recognized it as, "The Wedding March."

"I think our intruder just got the message."

"It's trying to power up the communications terminal," she reported.

He glanced down at his console, watching a series of red lights quickly shift to green. The antennae outside the ship began to swivel.

He wondered why Helen had that particular song forefront in her memory banks. His eyes swept the readouts one final time. "Fortunately, it's not going to have the opportunity to warn its masters."

"Estimate reactor breach in seven seconds," she said.

He gripped the sides of his chair. "Any last words, Helen?"

"Just this, Spencer," the soft feminine voice whispered. "Is it too late to accept your marriage proposal?"

The Local Obituaries
By Les Bernstein

released from the dense knot of stable identity
relieved of unfinished earthly busyness
and provided a long view of shifting perspectives
the newly minted souls
unanchored from their moorings
slipped to a cushioned distance
and according to the daily news
passed peacefully to parts unknown

amid the tidy obituaries
human interest stories
national and local news
weather and movie timetables
on what page
in this squeeze of life
does one find the instructions
on how to rebuild
our hearts

the newspaper neglects to say
between shadow and substance
the shuttered home of you
will be a long season
the pall will pull hard
time will arch backward
and streams of memory
engraved in our cells
will river throughout
a span too wide

Swap

By Aaron Pasker

Winston twinged as the doctor placed the cold stethoscope against his back.

"Deep breaths, Mr. Falk."

He breathed deep and exhaled long and slow.

"Your breathing is certainly improved. It looks like your body has integrated the new lung very well." Dr. Cain examined his chest, probing and pressing with frigid fingers.

None of Winston's replaced body parts had had any problems. Just the opposite. His arms were as strong as when he was twenty, his eyesight was again a perfect 20/20, his hair thick and full – the list went on and on.

"Good to hear, Doc," he said, putting his shirt back on.

"That's not all of the news." Dr. Cain frowned. "Have you still been feeling fatigued, dizziness?"

Winston froze in the middle of buttoning up his shirt and looked up at the doctor.

"Well, yes, some. But not like it was before the lung replacement. Sometimes just walking to the kitchen feels like a marathon. I thought maybe it was just an after effect of the surgery."

"I'm afraid not. I heard a slight arrhythmia that wasn't there during your last visit. I suspect your cellular degeneration has progressed."

Winston's pulse quickened at the news. So far, they had always been able to replace every affected part.

"Don't worry, Winston. Like I told you when you first walked into my office, I'm committed to saving your life. Replacing your heart will be just like everything else. We'll grow one from your augmented DNA sample, do a quick procedure, and you'll be fine."

"It's just that... my heart. What if the replacement doesn't work? Or my body rejects it?"

"The chance of rejection is very low. But we'll keep the old heart in cryogenic storage with the rest of your original organs. If an issue does arise, we can put it back in temporarily until we solve it."

Winston imagined his former body parts sitting in a freezer in the basement of a laboratory somewhere. He understood the reasoning – keep them on hand as a precaution, should they ever be needed. Still, it was strange to think about.

"When do we do it?"

"I'll do a full body scan to be sure, but based on my observations and the history of your disease spread, I would say soon. Very soon, if we want to continue to stay ahead of it."

* * *

Two days later, Winston entered the decontamination chamber. The door closed behind him with an airtight seal. Jets of white mist sprayed out of nozzles in the ceiling. After thirty seconds, the gas jets stopped and the exit door opened. Properly sanitized, he proceeded into the operating room.

The centerpiece of the room was the metal surgical table. The ceiling had an array of robotic arms with various medical tools attached to their ends. The walls were bare other than high-resolution cameras that allowed the surgeon to control the instruments and view the patient from every angle.

He climbed on the metal table and laid down.

Dr. Cain's voice came through the room's intercom. "Mr. Falk, we are ready to begin. Just lay back and relax. We'll be done in no time."

One of the robotic arms with a rubber mask at its end extended down and covered his mouth and nose. He heard the telltale hiss of oxygen and anesthetic flowing.

With one deep breath, the room faded to darkness.

* * *

A week after his surgery, he returned to the clinic.

Dr. Cain listen to his chest and asked, "How are you feeling?"

"Like a new man, Doc. The new heart is ticking away like clockwork."

"No more fatigue or dizziness?"

"No, I feel great."

"I'm glad to hear that." Dr. Cain put his stethoscope away. "It looks like your new heart has integrated well. That's the good news."

Winston tensed and stared at the doctor, waiting for his next sentence.

"Your pre-surgery scan showed an abnormality in your dura mater, the membrane that surrounds your brain. It appears the degeneration is starting to affect it. It's only a matter of time now."

Winston's new heart leapt into his throat. "So... so, that's it then."

"No, Winston," Dr. Cain said, laying a reassuring hand on his shoulder. "Not at all. I told you I would do whatever it took to save your life. I can, and I will."

"I don't understand. What do you mean?"

"I mean, we can replace your brain now, before the disease spreads to it."

"What? How is that even possible? Wouldn't I..." he pointed a finger to his temple, "be gone? Dead?"

"No, no, Winston," Dr. Cain said with a smile. "Your brain is an organ, and it can be replaced like any other without losing your memories, skills, and such."

"How? How would you do that?"

"First, we grow a new one. Consider it a 'blank,' if you will. Your brain is made up of two halves. My plan is to remove one half of your existing brain and replace it with half of the blank. With the aid of an implanted microchip, the old half will train the new. Within weeks the blank can reform the neural connections and it will be just like the original. Then, we will remove the other original half and repeat the process."

Winston considered the idea. "I'm not sure how I feel about that."

"If there were another way, I would do it, but this is truly the only option. And I suggest we get started as soon as possible before the degeneration starts to affect it. We want to retain everything we possibly can."

"Okay, Doc. Let's do it."

* * *

Three months and three surgeries later, Winston walked through the clinic doors for his post-surgery checkup.

In the examination room, Dr. Cain shined a small penlight into his eyes.

"Your vision has been okay, no problems?"

"I'm seeing just fine, Doc."

"Any slurring of speech or weakness in your limbs?"

"No, everything has been working just right as far as I can tell."

"And your cognitive function? Any memory lapses, blackouts, that sort of thing?"

"Like I said, Doc, everything up here," he tapped his temple, "is good."

"I'm glad to hear that." Dr. Cain put his pen light back in his lab coat pocket. "All signs show that you are recovering perfectly.

You're a brand-new man, Winston. Literally."

"You mean-"

Dr. Cain smiled broadly. "Yes, we've finally done it. We've replaced every part of the old you. No more cellular degeneration, no more surgeries."

"I'm done? I'm cured?"

A wave of relief swept over him.

"I want to do one last full body scan and I want to see you again in a month for a checkup. But yes, Winston, you're cured. I told you I would save your life."

* * *

Two weeks later, Winston limped through the doors of the clinic, an incredible pain shooting through his left foot.

The receptionist ran around her desk and met him at the door. "Mr. Falk? Are you alright?"

"No, something's wrong. Very wrong. Is Dr. Cain in?"

"He is, I'll call him right away." She offered her arm to him and helped him to a sofa. He slumped down as she hurried back to her phone and had a hushed conversation. A minute later, Dr. Cain appeared in the doorway.

"Winston, what's going on? Your checkup isn't for a couple of weeks yet."

"It's my foot, Doc. It feels like it's on fire."

"Come on back and let's take a look."

The receptionist brought over a wheelchair and helped him into it. Dr. Cain wheeled him through the door and down the hallway. Once they entered one of the examination rooms, the doctor carefully removed Winston's shoe. As the doctor peeled off his sock, he revealed a black, swollen foot.

"What's happening? What's happening to my foot?"

"I was afraid of this. Your last scan showed some minor signs of tissue breakdown on the DNA level." Dr. Cain dropped his head and sighed. "It was limited and I had hoped it would not spread, but it appears to be systemic." He stood and opened one of the wall cabinets.

"What do we do now? Do you have to replace my foot again?"

The doctor took a syringe and vial from the cabinet. "I'm afraid not. Any new tissue grown now would eventually break down in the same way. And I won't have time to refine my process before the breakdown progresses." He filled the syringe from the vial and turned to Winston. "Roll up your sleeve. This will help."

Winston pulled his sleeve up and the doctor gave him the shot.

96

The pain faded almost instantly. A wave of serene euphoria came over him.

"Whoa, what was that?"

"Morphine."

Winston's mind swam.

"What do we do then, if you can't replace my foot? Amputate it?"

Dr. Cain refilled the syringe and injected him again.

"No, I'm afraid not. I'll have to start over."

"What do you mean start over? We do all of the surgeries again?"

"Not we, per se. Winston and me."

"What?" Everything was going numb. "Doc, I'm Winston."

"Perhaps from your point of view, but one could say you're just a collection of experimental tissues grown in my lab."

Dr. Cain injected him again, then sat in a chair in the corner of the room.

He rubbed the bridge of his nose as he continued. "A failed experiment, at that. But I can start over with the original—the man currently in pieces in cryogenic storage."

"I... don't understand." He struggled for breath.

"I know, I know. But, he will, once I put him back together." The doctor stood. "I will have to refine my process and starte anew, but I promise I will be successful this time."

The room grew dark. "But I'm Winst-" He fell back on the table.

"Shh..." Dr. Cain leaned over Winston and gently rubbed his shoulder. "Don't worry, this won't hurt. You can just let go."

The world faded to black.

* * *

Winston Falk opened his eyes on the cold surgical table of the operating room.

"Welcome back, Winston." Dr. Cain's voice sounded over the intercom.

He tried to sit up, but pain radiated throughout his body. Every degenerating cell screamed in agony. He gave up the attempt and laid back.

"What happened? Did something go wrong with the brain transfer?"

"Yes, I'm afraid so. My tissue replacement program failed. But, not to worry. As I told you, I am committed to saving your life."

Pull My Finger
By Robert Walton

A veil of smoke-colored snow fell from the moon's shoulders onto round-shouldered hills. A lantern's golden light bounced and bounded through a tree-shadowed valley. Its light grew brighter, came nearer and finally illuminated a sleigh. It was Santa's sleigh—loaded impossibly full, but riding high on an icy crust.

With bells tinkling, harness creaking, and reindeer puffing plumes of silvery steam, the sleigh slowed. Santa pulled a thermos from his bag, opened it and sniffed. The cinnamon tingle of hot mulled wine tickled his nose and made him smile. He swigged from the thermos, then put it aside. He plucked a scarlet-bowed, gold-wrapped box out of his bag, grinned his merriest grin and offered it with both hands.

* * *

"That's enough, Mom."

"But the holo-vid isn't done yet, honey."

"I know."

"Is there something bothering you?" Ella smoothed her son's dark hair.

Jonah looked down. "It's just that ... well, I never get to open the present."

Her face fell into that harassed expression mothers have when events conspire to keep their children from being happy. "You know Amazon can't deliver during attacks."

"Yeah, I know."

"I'd have gotten you something—something good—but this shelter-in-place order was a surprise." She glanced at the environmental monitor. "And this attack seems worse than the others."

"It's okay."

"Maybe Amazon will get through when the all-clear sounds," she offered.

He detected the dispirited note in his mother's voice and looked up. "But I really like the part before the gift."

"I do, too, honey, I do too."

"Could you start it again?"

"That would be the third time today."

"Please? Just until Santa opens the thermos?"

"How about, *The Uncles*?"

He thought about this for a moment. At last, he nodded. "Yeah. *The Uncles* are fun."

"I'll put it on."

"Mom?"

She manipulated the remote. "Yes?

"Do I have real uncles?"

She froze, her mind awash with memories. "No, dear—not for some years."

"But I had some?"

She glanced at the bookshelf against the far wall, at the peacock blue bowl from Istanbul her brother in law Derek had given her for a wedding gift. "For a few months—they died shortly after the war began and you were born. They never saw you."

* * *

Colonel Ivan Andreyevich Peshkoff studied the glowing screens. "The attack is at its peak."

"Yes," Professor Ivanovsky grunted with satisfaction. "The old submarines will surface and burst like soap bubbles.

"These radiation levels are quite high."

Ivanovsky nodded. "The highest we've yet achieved and the winds are exactly right."

"Tell it to the North Koreans. They thought the winds were right, too."

"True. Using that supertanker last month, concealing its cargo and purpose, was really quite clever of them. Their meteorology was deficient, however.

"Deficient enough to kill their crew."

"Only half—the rest are recovering in Guantanamo, I understand."

Peshkoff again glanced at the radiation level readouts. You'd think that these repeated attacks would crush domestic resistance."

"Not by themselves."

"Why not? The guts of forty sub reactors will be spreading across their skies."

"No." Ivanovsky paused. "The Americans' defenses will protect them from any simple radiation assault we can contrive."

* * *

Ella glanced at the filters' monitor lights. Green. Functioning. Keeping out the poison. She sighed with relief. She knew this was a bad storm with radiation levels above anything experienced before. They would be confined to their apartment for weeks, well past Christmas, but thank God for the building's filters.

A hopping, leaping tune sounded from the hologram uncles. Uncle Bill had a nose flute plugged into his yawning right nostril. Uncle Tom buzzed his kazoo. Uncle Ed sang:

Oh, I come from Alabama with a banjo on my knee! Going to Louisiana, my true love for to see.

"What's a banjo, mom?"

"It's something like a violin, I think."

"Why does he have it on his knee?"

"Maybe that's an easy way to play it?"

It rained all night the day I left, the weather it was dry/ The sun so hot I froze to death, Susanna don't you cry/ Oh Susanna! Oh, don't you cry for me! For I come from Alabama with a banjo on my knee!

"Why should she cry?"

"Who, dear?"

"Susanna. He's coming from Alabama with a banjo on his knee. Why should that make her cry?"

She pointed at the hologram uncles to deflect—as all mothers do—a question for which she had no answer. "Look, it's time for them to tell jokes. They always have new ones."

Bald Uncle Bill leaned toward Jonah, grinning. "What do you call a baby insect?"

Jonah shook his head. "Don't know."

"A baby buggy!" Bill slapped his thigh and roared a laugh.

The corner of Jonah's mouth quivered.

Uncle Tom winked around his red turnip of a nose. "What do you call a sleeping bull?"

Jonah shook his head.

"A bulldozer! HA! HA!"

A half-smile creased Jonah's lips.

Uncle Ed, with his white hair catching a gleam from the monitor lights, extended his right index finger. "Pull my finger."

Jonah looked at him.

Ed smiled encouragingly. "Go ahead, pull."

Jonah wrapped his small hand around the imaginary finger and pulled.

A proud fart blatted through the quiet room. Bill and Tom and Ed howled with laughter. Jonah squealed along with them.

When they'd almost caught their breath, Uncle Ed again extended his finger. "Pull harder."

Jonah did. Flatulence, fruity and exaggerated, again ripped through the apartment's stale air.

Tears leaked from the corners of Jonah's eyes as he gasped for breath.

Ella smiled, not at the crudity, but at her son's pure laughter.

* * *

Peshkoff snorted. "We have a limited number of obsolescent submarines—old boomers that may be converted to rad-weapons. Why waste them if attacks like this one are futile?"

"Because, my dear colonel, today we have something new."

"We do?"

"As I said, the Americans' rad-hazard defenses are excellent, especially those in New York. Diversion fans, charcoal shields, filters, dispersal agents—they've mostly neutralized previous attacks. But, now we've engineered specialized microorganisms."

Peshkoff shrugged his indifference.

Ivanovsky smiled. "Imagine nano-piranhas, tiny monsters that devour filter fibers. They will allow this attack to kill tens of thousands, perhaps more, and pave the way for the final victory."

"You truly think this?"

"New York is their heaviest defended habitat. When we defeat it, they will have no choice but to surrender. Tens of thousands will die to save millions more. That's war."

Peshkoff chuckled. "Tens of thousands will die so that millions more may die—that's war."

"You're a nihilist, Colonel."

"I'm a soldier."

Ivanovsky shook his head. "I'm no monster, Ivan Andreyevich."

Peshkoff said nothing.

Ivanovsky continued, "Victory is at hand. You'll see."

"You've deployed your nano-piranhas?"

"Billions."

* * *

Ella sat at her apartment's table, bent over, head resting on her right arm. Her face was pale and calm, but a trickle of dark blood traced a line from her right nostril across her lips and pooled on the table's translucent, green surface. She stared straight ahead. The filter monitor's pulsing red light reflected from her unblinking eyes.

Jonah sat in the easy chair, his chin resting on his breast.

Uncle Ed, crouching across from him, smiled slyly, extended his right hand and said, "Pull my finger."

Jonah didn't move. The hologram flickered. Uncle Ed smiled again and extended his hand.

"Pull my finger."

The Same Tears Flowing from Older Eyes

By Donald J. Bingle

"What do you mean, you can't do anything?"

Marilee Collingsworth glared at the white-coated "specialist," all prim and professional. The doctor leaned back in his modern, ergonomic chair, hands folded on his over-sized mahogany desk. A matching credenza decorated with small *objets d'art* sat against the wall behind him. Framed diplomas and certifications of accredited specializations in various forms of pediatric medicine dominated the space above the credenza.

She reached out and clenched her husband Gary's hand, without taking her eyes off the doctor. "He's only three. He's hardly even lived yet. Our pediatrician, Dr. Steinman, he said that you were the expert in these cases, that you'd be able to help us."

Gary spoke up. "We have insurance, Dr. Tremmel. And Marilee, she's a stay-at-home mom. She can give him all the attention he requires during treatment and recovery."

Dr. Tremmel pursed his lips as if the conversation were inconvenient and distasteful. Marilee saw his eyes flick to the expensive-looking watch on his wrist. She wondered what could be more important than saving the life of her son. He cleared his throat.

"News like this is never pleasant, Mr. and Mrs. Collingsworth. Your son ..."

"Tag," Marilee snapped. "Our son's name—your patient's name—is Tag."

"Yes, Tag. Tag's condition has already progressed to a highly advanced state. While there have been a few successes in delaying the progression of this illness when caught quite early, I have nothing to offer you but palliative care—to relieve the severity of his pain—between now and his inevitable ... decline."

Her eyes filled with tears, but she fought to contain them there. "When we first contacted you, you said there were clinical trials. You said there was a treatment."

"That was before I knew how far the disease had spread in ... Tag. At this advanced stage, he wouldn't even qualify for a blind treatment study. Progress is being made. Within our lifetimes, we hope to be able to wipe out the scourge affecting your son, but I'm afraid we are decades away from that now."

"How long?" whispered Gary. "How long will he suffer before he dies?"

"We'll do our best to minimize the suffering. There's little point in being stingy with the morphine when there is no risk of addiction and the end result is inevitable, but we are talking a matter of weeks—two, three months at most."

"I want to take him home," Marilee insisted. "I want the rest of whatever time he has to be at home, not here in the hospital with ... strangers."

Dr. Tremmel's face relaxed. Marilee assumed it was because he was relieved he would not have to interact with her and Gary ... with Tag ... anymore. "Of course, Mrs. Collingsworth. Our Nurse Practitioner can teach you how to administer the morphine drip and we can arrange a service to come by for several hours a day to assist you in Tag's care if that is your desire." He pressed a button on the desk phone, then stood and ushered them toward the door. "Let me introduce you to my assistant, Loren. She can arrange everything you need."

Dr. Tremmel offered his hand to shake. Marilee ignored it, but Gary, ever accommodating, grasped it. The doctor inclined his head as they shook. "I'm so sorry for your ..."

"Don't you dare!" spat Marilee. "Don't you dare say you are sorry for our loss. Tag's still here. He's still alive and I'm going to make sure he stays that way, with or without your help."

Dr. Tremmel's face blanched. Backing away, he stammered, "I ... I never. I was just saying I was sorry for your *situation* and that I wish there was something I could do to help."

Gary tried to comfort her as Loren maneuvered them back to the reception room, where other people sat stone-faced as they waited for their own news. There, Marilee calmed down before putting on her most reassuring face and walking to Tag's hospital room, where she began the cumbersome paperwork releasing him to home care, to her care.

Gary was a good man, a loving man, but he was out of his depth. No, if anyone was going to save Tag, it had to be her.

* * *

She'd never spent much time online. As a mom, she was too busy taking care of washing, cleaning, and cooking, to fritter away time tweeting and texting or browsing and sharing. But she did know the basics. She could surf and search. She knew how to read articles online, even post some questions on the medical and support sites. Now, whenever she wasn't caring for Tag, she spent time combing through everything she could find about his ailment, including clinical tests and alternative medicines.

The effort was numbing and depressing. Dr. Tremmel hadn't lied to them. She could find nothing that was in the slightest encouraging or that discussed current trials he might join. Always, always it was "someday" there would be a cure. That someday was always decades away, though, and she only had a few weeks to save her son. The support groups focused on helping parents cope with suffering and loss, not on medical advice. And so her searches became broader, more desperate, more outside the box.

She began posting pleas for help on the alternative medicine sites. A few responses were easy to identify as scams. Still, she lingered over those messages, almost willing to let the senders scam her. She craved even the slightest hope, not that she could afford to chase false leads. Even with insurance, Gary already worked extra shifts for home care costs. They also hoped those double-shift dollars would let him take a few days off as the end neared. She knew work was his way of coping, as best he could.

One morning, after changing Tag's IV lines, she found a message and a link waiting for her from a woman she'd met in one of the online support groups. "Check out this site. Maybe it can help." She thought for a few moments before clicking through. She knew anonymous links let viruses, spamware, and spyware take over your computer and send your personal information to the Russian mob. The more she thought about it, though, the less she figured shills for the Russian mob were trolling medical malady support groups ripping people off. That's what porn and pirate sites were for.

She double-clicked. A site opened for a company called ChronoTek, where, apparently, "the future was now." Scrolling down, she saw that they had a few "payload" opportunities for sending items one way "into the future" on their inaugural series of commercial time travel runs.

It had to be a joke, but the site was both professional and detailed, including a lengthy legal disclaimer: "No guaranty of delivery. Substantial risks apply. Liability limited to the cost of shipment. Shippers must sign a waiver of damages for loss of shipment, including actual, consequential, exemplary, and punitive damages. Serious inquiries only. Transportation is one way only. Shipped items cannot be returned."

For a few minutes, she didn't understand why her online friend sent her this link—the support group wasn't the kind of thing where people shared Facebook memes, cute cat photos, or interesting posts and sites. Then, she gasped.

Tag's condition was incurable *now*. Tag's condition was terminal *now*. No treatment existed to help him *now*. There was no hope of saving him *now*. That's what all the doctors said, but they always softened the blow. Researchers are working hard on a cure. Promising drug trials are underway that one day could lead to a cure. What we are learning from the progression of the illness in Tag may one day help others ... Blah. Blah. Blah.

She didn't care about the future. She needed the future to be *now*. And, that's what ChronoTek promised, that the future was now.

If she could send her baby into the future, where his condition was treatable, curable, he could be saved. He could live a normal life.

She was desperate, but that didn't mean she wasn't skeptical, too. Before doing anything else, she researched the basics. ChronoTek appeared legitimate, with a research lab in the desert north of Las Vegas. It was a private company, so she found little detail about its business. At least news sites confirmed it employed several hundred people and did research projects for both private companies and the government. She googled the name of the company, along with words like "fraud" and "scam," but found no complaints. A more extensive search yielded a few postings by people ... like her ... wondering if the posting was serious.

Then the visiting nurse arrived for the day and they discussed Tag's condition. He was not sleeping well and moaned both while asleep and awake. They could increase the morphine drip ... again ... but the medication impacted his breathing. At some point, alleviating his pain would hasten his death.

She looked down at him on the bed. He was so little, so frail for his age. His sandy hair spilled out over his forehead, just above his closed eyes, puffy from medication, yet still baggy from lack of sleep. He hugged his stuffed dinosaur, his "wubby," the tiny arms of the faded and worn T-Rex as delicate and underused as his own. She had bought the inexpensive, but soft and colorful, toy on impulse during a hurried Christmas shopping run when Tag was only a year old. She realized now that it was unfortunately appropriate. Both Tag and T-Rex were doomed to extinction by forces they could neither understand nor control.

"Go ahead and increase the dosage," she murmured. "I can't stand for him to suffer."

Marilee cried for an hour after the nurse left. When she had cried herself out, she called up the ChronoTek website on her laptop, clicked through to the preliminary customer profile page and completed the information. Sure, it was desperate and stupid and, for all she had read, pointless, but she needed to *do* something. It wasn't fair to take it out on Gary, again, venting about her frustration and distress when he got home from a double-shift at work. She pressed "submit" without even re-reading her form.

* * *

"You did what?" Gary asked after staring at her for almost a full minute when she told him about her application to ChronoTek.

"Don't you see, Gary? Tag can be cured in the future."

"But ... but ... even if all of this is legitimate, we not only risk killing Tag in order to save him, we lose him either way. He'll be gone from our lives forever, an orphan in some unknown future."

Marilee shook her head. "No, no. Don't you see? The trip is only twenty years into the future. We can catch up to him. It's like putting him in ... suspended animation for twenty years while medical science advances to meet his needs. We send him into the future in a flash, when a cure for his illness will already have been discovered and perfected. We move into the future a second at a time, just like we always have. Then, twenty years from now, we go pick him up *just as he arrives* and get him the treatment he needs to survive." Tears fell from her eyes, but she made no effort to stop them. "Then ... then we can *raise our child* just like we always planned to do. Together, one happy family."

It was almost morning by the time they finished talking it out. Finally, Gary said: "Fine. Assuming we check this all out and it's on the up and up and assuming this ChronoTek company will even take human "cargo" and they can convince us that Tag will survive the journey, I agree it's our only hope. Can we afford it? I don't think Blue Cross/Blue Shield has ChronoTek in their preferred provider program."

Marilee hesitated a moment before responding. She had looked at the tables on the webpage showing cost per ounce. Getting to the future in a hurry wasn't cheap. But she didn't need to burden Gary with that, not right before another full day at work with next to no sleep.

"I'll get a job. Since I won't be taking care of Tag full-time. I'll talk to the insurance people—this saves them a lot of money if you think about it."

Gary tilted his head. She knew he was doing his best to be supportive, but she sensed his skepticism.

She continued on. "Maybe ChronoTek will give us a discount because of the good PR they can get out of doing this. I can organize fundraisers if needed. I will figure it out, Gary. I promise you that. I'll make sure that money doesn't stand it the way of our being able to raise our son, to have a future together, even if it's delayed a few decades."

* * *

And she did.

It wasn't easy. ChronoTek was hesitant about sending a three-year-old, physically unfit, terminally ill, human being into the future. They insisted on affidavits from Tag's doctors about his status, his ability to withstand the minor rigors of the journey, and the likelihood of a future cure. They insisted on a healthcare power of attorney from Marilee and Gary giving ChronoTek the authority to make any medical decisions necessary for Tag until such time as his parents regained custody. They even insisted on psychological testing to establish Gary and Marilee's competency. But, Marilee never blinked.

She pushed and prodded until they relented. She didn't know why they gave in. Maybe there wasn't as much demand for sending items one way into the future as they had hoped.

If there was a lack of demand, it wasn't reflected in ChronoTek's pricing. Gary kept working double shifts. They took out a second mortgage, drained their retirement savings, sold whatever they owned worth selling, and convinced local stores to set out donation cans to help defray Tag's medical costs. Marilee lined up a job, two jobs, to commence on Tag's departure.

And then the day came. Tears of sadness and hope all mixed into one wet, emotional farewell. Marilee hugged Gary so tight she was afraid she would hurt him. The timer counted down and they watched Tag, asleep from sedation amidst a motley array of the crates and collectibles chosen for the future by someone willing to pay a king's ransom for the privilege. Even asleep, he hugged his wubby tight to his chest. Gary didn't know it, but Marilee had sold the small stone in her engagement ring to cover the extra cost of the T-Rex, so Tag wouldn't be alone even for a second before they were reunited in the future. At the last moment, she noticed a Cheerio stuck to the side of his hand; she always kept a plastic bag of them handy for snacking in the car.

Jesus, she hoped she wasn't paying extra for that, too.

A flash of greenish light followed by a sudden drop in air pressure signaled departure. Marilee and Gary stared at the emptiness on the transport platform. A few minutes later, a tech arrived to let them know that the launch was a success and Marilee sobbed even harder as she pictured the future, imagining Tag being hustled into a waiting ambulance twenty years hence as they stood there ... no, here ... greeting him with the same tears flowing from older eyes.

After about twenty minutes, the tech suggested, gently, that it was time to go. Gary wiped his eyes and mumbled about getting back to work. Marilee nodded. Her first shift on her new job started in an hour.

* * *

Their lives were different without Tag. While Tag's absence hit them like a freight train, disrupting every moment, smashing normalcy into dust, Marilee refused to let herself grieve. Tag wasn't dead; Tag was alive. He was just far, far away from her, getting the medical attention he needed. He would grow up with them someday; they would be a normal family again, someday. Still, any reminder of his absence was like a punch on top of a festering wound. A wound that would not heal for twenty long years of loss.

They adapted without ever acknowledging Tag's loss. Marilee boxed up his toys and clothes and turned his room into a sewing nook. She made extra money making baby clothes for other mothers. The visiting nurse stopped visiting. She and Gary worked their jobs, did their best to pay their bills, and barely saw each other in passing as work and worry crushed them in their fog of unexplainable loss.

They explained Tag's absence by telling their friends he was in a special medical facility, but as time passed they had less and less need for explanations. They had no time for friends, for a social life. They had no time for anything but work and wistful looks at the calendar while they tracked the painfully slow progress of their own private limbo. They were temporally deactivated—their family, their life, on hold until they could be reunited with their son.

At first, Marilee stole spare moments, scouring the net for any sign of progress towards treating Tag's illness, but the information was too painful, the progress too slow. Worse yet, whenever she did check on the race for a cure, she found herself second-guessing their decision.

Was twenty years more than they needed to wait? Was it not enough? Had Tag even survived the trip?

She didn't know. She wouldn't know for twenty years.

She wept in secret as she watched other mothers in the park across the street, playing with their children. And even though the sun shined outside her window, her days turned dark and gray. She snapped at Gary too often when he shuffled through the door to sleep for a few hours before heading off to work again.

The world continued on, a parade of fires and crimes and wars and economic downturns marching toward the future. For Marilee, current events existed only as an irritant. Yet, the mindless talking heads of twenty-four-hour news droned on, somehow constantly amazed and incensed at events even though they repeated in patterns from time immemorial.

No light of joy flickered in Marilee's world until the nineteenth year passed since Tag's departure. For the first time, objective facts suggested her plan to save her son was coming together as hoped.

Slow and fitful medical progress had finally crossed a crucial threshold. Treatments existed for Tag's condition, though still expensive and not as efficacious as Marilee had hoped they would be by now.

As for transport, ChronoTek had publicly reported successful cargo arrivals of other shipments sent on shorter hops scheduled to arrive sooner than Tag.

Their sacrifice was coming to a close. They paid off the debt incurred for Tag's travel and began saving for his arrival costs.

No other news mattered to her that year. Not the burgeoning climate crisis, not the latest economic collapse, not the recall of cochlear implants by the largest purveyor of in-your-ear streaming music, or even the scheduled brown-outs and looming energy shortfalls in the wake of China's cyber-attack on the American power grid. She would see Tag soon. She would be a mother again. Gary would be a father again, not just a faceless worker drone. Once their twenty-year sentence ended, their life would reactivate—complete and filled with joy.

She barely spoke to Gary during the transport ride to ChronoTek the day of Tag's scheduled arrival, so lost was she in the wonder and anticipation of the moment. She saw a smile crinkling the edges of his face and knew that he felt it too. Their ordeal was almost over. Their day had come. Their life could begin anew even though, like an exonerated convict, the weight of wasted years pressed hard upon their weary brows.

They sat in the same seats they had twenty years before in ChronoTek's cargo bay as the arrival clock ticked downward. A young receptionist—about the age Tag would have been if he had lived without needing to skip ahead—brought them tea and dried cherries while they waited. It suddenly hit Marilee hard. She had literally waited a lifetime for this moment.

The future *was* now.

At t-minus two minutes, a yellow warning light strobed and the few remaining techs exited into the control area, a plexi-glassed room across the bay. At t-minus forty-two, an audible hum built to a bass thrum and the overhead lights flickered and dimmed. At t-minus eight, the air in the center of the cargo bay glimmered and wavered. At t-minus one, a green flash of light accompanied an enormous clap of thunder as a burst of air pressure pummeled Marilee.

Marilee involuntarily closed her eyes at the first flash of light, but she forced them to open despite more pulsing green flashes assaulting her vision. The thunder dissembled, rumbling to join the deep thrum, which continued to crescendo. As it did, she watched an array of cargo coalesce in the center of the room. Focusing her squinting eyes on Tag's position, she spotted his placid, sleeping face for an instant before another series of green flashes assaulted her eyes.

The thrum stuttered several times before transforming into a screaming falsetto whine. Then a solitary red light flashed and the cargo itself was pulsing, but not in syncopation with the continued green flashes. Static electricity played over the edges of the containers and equipment. One of the techs in the control room slammed his hand down hard on the console in front of him and the green light flashed yet again. The air pressure dropped in a sudden swoosh.

The lights all stopped pulsing.

The cargo bay was empty.

Marilee screamed.

* * *

She awoke in a hospital room. Gary sat next to her bed. He looked haggard and tired.

She tried to sit up, but a soft, firm hand held her back.

"Shhhh-shhhh, now. You just lay back. You'll pull out the IV tube if you move too suddenly."

A nurse stood next to the bed, looking first down at her and then at a bank of monitors above her bed. Marilee swiveled her head slowly—a throbbing headache protested—to look at Gary, who was biting his lip. He took her hand in his.

"What ... what happened? Where's Tag?" she croaked, her throat ragged and raw.

"There was a power fluctuation during the arrival. The computers dropped out during the resequencing and had to reboot ..."

"Oh my God," she cried, the pain in her throat matching the pain in her soul. "Tag ... Dear, God. What happened to ..."

Gary interrupted, his voice gaining in strength and volume. He used the same tone she'd heard Gary's father use once to command him to listen to something Gary didn't want to hear. "Dad Voice," Gary called it. Gary never had a need to use it on Tag, but he now used it on her. "They ... they have emergency procedures, back-ups for this kind of thing. You know, just like NASA. The computers couldn't resequence, but the propulsion system could still transmit. They punched up the emergency override and pushed the cargo forward to a later time."

She whispered this time. "Oh my God ..."

"They think the transmission succeeded. They think Tag is still alive." He faltered for a moment. "Of course, they can't know, not for sure, not until he arrives."

Marilee closed her eyes, imagining that brief moment when she saw her son in the cargo bay—the only instant she had seen him for twenty years. Tears streamed down her face as she clung to that image. "How long?"

Gary cleared his throat. When he answered, she could barely hear his voice above the whir and beeps of the medical equipment.

"A hundred years. Their emergency protocol automatically transmits a hundred years forward."

She heard herself screaming; fire burned her throat. She thrashed against sweat-soaked sheets; strong hands held her down. Then, the sharp pinch of a needle turned everything soft and she faded into darkness.

She never asked how many times, but that same process— awakening, realization, screaming, medication, blackness—repeated until the day came when she awoke and just lay sobbing in bed.

* * *

A tech from ChronoTek showed up one day to answer her questions. He remained quiet and showed no emotion as she vented about his employer. When she stopped, he simply asked: "What do you want to know?"

Her lip still quivered in anger, but finally, she spat out a question. "What happened?"

"A massive power spike on the main grid tripped the computers. The government says the Chinese were behind it again, but nobody is really sure yet. It takes a lot of computing power to resequence the chrono-transmission. The computers crashed just as that process was beginning. There was no way to complete it."

"But I saw him. I saw Tag. Why couldn't you just have stopped while he was there?"

"Resequencing occurs from the outside in, to the center of the load. You didn't see Tag. You saw a shell of him. If we'd stopped, he would have been incomplete. He would have been an empty shell. He would have been dead inside."

She felt like she was dead inside.

The tech waited a few seconds, then continued. "Our chief engineer hit the emergency transmit. It allows us to re-transmit any incoming signal forward in time, in case the equipment isn't operating properly or someone or something is encroaching on the physical space where incoming mass is resequencing. It simply bumps everything forward."

She clenched her teeth for a few moments to control her anger before continuing. "But, for God's sake, why a hundred years? Why not a minute or an hour or a day or ... a goddamn year? Why send things forward a century?"

The tech sighed and shrugged his shoulders. "The emergency protocol wasn't really set up with human passengers in mind. With cargo ... inanimate cargo ... you just want to send it someplace, sometime, out of the way. You don't want to go too far forward, but you don't want it to be too quick either."

"Why not?"

"Well, for one thing, you need to have time to fix the problem that forced the re-transmission ..."

"That explains an hour or a day or a week. It doesn't explain a hundred years. Why not just set it to re-transmit in an hour and do that again and again until the problem is solved?"

He nodded as if this question was expected. "I don't want to get all tech-wonky with you, Mrs. Collingsworth, but it has to do with thermodynamics. You probably remember from your physics class in high school about conservation of matter and energy. They can't be destroyed, just converted from one to the other. Well, when we transmit mass, we take it out of the universe as it exists at that time, so we have to input energy into the universe sufficient to offset that matter and, well with E equaling MC squared and all, that's a lot of energy. We do that up in the ionosphere, high as we can get, but it still creates a lot of waste heat. Of course, the opposite occurs when we receive. We have to pull energy out of the universe, so you'd think it might balance out, but it's like electricity transmission—just transmitting it to where it needs to be is wasteful and expensive."

"Expensive?" she growled. "You're talking about my son."

He nodded. "I know that, Mrs. Collingsworth. I'm just explaining why the protocol was set up that way."

"So, that's it?"

"No, Ma'am. We at ChronoTek, we want to make this right."

"So, what? You're giving me back my transport fee? That's what the contract says I get. But that won't do. I want my son."

"I know that. We know that. We can't send back your son. Nothing can ever go back in time. It would cause paradoxes. So the only thing we can do is send you, you and your husband, forward in time to meet your son. We can put you on a planned transmission just three months from now that will let you arrive just six weeks after your son."

"Three months?"

"That gives you time to get ready now and for your son to get healthy before you get there."

* * *

Marilee could hardly wait to tell Gary the good news when he arrived at the hospital. He walked in with a small bouquet of daffodils, his face set and grim, and she immediately assaulted him with a rush of words about what the tech had told her. Gary put the bouquet on the table beside her bed and held up both hands, palms out, gesturing her to slow down.

"I know. I know," he said, sitting down and grasping her left hand in both of his. "ChronoTek talked to me first, a few days ago."

"But, why didn't you tell me?"

He looked up at the corner of the room. "I can't do it, Marilee. I can't go. You know I love you and that I love Tag, but I can't go on chasing a dream that will never come true. For all we know, Tag's dead. For all we know, the transmission to the future will fail again. For all we know, Tag may still be days from death even if he arrives in the future, with nothing they can do about it."

Tears fell from his eyes. Still, he did not look at her. "All I've done, all we've done for the last twenty-some years now is work to make some tiny, tiny hope of a future as a family. I *am* my job now. I can't quit and risk everything ... leave everyone I know besides you and Tag ... and go to a future, where I have no job and will have no useful skills, on the infinitesimally small chance that everything will magically work out."

He finally turned to look at her. "I can't go."

She squeezed her eyes shut. "I can't *not* go."

"I know," he said, still holding her hand while they both cried. Then he leaned over, kissed her on the forehead, and left.

By the time she got home from the hospital, his clothes and their honeymoon luggage were gone. She was heartbroken but didn't blame him. Gary was a good man, but not as strong as she was. She would go into the future alone if she had to. She would go anywhere for her child. That's what mothers do.

She never saw Gary again.

* * *

Marilee sold everything she owned and put the money in an interest-bearing, long-term certificate of deposit. She wound up her affairs, said a few goodbyes to casual friends, and got ready to meet the future.

Finally, again, the future was now.

She arrived at the familiar location keyed up from both fear and anticipation. The techs at ChronoTek were pleasant and accommodating, reassuring her that all would go well.

This time, as the time counted down, she watched the empty visitors' galley and waited for the precious green light that would reunite her with her only child.

Flash.

The next thing she realized, an unkempt tech wearing a dirty lab coat bearing a ChronoTek logo scurried toward her, assisting her down from her perch on a ledge amidst the other cargo.

"You must hurry," he insisted. "It is dangerous here. They will notice the power fluctuation."

The ground shuddered after she took a few steps. The tech abandoned her and searched through the cargo. She was almost unbalanced by a whoomphing thud as the ground shuddered again. In the distance, she heard what sounded like gunshots cut a scream short. Something was terribly wrong here in this time.

She stumbled over to the tech ransacking the chrono-transported cargo. "Where's Tag? Where's my son?"

His eyes flicked down to a device on his wrist and he used a finger to scroll through a list. "No other passengers aboard this transport," he said as he turned back to the pile of cargo, chucking items aside as he searched.

"Not this transport," she insisted. "Six weeks ago. My son arrived six weeks ago."

The tech barked out a laugh. "Six weeks? Pre-attack. Could be anywhere now."

"What attack? Who attacked who?" she asked, then shook her head. She didn't really care about that. She only cared about Tag. She needed to focus on her questions. "My son, he was sick. They would have taken him to a hospital."

"Aha!" yelled the tech. He grabbed a toaster-sized piece of equipment and turned away.

She grabbed at his sleeve. "The hospital. Which way is the hospital?"

He brushed her hand away. "West, along the aqueduct. But I

wouldn't go there. Lots of casualties. Lots of predators taking advantage of them. Very dangerous."

More gunshots. Closer this time.

"Gotta go," said the tech, as he scampered away.

* * *

She never got to the hospital.

She found her way outside of ChronoTek's heavily damaged and abandoned offices. The area around the building was in shambles, not that she would have recognized much of it even if it hadn't been. A hundred years into the future was a claustrophobic place. Bombed-out ruins crowded against fire-gutted buildings. Half-demolished shanties leaned against the few solid walls that remained. The narrow streets were strewn with rubble and jammed with abandoned Segway-like personal transport devices. A thick, yellow miasma hovered above ground-level, blocking out both the horizon and the sun. She couldn't get her bearings; she had no idea in which direction she could find the aqueduct ... the hospital ... her son.

Almost a day passed before she found clean water. Another day before she scavenged any food—three packages of dried apricots under the magazine rack at a looted convenience store. She searched for the hospital but got nowhere.

At first, she avoided the people skulking through the haze. They were large and tough-looking, firing their weapons at the slightest provocation, even at the debris that sometimes rained down when the ground rumbled, conveying tremors from large explosions in the distance.

But, she needed information. Finally, she risked approaching a small group of scavengers and survivors working nearby. She was wary, but she needed them. It turned out they also could make use of her. The more scavengers a pair of guards could protect, the more supplies could be found. There was safety in numbers. Besides, she guessed that life on the streets was always easier when you had someone to watch your back, to stand guard while you slept, to share not only resources but information about where to find more. She knew she had no useful information to offer, but they didn't know that yet.

The group deflected her questions early on, even the simplest ones. She didn't blame them. She bided her time for several days.

Then, one evening as she bunked down with Trella, a woman just a few years younger than her, she could wait no longer. "I need to find the hospital."

"Hospital's gone. Not just destroyed, gone. Saw the crater

myself when Carter sent me on a long-range scrounging run one ... maybe two ... days before you hooked up with us. Nothing left but a twisted sign for Outpatient Parking."

"They targeted a hospital?"

"Wars ain't pretty." Trella looked her up and down. "Why do you need to go to a hospital? Are you sick? Did you get hurt in the rubble today?"

"I'm looking for my son, Tag."

Trella tilted her head to one side. "Why would you do that?"

"What do you mean? He's my son. I want to take care of him."

"That's not your job," replied Trella, furrowing her brow.

"Of course it is," replied Marilee. "I'm his mother."

Trella furrowed her brow even more.

Suddenly, it came to her. Given Marilee's age, Trella must think her son to be full-grown. Marilee held her hand up, indicating Tag's height. "He's not grown up. He's just a toddler. He's sick. I need to find him, to take care of him."

Trella shook her head. "That's not your job."

She still wasn't getting through somehow. She needed to try a different approach. "Do you have any children, Trella?"

Trella nodded. "Three. All boys."

"How old are they?"

Trella paused before replying. "Eight, ten, and thirteen, I think."

"You think?" That's when Marilee realized she hadn't seen any children since her arrival. Not scavenging in the ruins, not fighting in the streets. She did her best to keep the alarm out of her voice as she asked the next question. "Where are your children, Trella?"

Trella's eyes narrowed and her nose scrunched up in confusion. "Gone, too, of course. This place, this time ... they're no place for children. Too crowded, too dangerous, too little to eat. The government could do nothing to change the facts. This war, it was bound to occur sooner or later; everything is collapsing."

"Please," murmured Marilee. "Please tell me the government doesn't make you kill your children."

Trella laughed out loud, drawing an angry stare from the night guard near the front window. "No, silly goose. They don't even do that in China, not anymore. We sent them to the future. Far, far into the future, eons and epochs beyond when they say all of civilization has collapsed and the Earth has reclaimed the land and replenished itself."

Tag ... even if he had survived, he might have been sent forward, before the war broke out. He could be alone, abandoned in the far future. "You sent them away? To fend for themselves?"

"We sent them with teachers and farmers and caretakers to create a new civilization. It is our greatest accomplishment as a people. There is nothing for them here. There, then, they have clean water, clear skies, food aplenty, and no tribal, local, or national animosities to drive them toward war. They have an entire world to rebuild."

"How can you know that?"

Trella shrugged. "The targeting parameters excluded locations with pollutants, whether from radiation, poisons, or existing civilizations. You can keep going forward until you find a landing site that is not only safe but has been safe for tens of thousands of years. If conditions aren't right, the transport automatically bumps farther forward."

"But, how is that even possible? Don't there need to be computers at the other end to do the resequencing?"

Trella shook her head. "They figured out how to make that part of the payload more than a decade ago. Of course, there's still no going back."

Marilee had no intention of going back. Her focus was forward. Still, she hesitated before asking the next question—afraid of what the answer might be—but she had to know for sure. "What do I have to do to join him?"

Trella looked down at the ground, biting her lip. "You can't. The transmission centers didn't survive the first wave of the assault. This war has not only destroyed the present but it's also stolen the future from us ... from everyone who isn't already there."

"So, he's gone." The future had stolen her son. Marilee had sent Tag into the future to save him; she just couldn't join him there, in that fresh new world. All the years of work and worry crashed down upon her. The loss she always rationalized away constricted her chest. She would have screamed if she could, despite the danger. She teetered on the edge of uncontrolled rage.

Then, Trella looked back up at her. "Just know he's in a better place. All of them are. The children are our future. Isn't that what a mother should give her child? The future?"

Marilee closed her eyes in contemplation. Her past was a shambles filled with work and pain and regret. Her present, a constant struggle to survive in a hostile environment. But her son still wasn't dead. She still didn't need to grieve. Even if Tag had not yet landed, he was hurtling through infinity until he found paradise. She clung to that image. Her son had an unlimited future. What more could she wish him? She took a deep breath and let the years of struggle and anguish melt away as physical and emotional exhaustion overcame her.

She slept soundly for the first time in more than a century.

It Only Ends Once
By Winston Plowes

After turning over
a beach of pebbles,
I found you.

My treasure to keep polished
you dried into islands of hope
on my palms.

I will sew you into the bottle green leather
of laurel leaves
and swaddle you in peach skin,
stitched in gold and smelling of damp history.

Each morning I will settle into your depression,
dream under double rainbows
and count your fresh promises
before they melt into the sea.

And then, with every bow and curtsey of the tide,
the things we once both lost
from within our echoed hearts
will return to us remade.

Evelyn's Last Mitzvah

By Cari Greywolf Rowan

He sat on the stoop of his apartment building most days and watched people rushing by, lost in their own worlds. Most never gave him a thought or a glance.

"Being this old, one becomes invisible. It's a cruel curse," he muttered to himself. Jacob had lived in the old five-story walk up for forty-five years. Now, at seventy-five, he lived alone since the death of his wife nearly two decades ago. It had been a good marriage for thirty years. The silent home was a constant reminder he was alone. He thought, "How I miss her scent, her voice, the sounds of homemaking."

His friends had all either died or moved away. He had no interest in leaving his home. He was determined that the only way he would leave the home his wife had made for him was on a stretcher. He loved waking up in the simple apartment they had called home. The curtains she had made were now worn and threadbare in places, but they let in the light and lit his heart, evoking memories of her.

When the hydraulic jack at the shop where he worked had given way ten years ago, leaving him with severe multiple injuries, he wasn't sure he could keep walking up and down the five flights of aged, uneven stairs. His doctors urged him to move to an assisted living facility. But he was intent on returning home, to the lingering memories of his life with his beloved.

Once released from the hospital, his rehab consisted of struggling up and down those stairs. He'd count, one, two, three all the way to twelve, one excruciating step at a time. He'd rest at each landing, and then repeat, one, two, three to the bottom again and then rest.

As he regained some of his strength, the flights became somewhat easier, less painful, but he was no stranger to pain. The physical ache was a daily companion in his mechanics' labor. Emotional and spiritual pain piled on over the years was also far too familiar. He learned to make peace with both long ago. However, he couldn't make peace with his loneliness.

He spent his time sitting on the stoop day after day, often watching the elderly woman across the street. He could tell time by her. Every morning at ten, she appeared with a broom in hand to sweep the sidewalk in front of the apartment building where she lived. Jacob observed her transforming the mundane task into a ritual performed with care and devotion. Most people would have completed the job in a few minutes. She, however, swept to perfection, sweeping, and then stepping back to examine her work, then sweeping some more. Jacob respected her care and thoroughness, qualities he found lacking in too much of the world around him.

She looked spry for her age, which he assessed to be beyond his own 75 years. She was tall and thin, her white hair pulled back in a neat bun. Even though her clothes showed signs of age, Jacob appreciated how she paid attention to details. Now and then he would catch her eye and wave. She waved back and offered him a wide smile.

On a particularly lonely day, he summoned up the courage to venture across the street. He extended his hand and said, "Hello." She responded in kind, and then, not sure what to do, he shuffled up the block a bit and turned around to go home.

This became a new habit for him. He began to look forward to this routine. The little walk up the block and back was good exercise, and her smile and her greeting were good for his spirits. Day after day, unless the weather was too harsh, he repeated his new ritual. It left him feeling less alone. He began to think of her as his friend, and after a month, he stopped and said, "Hello," as usual, but then added, "My name is Jacob. I admire your dedication to keeping the sidewalk swept."

She smiled, and replied, "I'm Evelyn. I'm the super for this apartment. So I sweep, and unplug toilets and change light bulbs for all the 30-year-old couples that live here. They're all so well educated, but literally can't change a light bulb," as she gave a lighthearted chuckle.

Jacob was lost as to what to say or do next, so he muttered, "We live in a different world these days." Then, not knowing what else to say, he turned uttered, "Have a nice day," as he turned to walk up the block.

"You do the same," she called after him.

He left with a lighter step, his heart a bit less heavy. He liked the twinkle in her eye and her ready smile. He had a million questions he wanted to ask her, but his manners, from a different era, held them in check. His generation was more reserved than those that followed.

Each day, their conversations grew a tiny bit longer. Over the next months, he told her about his injury, losing his ability to work, his wife's death, and the loss of his only child who died so many years ago at age seven. Bit by bit, he found himself less lonely. Those five to ten-minute conversations became the bright spot of his day. Evelyn seemed to enjoy their repartee, always greeting him with a wide smile and that endearing sparkle in her eyes. But she spoke very little about herself, other than about her daily duties as super and her running commentary on the weather. She seemed to protect her privacy as sacred territory, not to be shared at the curbside. He respected that.

One hot summer day, she was wearing a short-sleeved dress. As he watched her ritually sweep the pavement, the tattooed numbers in faded blue on her bare left arm grabbed his attention. He had seen the same sort of tattooed numbers on his father-in-law's arm. He held back a gasp and ended the conversation to regain his composure. He didn't want to embarrass himself or cause her any concern.

Jacob spent much of that day pondering why the tattoo startled him. Maybe it was a reminder of his wife and her family who welcomed him so warmly. Maybe it was the contrast between his father-in-law's persistent slumped sadness and Evelyn's ready smile and spry walk. Maybe it was grief for a world that would let such nightmares occur. Surely, it was empathy for his pleasant neighbor. Intrusive thoughts forced themselves into his consciousness: stories passed down of what she must have endured surviving in the camps. Most likely, he concluded, it was a combination of all of that, and the recognition that, while she seemed so much more capable than he, she, too, was deeply wounded.

The next day, he found himself a bit hesitant to continue their social custom. He was still processing the many thoughts and emotions that those numbers, A105623, evoked in him. He skipped the morning paper as he weighed his hesitancy. But Jacob was never one to back away from discomfort. After breakfast, he headed down the stairs and sat on the stoop, waiting for 10 o'clock. Once she appeared, he walked across the street, and said, "Good morning, Evelyn, how are you today?"

She replied cheerfully, "Good morning, Jacob, I'm well, and how are you?"

A simple conversation followed about his health and her chores. As he moved to leave, he turned back and asked, "Evelyn, how old are you?" He knew it was a bold question, but she responded with that ever-present glimmer in her eye and motioned for him to come closer.

She spoke softly, "Can you keep a secret?" Jacob leaned in and said, "Yes, I can keep a secret very well." She smiled the widest grin he had ever seen on her face, and said, "So can I." She winked and returned to her sweeping.

Jacob walked up the block. Halfway home, he giggled to himself, the first time in many years. He and Evelyn continued their 10 am curbside conversations for another 9 months.

Then one day, while he was sitting at his table eating his breakfast, he heard sirens and noticed the flashing lights of an ambulance and a police car speeding to a sudden stop across the street. He abandoned his cereal bowl and hurried as best he could down the stairs. As he crossed the street, he saw a stretcher came out with Evelyn lying on it. Bleeding from her head, she still managed a smile for him. She tugged on the EMS responder's shirt and asked him to stop for just a moment. She motioned for Jacob to come closer and whispered, "99, that's how old I am," and then closed her eyes.

He watched as they took away his only friend, not knowing if he'd see her again. Realizing he forgot to ask what hospital they took her to, he could only count the days and wait. Each morning he watched the sidewalk grow with litter. He wished he could sweep for her, but his injuries precluded him offering up that gift.

On the nineteenth day of waiting, a man, about his own age, swept the sidewalk. He watched this man for three days before he crossed the street. After saying hello to the stranger, he was greeted with a robust, "Shalom." Jacob inquired about Evelyn. The man said, "My name is Isaac. Evelyn was my mother. She fell a few weeks ago and had a severe head injury. They did surgery but she never regained consciousness. She died two weeks ago. My brother owns this building and asked me to take over her job as super. So I guess I'll be seeing you around."

Jacob said, "I'm sorry for your loss. Your mother was the only friend I've had in some time." Jacob struggled to hold back his tears, the first he had shed since his wife died. Startled at first, he settled into the embrace offered by Isaac who said, "I'm sorry for your loss, as well."

The next day, as Jacob sat on his stoop, Isaac crossed the street and said, "Shalom. I haven't lived in this city for almost 30 years. I don't know anyone here. Would you like to share Shabbat dinner with me tomorrow?"

Jacob hadn't honored the Sabbath since his wife's death, angry with a god that would take so much from him. So he surprised himself when he heard words falling from his mouth, "I'd be pleased to join you. Can I bring some challah? There is a good kosher bakery just down the street."

"Excellent", replied Isaac, "I always use my mother's recipes, and she cooked the good, old style. It will be refreshing to share a meal. Come tomorrow at 6?"

"It's been so long since I shared a meal with anyone. I hope my manners are acceptable," Jacob shared.

Isaac chuckled and said, "Just come as you are. My mother learned to cautiously watch and evaluate people, no doubt a survival skill learned in the camps. I can trust her instincts about people. If you were a friend to her, you're a friend to me. I'm sure your manners will be fine. We both need new friends. Until tomorrow, then?"

Jacob hobbled across the street filled with a mix of emotions: grief at Evelyn's death was counterbalanced with hope for a new friendship. Isaac was more gregarious than Evelyn. Jacob hoped that would bring ease to the budding friendship and relieve him of the burden of carrying the conversation.

He searched through his closet for his best suit, worn but clean, and even pulled out a tie. It had been a long time since he honored the Sabbath. Not wanting to embarrass himself, he pulled out the old prayer book to refresh his memory. He slowly considered the words, "Baruch atah Adonai, Eloheinu melech ha-olam, asher kid'shanu b'mitzvotav, v'tzivanu l'had lik neir shel Shabbat. Amen."

The words, simultaneously familiar and strange, unleashed a flood of memories of his wife and son. He wept at their loss, at Evelyn's death, and for the loss of his faith. For the first time, he allowed those tears to flow freely. He heard his wife's lilting voice saying, "Blessed are You, G-d, Spirit of the Universe who has made us holy with Your mitzvot and commanded us to light the Shabbat light. Amen."

That night Jacob's dreams were filled with images of his wife and his son. He saw her closing her eyes, lighting the candles and circling her hands above them three times. He smelled her fresh baked challah. In his dreams, he was happy.

He awoke refreshed, his heart hopeful. He puttered about the apartment to keep himself busy and keep his anxiety in check. He couldn't remember the last time he had shared a meal.

Mid-afternoon, he walked to the bakery, returning with a challah loaf and some rugelach for dessert. Dressing carefully, he waited with child-like anticipation for 5:45, when he started his climb downstairs.

He was greeted by a warm hug from Isaac and ushered into the apartment. The aromas filled him with delight and memories. Isaac asked, "Would you like some tea or a glass of wine? I'm almost done in the kitchen. Fifteen more minutes and we'll eat."

Jacob accepted a glass of wine. The sweetness brought another avalanche of happy memories of his family. As he looked around the room, he wondered about Evelyn's life. He had shared so much and she had shared so little. He had never wanted to intrude. In the midst of his ruminations, Isaac announced, "Come, my friend, dinner is on the table.'

Jacob followed Isaac's voice to a large dining room with a table filled with enough food for a family of six. Isaac commented, "I may have overdone it with the cooking, but once I got started, I was filled with recollections of our childhood gatherings at this table. So, we will eat well tonight."

Isaac lit the candles, said the blessing, and raised a glass of wine, toasting, "To those we have lost and those we have found. Mazel Tov."

Jacob set about eating with a long lost relish for the taste and feel of the food. "Isaac, this is as good as my wife's or my mother's cooking. I feel very blessed and that is something I have not felt in a long time."

They spent the meal talking about their lives discovering they had much in common, including the deaths of their wives and a child. Jacob was surprised at how easily his words flowed. Isaac's warmth and ready friendship was a balm for Jacob's heart.

When both had eaten their fill, Isaac rose to clear the table, inviting Jacob to retire to the living room. Isaac returned with cups of coffee. "Isaac, thank you for an incredible meal and your companionship," Jacob said.

Isaac smiled broadly and said, "All my pleasure. It has been strange living in this apartment where I grew up. Sharing Sabbath dinner with you makes it feel more like my own place. Would you like to do this again next week?"

"Yes," was Jacob's automatic reflex. "May I contribute more to the meal next time?"

"No need. Bring the challah, which was excellent, and more rugelach. I'm a good cook and a bad baker," Isaac said with a big grin.

The following Friday, they shared another meal, deepening their burgeoning friendship and beginning a new ritual of shared Shabbat dinner.

Through the week, they continued their sidewalk chats. Isaac began joining his friend in stoop sitting and people watching. After a few weeks, Isaac asked Jacob, "Do you like to play cards. I've been invited to a poker game, low stakes and friendly. Would you like to come next Wednesday?"

Hesitantly, Jacob responded, "Yes, but it's been years since I played. Could we play a few games before so I don't feel dumb when I get there?"

"You may be many things, but dumb is not one. Of course, we can practice. Can I come over tomorrow afternoon? I'll bring the cards. Is two o'clock ok?" asked Isaac.

Wednesday night card games became a regular event for the two men. Along with Friday evening meals and almost daily conversations, Jacob's life was transforming. As he realized how empty his old life became, he started to examine why and how he had turned from his faith.

At the end of their next shared meal, Jacob asked, "Would you tell me how you kept your faith after all your losses? I walked away, angry and felt betrayed by G-d after my wife died. I tried to pray, but it felt meaningless. Sharing Sabbath prayers with you has re-awakened a yearning for G-d."

Isaac remained silent for long minutes which felt like hours to Jacob, who worried his comments had offended his new friend. "That's a hard question to answer," Isaac eventually stated, "I was furious at G-d after my wife died in childbirth. I stopped going to temple, stopped praying, no longer thought of myself as a Jew. It was my mother who brought me back. When I came for a visit a year after that loss, my mother was adamant about taking me to temple. She had arranged a meeting with the Rabbi. She promised he was not the typical Rabbi and she was right as usual. He let me talk for hours about my rage and pain. He never criticized me or made me feel wrong.

When he said to me, 'Our G-d can handle your anger. He understands and loves you even when you turn from him', something shifted in me. I felt like I had been struck by lightning but in a good way. I cried and the Rabbi held me as I sobbed. He was a righteous man who knew about being human."

After a long silence, Isaac added, "After that meeting, my mother talked with me for the first time about her years in the camps. She was firm in her belief that if she hadn't found meaning in her suffering, in the suffering of those around her, she would not have survived. She lived her life in joy and blessing despite her experience, or, as she might say, because of it. I decided that if she could live through those terrible days and still face the world with love, that I could do the same."

Another long silence before Isaac asked, "Would you like to go to temple with me?"

Jacob, tears gently rolling down his cheeks, turned his face to Isaac and grasped his hand. "Please, yes, please. Your mother initiated my journey back to the living. It is right that you should help me take the next step."

Isaac rose from the table, offered his hand to assist Jacob, and the two old men embraced and sobbed together.

Always Never Again
By Liz Perry

I just want it over so I can miss it again. The waiting is always the hardest part every time.

It's like a favorite movie coming on after the previews, a song harmonized in the car with a best friend, or an impromptu dance party while washing dishes as dinner cooks. There has to be a way to make the worst of this event fun, or none of it is fun. It never was fun, but I don't know what else to do. Every day I look at the calendar but it moves a lot slower than it used to.

When I wake up after a meeting about it, I can feel the sponges scrubbing my knowledge clean as I go about another day not telling them, and them not telling me. Although, I remember what it feels like to know. The forgetting is always the hardest part every time.

It's a surprise party, they say at the end. You're not supposed to know about it. That's why it's fun, we reasoned. Three days and the itch starts. Then two and everything sparkles. One to go and all I can do is breathe. When the bomb hits, I smile. It's a relief to witness it.

I watch my skin crackle and close my eyes to merge with the pain. Sweet, terrible pain. My family scream, but not so loud they can't hear me laughing. Sooner than I expect, but not so soon I don't panic, it's all over. I breathe in the stars, looking down at the wasteland that was home long ago.

I'm greeted again, cleansed.

We should move on. This isn't fun anymore. It's like picking at a scab when you're fifty.

They smile sadly as we release the old pain again. They didn't give us the technology to wallow. They didn't know death gets us off. They should have known.

"Okay, but this time, from the pilot's seat," I say, and they nod, as always.

Vision Board
By Michelle Tang

Her name was Lily Waterston and I hated her. It wasn't an active hatred; I wasn't plotting to accelerate my rusty old Camry when I saw her crossing the street or anything. No, it was a slow burn of resentment, a simmering cauldron of contempt, and more than a tinge of jealousy.

I knew her name because it was embroidered, bedazzled, or typed on handkerchiefs, leather bags, and binders around her room. I had cleaned her family's home for almost a year in order to save money for university. Lily's father worked in an office that my mother cleaned and had hired me on when he learned I needed a job. The house was palatial, all gleaming dark wood and sparkling marble. When I walked into the open hallway, the first thing to catch my eye was the round table in the center with the ever-present vase of lilies in full bloom. Sometimes elegant, tapered buds, other times bold-colored petals spread open like mouths, but always lilies. The smell of the flowers permeated every room, making me glad for the strong chemical aromas of the bleach and lemon-scented cleaners I carried.

The Waterstons didn't talk much, to me or to each other. With the cold marble, suffocating smell of lilies, and deep silence, I often imagined I worked in a mausoleum. I cherished the quiet, so heavy and thick it was like a luxurious blanket surrounding me. My home, a two-bedroom apartment on the wrong side of town, was a constant roar of chatter, filled with life's noises from my parents and three siblings. Our apartment had no flowers.

I always left her room until last, because even a passive hatred is exhausting. Lily's room was blinding in its brightness, as though the sun never stopped shining on her blessed existence. She was, of course, tall and model-thin; her clothes hung from her bony frame the way their designers, names I'd never heard of, had intended. She could have been a model with that face: all doe-eyed, full-lipped, and cheekbones sharp as sickles. Some girls in my situation might have tried on her clothes, strewn haphazardly about, as they rehung them in her walk-in closets, but I never had the inclination. After feasting your eyes on a gourmet meal, would you be satisfied with a loaf of bread? I was short, overweight, and full of anger, but I knew my place: Lily's expensive garments would revert back into their wool and cotton and silk threads upon touching my unworthy skin.

If she were in the room when I reached her door, she would draw herself up as though she had all the time in the world, then ease out of the room with a smile that had a hint of apology. It was that expression that cemented my feelings towards her, as though despite her beauty and wealth she was embarrassed I was there to clean up her detritus. That close-mouthed lip-tightening combined with prolonged eye contact was chock-full of acknowledgment: I was human, nearly her age, and she was regretful that our lives were so different. That smile told me she was sorry for me because unlike her, I was poor and plain.

I never spoke to her, not even when she used to ask me how I was doing. I'm cleaning your toilets so I can pull myself out of poverty, how do you think I'm doing? Lily quickly learned I was deaf to her overtures of politeness, but she always smiled at me as she left. In a silly way, it made me feel powerful, that my entrance into a room could cause its inhabitant to vacate.

I barely spoke to the family, but the traces of their existence were like ghosts in their wake, whispering tales of their lives. I knew from my mother that Warren Waterston was a lawyer, and was wading through War and Peace (the bookmark hardly making progress as the weeks went on). Amelia Waterston owned an art gallery and left rosary beads all around the house. Lily had gone to Brown University, although I didn't know what she studied or if she had graduated.

During one of my cleanings, I saw that Lily had hung up a Vision Board. It was a poster board on which wishful thinkers placed images of the things they wanted in life. The idea was that visualizing your desires each day would help with positive thinking and that you would then manifest everything on the board. I had wanted to try it, but couldn't spare the cash for magazines or art supplies. Vision boards are only for those already rich in time and money. I snorted at hers, nearly bare except for a magazine cut-out of a handsome old couple surrounded by children. Lily lacked for nothing; her only desire was for a long marriage and grandchildren. I admit a part of me was angry she hadn't needed to glue in a picture of a Porsche or a beachside villa, things I could only dream of having.

I didn't see her for a few weeks. I imagined her vacationing across Europe over the summer while I changed bed linens that hadn't been slept in, washed a sink that hadn't been used. Her parents were hardly home, and if they were they kept to themselves. The lilies had not been replaced in her absence, and when they turned brown and wilted I discarded them. With Lily gone, I could admire the beauty of the house, imagine that I lived there and chose to scrub my own tiles on hands and knees, rather than being the hired help.

Lily returned to the house in late August; there were fresh flowers on the foyer table and she had added onto her Vision Board. I stared at the diploma she'd cut out from somewhere, the stethoscope artfully glued to overlap it, and turned my back to the images. I'd not earned enough money to start school in September as I'd hoped. I was already a year behind my friends, what was another few months? To imagine Lily as a physician, wearing a white lab coat and making it look like high fashion, made acid burn all the way up my throat. To add to my disgust, her long, cornsilk hair was everywhere. I had to cut it out of the vacuum, shake it out of her blankets, and pull it out of her tub drain.

My mother saw my face when I returned home and knew I was in a foul mood. I never spoke of the Waterstons to my family: even at that young age, I realized speaking of their private life would ill-repay Mr. Waterston for his generosity. My mother made my favorite dinner and without much effort, my siblings cajoled me into laughter. At that age, I was so focused on our financial poverty that I was oblivious to other forms of wealth. I sat at the kitchen table that night, after everyone had gone to bed, and stared at a blank piece of paper in front of me, pencil in hand.

When someone like me considers all they want from the world, from life, the desire can be overwhelming. It's hard to imagine a thousand dollars, let alone a million. The entire endeavor is surreal and absurd, the sheer act of wanting so intense it precludes attempt, the chance of failure more painful than no chance at all.

I left the paper untouched.

Lily was in her room at my next cleaning. I stared at her. She'd put her hair into a baseball cap, and her wide, blue eyes were red and swollen. Her hands trembled as she unplugged her tablet and tucked it under her arm. Noticing my attention, she gave me a watery smile before yielding her room to me. Her vision board was now full of pictures: travel, a bridal party, a wedding gown, a baby. An image of a gorgeous couple drew my eye. After a moment, I realized that unlike the others, this was not cut from a magazine—it was a photograph. A handsome man had his arm around Lily and was gazing at her with love, while she smiled at the camera.

Despite my long hatred of the girl, I cleaned her room with extra care that day. The idea that someone, as blessed as her, could be vulnerable to heartbreak soothed the angry beast that was my envy. My contempt for her only grew—her life was perfect and she was crying over a man. I felt deep satisfaction at her unhappiness and was so guilty about it that I made sure her room was immaculate.

By the end of November, I'd made enough for my first year of school, and was able to buy small gifts for my family as well. I shared my family's excitement as they opened their presents. I'd received a wonderful present of my own, just in time for the holidays: I'd won a scholarship, which meant I could afford to quit cleaning houses and focus on my studies.

The last time I knocked on the Waterstons' door was just before Christmas. For a moment I didn't recognize Lily's mother; she looked as though she'd aged thirty years since I last saw her. She spoke to me in a ravaged voice as I took off my boots.

"Stephanie, you should know that Lily passed away last week."

I froze, one arm still inside my coat. "She what?"

"We were so hopeful, but the cancer came back. She'd tried an experimental treatment in New York over the summer, but it didn't work, and then there was nothing else the doctors could offer her."

Amelia Waterston was too far gone in her grief to see the shock on my face, to realize I'd had no idea Lily was sick. Later, I would find out that Warren Waterston had mentioned his daughter's terminal illness to my mother, had hoped that we could become friends. My mother had spared me this sad news in a misguided attempt to protect me, to take off the pressure of expectation.

In a daze, I listened while Mrs. Waterston spoke of her daughter's illness, reported her last days with such loving detail I might have been her confessor. My nemesis—beautiful, rich Lily Waterston—had been dying the entire time I'd been wishing for her life. I offered awkward condolences and extricated myself from the sight of Amelia Waterston's glistening eyes.

I cleaned in a hurry, the house's silence pressing on me the way the earth must when you are far underground. I cleaned her bathroom, but I kept her bedroom the way she'd left it: bed unmade, the imprint of her head still on her pillow, strewn with hair like cornsilk. Her Vision Board was complete now, the final blank space filled by the number twenty-two, covered in bright blue glitter. My throat thickened until it was hard to swallow and despite myself, my eyes filled with tears. Lily wasn't filling the board with the things she wanted to manifest—she was making a record of the things she would never see fulfilled, including her twenty-second birthday. When I finished cleaning, I didn't seek out Mr. Waterston for my payment—this was the only thing I could give them to show my sympathy. As I left the house, I passed by the hallway table: the vase of flowers was gone, leaving no sign that the lilies had ever been, save for a lingering scent that hung in the air like a memory.

Our Place

By Mark Towse

His left cheek tingled as the sun's light found its way through the dry, spindly canvas of leafless trees and illuminated the rock where he sat. There wasn't just a physical reaction to the heat, for a moment it altered his mental composition, an internal glow that drove away from the fog that blanketed his mind since he lost her. He smiled, a small crease, but genuine nonetheless, far from the well-practiced ones he forced when reassuring everyone he was going to be okay.

There were previous instances when he felt the beginnings of a genuine smile, but he had always stifled it—the combination of guilt and fear it brought meant the beginning of moving on and leaving her behind. He wasn't ready and questioned whether he would ever be.

He afforded himself the luxury of letting the fragile smile linger for a few seconds; this was their place after all.

Warmth engulfed him as he turned his face towards the sun, and with eyes closed he pictured her in all her original beauty and before cancer had devoured her from the inside. A playful smile flicked across her face, further emphasized by the tiny creases at the side of her eyes that he missed so dearly. Her eyes sparkled as they always did, even on her darkest days, and they had always filled him with hope.

She stood in front of him, leaning in with her curly auburn hair drifting across her face in the gentle breeze. Without taking her eyes from her, he could make out the sway of the trees, a mass of green and gold foliage floating behind. Her hair brushed his forehead, causing him to shiver as he had done a thousand times before. She pressed her lips to his right cheek, and they lingered for a while as she placed a leaf into his right hand. Her soft voice carried on the breeze, speaking only a single word and he snapped his eyes open, filled with hope at the audible whisper of his name, but only found the disappointment of being alone.

His right cheek felt warmer now—kissed by an angel, he thought.

The leaf he held was vibrant green and damp to touch as though coated in the early morning dew. It certainly didn't belong here, not now. He suddenly felt the same way, as though he was trespassing on times gone.

The last time they were here, it was early spring, and he had picked the greenest leaf he could find, one that was bursting with life, a representation of how he felt in her presence. He had given her the leaf and joked to never complain about not getting flowers. The one in his right hand was just as perfect.

There was an immediate and pleasant cool feeling on his chest as he placed the leaf in his shirt pocket next to his heart before he scrambled up the side of the mountain. They were never ones to follow a path. Life was full of so many variables, and they agreed to explore as many as possible. That's why Laura struggled so much with the routine of disease, and that routine must have eaten away at her soul as much as cancer consumed her body. At least she was free now.

His overriding emotion had been anger at the time, fueled by a belief that she had decided he was no longer worth the fight. He knew it was a selfish, knee-jerk reaction to being left alone but his reason for getting up in the morning had left. They had battled together for two years, and he hadn't been ready to give up the fight. There were even signs of improvement before she suddenly slipped away.

He climbed the summit once again, this time alone. At the top, a stump in the ground near the center of a small clearing brought a vivid memory back. It was here they had both agreed to bury a treasured belonging in an empty glass jar and come back in twenty years to see if it was still there. They liked the idea of longevity it symbolized—how arrogant they had been.

The ground was hard and dry, and initially, the flick of the penknife only managed to dislodge loose dirt until he found a trace of moisture a couple of inches below the surface. It was slow going, but a few minutes later he felt contact. He clawed at the soil surrounding the jar and finally exhumed it from the earth. He unscrewed the lid and emptied the contents onto the ground. Not much to speak of, just some cheap jewelry they had bought each other in the early years as a proclamation of eternal love. The bracelet and earrings were already falling victim to the tarnishing effect of time—a stark reminder that nothing is forever.

The letter inside was curled up, already conforming to the confines of its home.

He unfurled the paper and written in her unmistakable handwriting were just two words: Our place.

He fought back the tears and kissed the note before returning it and the jewelry back inside the jar, and as he reached for the lid, he remembered the leaf in his pocket.

The leaf was already dry and fading in color, not able to hold on to its previous perfection. It had its time of beauty, but it was time to let go now.

"I understand," he said and smiled.

A single tear fell into the central vein of the leaf, and as he guided the moisture through the entire venation, the leaf began to reinvigorate until it was back to its most perfect stage—as soft as her skin and bursting with color.

He quickly placed it in the jar and screwed the lid on, forever sealing their most perfect forms for all eternity.

"Bye, Laura," he said as he smoothed the ground over.

He sat there for a while before moving on.

Out of Dust

By Joanna Michal Hoyt

Translations from the journal of Cristina Fuentes:

April 7, 1954

My name is Cristina Guadalupe Fuentes Espinosa. I am ten years old. In this book, I will write the story of my adventures with my papi in El Norte where we are going tomorrow. We don't have money for me to go to school here, and in El Norte they will not let me go to school even if we have money. But, Papi says that is no reason to be ignorant. I read every day from the Bible, and now I will write every day in this book, and in El Norte... in the *United States*... I will learn English too. Papi says I have to keep learning, and I do what he says.

But, when he said to stay here with my Aunt Lancha while he went North, I said no. I told him he is all the family I have now and I am all the family he has and we have to stay together.

"All the family we have in this world," he said.

"This is the world where I live," I said. "Anyway, Aunt Lancha doesn't like me."

He said she did like me, but it was hard for her having so many children to take care of and not enough money.

I said I was old enough to take care of myself if I went with him, and in El Norte there would be enough money.

"It's not safe, where I'm going," he said. "You know I don't want to go."

I know that. I know he wants to stay here with me, but he has to go. He is very good at fixing things, but so are a lot of the other men who can't find work. He is very good at making beautiful things from clay, things that seem alive, but nobody pays money for things like that. In El Norte, there is work and money for everyone. There is more money for the people who had enough to pay the officials here so they could go to El Norte and stay inside the law, but there is money there even for people who have none here. I know that is why my papi has to go there. I know, too, that I have to go with him.

"It's not safe anywhere," I said. And my papi agreed to take me with him.

I have to stop writing soon and finish packing the bag that I will carry across the river and the desert. But, there is not very much to pack. Just clothes, tortillas, the Bible, this book, and the family bowl

Papi made with all the hands around the rim. Anyway, Papi is happy to see me writing.

April 15

We are here on a big farm in El Norte. We found an easy place to cross the river and a short place to cross the desert. I was hungry and tired, but we came to a town where Papi bought food and found people who spoke Spanish. Those people told us which way to go to find work, and Papi found this place before we were all the way out of money.

It is a good thing Papi brought me with him because I can help. Not in the fields though. Pedro is doing fieldwork and he's just thirteen, but Papi says I shouldn't do that. But, I can take care of Doña Lupe and Doña Marcela's babies. I can also boil the beans for the workers to eat at lunch and at supper, and I can bring good water to them while they're in the field. There's a water pump not far from the edge of the big melon field, but if you drink that water straight from the pump, you get sick-sick-sick. Doña Dolores drank some that way last month.

Doña Dolores doesn't have children who are still alive. She is a little bit crazy. Papi says not to stare at her when she talks funny, or when she stares at me. She has cracks, Papi says, but God has breathed into them.

Anyway, the water is safe if you boil it, so I do that. We have two great big pots, but they're too big for me to carry. We do have four little pots, though. And I can carry them even when they're full. I pump water into all the little pots and put them in my wagon, then pull them back to the bunkhouse and boil them. Then I put a big pot in the wagon and pour all the boiled water into it, and then I pull that pot out to the field and call for someone to lift it off the wagon; then I take the mostly-empty pot they've been drinking from back and I do everything again. Sometimes my papi comes to take the water pot out of my wagon, sometimes somebody else. When Don Fermin or Doña Lupe come, they smile at me and call me Senorita Fuentes the fountain girl. When Doña Dolores comes, she looks at me with her hungry face and doesn't say anything. And then they go away, and I go back to singing to the babies or to reading or writing in this book.

I have more books to read now because of my cousins. Doña Concepcion is my mother's second cousin, but I call her Aunt Chon because it is easier. Aunt Chon and Uncle Miguel came to El Norte with their parents long, long ago. They have a *casita* of their own on the edge of Mr. Martin's farm a mile up the road. They stay there all year, even in winter, to take care of his animals, and their son David goes to school with other Mexican kids who stay all the time in El

Norte. So, instead of sleeping in the bunkhouse with Papi and the other workers, I go with David every evening and eat supper with my cousins. I sleep on a pallet by my aunt's bed, the way I used to sleep near Mami when I was little and she was alive. And, I get to borrow books David takes home from school.

I won't have time to read much today because I have done so much writing. That is okay.

May 1

There is not much to write about today. The things that change from one day to another day are small. Yesterday Papi and the others picked rocks up out of the field and threw them into a big wagon. Everybody was tired and sore and even Don Fermin did not smile at me. Today they are planting, so they will just be sore from bending and not quite so tired. Yesterday, they were in the north field. Today, they are in the east field, which is a longer way to pull the water wagon. Tonight maybe it will rain, and they are hurrying to plant before the rain comes. I am not hurrying. I am waiting for the water to boil and trying to write so I will not be ignorant.

Today at lunch break, I told Papi I didn't know what to write, and he told me to think of three beautiful things every day and write about them. I will do that.

When Doña Marcela walked back out to the field after eating, she sang one of the songs about La Guadalupana that Mami used to sing. Her voice is very beautiful.

Last night, the moon was so small that it was almost gone, and there were no rain clouds. The sky was full of stars all low and close like fireflies.

That is two things. Papi didn't say to write only beautiful things that happened today. So, I will write about the family bowl that Papi made because that is the most beautiful thing.

Papi made it after my little brother Santiago—Chago--cut his leg playing in the river and got infected and died. I was seven then, still a child, and I stopped singing, stopped eating and stopped talking. Papi sat down by me and told me Chago and Mami and all the dead people are still with us, even though we can't see them, and after we die we will see them again. I said it would be better just to be dead right away and see them. He cried, and he went away. I was afraid I would not see him again. But, after work—that was in the three months when he had worked on the road crew before the weather turned bad and they sent him away--he came back and told me to come with him.

He took me to the raw bank where they had just cut the new

roadbed, and I helped him get good clay dirt out of the bank and put it in a big glass jar. After he'd soaked it with water, I helped him squish the wet mud and break up all the clumps. While we squished, he talked about Chago, and how he went straight from scooting on his stomach to walking without ever learning to crawl. He talked about the time when Chago carried a king snake home and Mami thought it was a coral snake and was very afraid. He also talked about the time he found the dove's nest and brought it back to see if we could hatch the eggs. Then Papi told me to sleep while the mud-soaked up water. In the morning, he went to work. While he was gone, I did what he told me to do. I saw the line that separated the clay water from the rocks and other kinds of dirt in the bottom of the jar. I poured off the clay water into a new jar and dumped out the rest. I did that over and over, and while I worked I sang every song I could remember Mami singing.

After the cleaned clay had dried while hung up in one of Chago's shirts, Papi took it out and started to shape it. Sometimes, he told stories about when he and Mami were young. Sometimes, I told him what I remembered about Chago and my abuelita and all the other ones who are dead. And while we talked, his hands shaped little figures in the clay and shaped another piece of that same clay into a round bowl.

The bowl is painted black like a night sky with no stars, and the people pressed all around the outside of it are the reddish color of the clay. There are spaces between their bodies, spaces full of shadows, but at the top, their hands are clasped together. Their faces look alive. One of the people has my face, and one has Papi's, and there are other people who look like Mami, Chago, and Abuelita. In between us, are five other people with faces that don't look quite like anyone I know— and I swear their faces change every time I look at them. Papi says those five are for all our people on the other side. The ones whose faces we don't remember.

Sometimes I think the people are holding on tight to each other so the wind out of those dark empty places doesn't blow them apart. Sometimes I think they are dancing.

The bowl stays under Papi's bed in the bunkhouse. The bunkhouse is crowded and ugly and smells like sweating people and mold, but people have their home things in it—Lupe's icon of La Guadalupana, and Don Fermin's guitar, and Papi's bowl that holds us all together. Sometimes while I wait for the water to boil I sit and I hold the clay hands of the people on the bowl. Sometimes when I touch Mami's hand, I can hear her singing. Sometimes when I touch Chago's hand, I can hear him laughing. And sometimes when I touch the hands of the other people, the ones with the changing faces, I feel something,

I understand something... I don't have words for that. I have words for everything else, Spanish words and now some English ones, but I don't have words for that.

There. That is a lot of writing. Now the little pots are boiling and it is time for me to pour them.

June 10

Now Papi and the rest of the workers are weeding all day every day. The melons will not be ready to pick for two more months, Don Fermin says. He also says harvesting will be hotter, harder work than weeding. When I am hot and tired pulling the water wagon, I think about eating a whole watermelon and spitting seeds the way I used to do with Chago.

I think about fruit a lot now. That's because on Mr. Martin's farm the plums are ripe, and the plum smell comes in the window of the room where Aunt Chon and I sleep. Sometimes the smell is almost too much because the air is so heavy with heat. And I go to sleep wanting plums and I wake up wanting plums. But, if Aunt Chon and Uncle Miguel want plums, they have to buy them. If the crew boss sees them eating plums or taking them away, they could lose their job and their *casita* too. Still, Aunt Chon says tomorrow morning, Saturday, when Mexicans are allowed to shop where the Anglos are, she will buy me a plum.

It is very different from home. Aunt Lancha had two pear trees in her backyard, and when the pears were ripe enough so we could smell them, we could eat all the pears we wanted and it did not cost anything.

Fruit is the easiest thing I miss. I miss the way the sky looked and the ground smelled back home. I miss Aunt Lancha even though she didn't like me. I miss fiestas in town.

But, I don't miss worrying about money. Here we always have enough to eat, and on Sunday special things like spicy sausages or plums, and still, Papi is saving money to take home this winter. He keeps half of his saving money in his shoe. I keep the other half in this book because that is what he said to do. I have almost stopped worrying but Papi has not.

Uncle Miguel is worrying too. He bought a newspaper yesterday and talked about it with Aunt Chon last night when David and I were all supposed to be asleep. I was hot and thinking about plums, and I heard him talking about the President. First, I didn't listen much. Complaining about the President is just what grown-ups do, in Mexico or here. But then he read a piece out of the newspaper—the

140

English paper—and I listened hard because that helps me learn English and not be ignorant. Some of the words were too hard for me to understand, but I heard some words I knew from David's books or from other newspapers. *Criminals. Invasion. Stealing jobs. Invasion* again.

Invasion...I knew I had seen that in David's history book. That is when soldiers attack. That is a very bad thing. Like when my abuelita's abuelita was a girl and the norteamericanos *invaded* Mexico and took a big piece of it away to be part of their country, and they burned the house where my abuelita's abuelita lived, and she screamed at night after that, and later she had a boy with blond hair and blue eyes who had the same last names as her because she wasn't married—not then, but she was married later, when she had my abuelita's mama. It was bad, too, when Papi was a boy and the soldiers burned their house down. That was the civil war though, not an invasion, which means it was all our people fighting, and it is not quite as bad... maybe, I don't know.

I got up and pulled my serape around me and ran out into the kitchen where Aunt Chon and Uncle Miguel were. "Where is the *invasion*?" I said. "How close are they? Can I get to Papi before we have to run?"

"You're supposed to be sleeping, not eavesdropping," my uncle Miguel said.

"But, if there are soldiers coming..."

My aunt sighed. "Come with me," she said, and she walked me out through the dewy grass toward the plum trees. And she explained.

It wasn't soldiers coming. It was us. Mexicans. The paper writers said people like Papi were invaders coming to steal jobs from the real Americans and maybe to steal other things

"Papi does not steal," I told her. "I do not steal." I meant to say it strong and angry, but I cried instead.

These are my three beautiful things from last night:

The smell of the plums.

The noise the crickets made all around us.

Aunt Chon holding me like her own and only daughter until I had finished crying.

June 18

I am too tired to write much, but these are four beautiful things from today:

Tomasito chasing butterflies on the edge of the squash field. He is four and he has a big laugh like his mama, Doña Lupe, and he doesn't seem to mind that he never catches the butterflies.

Doña Marcela's twins, José and Rosita, curled up together, sweaty and asleep, and smiling and not pushing each other for a while.

The star that fell down the sky while I walked to Aunt Chon's house.

Papi giving me an extra kiss before I went. He sat with me for a few minutes with the family bowl between us, not saying anything, remembering. He looked sad. I hope that was just from remembering.

June 19

I am writing because Papi told me to and because when Aunt Chon comes to check on me, if she sees me writing, she does not fuss around and try to cheer me up. I am not cheered up and I do not want to have to act like I am cheered up when Papi is gone.

She wants to make sure I do not run away after Papi. I am old enough to know I cannot run fast enough to catch up with the truck they took him away on, even if I knew the right way to go. Anyway, Doña Dolores says Papi told me to stay with Aunt Chon and Uncle Miguel, and even though she is crazy, I think that part is true.

This is what happened:

I left Aunt Chon's house at six-thirty this morning. We walked down the road with the light still new around us, and I sang a morning song Mami used to sing. But, before we got down to the fields, we heard trucks coming up the road, and David told me to get down in the ditch right away. He said it in a voice like Papi uses when there's no time to ask questions. I didn't ask questions. I hid, and he hid with me, and we heard the trucks going by. Even when they were gone he didn't stand up for what felt like a very long time, and when I asked why we were hiding, he didn't answer.

We got up and started walking again. The hem of my skirt was all wet and sticking to my legs and I kept pulling on it. And then Doña Dolores came running up the road towards us. She looked very very crazy, like all the cracks in her were getting wider and wider and maybe it wasn't just God breathing through them. She waved her hands at us like she was scaring chickens and said go back, go back, go back. And I said where's Papi, and she said he was gone where I couldn't go, which is what Jesus said to the disciples when he knew he was going to be dead.

I thought she said that just because she was crazy. I ran toward her, ducked when she grabbed at me, and ran past her. There was nobody in the melon field. Nobody in the squash field. No pot under the pump. The wagon was tipped up on its side. I ran to the bunkhouse.

There was nobody there. The blankets were gone from the beds, and the boxes and bags with clothes in them were gone, and Don Fermin's guitar, and La Guadalupana. There were gouges in the wall that hadn't been there before, and one window was broken. Papi's bowl was gone too.

I thought Aunt Chon and Uncle Miguel had lied to me. There had been a real invasion after all.

I looked for the bowl. I kept thinking if I could find it, I could find Papi. But, all that I found was a shoe with the heel ripped out—a shoe that had been Don Fermin's— a dirty diaper that must have been José's or Rosita's, and a crumble of clay-colored dust on the floor.

David and Doña Dolores found me sitting on the floor with those clay crumbs in my hand. I wasn't crying. My eyes felt hot and hard and dead.

Doña Dolores held out a wadded-up bandanna, and I thought it was for me to cry in. I shook my head. Then she unwadded the bandanna and pulled out what was inside. A piece of the bowl. The piece had me in it, except for my left arm, one of the people-who-went-before, whole, and another left arm that I knew had been Papi's because he was on the right side of the other person on the right side of me. I held onto his clay hand while Doña Dolores told us what had happened.

The men with guns came at sunrise when Doña Marcela was nursing the twins and everyone else was pulling their shoes on to head out to the fields. The trucks came loud, loud, and pulled up all around the house. Somebody shouted in English, which most people didn't understand, and then they said it again in bad Spanish: "Come out in ones with your hands up, don't make any jokes (she thinks that wasn't the word they meant) or we'll shoot."

Don Fermin was the first one out that door, moving slowly and holding his hands over his head. He did not say anything because he didn't know what they might think was a joke. The people inside waited to see if the men would shoot him anyway, but they didn't, so another man went after him, and the gunmen didn't shoot him either. They shouted for everyone else to come on out, hurry up. Papi didn't come right out because he was putting things into his bag. He took out the bowl and looked at it like he didn't know what to do with it, and then two of the gunmen came in and grabbed him. They dropped the bowl on the floor and it broke. They stuffed most of the pieces into his bag, but they missed the piece that went under the bed. Doña Dolores saw that before they made her come out too.

By the time Doña Dolores went outside, our people were standing with their hands held up behind their heads. The men with

guns were feeling them all over to make sure they didn't have guns or
knives or anything—they took away Don Pedro's whittling knife,
Papi's pocket knife, and everybody's razors. They were going to feel
Doña Dolores too, but when they went to touch her she was afraid, and
she screamed and fell down. That was for real, but when they backed
away, she did more screaming and rolling around and acting crazy so
they'd stay away. They didn't touch her, though one man kept a gun
pointed at her. And then they made all the people pile into the backs of
their trucks, shoved in tight like steers going to market. But when they
tried to make Doña Dolores go, she acted crazy again and they left her.

Papi told Doña Dolores to give me the piece of our bowl that
was left and to tell me to stay with my aunt and uncle. He said it in very
fast Spanish and she thought the gunmen didn't understand. Then they
put things like cages over the backs of the trucks where the people were
and they drove away. Doña Dolores couldn't ask where they were
going because she had to keep acting crazy. Don Fermin did ask. She
said they didn't answer. Maybe she said this so I wouldn't go after him.
She wouldn't even point which way they went. David made me stop
shouting at her to show me, and he walked me back to his house.

Aunt Chon went back to look for Doña Dolores and see if she
needed help, but Doña Dolores was gone, I don't know where. I hope
she is safe. But if it was a choice between her and Papi, I would want
him to be the safe one.

June 20

There are stories in the newspaper today about *wetbacks*
getting arrested. Aunt Chon explained that means us, because of
crossing the river—though I was not wet when I crossed because I sat
high up on Papi's shoulders. One story says that the President had to
send out the gunmen to push back the *engulfing tide* of illegal aliens. I
am learning a lot of English and I do not want to, I do not want
anything about this country anymore, I just want to be safe away from
it with Papi. But I can't do that.

The other story talked about *aliens* being kept in big dirt yards
near the cities that have bus and train stations. One is almost an hour
west of us even for people in trucks, and the other is about that far east,
and the papers didn't say which people went where. It said some of the
men that were arrested acted like animals and threw rocks at the
newspaper people. If I had a rock I would throw it at the men with the
guns instead. Only then maybe they would shoot people, so maybe I
would not.

Papi, I think, would not throw rocks at anyone. But they

should not keep him out in the dirt like that. They should not make him go back to Aunt Lancha's house without me, and without his pay for the week (they were supposed to pay him on the day when they took him away instead).

And what if somebody else throws rocks and Papi gets shot?

Aunt Chon says to pray instead of worrying. Padre Vincentio said the same thing during the Mass, and again after to me when Aunt Chon took me to see him. But Padre Vincentio's father is not standing in the dirt somewhere with gunmen around him so it is easy for him not to worry. Padre Vincentio has a telephone, so he called some places and tried to ask about Papi, but they said they didn't have a list of names, and they wouldn't take a message, even if we could have thought of a safe message to leave.

Aunt Chon hugged me and I pushed her away. She gave me a plum and I tried to eat it but I cried and choked instead. She tried to talk to me but I ran to my alone place under the juniper and I held onto Papi's clay hand, and when I came back I started writing right away so that she would leave me alone.

June 21

I am not going to tell Aunt Chon what I saw, because she would maybe think I am getting crazy like Doña Dolores. But I think what I saw was real and not crazy. I do not want it to be real, but I think it is.

Yesterday when everybody else was gone to work or to school and I had swept the floor and washed the dishes and put the beans on to soak I sat down and held Papi's clay hand again and I tried to pray. I am not good at praying. But I could feel Papi's hand getting warmer, and then I felt like I fell into a hole in the ground, like the time I was eight and fell in the cistern where the boards on top were rotten and I thought I would die there but instead Papi found me. Only this time when I fell through I found him.

I must have been hanging in the air like an angel—no, not really like an angel; angels talk to people and tell them not to be afraid and give them good news and keep them safe, and I did not have any good news and I was afraid and I shouted for Papi but he could not hear me at all. I could hear him, though, and see him.

He was still in one of those cage trucks, in a long line of cage trucks bumping down a dusty road. There was dirt on his face and his hands and his clothes. There wasn't dirt in his hair because he didn't have any hair. His head was all bald and sunburned. One of the newspapers said they were shaving people's heads so they couldn't come back to El Norte without being recognized. Papi looked older and uglier and sadder being bald like that. His head drooped down and his shoulders drooped down and he held something in his hands. I looked all around the truck and all I could see was tan sand with bits of dead grass growing on it like fur on a mangy animal. Somebody in the truck was cursing, and somebody was praying the rosary out loud, and Papi wasn't saying anything at all. I thought it was maybe a rosary he had in his hands, but when I looked closer I saw it was a piece of the bowl. He was holding my clay hand.

Then the truck stopped. Papi put the piece with my clay hand in his pocket, and he kept his hand on it there. Three of the gunmen got out. They unlocked the cage and unlatched the back of the truck and said to jump down.

"Here?" said the man who'd been swearing. "But we left Mexicali more than an hour ago, and out here..."

"You won't be back over the river in a hurry, will you?" one of the gunmen said.

One of the other gunmen reached up to help a woman get down out of the truck, and he looked like he wanted to cry, though maybe that was just from being hot and dirty. "What about water?" the woman asked him. He gave her a big bottle and then he walked away looking even sadder and climbed into the front of the truck. A man asked the other gunmen for water, but they didn't give him any. Another man tried to climb back into the truck, but they hit him and he stopped.

When my papi and all the people with him had gotten down out of the trucks, the gunmen got back in the trucks and drove away. The dust shone in the sun like stars falling. I could just see and hear, not feel or smell, but I knew how hot it must be from the shine in the air and the way the people breathed. They stood there, looking all around for shade, but there wasn't any, and for water, but there wasn't any.

Someone said it would take too long to get back to Mexicali, and someone else said it would take longer to get anywhere else, and Papi didn't say anything, but he took José on his shoulders, with his extra shirt spread out over José's head to keep the sun from beating on it. That way Dona Marcela just had Rosita to carry, and she tied her in a sling in front of her. Then they all started walking back up the road. I wanted to be there with him and have José back in El Norte with people who would try to talk to him and feed him plums. I would not sit on Papi and make him tired. I would walk beside him. I would help him.

They walked and walked for a long time, and they went slower and slower. Rosita started to cry, and instead of singing to her or taking her in her arms Doña Marcela put her hands over her ears.

I remembered something then. I opened my eyes, so I could see the casita as well as the desert, but I kept my hand tight on Papi's clay hand, and even with my eyes open, I could still see the desert light. I found my Bible and looked in the very first book for the part where they send Hagar and her baby out in the desert without enough food or water or anywhere safe to go. There was a light around the words, the way that sometimes there's a light around the clay things Papi makes. I can't put life into things with my hands the way he can, but sometimes I can with my voice. So I read the words out loud. I read this:

"When the water in the skin was gone, she put the boy under one of the bushes. Then she went off and sat down about a bowshot away, for she thought, 'I cannot watch the boy die.' And as she sat there, she began to sob."

I was starting to sob then too, but it was not the time for sobbing, it was time for reading. I read the good part too: "Then God opened her eyes and she saw a well of water. So she went and filled the skin with water and gave the boy a drink."

I shut my eyes and saw the desert again, and Doña Marcela with her hands over her ears. I waited for clouds to come over the sky, or for someone to see green trees in the distance and know there was water, or for a truck full of kind people with water jugs to come down the road. I said the good words again and again, but none of those things happened. The people kept walking, and the baby kept crying, and the sun kept getting higher in the sky, and the clay hand in my hand felt dry as dust and I thought it was going to crumble apart.

After a long time, with me saying the words dry-mouthed and gasping, and them gasping and not talking, the land started to twist around them: a big slope of sand went up on the left of the road, a big slope of sand went down on the right. The sun was coming from the right, so there wasn't any shade for them. Papi's eyes looked wrong like he wasn't really seeing the things in front of him. *Do something*! I said to God again. But all that happened was that Papi stumbled. Someone took José off his shoulders. He straightened up and took a few more steps, but then he stumbled again and fell on the edge of the road. He flailed out with his arms to catch himself, and I saw the bowl shard in his right hand fly up and away, and then down, down into the sand that sloped away. And then I couldn't see anything at all. I had fallen back through the hole and Papi was gone.

July 1

Every day I cry. Every night I want to dream about Papi and I do not. Instead, I dream about water that disappears when I try to touch my hand or my lips to it.

Every day I read something in the Bible or in David's books and I write something in this book because that is what Papi told me to do. When I can't think of anything beautiful I write that I can't think of anything beautiful.

Every day Aunt Chon makes me get up and makes me eat. Because I have eaten, and because I have to do something with the day, I work a little in the house. Although, she would not make me do that.

Every morning and every night I put my hand on Papi's clay hand, but I do not feel any warmth. I do not see anything. I do not keep it in my pocket anymore because it was flaking into dust there. Now I keep it by my pallet but it is flaking into dust there too.

Translation of a letter from Angel Felipe Fuentes Ortiz to Cristina Guadalupe Fuentes Espinosa, care of Concepcion Soledad Navarro Reyes

July 15, 1954

To my dear daughter:

This is to tell you that I am all right. Your Aunt Lancha gave me the message that Padre Vincentio called into the town hall here saying that you were safe at your aunt and uncle's house, thanks be to God. But she didn't have a number to call the priest back, so I am writing you this letter instead. Write back to the town hall, not to your aunt's house—by the time the letter gets here it may not be your aunt's house anymore; I am looking for work, so is she, but I do not know if we can pay the rent next month. Write, but stay where you are. I am sorry, but there is no money to buy you a ticket, and there is no money to keep you here. You know your cousins Raul and Felipe were working in El Norte and sending money home to your aunt Lancha. Well, Felipe came back with his head shaved, and Raul has not come home at all. Felipe was lucky: the train he was on left people right in Nogales, so he could call from the church there and tell his mother he was all right. Raul... We hope Raul is all right.

I did not want to tell you anything about the danger there is for people who are sent back, but Lancha tells me the papers have stories about the people who died from being left in the desert in the heat, so you will already know and be worried. Don't worry. Raul wrote his mother a letter the day those people died in the desert, so we know he wasn't on those buses. And I am safe, I am all right. They put us in the desert too, but not so far in, and we found water. How we found it is a

148

strange story, but I think you will believe me when I tell it, Cris.

I hope you still have the piece of the bowl I gave Doña Dolores to give to you. I kept the other pieces, and I held your clay hand and asked God to keep you safe. I was still holding that when they put us out in the desert and we started walking back. But I fell, and it flew out of my hand and off the road in a place where the slope dropped off steeply. I felt as though I was losing you again, and I ran after the piece, and then my feet slid and the sand slid under me and I went down, down, and I didn't know if I was strong enough to climb back up. When I stopped sliding I kept my eyes closed for a little while because I was afraid to look up and see how far I would have to climb. But they were shouting to me from the road, and I had to sit up and open my eyes. And I saw an opening in front of me, going back into the sandbank. Just a little opening, one I could go through on my hands and knees. But it was dark inside that opening, and I thought how cool it would be, and I crawled in. And just a little way inside the rock lifted above me and I could stand. It was cool there, blessedly cool, and I smelled water.

Cris, you have the gift for words, you could say better than I can how I felt when I heard the water. But you know from the Bible, *At the scent of water, he shall revive.* And I did.

I called, and the others came, and we drank, and we rested in the heat of the day, and then we started walking again, and before we could get badly sick from the cave water we came into the city, hot and filthy and sick and tired and very, very glad to be alive. But I was not as glad as the others, because I did not know what had happened to you, or even to the little piece of you that I had left in the clay.

Well, that was foolishness. You are safe. I love you, Cris. I will tell you how much I love you when I see you again. I do not know when or how, but I will see you again.

~Author's Note:

Operation Wetback really did happen in 1954. The Border Patrol rounded up close to one million undocumented immigrants from farms and factories across the country, shaved their heads and shipped them deep into Mexico. 88 people died after being left in the desert on a blistering hot day. Many more survived—but some of them were separated from their families and didn't get word from their relatives for many years. I made the Fuentes family luckier.

The Blade

By Leah George

Lonely, bitter, angry and afraid
A longing look at the evil blade

A testing strike through a snow-white sheet,
A frightened glance into death's retreat

A light crossing through the inner wrist,
Anger flows through a clenching fist

The edge brought down with shaking fingers
For a moment, loneliness lingers

First, one slash and then the other is made,
The razor glints, and with blood, it is paid

Dark red surges from the broken vein
Eyes closed tight in expected pain

The spill swallowed greedily at first
By the smooth pillow quenching its wicked thirst

Desperate eyes search a darkened room
Hands Grasp as the pain blooms

Innocence stolen with each brutal thrust,
As was love, beauty, and moments of trust

A bitter surge through a dying heart,
For a life beginning, ripped apart

Remembered laughter rings through the mind
As does love, friendships, and those who've been kind

A silent prayer tumbles through whitened lips
As the numbing coldness begins its grip

A last glance at hurt held so tight
Leaving no room for grace or for light

Thick lashes rest now on a pale cheek;
This was the wrong peace to seek

What once was stolen in ugliness and strife,
Was given this time at the end of a life

Now no more anger, pain or fear,
Only the silent fall of red tears

No love or laughter to cling onto tight
Just a blade edged with red, proving its might.

Home

By Melissa Schell

The closer I got to home, the tighter my insides knotted together. A lump of dread had settled in my throat the past few days, but I wasn't sure why. I gripped the steering wheel tight as I drove through the quiet neighborhood.

The house was eerily quiet when I walked in. I expected one of my five roommates to be up. Yet, nothing moved or made a sound in the darkness. Maybe I was anxious because this new place still wasn't a home for me. I decorated our rooms with pretty little purple lights, installed shelves for our knick-knacks, and arranged all my stuffed animals, but the pieces still didn't fit together. This place wasn't my home.

I made my way upstairs and into our bedroom. Seeing Scott peacefully asleep, curled up in a corner on our new queen-sized bed, released my inner tangle. My heart fluttered. The sight took me to a better time and place, years ago now.

* * *

"Hey... can I tell you something?"

Sunlight streaked through the bedroom window. Soft music floated across the rays. I lifted my head from Scott's bare chest, taking in his smile, our naked bodies curled together.

It was our first time alone together at his house—a rare occurrence for two teenagers. The house was peaceful without his bipolar mother screaming about something and his anger-ridden father roaring back at her. We had nothing to be afraid of that moment.

"Of course, you can tell me anything."

"I think you're beautiful," he said and ran his hand across the small, almost uniform scars on my hip. I fought the urge to pull away and hide them out of shame.

"I'm sorry this happened to you. It makes me sad knowing somebody hurt you enough to make you want to hurt yourself like this. But, I still think every part of you is wonderful."

I squeezed him closer.

"Thank you. I know you'll never hurt me like they did."

* * *

Looking around now, I couldn't believe we moved in together after years of living with his parents. It had been a faraway dream for so long, but now it was finally here. I climbed over the bed to gently kiss his forehead. As my lips touched him, he startled awake. I ran my fingers across his head.

"It's just me."

He sat up, glassy-eyed and reeking of alcohol. A flood of disappointment replaced the flutter in my heart.

"You're drinking again?"

He drank yesterday, the day before, and the day before that. I wouldn't mind if it didn't make him so angry every time.

"I mean, I only had a couple of drinks, that's all."

"You've been drinking every day since we moved in. I'm really starting to worry about you."

"Hey, whoa, I only have a few drinks here and there. I don't get trashed every night."

"This is serious, babe. You can't let this get out of hand. It's like you always need alcohol now. Every time we go out somewhere, every time we hang out with friends, and now every night at home, you always need a drink."

"You need to relax." He jumped up from the bed and chugged the water bottle from the nightstand. "You've been so wound up since we moved here, just fucking chill." His voice growled with annoyance. "You're jealous. I only work once or twice a week and have been able to drink and hang out with everyone here more than you have."

"Jealous? You think I'm jealous of your alcohol dependency?"

"Stop calling me a fucking alcoholic. It's not fucking about that. You know what it's about? You're resentful of my life and that's why you've been so depressed. Don't worry, little princess. You'll be here for plenty of fun times, I promise. Maybe then you'll get some sense into your head instead of wanting to kill yourself like you told me the other day. Stop being dramatic just because you have to work sometimes. I mean, I work sometimes too. It's something you have to deal with."

He tried to take me in his arms, but I pulled away. I let him rub my back instead. I still couldn't get past the slur in his speech though.

"Jane is coming over tonight," he said.

Jane was a new *friend* of ours. We started sleeping with other people when we were plastered. We'd grown unhappy with each other, especially when it came to sex. We were black and white--I was vanilla, and he was dark chocolate. We thought sleeping with other people might remedy our differences.

He gave these encounters more meaning than I did and was convinced they could lead to polyamorous relationships, but I saw right through it. I knew they were only progressing the countdown on the ticking time bomb of our relationship. We prolonged this life together like a coma patient who would never wake, and I unconsciously wanted to pull the plug. In the back of my mind, I longed for the death of us.

"You didn't tell me she'd be coming over tonight."

"Yeah, I forgot."

"Well, what if I don't want her to?"

"Why wouldn't you want her to?"

"I wanted to spend time with you."

"Well, she's coming over whether you want her to or not."

"No, she can't come over."

"Excuse me?"

"I said, your little fuck buddy can't come over."

Those words set his eyes ablaze. His face reddened to match his hair. The plastic water bottle crinkled under the pressure of his hand, and then water splashed over my face.

I froze, mouth agape, unsure how to react. Water dripped down my neck and shoulders. Any time I grew tall and stood up for myself, he would knock me right back down. The water ran down my chest. I headed towards the dresser in the room across the hall to grab some clothes. As I walked past him, he grabbed my arms.

"Let go of me!" I struggled to get out of his grip. My skin burned as his fingers dug into me, resisting my attempts to escape. I twisted my arms free, but then he grabbed me around the waist.

"Don't you dare try walking away from me!"

"Fuck you, let go of me!"

I pried myself from him and ran through the doorway into the other room. I slammed the door behind me and locked it. The door vibrated as he started pounding it. I imagined a monster had crawled out from beneath my bed, and now he was coming for me.

"You better open this fucking door! I swear to God, if you leave this house, it's over!"

He kept twisting the doorknob and pounding the door as I stuffed some work clothes for tomorrow into my purse. I could figure out the details of tomorrow as soon as I could figure out an escape plan.

His empty threats weren't affecting me at this point. Normally by now, I would panic and cave into him. This time, I wanted it to be over. This wasn't my home. This wasn't my room. These weren't my things. Jane wasn't my girlfriend. And this… this doormat of life was not my life.

Once I had shoved a pair of pants and a shirt into my purse, I stopped to think over what to do next.

Silence swept back over the house as he gave up on trying to open the door.

How has it gotten to this point? When did it get this bad?

When was the first crack in our foundation? Was it when we decided last year to open our relationship up to include other people? We agreed we couldn't meet *all* of our needs for each other, so maybe we needed more people to help with our shortcomings.

What kind of healthy relationship can't be mended by the two people in it?

* * *

"I really think we should start seeing other people," Scott said.

"It's just ... You don't satisfy me anymore. You barely ever want to have sex, but I need it. I need it every day. And I can't be happy if I can't have that."

He began this discussion after I told him for the second time that day I didn't want to have sex. I laid in bed, staring at the wall, wondering what was wrong with me. I knew he was right. I was so depressed that I barely had enough energy to make it to work every day, let alone have sex. A couple of times a week was all I could manage. I should have wanted it more, but I didn't. All I could do was curl up in bed every day for hours on end.

Zoloft became my new best friend, but a little pill wasn't going to magically fix my world. I knew this. I knew I was broken beyond repair.

He sighed and sat on the bed next to me. "I know you want this too. You've told me before you're a very affectionate person, and I can see that. You need another person to be affectionate with, and I need another person to sleep with. I think it would work out for both of us."

Maybe he was right. I did need to be with someone else. I didn't see it then, but what I really wanted was someone else besides him.

But, Scott was all I knew. We had been together since I was 15. I couldn't leave him. I had to make it work. We always made it work before. I stood by him as he worked through anger issues when we first started dating. He didn't leave me because of my panic attacks from anxiety nor my not-getting-out-of-bed-for-days-on-end depression. Maybe we could make this work. Maybe another person would make us both happy.

* * *

We started seeing Jane last week. I didn't have a connection to her like I did with the first girl we dated a polyamorous couple.

Maria.

I had high hopes with Maria. She became my temporary escape from Scott. She stood up for me whenever he put me down. Jane wasn't Maria. I didn't want to sleep with her all the time or drink with her every night like he did.

My heart numbed more with each passing day. Nothing mattered anymore.

* * *

I looked at the door and slowly unlocked it. I didn't hear him, but as I opened the door, I saw him still waiting in the hallway. I rushed to pass him and get down the stairs, but he grabbed me as soon as I came out.

"Don't do this," he pleaded.

I ripped myself out of his grip and ran through the dark house and back to the front door. I wondered if our roommates heard the screams or not. I wondered if they were sitting in their rooms, trying to ignore us, or if they were worried about us. They must have thought all of this fighting was so out-of-character.

Everybody saw us as the high-school sweethearts. Destined to be together forever. We were the most fun couple to hang out with, and the couple that never argued—at least not in front of anyone. But, they never saw what went on at home. They couldn't recognize the disappointment in Scott's eyes when I did or said something he didn't agree with. They couldn't see the terror growing in my heart as we edged closer to home where I knew he'd punish me for my disobedience. How many nights had ended this way?

* * *

"You know," Scott said as we walked into his room, returning late from hanging out in our friend's garage one night.

Oh, boy, here we go.

"You don't have to embarrass me in front of all our friends like that."

"What are you talking about?" I always tried to play dumb to avoid another argument.

"I mean when you got upset because I was joking with you. Everybody could tell you were upset because you're terrible at hiding

156

it."

"Oh, you mean when you called me a bitch?"

"Come on, lighten up. Me and Alyssa joke with each other all the time."

"Right, but she's just your friend. You don't say things like that to your girlfriend, whether you're joking or not."

"Yeah, well maybe I don't have to joke about it because it's true. You're being such a bitch about it."

"Don't you dare call me that again."

"Or what? What are you gonna do, bitch?"

I slapped him across the face.

All I remember after was that fiery, wide-eyed gaze as he grabbed me and threw me across the room.

* * *

Once I got outside the house—that wretched house—I rushed to my car and started the engine. He had been on my heels this whole time and ran over to the passenger door as I backed out of the driveway. He grabbed the door handle. A sudden cracking noise made me stop the car. He came over to the driver's side, holding something in his hand, and opened the door.

"You broke my fucking door handle? " I sat in disbelief.

"I was trying to open the door! Please, just stop and listen to me! I'm sorry I threw the water in your face, but come on, you threw something in my face too. I mean, metaphorically anyway. Look, we agreed to see other people, you told me that was okay. So, you can't go around calling Jane my 'fuck buddy.' She's our friend too, she's more than a fuck. Where are you even going right now?"

"Does it matter? I'm going away from you. I can't do this anymore. I can't deal with your drinking, the fights we have every night, living in this awful house. I can't, so I'm... I'm leaving." I reached over to close the door. A look of desperation spread across his face and he hurled his head into my car.

"What are you doing? " I grabbed the keys out of the ignition and jumped out. He continued smashing his head. I tried pulling him away to get him to stop.

"You're making me do this. You're hurting me, and I can't show you any other way how much you're hurting me right now."

"Please stop," I begged.

His eyes bored into mine but all I could see was a large lump and blood trickling down his forehead. His soft features hardened as he pulled something from his pocket. It took me a second to process what he did.

I locked onto the hand holding the object. It was a slim, silver dagger. Then I lowered my gaze to his forearm. Bright red blood gushed everywhere.

He never took his eyes off mine as the blood ran down his arm and dripped onto the driveway.

"Oh my god! What have you done! Oh my god!"

He said nothing and stood motionless. I thought he would let himself bleed out if I didn't act.

"Okay, okay, let's go back inside. Let's wrap that up, and… and get you to the hospital or something, I don't know. Fuck."

My panic-mode subsided as I began to focus more on how I was going to fix this.

His face curled into a relieved smile.

"That's my girl," he whispered. His warm whiskey breath crawled over my neck. He leaned on me and I helped him stagger back inside.

The Silent Neighborhood
By Benjamin R. Barnes

I'm writing this message to the man who keeps sneaking into the house. I assumed you would find it here on the kitchen table. I don't know how long you've been coming and going. I don't know who you are or even what you look like; I've only caught glimpses of you out of the corner of my eye. You're fast, and you're quiet, but I still know.

A man knows when another man is in his home. Maybe you're watching me pen this right now. I wanted to make sure you understand that I'm not scared of you. I was at first. I've been in the house by myself for so long that I didn't know how to react to the presence of another person. I decided that this might be a good way to try to communicate with you since you don't answer when I call out to you. It breaks the silence in the house, and it feels out of place. I won't do that anymore.

I'm going out for a few hours to collect my thoughts and raid a few places for food, books, and booze. I'll leave the pen here for you.

* * *

Well, I'm back. I'm not surprised that you didn't respond yet. I guess that I haven't given you much reason to open up to me. Once you get to know me though, maybe we can get along? I'll keep leaving this running note out for us until you respond, or I quit catching signs of you, no matter how long that takes.

I can't believe I'm saying this to a stranger, but I don't mind sharing the house with you. I'm surprised that I feel this way, but I've been by myself for so long. You can come out. We can talk.

I'll start:

Sharon and I raised the kids in this house. We bought it because it was right across the street from the playground. All three of our kids spent most of their summers and afterschool time out there. Now the playground sits there, silent. Our kids moved out twenty years ago, but other kids still played there. It was comforting when I could look out the window and see happy families with children chasing each other like maniacs. Now the neighborhood is as quiet as the swings, slides, and climbing bars across the street.

I get drunk every day now. It helps… or it doesn't. It's hard to tell. I'm half in the bag right now, or I wouldn't be telling you my life story. Losing Sharon isn't easy for me to talk about, but it feels better to have it down on paper. Maybe it'll stay on the paper now, instead of running through my mind on a continual loop of self-loathing and melancholy.

Anyway, I've been thinking about it, and this hasn't been much of an apocalypse so far. It's nothing like what they promised us in the movies. There are no zombies, there wasn't a nuclear war to kick it off, and aliens haven't invaded, probably. People just got sick and died.

Sharon got sick very early on and died quickly. She was fine that Monday, but by Friday she had wasted to almost nothing. The fever burned her up, consumed her.

Losing her was hard. Living without her has been harder. The whiskey is making me maudlin and tired, so I'm going to stop writing now. Before I go, though, it's important to me that you know that I'm a pretty good guy. I'm harmless. I'm going to go to bed now. Help yourself to anything in the cabinets. I found a ton of supplies in a church pantry today. I'm leaving the pen for you again.

Signed,
Alfred Perkins.

* * *

Still not going to write back, eh? I think I saw you again this morning, but it's hard to say. I'm hungover, so I'm not at my sharpest. You're like a goddamn bat, flitting around in the periphery of my vision. I suppose that maybe you have trust issues, but that doesn't explain why you keep coming here. There are tons of empty houses.

What are you doing in my house? Where are you hiding? Sometimes I think you're in the walls, or maybe the attic, or stuck up in the corner of the kids' room lurking like a spider on the ceiling.

To be fair, I'm still not certain that you're real. Maybe I'm just lonely, and my subconscious invented you. If so, it's made the last few weeks more entertaining.

Your move, stranger.

* * *

That was not OK! Not at all. I saw you in the mirror, just like you wanted me to.

Scaring a guy while he's shaving isn't very becoming of a guest. I've been trying to be nice to you, and then you go and do something like that. Do you know what the worst part of it was? I only saw you for a second in the shower-fogged mirror, but you looked exactly like a clean-shaven me. Who are you?

* * *

You know who I am, Alfred.

* * *

I knew you were real! Now I have proof. Your handwriting sucks, by the way.

I still don't know why you're following me around. I saw you again today while I was at the library. It's even quieter there now than it was when librarians policed it. For some reason, I kept dreaming about a word last night. *Doppelganger.*

I walked to the library and read up on it. I've started thinking that might be what you are. Crazy Germans and their myths.

* * *

This time, I heard you before I saw you. At first, I thought it was a mouse, but there you were, walking through the stacks of books. I didn't see your face, but you're me, damn near at least. I don't think that you saw me, but I also don't think it was a coincidence that we were both there at the same time.

If you're here to become me, to steal my life, I think you picked the wrong guy. Anything of value in my life vanished long ago. If you want to be me, move into an empty house and spend your time drinking hard liquor, reading books, and living a silent life in a silent neighborhood.

Just know that if you come for me, I will defend myself. I've got a handgun, you know. Who are you? No more games.

* * *

I'm everyone and no one. I'm you; I'm your mother. I'm glad you think that I'm real because I've been questioning if you're real for weeks. It's only a matter of time until one of us makes a move.

With deepest devotion,
A.P.

* * *

You're right about that; one of us is going to make a move.

The way you sneered at me today was the last straw. At first, I thought you were going to vanish from the mirror again, but you stayed. I couldn't believe that you were there, in the flesh, when I turned around. Then you gave me that evil grin. You were so confident, even when I leveled the gun at you. The look on your face scared the hell out of me. Do I look that scary?

I took a shot, but you were too fast again. I think I figured it out, though. Maybe I'm not as harmless as I thought.

If your face is my face, then I know where to find a steady target. Maybe it'll kill us both, but I think I'm finally OK with that. Either I've finally gone crazy from alcohol and loneliness and invented a companion, or you're real, and you're probably going to kill me anyway. I'm going to do it now, but I'll leave the pen so that you can have the last word.

* * *

Wunderbar.

Wendigo

By Joshua George

I.

"It consumed my family. It took each of them, savoring their flesh and their spirits. They offered little resistance, as resigned as men facing an avalanche. It came first in the summer for my wife. She saw its face and said simply, "I knew you would come. My husband has cursed us." The beast waited outside the wigwam as his victim retrieved my tomahawk and stalked behind her as she walked into the woods. After several miles, she stopped in a clearing where our family gathered berries. She laid the weapon at the beast's feet. My beloved wife dropped onto her knees, a prayer to *Gitche Manitou* on her lips. It did not save her.

The nourishment she provided sustained him for a season but did not wholly satisfy. Eventually, the hunger returned. My sons were next. This meal the devil-spirit played with, consuming the souls before the bodies. My eldest was forced against his will to butcher his own brother while It watched. The beast fed but was not sated by just one body. It snatched the stone blade I wore on my hip and buried the weapon into my remaining son's chest and ate him too. The boy had been too distraught by his own actions to offer any resistance. My remaining family knew they could not escape their fates. You cannot outrun a creature like this, nor can you hide from it. The monster knew this, and the fear was almost as sweet as their bone marrow and flesh.

My eldest daughter was the last one to be consumed. It was deep into the dead season and the girl had watched as our family had been devoured as easily as the leaves had fallen. The beast came and dragged the girl from her seat near the fire out into the snow to make her suffering long and lavish. She spat into its face and demanded to know why I did not protect her, why I was so weak. The words did nothing. I could do nothing as my only remaining family was torn to pieces.

After there was little left of her sans splinters of bone, the beast began a contented slumber. I was in control of myself again for the first time since my curse had manifested. Crows paced over the ground, looking for any morsel hidden in the snow. I walked to a nearby creek and began to wash the blood from my face and body. A bit of bone had become lodged in my gum. I removed it sharply. The bleeding lasted a moment and stopped. I paused my bathing, focusing on my reflection in the water. Despite the feast the devil-spirit had used my body to eat, I had become emaciated and withered. My skin was pale, fetid and frost-bitten. The hair had begun to fall from my head, my teeth and nails had turned a deep shade of rotten yellow. I accepted these things. I could not bear, though, the evidence of my crime which stained my skin and clothes. The stream seemed to lack the power to cleanse.

I stepped from the creek and walked back home. I went to my wigwam, where my wife and I had slept after my exile and before her death, and retrieved the stone knife. It was a weapon with history and I found it fitting for the job. I held the handle tight and pulled the blade across my throat.

Dropping to my knees, I prepared to embrace death. The pain was fire. I was wrong, though. I felt the skin stretch and connect over the ragged gash, leaving no wound. The beast stirred in my heart, tossing in its sleep. I made another attempt, slitting each wrist to the bone. These too knitted together before much of my blood stained the snow. *It* awoke and It knew what I had tried. The beast began to assert its sovereignty over our body. I understood then what my obligation was."

Edward laid the sheet of paper back on the table and looked at the man across from him. "It's decent, Jack. I mean, it seems a little dramatic, but I think that's something you can probably work out in the next draft." Edward had thought he was simply coming over to share a few drinks and pursue a shared interest with his friend. He'd been a little surprised when the man asked him to read a short story he was writing. "And I am not really sure where it can go from here. Also, who the hell is Gitche Manitou?"

"Gitche Manitou is essentially God," Jack said, pouring himself a little more bourbon, which was the same color as his skin, before leaning over to top off the other man's glass as well. "Sort of. He's also kind of like the Force from Star Wars. He's from an old native American religion, Midewiwin."

"I'm not even sure that I can say that." They both laughed at Edward's awkward attempts at the word.

"You're close. Work on it, you'll figure it out. And I haven't really decided where I am taking it yet. You'll have to see the next time you come over. Anyway, we both know why you're really here. Come on, I'll show you." Jack stood up from his recliner and led Edward out of the living room.

When Edward had arrived, he had been impressed by Jack's house and that feeling had not faded. It was large for a bachelor's pad and well appointed. The kitchen's bar was stocked with top-shelf

164

liquors and there was a pool out back, ready for warmer days. It would be another couple months until winter ended, but Edward could already imagine cookouts with scantily-clad women. Most intriguing, though, was Jack's massive collection of antique knives and swords. When Edward had heard about these at the bar, he'd asked if he might be able to come and see them.

"They don't do me any good if people don't come over to see them. Hell, I might even crack open some of the good stuff for you," Jack had said at the time.

Edward was guided into a room whose walls were lined with racks and glass-topped cases. There were weapons from every culture represented: a kukri, a German saber, a katana, a Roman gladius. Jack picked up a machete in an olive-colored cloth sheath with dark splotches near the bottom. "See those stains there? That's blood. This thing is stamped 1944. I'm betting it saw combat in the Pacific theater."

"Oh wild. I bet it's haunted," Edward said. He let his eyes drift from the weapon in Jack's hand and towards a case in the corner. "Hey," he said walking over and pointing, "is that the knife from your story?"

Jack put the machete back onto its rack and walked over. He opened the glass lid and withdrew the piece reverently. "Yeah, it is. This is actually the piece that started the collection. It was a gift from my father before he died." He turned the stone knife over in his hands for a moment before passing it to Edward. It was a rough stone blade affixed to what appeared to be a bone or antler handle.

"I'm sorry to hear about that, man. Was it recently?"

"Oh, no. Don't worry about it. I was pretty young when he passed away. I actually barely remember him. But yeah, it's my favorite piece. It's totally authentic, too." He reached over and plucked the weapon from Edward's hands and placed it back into its case. "Well brother, I think it's time we go finish our drinks. I have work in a couple of hours and they won't appreciate it if I have to crawl in."

"Lawyer." Edward had known Jack for a year or so from a bar in town, and in that time, Jack had never revealed what he did for a living – or much else about himself. The two got along well, though, so Edward had never given it too much thought. "Now that I've seen your house, it seems safe to eliminate most minimum wage jobs."

"I am no lawyer. Too boring. But hey, even if you got it right, I wouldn't tell you."

The two men finished their drinks. Before he walked out of the door, Jack asked him to come back in a few days, when he hoped to have the next piece of his story ready. "A few days it is," Edward told him, waving. "I'll bring the bourbon next time."

II.

"The shaman wore the face of a demon over his own, carved from wood and adorned with hide. This was to frighten the demons from me if my actions had given them entry. It had been crafted solely for this occasion. In his hands, the old man carried ashes from the fire, and these he rubbed onto my face. They were to sear away any demons who braved the mask. I had been fed a meal of berries and nuts before the ceremony had begun. These were to sate any demons who refused to be driven away, hoping they might leave on their own. My hands had been bound, and I was placed sitting near the flames.

The dance began. Men assembled around the fire, their faces obscured with masks akin to the one worn by the shaman. The drummers set a slow pace at first. The dancers circled the fire backward, one hand towards each the Sky and the Earth. The tempo of the drums increased steadily. The men began their song, a haunting wail, beseeching the devil to leave. While they danced, I struggled.

Something in my spirit fought the ceremony. It felt itself being expelled from my flesh and my soul. My nose began to bleed, and then my ears, and then my eyes. My stomach rejected its contents. I tried to focus my mind onto the shaman, to accept and aid the power of the ritual, but my mind was awash with a desire for violence. The demon spoke with my voice, invoking death and famine on everyone present. The tempo increased. The volume of the singers rose painfully, drowning out the beast's threats.

The shaman loomed over me. He grasped a handful of my hair and pulled my head back, eyes locked with mine. Shadows cast by the fire played across the mask. With his other hand, he poured more ashes on my face and into my mouth. "I invoke the *wiindigookaanzhimowin* by the virtue of *Gitche Manitou!*" The beast's struggle subsided with these words, and the shaman released his grasp. I collapsed, face into the dirt, unable to catch myself because of the bonds.

At that, the dancers broke from their labor and gave a whooping cry. Another dance began, this one of celebration. There was no concern that the ritual might have failed, as our tribe was renown for the power of its shaman. My wrists were freed and my face cleaned. I was led into the shaman's wigwam to await a final judgment of my purity, though none in the camp showed doubt. Outside I heard the sounds of jubilation, but I was not so certain the matter was resolved. If I was found tainted despite such powers being invoked, I would be put to death.

The shaman entered. There was no mask on his face. He carried a pipe in his hands, and the smoke collected into a dense cloud around us as he sat before me. For several minutes, he said nothing, seemingly oblivious to me and the sounds that drifted in from outside. When he finally spoke to me, he simply asked, "Did it leave you?"

"Yes, medicine man."

The shaman looked into my eyes, measuring me. I met his gaze, frightened to look away. The old man shook his head. He had seen something he did not like. "You are not clean." We sat in silence for a time. None interrupted us, though the wigwam was not far from the fire and the dancing and the music. He passed me the pipe and rose to leave. "I will speak to the chieftain. The choice is not mine." I took a long drag on the pipe.

After a time the chieftain came into the wigwam. He sat before me and motioned for the pipe. I passed it over to him. The big man had wounds on a cheek and one thigh that had been rubbed with an earthy poultice. "I am sorry that I have done this to you. You were not ready for the test I offered you. I should not have pushed you. Because of my part, I cannot put you to death, though I am obligated to. Instead, you must leave the tribe. Take your family and any who are bonded to you and leave tonight. You are an exile, and in case your taint has spread, so are they. Goodbye, friend. I am sorry." I accepted his generosity and left. I told none besides those who would leave with me of my fate so that the rest might continue their celebration."

Edward took a draw off his cigarette and handed the paper back to Jack, who asked, "What do you think?"

"You have me interested. I can't really imagine what people dancing backwards look like, though. Was it the moonwalk?"

Jack grinned. "More or less, I guess. There's still a troupe who knows it. Maybe I'll take you to the reserve some time, let you see it in person." He drained his glass. "Still not sure why they do it backwards."

"Ha! You grew up on a reservation, then. That's where you learned all of this stuff. Do you believe in Midewiwin, then?" Edward finished the rest of his drink. He had brought a bottle of them this time. He grabbed Jack's glass, filling them both.

Jack grinned at Edward's practiced pronunciation. "I guess it's as likely as anything else. My father believed, though. Used to tell me stories about the Sun Spirit, who was kind of like the religion's Jesus, bringing people back to life. I think it's interesting." Jack reached out to accept the glass Edward offered him, but it slipped in transition, shattering on the wood floor.

"Oh, damn it! I'm sorry. Let me grab a towel and clean that

up." Edward stood and dashed towards the kitchen to grab some paper towels. It took him a moment to find where they were tucked away on a small holding rod under the sink. Before he could return to the living room, he heard Jack curse loudly.

"You okay?" Edward walked into the room to see Jack, one hand holding most of the pieces of glass, the other covered in blood. A large shard shone red on the floor. "Oh, Jeez. I'm sorry, Jack."

"Accidents happen, Ed. I'll survive." Jack stooped and retrieved the bloody glass from the floor with his injured hand. He went to the kitchen to toss the shards in the trash. By the time Edward finished cleaning the floor, his friend returned with a large bandage across his left hand, over the area above the thumb and below the pointer finger.

"Let me see it – is it bad?" Edward peered toward the hand, but his friend shoved it into his pants pocket.

"It's not worth worrying about, except as evidence that we're probably done drinking for today. You hungry?" Jack asked. Edward nodded, grinning guiltily. "Good. You're buying. I'm thinking gyros."

III.

"We stood on the wooded ridge above the rival's camp, looking down into it. The Sun had fallen and we were within the trees. We had not been seen approaching. In the village, women and children went about mundane tasks while the men sat around the fires eating deer they had stolen from our grounds, in defiance of our warnings.

Our chieftain looked to us and indicated with his spear to a man sitting in a place of prominence among his peers. "He is the greatest warrior of their tribe. I claim him for myself. Any other, you may kill." We readied for action. Our leader held his spear aloft, pointing to the Sky. As it fell, its point leveled toward our rivals, we charged.

The enemy was not lethargic. Before we reached the village, warnings were called and men gathered their arms to meet us. Arrows filled the air. A man threw a javelin at me, but I slipped from its path. When our two parties met, he was the first I killed.

The battle swept into the town, and the women fled before us with their children. Their men were brave though, and some of our warriors were struck dead. In the center of the melee, a hole formed around our chief and his target. The sharp sound of wooden spears snapping off each other filled the night. Both men moved with grace and speed in the moonlight.

Our leader was the first to err. His opponent's spear cut a shallow path across his face. He managed to deflect the next blow and retaliate, though more slowly than before. Blood flowed freely onto the ground from the wound. None of our men were immediately able to break away and help him.

The enemy champion saw that our chieftain would not be able to resist for long now that the first blow had landed. Feigning high, he stabbed through my leader's guard and into his leg. The chieftain collapsed to his knees, dropping his own spear in the fall.

The rival withdrew a stone knife from a pouch at his waist and took a step towards our chieftain, ready to execute the disabled man.

Burning with panic, I overwhelmed the man I was matched against and struck him dead. I turned from him before he'd fallen and dashed towards the man with the knife. He was too assured of victory and didn't know I was bearing down on him until my tomahawk buried itself in him.

I stood over my chieftain until the battle moved past us and then knelt to probe his wounds. From what little I knew, they did not look to be beyond what the medicines the *manidoog* had given my people could cure. A young medicine man was close by to attend to our wounded, and I signaled him to care for the injuries before I rejoined the melee.

The battle had begun to slow and I saw that our tribe had won the day. Our dead were much less numerous than theirs', and what was left of the enemy tribe were fleeing from the village. They had paid very dearly for their theft.

The chief came to me as the men swept the village for supplies they could take. He supported himself on his spear and walked with difficulty. "You have saved my life. I owe you a boon." He led me towards the center of the town, where our people were gathering our dead and organizing the construction of a *jiibegamig* to honor them. Still lying where it had fallen, though, was the body of the rival tribe's champion. As my leader limped towards the corpse, many of our tribe turned to observe, speaking in hushed voices about the powers he was about to invoke. "Chieftain's right," I heard them whisper. First, he pried the stone knife from the dead hand which clutched it. He hefted the knife for a moment, feeling for its weight. Then he began to pry open the champion's chest. After a few moments of work, he withdrew a wet heart from the breast. He turned and approached me with these items in hand.

"First, I offer you this knife. It is a token for ability." I took the knife and put it into a sack at my waist. "I offer also this heart, a token for bravery. If you consume it, you will gain the power it held in life."

He extended the red mass to me. I took this into my hands and began to raise it to my mouth.

Before I could do as I was told, the medicine man declared, "What you do is anathema. Fortune should not be confused with fitness for the bargain. He is not ready. He will be Wendigo."

"He is ready. He overcame that man who I could not best. He will not be Wendigo." The congregation muttered their accord with the chieftain, and the healer argued no more. I raised the heart to my mouth and ate it."

"This is the best one yet, Jack. If you fill in the gaps between each episode, you could get it published. " Edward reclined in his chair, sipping his bourbon. He had asked if they were better off refraining from drinking after the accident two days ago, but Jack had insisted on breaking out the best bottle of his collection.

"Actually, that's the entire story. I'm not getting it published, either. I wrote it just for you. I thought it was important that you heard it." Jack eyed Edward oddly from over the top of his glass.

Edward laughed. "Important for me to hear? I knew it. You're taking me to the reserve to see that dance, right?"

"No, nothing like that. I just wanted you to have an idea of where I come from," he said.

Edward shrugged. "If it's personal, thank you for sharing it with me." The bourbon had made his mind a little fuzzy, and he felt as though he might be missing something. "How's your hand, by the way? I never saw the cut. It all happened too fast. And by the way, because I didn't say it enough before, I'm sorry about that."

Jack shrugged. "Don't be. It was nothing. Seriously. Look." He tugged the bandage off the wound and showed Edward his hand. There was no cut there, not even a scar. The bandage was also entirely clean, as though it were new.

"What the hell? It's only been two days. You acted like it was serious, man." He ran his hand through his hair, confused. "Were you hamming it up?"

"It was deep if that's what you mean. And that brings us back to my story. I need to show you this." Jack reached into his jeans-pocket and withdrew the stone knife. He placed the blade against his wrist and looked pointedly at Edward. "Watch."

"You're kidding me. Stop that. What do you think you're doing?" When the blade pulled raggedly through Jack's wrist, Edward leaped up from his seat. "What the fuck are you doing? This is a joke, right? What..." He trailed off sputtering, staring at Jack's wrist. The flesh was knitting itself back together. Jack wiped the trace of blood off on his pants, and it was as though there was never a wound there.

"I needed you to hear the story so that you would understand. I am not doing this because of anything you did. Someone has to be its food from time to time, or its hunger builds and it won't stop with a single person. Do you understand what I am telling you?"

Edward fled toward the front door. When he pulled on the knob, he found that it would not open. He screamed for help and pounded on the door, but when he looked behind him, Jack was standing there, waiting patiently. "Get away from me! What are you?" Edward screamed and tried to shove the other man out of the way, but found him as immutable as stone.

Jack put his hand on Edward's shoulder, holding him still effortlessly. "I am sorry. The fear is also part of this," he said over Edwards screams. "It is food too, just like flesh. I'll try to make this fast. You've been a good friend. That's why I told you the truth, even if it was only in that story."

Then the Wendigo came.

Hope, a Lesson
By Bernadette Fah

We eat hope for lunch
because maybe by dinner people haven't left yet;
then we throw up resentful mountains of hurt,
our stomachs scarred.

Sometimes I can't tell orange from grey, and every meal is bittersweet.
I want to tell you that even when it's at its worst,
when the only thing on the menu seems to be your fist
crammed in your mouth to stop yourself from crying,
there are small bits of relief under the salt of blood and bone,
and you will eat those crumbs, those morsels, like they're the saddest
diamonds in the world.

If we are what we eat, then you will know that someday,
from the inside out.
You'll understand what real brightness tastes like and
how the core of an orange day feels. That day, you'll realize
your fists were strength and your tears were courage.
You'll know why hope is the bitterest meal.

Confused

By Erica Marchant

My heavy eyes flutter as I adjust to the surrounding darkness. A dim light reflects off the wall opposite me. The soft surface beneath me radiates with warmth, but I am not comforted. My heart threatens to thump out of my chest. In the silence, I hear ticking.

What time is it?

And smell something sweet.

Where am I?

I urge my body to move, but something weighs me down.

Am I in bed?

A slight sigh escapes my lips and I wiggle my toes. Then my legs. I'm not stuck.

Just a blanket.

I rub my eyes relieving the throb in my vision, but the dull ache in my head won't cease. I nudge the blanket aside; a coldness sweeps across my exposed skin.

The nightgown I'm wearing is crumpled up around my hips. I feel laid bare, violated, and I still don't know where I am. My gut tells me there is a reason I am here, though. Something is familiar, yet I can't grasp it. I can't recall what it is.

The cold floor startles me as my feet touch down. Shivers run up and down my spine.

Why can't I remember?

"Hello," I whisper. "Is someone there?" My voice is coarse, arid as if it's been locked in a dusty, old forgotten storage cabinet.

I think there's a noise, like static. But only silence responds.

The tiny cascading light gives away no clues. Reaching along the wall, I grasp something fuzzy and warm, like it just came out of the dryer.

A clean linen scent sweeps past me. I brush the softness against my face.

A bathrobe.

I put it on.

"Explore," echoes in my ears.

My bare feet slide against something on the floor, also fuzzy.

Slippers.

I slide them on and my feet warm. Again, a sense of familiarity takes hold and something compels me to continue forward.

I need to remember why I am here.

Inching my way through the darkness, I glide my hands along the wall for a light switch. I cannot find one.

The darkness keeps my heart racing.

This isn't right.

My hand rubs across something, but it's not a switch. Nausea hits me like an ocean wave and I jerk away. A sticky, wet substance holds tight to my fingers.

It burns.

My fingertips rage with fire, and it runs the length of my hand. I try to wipe the slimy substance on the bathrobe, *my bathrobe*, but it won't come off. The ache surges as I rub the now raw skin against the fabric.

"It's so painful," I scream out, my voice surprises me. Clutching my other hand against my mouth, I listen for someone or something.

I try to will the pain away, and a tear escapes. That's when I hear it; crying, in the distance.

I wipe at the single tear, tilting my head like an animal straining for the faintest of sounds.

I know that crying.

Distant and hallow, it disappears as the rate of my breathing increases. My lungs seize.

Get control before someone hears you.

My mind reals with confusion and I realize my hand has gone from searing pain to numbing coldness.

What is going on?

I try recalling my last memory. Nothing. Just darkness far worse than my surroundings. I can't even remember my name. I focus on the faint light cutting the blackness. My breath heavy, while clutching the wall I make my eyes follow the cascading light back to a small window inches above my head.

"Somebody help," I yell. "Please, please help me."

I no longer worry they will discover me, I worry they won't. I need to see someone before the panic robs me of all sight and I exhaust the last bit of oxygen pulsing through my veins.

No one comes. The distant crying returns, throbbing into my skull. Now hyperventilating, I have an urge to grab a brown paper bag, but I fall to the floor.

I don't know what time it is or who I am, yet somehow I know this won't last forever. Panic attacks run dry within 10-20 minutes. The irrational part of me, however, wants to bang my head off the wall to make it go away, but I wait for this helplessness to subside. Perched against the wall, head in my hands, and knees curled up into a ball, I continue rocking until my breathing slows and my tears dry into salty stains on my cheeks.

I called for help, but no one came.

Is it worse to be alone and afraid, not knowing who you are, or to find someone is there watching?

What is that?

A noise crackles from above me this time. I jump up searching for the sound. I almost touch the wall again and then remember the burning slime.

My blind eyes enhance my other senses. The crackling blends into a soft scratching, like a cat kneading a soft bed.

I have a cat.

That's right. I remember her. Sadie. I make kissy noises, reaching my hand forward into the darkness, desperate to touch something familiar.

Is she really here?

The scratching stops. I am still alone.

How can I remember a cat if I can't even remember my name? And where is here? I don't realize the distant crying faded until it returns, unrelenting and urgent.

"Hello?"

"Hello?" echoes back to me from nowhere and everywhere.

"Who's there?"

Again, only silence responds.

Pull yourself together. You have to pull yourself together.

Shaking settles into my fingers and runs up my arms. I curl them around my body, knowing the only way to go is towards the light, towards the crying.

Fight the fear, I need to know.

I believe things will make sense when I move towards the light.

Don't just stand here confused and shaking.

My panic attack fades and my breath steadies. With a few deep inhales and exhales, I turn to face the soft glow shining through the tiny window. This intense fear threatens to paralyze my mind again, but I step forward.

One…

Two…

Three…

I listen.

Still nothing. The small window grows in size. It is not a window, but a door.

Has it been open this entire time?

The faint crying echoes around me, yet somewhere distant. It grows louder.

I step in front of the doorway and light blinds my eyes in a sudden flash. I raise my arms and turn back towards the darkness. I don't want to look.

You must look.

Bracing myself, I force my way through the door but slam into a wall instead.

What the . . .

An aching spot spreads across my forehead and my knee. I brush away my frizzy bangs to rub my head.

A blank, white wall where the door had just been. There's no end and no beginning, it continues on forever in both directions.

"Who is doing this?"

The crackling echoes behind me in response. Less like a cat scratching this time.

This isn't real.

My fingers still ache from the sticky substance, and now also does my forehead and knee. I wipe tears away from my raw eyes and see red, bloody, and peeling fingertips. As I walk the length of the blank white wall, away from the darkness, my hands swipe against something hard.

Framed pictures.

A woman in a shin length, flowing red dress stands alone in a dry grass field. A river in the distance. Her smiling blue eyes shine in the midday sunlight and her flawless skin sparkles. She isn't looking into the camera, but at something beyond it.

In the next, the same woman in the red dress stares up at a man. She appears content. The same serene field, void of flowers. His arm across her's. His white shirt, unbuttoned at the top, hides under a blue blazer. A wedding ring on his left hand reflects the same midday sun.

In the last, they wrap one arm around each other and cradle an infant between them. He, wearing the same white shirt and blue blazer, gazes down at the infant. She's no longer in the red dress, but a wide, beige peasant style shirt and dark pants. Her now vacant eyes stare up at him. No smile adorns her lips.

There's a fourth. Except this one doesn't hold a picture. "Please . . ." My lips quiver. I don't know what I'm begging for, and yet I do. It's there like a lost word unable to reveal itself when needed the most.

In the mirror, I see my withered face. The same face from the pictures, only older. Dark circles surround my eyes. Dry tears stain my cheeks. I'm not wearing any makeup, like the woman in the pictures. Though why would I be? My deep, vacant eyes burn red with sadness. The same vacant eyes looking up into the man in the last picture.

A white bathrobe cloaks my aching body. I'm not sure how it ever fit into that red dress.

The distant crying grows closer.

Shut that baby up.

A flash occurs on the edge of my vision.

It happens again. Continuous, now with some pauses.

I spin and see a soundless TV playing in muted tones across the room.

Vanilla and cinnamon waft through the air. My stomach rumbles. With deep inhalations, my nose searches for the sweetness as I move back along the wall bumping into a brown microfiber couch.

That wasn't there before. Was it? What is wrong with me?

A silent cop drama in a blurry haze plays on the flickering screen. It's familiar.

I've seen this episode before.

A man reaches out while an officer holds him back. His familiar blue suit taunts me. It's dripping wet, though it isn't raining. Someone, taken away on a stretcher, causes him pain.

The crying continues. The scene rewinds.

I am supposed to do something.

I reach for a glass of water on the shabby black table beside the couch when a voice booms across the empty space.

"What are you doing?" It asks. "Tell me what you see."

My heart throbs in my ears. Condensation, or sweat, makes the water glass slick in my hand.

"Who's there?" I spin, searching for the voice. I almost expect to see the picture man in the white shirt and blue blazer. The same man on the TV.

No one responds. The room still empty but for me.

Back on the TV, the show zooms in on the stretcher. I see her lifeless eyes above an oxygen mask. Red dress peaking beneath the white blanket. Just like my red dress. The one I don't remember wearing.

My lifeless eyes.

Heat rises up my neck and settles around my head.

I search for a way out. Four empty walls. There's no escape. The vanilla fragrant air overwhelms me and the panic regurgitates from me once more.

"Why? Why me?" I yell at no one.

"Sit Down, Melody. Please. Calm down."

"No." I shake my head.

Oh my god, Melody! My mother named me after my grandmother. Gigi's parents were orchestral musicians and wanted to name my grandmother something that reflected the music within them. Gigi never developed the same love of music. She died when my mother was young. I remember this now. How do they know my name?

"Sit," the voice says again. "The couch is comfortable and safe."

Another voice shouts "Go to hell." The cop drama. Sound now emanates from the square flickering screen. It was as if my ears were in a vacuum and the vacuum released. "Where is he," The distraught man in the wet blue suit screams towards the stretcher. "Find him, you need to find him." He pleads with the two officers still holding him back. The crying fades in and out like an echo off cavernous walls.

It was just the show. It looks so real. I'm the only one here.

I want to resist but sit anyway. Relieved, yet still confused, I'm lost in the episode before me and swear I've seen it before.

The sweaty water glass grows heavy in my hand. I bring it up to my lips and stop before taking a sip. The water. My gaze freezing on the still water forgetting the performance on the screen.

Drops fall into the serene surface breaking the otherwise placid liquid. A whooshing sound fills my ears, blocking out the TV and the crying. Tears flow from me like a river.

There was a river.

I can't focus my thoughts. The whooshing swallows me, drowning me. My eyes strain against closing. Breath seizes in my lungs. I mustn't sleep. I need to fight the river.

The glass shatters beneath my feet snapping me back. I jolt upright. The bright light fades and an ominous glow casts shadows about the room. I attempt to stand on my shaky legs and my slippers soak up water. It rises to my ankles.

"No." I turn to jump back on the couch but it's gone.

What is happening?

The whooshing sound brings with it a louder incessant crying. Fervent water rushes around, soaking the hem of my dress at my shins. My red dress. I don't remember putting on the red dress. I push my hands against my ears but cannot muffle the crying sound.

"Help! Please help me. Someone help me. Make it stop. Make it go away."

I can't swim, I can't breathe. I will pass out in this river and drown.

The water rushes past my knees, growing deeper. The cold

sends shivers through me. It hits my waste churning around me, threatening to drag me down and take me under. It's dizzying as it rises to my breast, my neck. Pulling at my dress.

Don't pass out. Get a hold of yourself. Look for something that can help you.

Tread, I tell myself, kicking.

Fight the current.

My arms are pressed against my body as if holding onto something. I cannot stay afloat.

The river pulls my feet out from under me and I release myself to the current, letting go of whatever I was holding. I let the rushing river take me. There is no use fighting it.

My teeth clatter. My body numbs.

I don't care anymore. I let go of all that I don't know, all that is, and all that never will be. I hope no one helps me. I take my last breath and slip under, watching the blurry sky disappear above me. It's over. No sound of rushing water. No crying. No disappointment in my husband's eyes.

I'm peaceful inside my mind. I don't question what has happened or who I am, no longer needing it to make sense.

Then, I hit something. My body thrashes against a cool, hard surface. Rolling over, I choke and throw up bile and water.

My red dress and my hair are dry. I draw in a bitter, stale breath, my aching chest heaving. So much pain.

Am I dead? Death wouldn't be this painful, would it? It couldn't.

I'm shivering on a cold linoleum floor. This is my floor. My kitchen floor.

I'm, I'm home.

This is my house. I recognize it. 10 Mountain Drive. I've lived here for 6 years. The familiar vanilla and cinnamon fragrance fill the air once again. And something else, like berry. Blueberry. Such a sweet fragrance. I miss that scent.

The open windows above my kitchen sink sparkle with a glorious light. Sadie, my cat, bathes in the dust speckled sunrays. Beyond the window, a bird chirps, hovering above his feeder. Wind chimes clank in the sorrowful wind outside.

Home. Quiet. Home.

"Hello, are you here?" I ask.

Warmth filters in from the living room. The crackling fire greets me in response. Still shivering, I stumble toward the fireplace and stand by the flickering flames, relishing in the silence.

The floor shifts and I stumble forward.

The walls shake around me and the crying returns.

No, please don't take this away from me.

But it was never this way, how I'm remembering it. Light and warm, full of the sounds of spring. My mind is lying to me. I run from the quaking and cradle myself in a door frame as the sun fades and the fire dies.

The shaking subsides and I throw myself against a darkened window, banging the glass and screaming at whatever is causing this.

"Don't take this from me. Don't do this to me."

My heart pounds in rhythm with my beating hands. The incessant crying returns, increasing with each heavy breath I take.

"I can't take it," I try to say, but only sobs roll off my tongue.

A dank, burning aroma fills the room and my fingers prickle with pain again. The air grows cold around me. White puffs bellow out from my mouth and disappear as fast as they form.

It's an illusion. Someone is playing tricks on me.

"I'm Melody Chambers," I say, mostly to remind myself I know who I am. "I was just at my house. Who is doing this? Show yourself."

Still, no one appears.

"I have a husband. Call my husband. He's taking care of our son."

Now I remember. The shaking returns and I wrap my arms in my fuzzy bathrobe.

I remember.

I pick up the chair from beside my hospital bed and throw it against the window but it doesn't break. I'm staring back at myself. I try again. Déjà vu rushes through me and I think I've done this before.

The memory overpowers me and I scream for my baby.

"Calm down Melody or we must sedate you, again." This voice is real.

"Let me out," I scream. "Let me out." I pick up the chair again.

A rattle and jangle sound echoes behind the now visible door. Two men in white come rushing in. I try to break free.

Eyes wide, they thwart my escape as both men grab me and hold me back.

It can't be true what I've done. "Find my husband," I tell them. "It isn't true. I don't know what I've done. Where's my baby?"

But I do know. I push against the men, adrenalin now in control. A woman in a long white jacket covering a red shirt and black skirt enters behind them. Her hair pulled slicked back in a perfect pony. She's holding something behind her back.

180

"No, no. Get away. Get away from me."

I break one hand free. I smack one of the men on his head. Scratch the other in the face. Fight to break away. Yet, I know this is a fight I never win.

They get ahold of my hand, pin me down, and something pricks the side of my arm.

The fight drains out of me—like I'm dying—taking my spirit with it. This has happened before. I glare up at the doctor holding a long empty needle and behind her, I see his face. Disappointed, scared, and crying.

"Why won't you help me?" I ask him. But my eyes grow heavy and my body slips away. "I'm sorry," I mouth and then "I love you." It all fades to black.

* * *

Sam turns off the TV. He grabs his keys and pauses in front of the three framed photos hanging on his deep ivory-colored walls. From the small window above his front door sunlight cascades across each of them reflecting the settled dust. Each picture increases a wistful longing within him. Melody in that gorgeous red dress. He didn't know. How much he wishes he knew.

As he locks the door behind him, he dreads today's visit. It won't be any different from the last.

* * *

Sam walks away from the room as Melody whispers I love you.

If she loved me, how could she do that to me?

Back in the observation room, he grabs a tissue and wipes his eyes.

"She does this every time." He says this more to himself than the psychiatrist. They met once when Melody was first admitted and have only spoken on the phone since.

"Yes. It appears she wakes up after each fugue and replays the same scene over and over again. Never changes. I've tried telling you over the phone."

"I don't understand." Sam watched her in horror through the two-way mirror as she ran around her room, hysterical, seeing things that weren't there, talking to imaginary people that didn't exist.

"What is she seeing, what is she doing?"

"I can't say for sure. The few times she's come out of it, she's brought up the baby and the river. And she's asked for you. When she tries to confront it, she loses herself again. We haven't been able to break this cycle."

Sam shakes his head, remaining silent.

"I believe her mind is replaying the last moments when she lost control. The temporary blindness, burning her hand making a pie, covering her ears to block out crying from your colicky baby."

"He was just a baby." Sam sniffles.

"She drops her water, mimics swimming and letting go. She's confused until she realizes where she is and why she's here. To her, it's always new. Every time. She can't fight her way out of it and it ends up in hysterics. We have to give her something to calm her down. But, unfortunately, it puts her right back into an amnesiac state when she wakes."

"That river," Sam repeats. That day he found her floating in the river. Mumbling. Hypothermic from the cold. It was the worst day of his life. His baby. His boy. Gone forever. She struggled after the birth, but he never imagined she could do what she did.

"We've been unable to reach her and I am afraid her psychosis is progressing. These fugues are lasting longer, and when she comes out, each episode increases in intensity. The trauma of drowning your child is so painful, her mind is shielding her from that pain. She doesn't want to remember. Until she does, I don't know if she will ever come back."

Sam stares back through the one-way mirror at his wife almost comatose and drooling on her bed. Bright light glares off the padded white walls of her cell.

"She'll never return to me?" He asks.

"I don't believe she will."

"I can't live her nightmare any longer. Thank you, doctor. I won't be visiting again." Sam shook the psychologist's hand before walking away, leaving behind his lost love and the memory of their 4-week-old little boy.

* * *

My heavy eyes flutter as I adjust to the surrounding darkness. A dim light reflects off the wall opposite me. The soft surface beneath me is warm, but I am not comforted. My heart threatens to thump out of my chest. In the silence, I hear ticking.

What time is it?

~Author's Note:
While this is a fictional story, [1]postpartum psychosis is real. It is a rare illness that affects 1-2% of moms after birth. Along with the symptoms of postpartum depression and anxiety—which occurs in 20% of births—psychosis causes hallucinations, paranoia, hyperactivity, severe mood swings, and delusions. While most moms with this illness are not violent, there is a 5% suicide and 4% infanticide rate. If you or someone you love needs help, contact your doctor, local emergency number, or an emergency hotline https://www.postpartum.net/get-help/in-an-emergency/. With help, postpartum psychosis is treatable and temporary. This fictional dramatization is an extreme and rare result of untreated psychosis.
[1] Information on Postpartum psychosis
https://www.postpartum.net/learn-more/postpartum-psychosis/

Petals

By Michael Riley

Ticking from the cooling engine marked time's passage as he sat in the driveway staring at the darkened house. His house. What he hoped would one day be their home. The small ranch stood before him cold and lifeless, a mirror to the man he'd become.

The clock on the dash read 2:30.

He climbed out of his car and walked a crooked path up the sidewalk, passing the unkempt grass and scraggly hedges without notice. Twice he dropped his keys while struggling to unlock the door.

She could have at least left the porch light on!

He stumbled into the living room—lit only by light spilling from the entry to the kitchen—and staggered through the cluttered space. Past the couch piled with blankets and a pillow where he slept many nights. Past the end table with long-dead flowers, their dried petals layered in a thin, dusty coating at the base of their vase, messages of sympathy clinging to withered stems. Past the crib still unassembled in its box, leaning against the wall that separated the room from the kitchen.

I really should do something with that.

He would tomorrow. There's always tomorrow.

The last couple aspirins rattled in the bottle before falling into his hand. He popped them into his mouth and chased them down with water. This became the new norm: chase the day's pain away with the contents of a bottle and forestall the next morning's with the contents of another.

How did this happen?

He already knew the answer to that.

Lost in the foggy recollections of the recent past, he didn't realize the glass slip from his hand until it shattered against the tile floor.

"Shit!"

He waited for her to storm in and berate him, bracing for the questions. She never came. Disappointment crept over him. Any reaction is better than the silence they lived in now.

They were done, he knew that, but he still loved her. Even if she didn't return that love.

He crept down the hall to check on her before retiring to the couch, something that also became the new norm. When he peeked around the doorframe, he saw the empty bed in the center of the room, its comforter pulled tight and smooth, and pillows meticulously aligned.

He couldn't remember the last time they made it.
He kept toward the bed, confusion creeping in.
Where is she?
Scattered red spots broke up the solid white comforter. He bent down for a closer look.
Petals.
Images that felt too far in the past flashed through his mind. The bed covered in rose petals. The trail of them leading from it toward the bathroom. The wonderful surprise left for him to discover. The last joyful night between them he could remember.
He retraced those same steps.
He didn't notice the dry whisper of crunching petals beneath his shoes.
In the exact place where the pregnancy test marked the start of their family, now rested a single folded paper note. He picked it up off the floor in front of the bathroom door.

I'm sorry.
I never stopped loving you.

Stunned, he stared through the slim opening between the door and its frame. The glimpse beyond offered only the view of a mostly empty wine glass on the counter and a candle burned to its base. She'd replicated the scene down to the last detail.
Could they go back to that night and start again? It wouldn't undo what happened, nothing could. The pain of their loss would be forever with them, but the suffering they inflicted on each other could heal. In time. Together.
For the first time in a long while, he hoped they might make it through this.
Their new journey would start tonight.
The door creaked open under his light push.
The crimson stained bath water meant he would start that journey alone.

Marionettes

By Michael Simon

Somewhere in the predawn haze, an Arctic Tern chirped. The upbeat notes slipped through the trees like a spring breeze and yet failed to crack our grim demeanor. Since strapping on the skis, neither of us had spoken a word and the rasp of fiberglass over hard-packed snow served as the only reply to our feathered friend. After two months, the daily trek had taken on religious overtones.

I watched the rising sun peel back the darkness like a curtain being raised, revealing a bleak and desolate coastline. The hill sat two miles north of our cabin and provided a full view of the Beaufort Sea.

At the crest of the hill, the used car salesman from Vegas abruptly held up, and I slid to a stop. Using only his elbows to balance on his poles—a skill he would never have mastered in the Nevada desert—the big man opened the black case that hung around his neck and took out the binoculars.

Every morning I held my breath.

"It's not just cloud." His matter of fact tone carried an ominous edge. And confirmed my worst fear.

My hands started to shake. "Are you sure?"

He turned and showered me with a look of disdain. Even after all this time, those blue eyes gave me the shivers. Having ridden roughshod over frailer humans his entire life, James despised weakness.

"See for yourself." He shoved the glasses at me.

I wanted to throw up but I took them anyway.

Gray clouds rolled across the sky, propelled eastward by prevailing northern winds. But what caused my stomach to lurch had nothing to do with the cruel and inhospitable weather. Rather it was the faint silhouettes of figures framed within those vast cumulous clouds. They looked the same as I remembered; hazy and contorted, advancing relentlessly forward.

"Bastards," I whispered.

Two years ago, they appeared off the coasts of every continent. Scientists and pundits declared the legions of marching figures the beginning of a new age. Experts affirmed them to be enlightened aliens making first contact or, at the very least, telepathic greetings sent from across the cosmos. Religious leaders proclaimed the second coming and people stayed glued to their TVs or made a beeline for the water to watch the *revelation* firsthand.

"Like bloodhounds," James said. "They never lost the scent."

186

I bit the inside of my lip to keep my emotions in check.

The BBC described them as 'rows of marionettes, marching in formation with crude, spasmodic steps—the actions a parody of human movement.'

The coverage was twenty-four-seven, and we watched as the minions advanced robotic-like toward the coast, their fuzzy outlines growing ever larger in the pale Californian sky. Their faces, surrounded by a soft, reddish hue, remained blank and expressionless.

After hours of screaming anticipation, their shadows touched land.

And people began to die.

They fell by the thousands. Anyone touched by the shadows succumbed immediately. It spread fast, like a nuclear detonation. Entire communities ceased to exist. Nothing could stop the advance.

Most victims passed quietly, slipping peacefully to the ground as if settling into bed. Others vanished into nothingness in the blink of an eye. But what riveted everyone's attention was what happened to a select few. Those unfortunate ones, scattered across different lands, simply burst into flame. It was like someone poured gasoline over them and tossed a match, except that no one did. Before the last television station faded into static, people got a good look at the charred corpses twitching in the middle of downtown streets. Their screams may have lasted only a few seconds, but the echoes reverberated around the planet.

Our civilization, in the making for thousands of years, descended into chaos. Throngs of terrified people surged inland. Cities burned. But the legions of marching marionettes, oblivious to the carnage, trudged relentlessly forward, sowing death and destruction with every clumsy step.

Inside the cloudbank, I could discern the familiar voluminous shapes, the same jerky movements. Suddenly it was hard to breathe.

"We'd better get back," James said, sounding both angry and frustrated. "The others would want to know."

As I skied down the hill, my brain refused to form coherent thoughts. This was supposed to be a safe refuge. They weren't supposed to find us.

* * *

"Christ!" I exclaimed. "I haven't seen this much food since we broke into that school cafeteria in Regina." The wooden table overflowed with steaming pots of soup, and plates of pasta.

Maggie frowned in my direction. "I'll thank you for noticing,

Calvin, but there's no need for swearing with young ears around. You'll mind your words in my kitchen."

"Sorry," I said, chagrinned, as I slid into the seat next to the woodpile. Maggie's daughter Rachel made a show of rolling her eyes.

"I've heard swear words before, mother."

"Not in my house." Maggie wiped her hands on her apron before taking another pot off the cast iron stove.

I winked at Rachel and whispered, "That's what mothers do. They're the word police."

She giggled. The thirteen-year-old had a crush on me ever since James and I pulled her and Maggie out of a burning car on the outskirts of Juneau.

At first, Maggie was apprehensive about her daughter's infatuation until she saw where my values lay. I may be only four years older but Rachel and I were separated by a lifetime of experience.

The corollary was that Maggie treated me like an adopted son and even though she was nearly forty, it was hard to think of her as anything but family.

I marveled at the irony. *The end of the world and I'm living with two unattached females, one entering puberty and one trying to be my mother.*

Next to me, the chair jostled. Wilbur and his ever-present smartphone sat down. If he noticed the feast over the beeps and whistles of his game, it didn't show.

We picked him up several weeks after the girls, the last surviving member of a group that made a stand just north of Fairbanks. Their canned food was infected with botulism, and Wilbur got to witness his family's final hours of poisoned agony.

He told us his name but not much else. Most of the time you could find him cloistered away in some unoccupied corner of the cabin playing his game. Needless to say, he didn't interact with the rest of us. He did manage to hook his up game to a warped solar panel on the roof so he could play practically nonstop.

"Everyone sleep well?" Maggie tossed the question over her shoulder as she shifted pots on the stove's only burner. Everyone understood the unspoken question; did anyone actually get any sleep, or did we pace the confines of our small rooms like convicts the night before our scheduled execution?

A chorus of 'ayes' answered her.

She smiled and shoved a log into the side of the stove.

"Can't be much left in the storeroom," I said. "Considering what we've been eating the last couple of days."

Her pleasant expression never cracked as she carried a

steaming bowl to the table. I swear that women could smile through a root canal.

"Getting pretty empty," she admitted and then winked at her daughter. "Don't worry, I've saved the last chocolate bar for us."

Rachel tittered.

It didn't matter. None of us would be making another run into the village for food.

Maggie squeezed Rachel's cheek and exchanged a meaningful look with me. I didn't say a word.

Three days had passed since James and I returned to the cabin with the news. Oddly enough, the group took the report calmly. No hysterics. No crying. I wondered if, after two years, we were simply tired of running.

To her credit, Maggie fed us like kings. Wilbur remained occupied with his game and I watched the marionettes grow larger in the sky. Like a well-heeled army, they were advancing on our humble abode in a grim and determined fashion.

The screen door screeched open and the familiar frame of the car salesman filled the archway. He carried a melancholy mood at the best of times, but the unsavory look he brandished about the room was harsh even for him.

"Shadows have reached the village," he announced brusquely. "Road's cut off."

His face hidden by the handheld, Wilbur snorted, "As if there's somewhere to go. We're at the edge of the world for God's sake."

The tips of James's ears turned red and I knew when it was time to intercede. "Wilbur's got a point. Short of swimming across the ocean, this is as far north as we get."

The big man turned his glare on me. The amount of vehemence in that look required a lifetime of practice. "So, what now, college boy? You going to just sit back and accept it? Maybe spend the last few hours talking about the *good times* and our last road trip?"

I learned long ago not to back down. His kind dominates the meek and mild. Still, I had to talk around the lump that formed in my throat. I couldn't hide from the facts. "You asked the same question in Colorado after the nuclear plant went critical and the fallout almost got us. And in those hick towns in Montana and Alberta ... you remember the *discussion* we had at the church after the fire." I shivered at the memory. James tensed even more, like a lion about to spring.

"Not to mention Juneau, Whitehorse and all the other ghost towns? When we walked past the corpses festering in the streets ... All the way from California ..." I took a deep breath. The parade of memories created a tremor in my voice and the girls stared at me wide-eyed.

"James, dammit, there's nowhere to run! The sea is at our back and the road is blocked. Even you can't outrun those demons across the tundra. Unless you're Moses in disguise and plan to separate the seas."

"Bah!" He threw off his parka and stomped across the kitchen. "I should never have saved your ass in the first place." His voice trailed into a whisper. "Silver spooned punk ..." He used a napkin to wipe the sheen of sweat off his forehead. "Freaking weather is unnatural," he declared.

I hid a smile, recognizing his familiar ploy of changing topics when he felt cornered. "Look at me; I'm sweating in the bloody arctic. It's sunny for the four thousandth day in a row."

Wilbur snorted again, this time in obvious agreement. Then again, they were right. Since the first sighting, it had been nothing but sun and cloud. No rain. No snow. Nothing. It was if someone had a giant weather machine and pressed the pause button before stepping out. Two years ago.

The bluster went out of the big fella and he slumped into the chair at the head of the table. His eyes seemed distant for a few moments before he noticed the feast. His gaze flicked to Maggie before coming to rest on me.

I shrugged.

Maggie found space in the center to lay down a plate of rolls. Then she removed her apron and invited everyone to dig in.

Wilbur paused his game and grabbed his utensils.

It was Rachel who asked the obvious question. "Are they are getting closer, Mr. Kennedy? The shadows I mean, are they're coming this way?"

James was ready to spit back a caustic remark when Maggie's throat clearing caught him up. "Yeah ... well, a little. The direction—"

"Now, Rachel." Maggie leaned in to ladle some split pea soup into her daughter's bowl. "Remember our manners. Mr. Kennedy just got in and needs to catch his breath. There will be plenty of time to talk about shadows later."

"Yes, Mother," Rachel murmured.

We ate in silence until Wilbur's game started beeping.

"Battery's low," he mumbled, pulling away from the table and hustling out of the room.

"Where's he going?" Rachel asked.

James grabbed a roll. "Haven't you been paying attention, missy? He's climbing up the roof to reconnect his do-dad to the solar panel he's got taped to the smokestack."

"How'd he know how to do that anyway?" I asked. "He's got about ten different wires up there."

"Easy," Maggie said. "He was in the university like you, Calvin. Third year at MIT. Must have been doing well too because he mentioned something about an internship at NASA."

"And you know that because—"

"Because I asked him."

I blinked. "Well, I'm glad he talks to someone around here."

"Why does he keep playing that game all day?" Rachel asked.

James snickered. "Because he's acting like an ostrich burying his head in the sand. He's hiding from—"

"Carrots, James?" Maggie thrust the bowl under the man's nose. "You look like you could use some fiber."

"Huh? Uh, thanks. I was just speculating ..."

By the confused look on Rachel's face, she had no idea what just happened.

"Maybe Wilbur's still in shock," I said. "We did pull him out of a bad situation."

"Get off it," James sneered. "You show me anyone here who hasn't survived a *bad situation*. We've all lost family and friends, and that's not the worst of it."

His voice trailed off but I could tell he wanted to say more.

An awkward silence followed as the four of us tried to eat. But without an actual appetite, it was hard to do.

* * *

Maggie and I leaned over the deck rail and stared into the sky. Legions of fluffy white clouds swept across another pale blue morning. High above them, the indistinct forms of shuffling mannequins marched inexorably forward. Beautiful sirens of death.

The wooden rail under my arms felt cool and rough, but the sight of those marionettes gave me goosebumps. I dropped my gaze and stared at the weathered decking.

Maggie rocked slowly on the balls of her feet, using her elbows to pivot against the wood. "Mr. Kennedy says the shadows will reach the cabin tomorrow," she said quietly.

I caught her eye. "He told me."

She started to tremble. I wanted to comfort her like a real friend would do. But I was too young. "How's Rachel?"

She forced a smile. "I found an old cryptogram book in the closest. She's busy working on the puzzles."

Like a normal thirteen-year-old.

"That's good." I rubbed my hand across the old wood. "What are you going to do?"

A sudden sob escaped her lips and she hurriedly put a hand to her mouth. I started toward her but she waved me back.

"I'm okay." She inhaled a deep breath. "This day was bound to come. I tried to prepare but," She wiped a tear away. "It's not something one can practice."

"I know."

She gave me a smile and her eyes twinkled. "Calvin, I wanted to tell you something. You've been a real gentleman these past few months. In fact, you've been the only sane person around. Wilbur has been a deaf-mute twenty-three hours a day and Mr. Kennedy has been, well, himself. I'm glad Rachel took a liking to you." She paused and her expression darkened. "That by itself saved me some of the worry ... some of the pain." She turned to stare at the apparitions in the sky.

"Tomorrow, I'm going to take my little girl to that hill just west of here, the one with the pretty blue flowers poking through the snow. I'm going to sit her down with her back to those ... things. Then I'm going to tell her about the day she was born and how excited her daddy was. I'm going to describe how she learned to ride her bike and what she wore on the first day of kindergarten."

Tears rolled down her cheeks. She made no attempt to wipe them away.

"We're going to have a mother-daughter day, for as long as it lasts."

A lump of fear formed in my gut. I had to ask. "Maggie, aren't you frightened? The way some people died ..."

She shook her head. "I believe they were the evil ones, Calvin, those who lived outside His Blessing. The vast majority passed on quietly. We have nothing to fear."

"How can you be sure?"

She took my hand in hers. "After forty years, you learn a few things. I've led a boring life, some would call a safe life. And Rachel, well, she's just a kid. We'll be alright."

We stood there for a long time, hand in hand, staring into the abyss.

* * *

When I walked back inside the only thing that had changed was Wilbur. The computer nerd had moved from one side of the room to the other, the game clicking and beeping happily in his grasp.

I shook my head.

Hours later, the sun drifted down the western sky as afternoon gave way to evening. The snow crunched under my boots as I wandered aimlessly among the trees. I patted together a snowball and threw it at the nearest tree. My teenage body was full of useless energy. If I were ten years older they'd call it anxiety. I called it fear.

I bent down to grab another handful of snow when a sudden cry rang out. I dropped the snow and bolted toward the sound. In seconds, I burst into a small clearing and spied James carrying Rachel in his arms.

Eyes wide, he looked shocked to see me. Rachel looked flushed and shaken.

"You bastard!" I yelled. Pulse-pounding in my ears, I bent down and picked up a branch. He was half a foot taller and fifty pounds heavier but I didn't care.

James held up one hand. "Wait, Calvin." He carefully put the girl down.

Rachel turned and hugged him. "Thank you, Mr. Kennedy." Then she waved at me and ran back toward the cabin.

I stopped in my tracks. *What the hell?*

James straightened his parka before meeting my glare. "I, uh, was out walking when I heard her call for help," he explained. "I found her up a tree. Apparently, she was trying to catch a squirrel when she got stuck. It took me ten minutes to convince her to jump. That's when you showed up." His jaw tightened. "Calvin, I know what you think of me. What everybody thinks of me. But I swear I would never ..." He cleared his throat. "I only wanted to keep you guys safe. Even acting the way I did, being an asshole, I just wanted to protect ..." His words fell away and his shoulders slumped.

The moment felt surreal. After traveling with this guy for two years, through cities and towns spun from Dante's Inferno, I was seeing him in a new light. I finally understood why the big man from Nevada was running so hard. He was terrified. Terrified of suffering the fate of so many *undesirables*.

But I could see straight into his soul. Though deeply scarred, something remained in the core. Something honorable.

I grasped his hand. "You're going to do fine tomorrow, James."

He looked at me, eyes hopeful. He wanted to believe. Needed to.

"Don't worry," I repeated. "It'll be okay."

Our hands dropped and I turned back to the cabin. As I trudged through the snow, I knew he was staring at my back, and counting down the minutes.

* * *

When I woke the sun was shining through the window.

I felt a spasm of panic. How long did I sleep?

I hustled into my clothes and, still buttoning my shirt, barged into the kitchen.

"Hello?"

"Anybody here?"

No answer.

On the kitchen table, cleared and clean, sat the last chocolate bar.

I smiled. Mother and daughter were on their way to scale a certain hill and Maggie had left a parting gift.

"Bye, guys," I whispered. "See you soon."

I sat down and ate the last piece of chocolate in the world.

"James, Wilbur," I called.

Only the soft rustle of branches outside the window answered.

I tucked in my shirt and stepped outside.

To my surprise, Wilbur sat in the old rocking chair, feet perched on the railing. His phone was nowhere in sight.

"Wilbur?"

"Mr. Kennedy left for town about two hours ago," Wilbur said. He didn't take his eyes off the clouds. "He said he couldn't wait for a lazy college kid."

"He went into town?"

He turned. Wide, dilated eyes betrayed his inner thoughts.

"He left a message for you."

"Yes?"

"He said he'll be waiting on the other side, and if you were wrong, he was going to kick your ass."

I couldn't help it. I laughed. The big man had decided to face his fear head-on.

Wilbur stared at me, his eyebrows knotted in confusion.

"I see you're not playing anymore," I said.

He shook his head. "Finished twenty minutes ago."

"Finished, or decided enough was enough?"

"Finished. All twenty-seven levels, all on the *impossible* setting." When I didn't look impressed, he continued. "Nobody here knew it, but back at school my friends and I designed the game. It was cutting edge, incredible graphics, humorous, challenging, customizable ... Apple bought the distribution rights. It was going to revolutionize the gaming world."

I didn't follow. "So, you wanted to play it till the end?"

"We engineered the settings so anyone could play, from three to ninety-three, from kindergarten to genius. *Impossible* was the ultimate. We put it there as a joke knowing it couldn't be beaten. No human could defeat our computer. The math was perfect." His gaze turned inward. "After watching my family die, I knew I needed something more to keep on living. The only way I could do that was by playing this stupid game, and beating it. I wanted, no, I needed to prove that science is not always the answer. Sometimes there's faith."

In my mind, the fog lifted and I suddenly understood. "And now?"

The old wood creaked as he leaned back in the chair. "Now I'd like to sit here for a while and watch the clouds."

I smiled and stepped off the porch. Above us, the figures loomed like mountains, moving limbs fantastically huge. My knees began to shake. "Wilbur, I'm going for a walk."

"Goodbye, Calvin."

I headed away from the cabin. Away from the clouds.

"Calvin!" Wilbur leaned over the railing.

I looked back.

"Thank you," he said. "For taking me in."

I waved and he disappeared into the shadow of the porch.

My legs took me north. I wasn't quite in a hurry and yet I dared not stop. Something terrifying nipped at my heels. The trail to the sea was fairly straight but it still took the better part of an hour to reach the rocky coastline. The winds picked up and I realized I should have brought a jacket.

Turning around to gaze at the advancing marionettes was in itself a test of courage. I had not created any separation. They towered over me, omniscient and threatening.

I noticed something else. Instead of numbering in the thousands, as they did on that very first day, there were but four figures left in the pale blue sky.

My brain drudged up the analogy. *Four Horsemen of the Apocalypse.*

I traced a path along the shoreline before coming to an extended point that stabbed deep into the water. Icebergs floated past like unchained islands. Our small canoe lay on its side in the wild grass. Strange how the sky remained clear, the air warm, and yet the snow refused to melt.

Only two figures remained in the sky.

"Maggie, Rachel." I fought back tears. My last true friends.

"Be safe."

The wind rustled my hair and pelted me with frigid spray. I watched a large iceberg float close to the shoreline.

On impulse, I pulled the canoe into the water and paddled hard for several minutes. The land drifted away.

My breath caught in my throat when I realized there was but one apparition remaining. Wilbur was gone. Only one human left on the planet. Mankind's reign was ending.

My hands trembled. I put down the paddle and watched the last shadow race across the water. We had run for two years, but it was relentless.

It had a job to do.

As the sun began its final descent in the west, and the golden hue of vermillion clouds faded from the sky, the winds were stilled as by an unseen hand.

The apparition bent down, its descent making it appear even larger. Soon it blocked out the entire sky. A dark stain, like a consuming plague, drew swiftly across the stillness. Heart pounding, I watched it close on me.

A fraction of a second before I became one with the darkness, I saw the eyes of the marionette twinkle with beams of golden light. Somewhere in the distance, trumpets sounded and a voice whispered, "The time of waiting is over. The Gates have been opened ..."

Pearl Teardrops

By Cari Greywolf Rowan

Cloaked in a soft, rich black shawl,
approaching the meditation room,
peace exudes from her delicate, aged body.

Her phantom-like entrance goes unnoticed.
An ethereal being gliding through the space
to a chair kept in sacred holding for her.

Like mala beads, she holds her pearls
with light, gentle caressing
between her wrinkled arthritic fingers.

She is present in the room
and simultaneously transcendent~
a woman embraced by paradox.

Her senses explore realms
out of reach from humanity in this age
of technological modernity and speed.

Her rarified territory is the epitome
of slow—in timeless eternal spaces
that defy definition and limitations.

She releases each worn jewel's
teardrop into her welcoming hands.

The small round gems, inaudible,
wail for her losses, weep for her joys,
and spread mercy through her fragile skin.

The veil between life and death grows
thinner, and she experiences the difference
between joy and sorrow dissipating.

Her heart opens more fully to life,
no longer fearing that which is
another shift in ever-changing consciousness.

She sits long after the room emptied,
overflowing with peaceful acceptance
and the grace befitting her pearls.

Vengeance is Mine
By Michael Riley

The winding road in the hills belonged only to the lone black sedan that traveled it at the late hour. Silence enveloped the car since John's wife had slipped into a dream in the passenger seat next to him. He stole a glance over at Rebecca, taking a moment to appreciate her beauty in the soft glow from the dashboard lights and the pale moonlight filtering through the window. She wore her hair up that evening, and even now as she slept it revealed the graceful slope of her neck that flowed into and through her shoulder. The strap of her black dress had slipped down her arm, revealing her smooth skin. She was the depiction of tranquility, and his heart matched her appearance perfectly. He had found peace in his life during their four years together, a peace he had never known in his thirty-five years before. He rested his right hand on her knee and allowed his thoughts to wander as he drove down the road through the wooded hills that would lead them home.

The yellow flashing lights burst into view as he rounded the curve, catching his wandering mind unprepared. He instinctively jerked the wheel to the left, throwing the car hard into the oncoming lane. Tires skidded against the pavement and the squeal of rubber against road filled the car's interior. The sedan narrowly avoided slamming into the back of the broken-down vehicle by a paper-thin margin.

John guided his car back into his own lane and pulled off onto the shoulder. His heart pounded in his chest and the sudden rush of adrenaline coursed through his veins.

"What happened?" Rebecca yelled, her voice a mixture of fear and confusion.

He sat in silence for a moment, slowing his breathing and calming his heart. "Someone stopped in the middle of the road." He tilted his chin upward, eyes locked on the rearview mirror illuminated by the headlights from the car behind them.

She turned and peered out the back window. "Are they ok?"

"I don't know. They won't be if they don't get that car off the road though."

John put the car in park, unlatched his seatbelt, and opened the door. "Wait here."

The interior light illuminated his wife's concerned expression. He headed off the objection he knew was coming, making a promise he intended to keep. "I'll be careful."

With that, he stepped out of the car and shut the door. She watched as he disappeared behind the lights of the car behind.

He was unable to ascertain if it had just been abandoned there until he walked past the front. The owner was inside, seated in the driver's seat with the window rolled down, his phone pressed against his ear. The breeze carried his mumbled words. On John's arrival, the man snapped his phone shut and quickly stashed it in his jacket. The darkness of the car's interior concealed the face of the stranded motorist.

"Everything alright?"

"Yeah, I'm good. Same can't be said about the car though. Don't know what happened. Driving along and all the sudden it just died. It was all I could do to keep it on the road," the man explained. "I got a tow truck on the way, it should be here in about twenty."

John stepped back from the car and looked down the short stretch of road that disappeared around the corner. "That's fine, but we really shouldn't let it sit here in the meantime. That's a pretty sharp turn back there. Tell you what, give me a minute to pull my car back around the corner where people can see it and I'll help you push yours off to the side."

"That'd be great, man. Thanks."

John nodded to the man and turned to walk back to his own car, never registering the creak of an opening door or the crunch of gravel underfoot from behind him. He'd made it halfway back when the smooth passing of metal against metal chased by the rapid snap of the slide locking into place sliced through the silence. The sound of a round being chambered was unmistakable; it was a sound he knew well. He stopped.

"Let's not try anything foolish."

Using a skill set honed in his previous life, he deduced that the cold, flat voice emanated from just under ten feet behind him and about two feet to his left.

He quickly surveyed the surrounding area. He stood almost exactly in the middle of the lane, leaving six feet between himself and the shoulder. The edge of the woods lay another twenty feet beyond. He would never make it. A hundred and sixty feet of the open road lay between him and his car, so making a break for that would be a long shot as well. Above all else, there was Rebecca. If he ran, there was nothing standing between the assailant and her.

Fuck! How could I have not have seen this coming?

He forced the thought from his mind. There would be a time to reflect on what he missed and chastise himself for his lack of attention, but now he needed to focus on how to get out of this. If the man had wanted him dead, he would have been already, so his life was not in immediate danger provided he could keep his cool.

"You're calling the shots," he replied to the stranger.

"Smart man. Walk in a straight line to the passenger side of your vehicle and keep your hands at your sides where I can see them. I will remain ten feet behind you until you get to the window. I will then flank to your right along the tree line. You will ask your wife to open the trunk from the inside, then you will circle the front of the car and get into the driver's seat. Do you understand the directions that I have given?"

It was obvious the man on the other side of the gun knew exactly what he was doing. "I understand." John forced his voice to remain calm.

He walked back to the car, all the while searching the scene around him for something he could use to his advantage.

He approached the passenger side window as instructed and the footfalls behind him moved to his right and further away toward the tree line, keeping him exactly between the stranger and Rebecca. He motioned to his wife to roll down her window.

"Hey, hon." His voice was steady. He knew exactly how this would play out. "Can you pop the trunk? I have to get the tire iron."

Rebecca leaned over to the driver's side, searching for the release. As soon as her attention was diverted, both he and the stranger went on the move. John followed the instructions he had been given, and the footsteps from behind rapidly covered the distance to the back passenger side door. A quick glance back over his shoulder revealed that he was no longer in the crosshairs, and the assailant now held Rebecca in his sights.

Nice move. Exactly how I would have done it.

With a simultaneous click, the trunk and the doors unlocked. The man opened the back door with his left hand, never wavering with the aim of his right. He extended his palm flat on the trunk lid, slamming it shut before climbing in the car.

John had just reached and opened his door when the man pressed the gun against the back of his wife's head.

"Don't turn around," the cold voice from the back seat commanded. She froze, the color draining from her face.

John took his seat behind the wheel.

"John?" Her voice was equal parts panic and confusion.

"We're fine honey. Just do what he says."

The voice from the back agreed. "That's good advice, Rebecca. Stay calm and face forward. With your left hand, take your cell phone from your purse and toss it over your shoulder into the back seat next to me. Edward, place both your hands on the wheel."

She did what she was told.

"Good. Now reach into Edward's right front pants pocket and do exactly the same with his phone."

A look of puzzlement crossed her face, but once again she did as she was instructed to do.

"Thank you, Rebecca." the man from the back said. "Edward, with your right hand, tilt the rearview mirror up as far as it will go."

John complied and was rewarded with his first opportunity to get a good look at his captor. The light from the car behind reflected by the mirror lit up the face of the man. It was only a glimpse, but it was enough. The man was young, perhaps in his late twenties, and judging by the distance between the top of his head and the roof of the car, John deduced he was short - five-six, maybe five-seven at the most. He was thin and had a face that would be easily forgotten under most circumstances. The only characteristic that would be readily remembered was a crescent-shaped scar wrapping around the outside of his right eye. John committed these details into his memory.

"I trust you know where we are going, Edward?"

Rebecca interjected before John could answer. "You must have us confused with someone else! He isn't Edwar-"

"Quiet! You will speak only when requested. I assure you that there is no mistake. Edward Shields is the man that I was instructed to bring in, and Edward Shields is the man sitting next to you."

She did not offer another word of objection but her frown and closely knitted eyebrows gave away her disbelief.

"She doesn't know, does she?" The sense of amusement in their kidnapper's voice was unmistakable.

"No. No, she doesn't."

"Interesting. Perhaps you can fill in the parts of your story that I don't know as we go. We have a long drive ahead of us and plenty of time for your wife to get to know the real man sitting beside her. I'm sure you know the way to the warehouse."

"I do."

"We had better be on our way."

The man was right, they did have a long way to go. It was a six-hour drive to the warehouse and, for the moment, time was on John's side.

* * *

At a quarter past four in the morning, the black sedan cruised across the endless wilderness alone. Except for the rare passage of an oncoming vehicle headed westbound on the road toward the mountains, there were no signs of human existence. They had been on the road for just over five and a half hours and were quickly approaching their destination.

The hours had passed slowly for John as he listened to their captor tell the tales of Edward Shields, the man whom he had left buried in his past. The man in the back seat did little to mask the exuberance felt in ensnaring his prey, recounting each of John's exploits more savagely than the last. Though embellished, at their core they were all true.

There was a time he'd hunted men. For over a decade, he used his expertise as a tool to enforce his employer's wishes when death was desired. He had been methodical in the planning of his work and ruthless in its execution.

The stories themselves were not the cause for his agony. He had long ago come to terms with the man he once had been, and the final acts of Edward had been those of repentance and restitution. The tears that rolled down Rebecca's face cut him far deeper than the memories of the lives he had taken. He was not the instrument of death he once was. She had changed him, unknowingly becoming the killer of the killer.

He held little hope they were going to make it out of this alive. The man in the back was obviously well trained, however, his dangerous mixture of inexperience and overconfidence may have provided John an opportunity to exploit. He talked too much and, perhaps with a little prodding, he could force him to make another, far more serious mistake.

"You seem to know a lot about me. Obviously, Mr. Montoya prepped you well in anticipation of our meeting. I don't, however, know anything about you. How about a name?"

"You don't need to be concerned with that," came the sharp reply.

"Hey, you got me. The greatest killer in the history of the organization. Wouldn't you like the legend to know the name of the kid who did him in?" John played both to the boastfulness that his captor displayed on their journey and to the inexperience of his youth.

"Haywood. Haywood Jablomey. Now shut the fuck up and drive."

John snickered in his head at the juvenile response and the flash of anger conveyed with it. He allowed a mocking grin to tease the corners of his lips. The man was wise not to give his real name but foolish to not understand his name was not what John was after.

"That's what I thought, you little chicken shit," John mumbled, his voice barely audible over the sound of the tires on the road. He deliberately glanced over to Rebecca and gave her a wink knowing full well that Haywood would see it. In fact, he counted on it. Her eyes widened and her jaw slackened. He buried the feeling of guilt for the horror her face revealed.

"What the fuck did you just say?" Haywood boomed.

That was the reaction he was hoping for, in more ways than one. Haywood may have been well trained, but he also was hot-headed and lacked the sharp focus only experience could provide. The voice that came from the backseat was no longer from directly behind Rebecca - he had moved to the center so he could hear what John was saying. He was getting sloppy.

"I didn't say anything."

"Right. Enough small talk. We'll be there in ten minutes. Keep your mouth shut for the rest of the drive. You should really save your voice for the screaming that will be coming soon."

The cockiness was showing signs of being forced.

John had no intention of speaking any further. All that was left to do was to wait for the perfect moment to act. He silently guided the car toward the small town on the river, past which lay the warehouse and their fate.

The town of South Bank was nestled along the southern shore of the Missouri River in Northeastern Montana, small and isolated from the rest of the world. It appealed very much to the man he once had been. With just under a thousand inhabitants and expansive wilderness surrounding it, it had once afforded him the luxury of solitude. Its proximity to the Canadian border also made the area a natural fit for smuggling, which in his past life had indirectly provided him with a substantial living. He knew the town well and the surrounding hills even better and was already two steps ahead planning their escape through the rugged terrain to the cabin he had once maintained in secret ten miles from town. He had little doubt it remained undisturbed.

All was still and quiet in the early hour of the morning, the single stoplight in the town's center blinked red in all four directions. He studied the dark storefronts and deserted streets as they passed, all of which appeared exactly the same as they did in his memories. The only thing to the north of the bridge crossing the river were a few homes and a church, followed by five miles of a hilly, winding road that led to their destination. He gradually and almost imperceptibly increased his speed as he crossed the bridge and drove up the steep hill toward it.

The small church's letter board backlit against the dark sky caught his attention as they crested the top of the hill, as did the oddity of the message that was written on it.

> "Dearly beloved, avenge not yourselves
> but rather give place unto wrath:
> For it is written, Vengeance is mine;
> I will repay, saith the Lord."

"They spelled Montoya wrong," Haywood mused aloud. Apparently, the sign had caught his attention as well. He chuckled at his own joke. "Vengeance belongs to the one whose six million dollars you stole."

Perhaps there would be a time when that story could be told: the theft from Montoya and the anonymous restitution paid to the families he had a hand in destroying. He desperately wanted to redeem his shattered image, to once again have Rebecca look at him the way that she did before this ordeal had begun. This, however, was not that time. This was the time to save her.

John stood on the brakes. The sound of screeching tires filled the car as the seat belt cut into his chest. Out of the corner of his eye, he saw Rebecca's long blond hair whipped forward before being eclipsed by the body of their captor flying from the back. The hand holding the gun led the way. John had one chance to seize control of the situation, and until this point, it had played out exactly as he intended.

The gun struck the dashboard, the force of the collision jarring it lose from the hand of their captor. John had already let go of the wheel and extended his right hand to where he had anticipated the gun would meet the dashboard, ready to grasp it. With his left, he deftly unlatched his seatbelt, preparing to turn and strike.

At that moment, it all went wrong. Their captor, now with his upper body wedged between the front seats, twisted to his left to face John. In the process, his right elbow buried itself deep into the inside of John's thigh, tearing his foot off the brake and onto the accelerator. The full weight of the man bared down heavily on his leg, driving the gas pedal to the floor.

The engine roared and the barreling car veered to the right and off the road, bouncing down the steep decline of the ravine. He wrestled to regain control, but with a loud metallic pop that he felt through the steering wheel more than heard, the front axle snapped under them. The driver's side wheel folded inward under the car.

The world spun as the sedan's unsupported frame dug into the soft ground and violently began to roll. A whirlwind of shattered glass and debris sliced at his skin and the sound of twisting metal drowned out Rebecca's screams. His head snapped to the left and smacked the window, flooding his vision with stars that quickly faded to black. For a moment, he was floating through darkness, his arms and legs weightless as he sank into the void. He heard only silence. He felt no pain, no fear, and then finally, he felt nothing at all.

* * *

A soft glow filtered through John's eyelids, flooding his field of vision with a sea of red. The light warmed his face and radiated through his body. Without memory or thought, he existed solely within himself and the light, and in its peaceful warmth, he was complete. He slowly opened his eyes, allowing the brilliance to engulf every inch of his being. It was the most intense light he had ever seen, one which he could physically feel caressing his skin, yet he found that he could stare into it without discomfort. He lay flat on his back, suspended above the ground floating towards it, drawn to it both physically and spiritually.

He turned his head and peered at the landscape from which he was rising. The trees of the forest were faint, vague shadows drowned out by the omnipresent fog. Beyond them, he could just make out the winding of a river fading into the horizon.

The river.

The thought held only vague meaning with no context. It floated across the stage of his mind, fading away just as the landscape around him. There was something about the river though, something that demanded to be remembered.

A smudge drifted up through the trees toward him, accompanied by the acrid and oily scent of something that he could not quite place. He shifted his attention briefly from the light that was drawing him ever closer to wherever it was he needed to go, and toward the smudge of gray rising from beneath the trees between him and the river beyond.

Fire! That smell is burning rubber.

Just as before, the thought carried fact without meaning. He concentrated harder on the scene playing out beneath him. The more focus he gave to the smoke rising through the trees, the darker it appeared and the more pungent its smell became. It was closer than he first thought, maybe fifty feet below.

It's a car. It's my car!

The realization of what it was he was witnessing snapped him out of the bliss provided by the light. The memories of the last six hours flooded back into his mind like an endless torrent from a breached levee.

"Rebecca!" His scream shattered the serenity of his ascent. The light around him dimmed as its pull weakened, reaching a balance that left him suspended and motionless above the sedan, fully engulfed in flames. He looked toward the road he had recently traveled and the deep grooves sliced into the soft earth of the hillside. There was debris of broken glass and twisted steel littered along its path from the car as it had rolled to the tree line below, ejecting him along the way. There were no other bodies along the hillside. He was positive she never made it out of the car.

The light intensified in its brilliance and pull. Once again, he began rising through the air.

No!

The thought was forceful, powered by rage that was boiling up through his sorrow. He turned away from the light. Extending his arms toward the ground, he strained with every ounce of his strength to reach toward the earth. He was not willing to succumb; there was one final job he needed to do.

The light faded and he began to sink back toward the ground. With every inch he descended, the landscape around him darkened and the pain in his body increased. The agony of the impact of his head against the window was now accompanied by the slicing of the glass that had carved deep into his face. Thundering pain pulsated through the left side of his head, blinding his vision and dimming his consciousness. When he finally made contact with the earth, the light was gone. He only held a vague awareness of his situation and once again sank into the silent and painless void of unconsciousness.

The light that penetrated his closed eyelids was not the same as the last time he had awoken, nor was the warmth on his face as peaceful or serene. He forced his eyes open and was greeted not by the light of a tranquil passing from the shattered physical body he left behind, but to a searing blaze devouring what was left of his love. His head pounded mercilessly and his battered body ached. The dream of his death that felt so real only a moment before now quickly faded from his mind.

It had been no dream, John had died at the bottom of that hill and deep down inside he knew that. Edward however lived on.

* * *

He surveyed his surroundings. It was still dark and, judging by the intensity of the fire and the lack of response, he figured he had been unconscious for only a few minutes. If he wanted to escape, he would have to move quickly. He took his bearings and set out for his secluded cabin.

He planned while he made his way through the dense forest. It was almost nine o'clock when he finally reached the cabin, and although he was overcome with exhaustion, he had made better time than he had expected.

The cabin had been well built and meticulously boarded up against the brutal Montana winters and wildlife. The heavy wood door was still secured with a padlock and the exterior appeared to be undisturbed. He limped to the back of the cabin, and after a brief search under a stack of rotting firewood, he retrieved a key that would grant him access to the inside.

Darkness shrouded the inside of the cabin, wrapping its contents in a blanket of shadow. He breathed in the stale, musty air, and ran his fingers over the thin layer of dust coating the small wooden table in the middle of the room as he walked by. The layout had been ingrained into his mind and light was not necessary in order to navigate through the space.

 He took four steps past the table to a small bed along the far wall and gingerly sat down on the mattress. He should have been retrieving and lighting the gas lanterns on the mantle of the stone fireplace or checking on his store of preserved food and water stashed away in the basement. He could not. He was frozen to the bed, alone and in the dark.

His body grew heavier with each passing moment that he sat in the silence, and now that all was quiet around him, his only thoughts were of Rebecca. The image of her asleep in the seat next to him, the underlying panic of her voice at the arrival of their captor, and the tears that streamed down her face as who her husband really was had been painstakingly revealed all taunted him in the darkness. For the first time since this ordeal had begun, the crushing weight of loss and regret fell upon him.

There was so much to do. The truck in the shed, the long quiet generator, and the hollowness of his stomach were needs that warranted his attention, but those took a back seat to his exhaustion. He felt himself slipping under without the realization that he was even laying down. Sleep came for him, the lure of the peace and comfort of unconsciousness too forceful to deny.

Rebecca's scream reverberated through his head and lingered hauntingly in the inky, still blackness of the room. He snapped awake and sat up, earning a reward of pain that sliced through his confusion. The dream of her fiery death still echoed through his mind. He forced the thoughts away and forced his body to its feet. Now was not the time to mourn. The nightmares and regret could have their way with him later.

He crossed the darkness by memory, lifted the lantern from the mantle, and proceeded to the table, where he primed and spared the lamp to life. The white-hot light pierced the darkness, blinding him for a moment and causing a fresh wave of pain to erupt in his head. He restricted the flow and softened the light. The steady burn washed the room in its warm glow.

The room was unchanged from his memory: the table at which he sat with its single chair, the small bed pushed up against the far wall, the stone fireplace with its iron grate tucked within, hovering over a pile of ash from a fire long ago. This was at one time not only his home; it was his refuge, a place of safety and seclusion. That was not why he came back here now though. His reason for being here had solely to do with what lay under the house rather than with what was contained within the walls of its single room.

He looked at his watch. 4:30 AM. He had slept for nineteen hours. While he did need the sleep, his plans would have to be adjusted for the shorter time table he was now presented with. Restoring power, a shower, or attempting to get the old truck out back revived were luxuries he could no longer afford. He rose from the table, ignoring the protests from his many bruises and cuts, and got to work.

Moving the bed, he uncovered a trap door. A creaking wooden staircase led him below. The light from the lantern he carried cut through the still darkness of the basement and revealed the tools of his trade. They hung on the wall, black silhouettes lining a wall of gray stone. He set the lantern on the steel counter that ran the length of the wall where the rifles were mounted and stepped back, momentarily contemplating which one would best serve him.

He took the Barrett M99 off the wall. It was heavy in his hands and at twenty-three pounds would be a long carry over rough terrain to the warehouse, but it was his most trusted rifle. He laid the gun on the table and began the process of stripping the weapon. He cleaned and oiled the weapon with care, placing each part into its proper place in the case. The ritual overtook him, focused him on the task to come, and provided comfort for the pain. He checked his watch: a few minutes before five in the morning.

He stripped the torn and bloody button-down shirt and dress pants from his body and walked to the nearby closet where he donned a black sweatshirt and rugged camouflage pants. Grabbing a knapsack from the shelf above the clothes, he packed some food and rope. On his belt, he attached a six-inch tactical knife, and on his head, he placed a plain black cap.

He left the cabin as dawn broke across the horizon, laden with the rifle on his back being carried on its final mission.

* * *

He emerged from the woods near the church, his rifle concealed in the brush and his provisions consumed on his journey. His diversion into town was unnecessary - the most direct route to the warehouse would have kept him on this side of the river - but the opportunity to do a little reconnaissance was a chance that he was willing to take.

The church's sign and its admonishment went unnoticed this time, but the black patches of rubber left by the skidding of tires on asphalt were not. The scene of her fiery death below forced its way to the front of his mind and carried with it a fresh wave of agony and rage.

Not now. Focus!

He pushed the memories and emotions down, forcing them into the deepest recesses of his mind. He could grieve later. His full attention now must be directed toward the bridge and the awakening town beyond.

His first stop was the rundown convenience store just over the bridge. The alarm chimed with the opening of the door as he entered. Edward poured a cup of coffee from the glass pot and picked up a newspaper from the rack at the counter. He pulled down his hat to conceal his face and, more importantly, the gash on his left temple. Just another hunter getting a coffee on his way to the woods.

The cashier was young, no doubt the underachieving kid of the shop's owner, biding his time in the family business until he could get out and explore the world. He hunched over the counter, face buried in his phone and the cords from his white earbuds draping down the sides of his face. He was either completely oblivious to his customer or was completely uninterested in working. Edward wouldn't have been surprised by either.

"Hey, you gonna ring me up?" Edward asked, trying to conceal his annoyance.

There was no response.

He pulled three singles from his pocket and left them on the counter before walking toward the door.

"Keep the change, kid."

Again, only silence returned to him.

He walked out, coffee in one hand and the folded paper tucked under his arm. Ideally, he would have much rather had a vehicle to conceal his presence while he surveyed the activity of the main street of the tiny town, but his options were limited. He casually strolled down the block, found a bench in front of a quaint barbershop, and sat. He rested his coffee next to him and unfolded the newspaper, acting as if he were reading.

He studied the street, the people going about their business in town, and searched for signs that something was amiss. The signs would be subtle and overlooked by the untrained eye, but a skilled hunter always spots his prey. If his presence here was suspected, the organization would be searching.

He noted the cars on the road, the turns they made. He watched the people carrying out their business, the stores they entered. He found nothing out of the ordinary on the streets, but as he looked down to pick up his coffee, the headline of the newspaper he had been holding screamed to him.

FATAL ACCIDENT ON HILL STREET CLAIMS LIVES OF TWO

His attention abandoned his surroundings as he focused on the story before him. The details were wrong, however, he could not have done a better job of telling the story himself if his goal was concealing his presence. There were two dead, a man and a woman, burned beyond recognition when their car had run off the road and hit a tree at high speed. That much was correct. However, he did not die in the accident as the article told. He was thrown free from the car as it rolled. It could be days before the second body would be identified as not his. Nobody was looking for him.

He folded the paper and rose from the bench, tossing the news in the trash can beside it. There was nothing more to gain by remaining in the open. The hunt was on and his prey was unaware they were being hunted. He would tread only in the shadows until the moment he could strike.

* * *

The sun grew heavy in the early evening sky, its warmth fading on his back. He looked down on the warehouse from his perch on a hilltop a hundred yards to the west. From this distance, the shot would be easier than his decision to pull the trigger. He laid prone and motionless, waiting, his weapon at the ready, trained on the door. For hours he had remained patient, waiting for the opportunity to present itself. He checked and rechecked the distance and conditions. Every distraction he presented himself pulled his mind from the sound of

Rebecca's last screams that were ever present in the background of his thoughts.

A door opened and two men emerged. He immediately dismissed the first, a short man with rather unremarkable features, and focused his attention on his companion. Enrique Montoya was unmistakable, a towering form whose presence and swagger commanded a sense of intimidation, even at this distance. He wore an expensive suit and removed a cigar from his coat pocket.

Like clockwork.

Every afternoon at this time, the boss emerged from the warehouse to enjoy a cigar as the sun set behind the hills. Today was no different, but it would be his last.

Edward sighted his prey through the scope. The two men stood facing each other, Montoya's front visible to the hunter, the other man facing away. He checked the wind and distance for the final time. The air was still, and the hunter's heart was slow and calm. The prey stood motionless and oblivious to his imminent demise. Edward's only regret would be that Montoya would never know.

He was one with the rifle. He relaxed his diaphragm, releasing the air from his lungs in a long, smooth exhale. He pulled.

Nothing.

Without breaking his visual link with his target through his scope, he slid his thumb up the grip and felt the safety switch. The switch had been set to fire. He quickly ejected and chambered another round. His pulse picked up and he struggled to reset. He again sighted his target and lined up a headshot. He squeezed and was met with silence.

Montoya must die.

Edward abandoned all concern for the prospect of his own survival. He would have to be swift and stealthy. He unsheathed his knife and descended the hill, picking up both speed and sound as he went. If he could avoid being heard until he broke the clearing between the tree line and the target, he could still make the kill. The hint of a smile curled the corner of his lips as he made his way down the hill. His vengeance would be carried out face to face, intimately, at the point of his knife.

He broke from the tree line in a full sprint, positioning himself directly behind the unknown man. From this angle, he could not see Montoya, but he knew that meant Montoya could not see him either. He covered the remaining thirty yards in seconds, weapon in hand. Neither man seemed to hold any awareness of his approach.

They were so engrossed in their conversation that they never saw him coming. Edward sidestepped to create an angle of attack around the man facing away from him and brought the knife over his head, clenched tightly between his hands. He jumped, and with the full weight of his body, drove the knife down through the top of Montoya's skull.

It plunged through nothing but air.

Edward crashed to the ground, his body hurling unimpeded through Montoya. He rolled and sprang to his feet. The two men stood before him continuing their conversation as if nothing happened. He pounced upon his prey once again, slashing an arc through the air, slicing deep through his victim's back.

The knife emerged clean on the other side. The body offered no resistance.

Edward's body went numb, the knife clattering on the ground after falling from his hand. He stutter-stepped backward. He stared in disbelief at Montoya, who carried on his discussion with the shorter man, impervious and oblivious to his attacks.

The shorter man. With a crescent-shaped scar wrapping around the outside of his right eye.

Realization struck Edward with the force of a bolt of lightning. The dream he had while unconscious after being thrown from his car, the corner store clerk who couldn't be bothered to look up from his phone, the rifle that would not send its bullet screaming through the air were all clues that now revealed his fate, all ignored in his quest for vengeance. Above them, rose the sign from the church: the unheeded warning.

The world faded, the crispness and brightness of the fall afternoon darkened around him. He again found himself entering the blackness, but he was not drifting painlessly through it. This darkness was a physical force, wrapping itself around and cutting into his flesh, pulling him down with a force much greater and more sinister than that of the light. He thrashed helplessly as its grip grew tighter.

He heard only his own terrified screams. He felt only his own pain and fear, and finally, he felt the pain of his victims. Forever.

Lullaby for a Dog
By Jennifer Bradpiece

I will revisit a place
I wanted to stay.
I will take you with me.

I sink into the cloth hammock:
the cloudless sky, the Moroccan lantern
above my head
and the wooden slats breaking the sun's light
are all impossibly blue.

The Formica table is cold as January—
your ears are late July.

The hammock sways above your head
like a half-moon on a rocker.

You turn your dewy nose up
to nuzzle me, before a furtive flicker
of motion steals your eye:

A quail bobs its plumed head
as it parades down the soft dirt pathway.
You are captured by the staccato
motion of the bird until the sun warms
your back and tumbles you onto your side.
You stretch out, front paws reaching
over shaded cement.

You hear voices murmur.
There is the clamor of metal.

The long sprig of foxtail leaves
bends down just low enough for
you to take between your teeth.
As you chew, the earthen taste of oat
hay seeps like tea onto your tongue,
such a different flavor from the
sweet and coppery green grass near your tail.

As your eyes begin to close
the Joshua Trees tease you
running wide figure eights in the breeze.
They look as your plush toys might
if they came to life and ran panicked,
puffy limbs waving, blind from the time
you chewed out their eyes.

The afternoon folds into dusk so slowly
each distinctive color and turn of shadow and light
is visible as individual beads on a child's abacus.

A faint, awful sucking sound. A vial
is filled, then another.

But come back with me
to the warm pavement below.
Well, cooling now.
Now the moon and sun face off
gently, and the sky goes indigo.

The silence here is so dense, listening
is like biting into rawhide. Over my head,
suddenly two sparrows . . .

Grasp

By Aaron Pasker

"Mr. Helms, where were you when the incident began?"

The lights shining from above the stage were so bright I could barely make out the audience. They were faded shapes in the distance, sympathetic shadows looking to hear my story. I saw these gawking fan types on television talk shows every day. They didn't care about me, not really, they just wanted to see the next big thing. Today I was it. Tomorrow there would be someone else to stare at.

"In a bathroom stall on the second floor. I was working late, just trying to get some stuff done so I could head home for the weekend without worrying if Monday was gonna be a shit storm."

The interviewer raised an eyebrow at that. "Working on New Year's Eve?"

"We all do, double holiday pay and all that."

She picked up a pen and pad from the table between us and started scribbling notes. Seemed like she wanted to document every word I was saying. Couldn't blame her, it was a hell of a story. This kind of story, my kind of story, usually ended in tragedy these days. Not this time though.

"And what do you remember about that moment? That moment when it started?" She asked without looking up from her notepad.

I remembered the crack, crack, crack, echoing in the distance.

"It was the noise, the pops and bangs. Not normal for an office. You know what I mean?"

"Pops and bangs?"

"Yeah. Just crack, crack, crack." I snapped my fingers with each word for emphasis.

The audience inhaled in anticipation. Those dark silhouettes beyond the lights already knew what was coming. Hearing it first-hand though, that's what they were really here for.

"And then what did you do, after you heard that?"

"At first? Nothing. I finished my business in the bathroom and headed back to my cubicle. I should have known right away that something was wrong, but it took a little while. It was only after the noise kept coming. Bang, bang, bang. That's when I knew something was wrong."

"So after that, after you sensed something was wrong, what then?"

The audience leaned in, ever so slightly. Their eagerness to hear the next tidbit was palpable. That's what everyone wanted, more of my story.

"I thought I better check it out, you know? See what was going on. So I took the stairs down to the first floor." The audience let out a collective gasp. "I know, I know." I held up my hands. "In retrospect it was dangerous, but it's what I was trained to do."

"Trained?" She looked up from her notepad. "You mean in the Marine Corps?"

Yeah, in the damn Marine Corps. Where I was trained to kill, so people like you can sleep safe and tight in your homes at night. Without the worry. Never having to worry. When was some rag-head was gonna drop a mortar on you? You got to snore the night away in peace dreaming about rainbows and unicorns.

"Yes, ma'am, we run toward danger when any sane person would run away."

The roar of adulation from the audience was deafening.

"I see." She wrote another note. "What happened next?"

"I got down to the first floor and the hallway by the stairwell was all clear. I crouched by the wall there to reassess the operating area. There was still yelling, and those same bangs and pops, coming from the foyer. I inched my way down the corridor toward the noise."

Bullets whistling by my head, shattering glass, and tearing metal. Chaos.

"From what I understand you did go into the main foyer after that?"

"Yeah, and I almost I hadn't. Almost. It was hell. Bodies slumped everywhere. Pop, crack," snapping my fingers can clapping, "Pop, crack. And bangs. Everyone screeching."

Burnt powder and hot brass. The last frantic screams of dying boys.

"What did you do once you entered the foyer?" she asked.

The audience hushed.

"That's when I saw him."

"Saw who?" she said.

Damn insurgents. Coming out of nowhere, everywhere. Shooting up the whole damn place.

"The terrorist. I knew I didn't have a lot of time. He looked at me. Right at me. I saw the fear in that bastard's face. He knew I was coming for him. He knew I was gonna end it."

"And so you attacked him?"

"Damn right." The dark wisps beyond the lights let their adulation roar. "I went after that terrorist son-bitch with everything I had."

"You call him a terrorist again. That's a strong term, Mr. Helms. Many might even think that term offensive."

Has she ever been ankle deep in a pool of her buddy's blood?

"Offensive? I don't give a damn. I've seen enough of 'em to know."

She leaned back in her chair and raised a hand to her chin as if pondering her next question. After a few moments, she asked. "Was he armed?"

"Armed? Hell yeah, he was armed!" I slammed my fist on the table between us.

We're gonna die. They're everywhere. WE ARE GONNA DIE.

"Mr. Helms, please contain yourself!" The audience pulled back and hissed at my outburst.

"Sorry. I'm sorry. Sorry, sorry." I pulled my fist from the table with the screech of metal scraping on metal. "Do you want me to continue?"

"Please do. Now, do you realize no weapons were found at the scene?"

"Those sneaky ass killers? Hell no, I'm not surprised. They leave evidence."

She scribbled another note on her pad before continuing, "Didn't you hear me? No weapons were found. You're not surprised by that? How could he have been armed?"

They swarmed the Humvees. Armed. Innocent. Just words. Sooner or later everyone was a part of it, civilian wasn't term that applied anymore.

"Maybe you should check your facts. I just know what I saw."

"I see," she continued writing, "You said you attacked the man after you saw him?"

Live or die. Choose.

"It was him or me. So I ran right at him, didn't give him any time to react. Tackled him right then and there."

The faded shapes behind the lights rose to their feet, giving glorious adulation. They knew. They understood, if even for this brief moment.

"Is that how you got that gash on your eye?"

"Yeah, Haji son-bitch threw a wicked haymaker. Caught me right here," I tried pointing to my left eye, but in the moment my arm failed me.

"Punched you?" she asked.

"Yeah, right in the eye."

"Didn't use his supposed weapon?" she asked.

"Supposed? Supposed my ass!"

What the Hell is she thinking with this 'supposed' crap?

"Anyway, no, he punched me. It was a hell of a punch to, I'll tell ya' that. That swing rang my bell pretty good."

She wrote more notes as if every word out of my mouth was of vital importance.

"I see. After you tackled him, and he punched you, what then?" she asked.

The audience leaned in, eager to hear the gory details.

"I got my weight right on top of him. Pinned him down. Then... well here comes the ugly part."

Blood gurgling out of his eye sockets, filling the floor of the Humvee. It was everywhere, covering my hands and arms.

"Mr. Helms?"

"Sorry," I said, shaking my head clear, "I lost my train of thought there for a second."

She lifted a briefcase from the floor beside her and placed it on the table between us. She opened it and pulled some photos out, placing them on the table for me to see.

"Do you recognize this?"

The photos showed a man's head, what was left of it anyway, the face was covered in blood and the eyes missing.

Die. Just die. You and all your crazy fucking buddies.

"Yeah, that looks like the terrorist. Once I tackled him, well... I had to do what I had to do. I was unarmed, so it was the only way."

"That's... very visceral, very violent, Mr. Helms," she said.

"I had to be. With people like this, it's kill or be killed."

Kill or be killed. That's it, that's all there is to it. We knew it, they knew it.

The audience gave a standing ovation. I tried to stand and take a bow, but my tired legs kept me in my seat.

I continued, "And then there was the screaming."

That was the worst part. Echoing in my ears for ever since.

"The screaming?"

I shifted in my metal chair with a rattle. You'd think a fancy television show could afford better furniture. When I was a little more comfortable I continued. "Yeah, the screaming. Do you deer hunt ma'am?"

"No, I can't say I ever have."

"Well, I do. And I'm a pretty damn good shot, but even I miss the mark once in a while. Sometimes instead of getting a clean shot through a buck's heart, you'll hit 'em in the spine. The buck will fall, paralyzed but still alive and in terrible pain. They scream this awful, tortured scream. It's the worst, most horrific scream you can imagine. That was the sound he made as I gouged into his eyes. It quieted as he died, but then new screams filled in. The other people in the foyer, those frightened survivors. It enveloped me." The audience cried and sniffled. I didn't blame them.

"And the man you killed, did you recognize him?" she asked.

"No. Before I got to him there was too much adrenaline, my heart was racing like a Corvette engine. After, well, afterwards his face was covered in blood and bits of grey matter."

"Would it surprise you if I told you the man was Sam Hasan?"

"Sammy? Really?"

I saw Sammy around the break room every day. We'd drink coffee and talk about football. Usually, he'd go on about how his Packers were gonna stomp my Bears. Unfortunately, he was usually right. I never thought him to be one to turn Crazy Terrorist.

"Hard to believe. I thought he was one of the good guys. You just never know, I guess."

She wrote several quick notes after that, then said, "The police officers at the scene say that when they arrived you were standing over him, covered in blood."

"Sounds about right. Messy business, but someones gotta do it. The officers were nice enough though, they got me out of there right quick. Probably for the best. If there was another one of 'em son-bitches around probably good to just let the police handle it."

She kept writing for a full minute after that. When she finally finished she handed me something.

"Mr. Helms, would you sign this? It states everything you just told me, and that you are signing it willingly, of sound mind and body."

I took what she handed me. My book, my biography.

"Sure thing," I said as I signed it, "You guys work fast."

They really thought I was some kind of hero. They didn't get it. I was just doing what I was trained to do. The kind of things they would never have to because people like me were here to protect them.

"I think we have everything we need here. Officer Williams, you can take him back now."

The personal escort backstage was a nice touch, though unneeded. I whistled my favorite ditty as we left, *America the Beautiful.*

The Sticker
By Samantha Pilecki

Losing your faith is a lot like losing your best friend. Millie knew this because she lost both on the same day.

It was at Abby's sleepover and Millie's legs were hurting again. She stood and waited because there was nothing else to do but stand and wait until *they* called her back in. *They* being Abby and Sofia. *They* were in the bedroom, behind the door, talking about something.

Probably boys. Abby knew she didn't like to talk about boys. There was no time for boys. Millie studied the door and the happy cat stickers she and Abby stuck on it in kindergarten. The fat cat peeking out of a donut was beginning to peel at the corners, tempting Millie's index finger to tear at it.

God, her legs hurt. Whenever Millie stood, her legs hurt. She bent over to rub her calves, but of course, that did no good.

She hoped it'd only be another minute of standing in the dark hall, the only light a soft glow from Abby's froggie nightlight at the end. She met Abby in Tadpole Pond Preschool, where they received those nightlights, and had been best friends ever since. They had both performed, mortifyingly, for the second-grade dance recital last year, went to the same church, and liked cats instead of dogs. But now their bond was wearing thin. Millie traced her finger over the sticker's edge. They hadn't been spending enough time together. She blamed herself. It was the time away from school. The scans. Her legs. The pain.

"But, it's just the county fair."

Sofia's voice. What was she saying about the fair? Millie leaned closer to the door.

"You don't know her. *I* know her. I know what she's been through."

That was Abby's voice. Standing up for her, no doubt, against Sofia. The outsider. Who was Sofia to encroach on their friendship? Sofia had a *dog*.

"Why can't she go to the fair?"

"She won't have fun," Abby continued from behind the door. "Her legs will hurt."

Abby would go to the fair without her? Because of her legs?

Millie began to pick at the donut-cat sticker. Its tail was sticking straight up and was gummed dark at the edge.

Her legs, her legs, her legs. Nothing for the past year, except her legs.

A deadened weight settled in Millie's stomach, pressing on hurtful nerves. Was Abby her friend anymore?

Sure she was. Millie remembered when they both won dolls at St. Mary's bingo. God wouldn't let anything happen to them. He was on their side. They were friends, pure and simple.

"You're right," Sofia said. "It wouldn't be fun, even for us, if she came. What would we do?" She snorted. "Sit and watch the pig race the whole time?"

"No rides. No running," Abby sighed. "I know. I just feel bad."

Abby didn't sound like she felt bad. She sounded...lofty.

The cat's tail was completely dislodged from the door and Millie peeled the whole sticker off with one smooth rip. The sense of accomplishment was short lived.

"I just wish she had other friends," Abby said. "Real friends."

The cat stupidly smiled up from Millie's thumb.

Pain bloomed in her calves. It was just as she had expected. She wasn't good enough for Abby or anyone anymore.

The certainty that she and Abby were two halves of a whole– that protective balance of supposed friendship - was now severed like an artery.

The cat sticker gave no answers. No reassurance. It was old and had been peeling. Why had she picked it? There was nowhere to put it.

Please, God. Please stop the pain. Defeated, Millie slumped to the floor.

"Millie?"

Mrs. Schaeffer. Abby's mom. Coming up the stairs, her phone in her hand, looking alarmed.

Don't ask me why I'm sitting out here on the floor. Please. Just don't.

Mrs. Schaeffer didn't. She looked at Millie the same way Sofia had looked at her. Pitying. And maybe a little scared, as if cancer was catching.

"Your mother's coming. I'm sorry, Millie. You won't be able to sleep over. Your mother...she got the results of your scan."

Millie folded the cat sticker in her pocket and stood. The pain came back. The one constant companion left to her now.

"I'll just get my stuff," She kept her voice happy.

The scan wouldn't be bad news because God wouldn't let it happen.

Or maybe He would.

Tenacity of the Species
By Michael Simon

The realization exploded in my brain. *I'm the last of my kind.*
In retrospect, humans were an accident of nature. Unlike the
dinosaurs that ruled for millions of years, we were never meant to
survive long on top of the food chain. Especially since our brief tenure
was punctuated by war, genocide, greenhouse gases, polluted oceans,
and nations battling nations over splinters of land. Only the romantics
and idealists harbored any notion of bringing all the countries together
in peaceful harmony. Little did they know all it took was an alien
invasion.

In the cave, the temperature hovered around freezing. I slid
into a sitting position against the rock wall and listened to the rats
scurrying in the darkness. Outside, the city burned.

I recalled how, in those early days, our self-serving politicians
put aside their differences and forged a planet-wide alliance. Even they
understood the need to marshal all our resources to have any chance of
combatting their incredible technology. And still, the aliens pushed us
to the brink of extinction. In a few short months, they destroyed what
millions of years of evolution had crafted.

Even now mechanical and biological units searched the ruins
of the city. They wouldn't stop until they exterminated our entire
species. I had eluded them for months but now, like the fox at the end
of a chase, my battered body screamed for rest. I ran my hand along the
jagged rock wall and shivered as the cold penetrated my tattered
uniform. The smell of death lingered like an omniscient poison. The
Coleman still worked, and I coached a small, blue flame into existence.
In the gloom, it resembled a beacon of hope. Like Earth before the war.

A warped tin cup was all I had to scoop water from a stream
that snaked across the cavern floor. I placed the cup on the burner and
soaked up some heat with my hands. The small flame twisted and
jumped and, in its dance, I saw silhouettes of fantastic alien ships and
indestructible machines.

First detected by Hubble, the spherical objects that entered our
solar system were not asteroids as first thought. The President
announced it on Christmas Day; an alien armada was on an intercept
course.

Space probes sent back pictures of their fleet, and we bore
witness to the immensity of their vessels, each one bristling with
bizarre and ominous weapons. To a warring species like man, the

holographic images struck a deep, instinctive cord. The aliens blasted the probes out of existence.

As the UN beamed off peace proposals, the generals, buried deep in the war rooms of the world, began preparations of a different kind. Humanity had two generations warning—fifty years—however, evolution had battle-tested our genes. We would fight to the last man, to the last breath ... to the end.

We couldn't close the technological gap before the aliens arrived, but it didn't stop the generals from trying. In a matter of decades, millions of drones filled the skies, and hundreds of killer satellites prowled Earth's orbit. Factories worldwide shifted to military fabrication, producing tanks, planes and every manner of projectile weapon. Five billion people received basic training. Hectares of landmines bracketed our cities, and we seeded even the oceans and waterways with explosive charges.

I dropped in my last tea bag when the water boiled and used my knife to squeeze every ounce of flavor from the packet. A faint cinnamon smell filled the air. The can of spam in my jacket pocket was the last bit of food I procured from a razed strip mall outside Toronto.

I tore off tiny pieces and savored every bite.

Licking the last crumbs from my fingers, I leaned back and closed my eyes. I remembered the *Before Time*; sitting around a table with my parents and brothers, laughing and joking. Brothers. I took a few seconds to remember their names. And my mother and father, their faces were fuzzy now after so much had happened. But once, we were a family.

I groaned and cast the illusion away. The aliens had killed my memories, along with most of the population.

My second family was different: raven-haired Jamie, Indian Dave, and diminutive Katherine. Selected at the ripe old age of eight, they grouped us together, taught us together ... injected us together.

The generals placed their bet on conventional weaponry, the tanks, planes and weapons of mass destruction. The scientists, however, went a different way. Being human they did what came natural, they searched for a way to cheat. They looked for an edge and what they found was a new weapon; me and those like me. 0.0001 percent of the population to be exact. We had the abilities they could magnify and manipulate.

The surgery and hormone therapy produced predictable, and some not so predictable, side effects. I smashed into puberty at ten and those memories still give me nightmares. By fourteen, we could predict tarot cards and memorize phone books. At sixteen we levitated cars without breaking a sweat.

I killed my first person on my twenty-fifth birthday. The victim was one of the infamous paparazzi who lingered at the gates of secret government sites, waiting for that singular moment. How he sneaked into my room and scare Jamie I'll never know. I woke up and reacted without thought.

My instructors were ecstatic. They called it a psionic bullet, a tiny packet of energy erupting out of the quantum field. Like an invisible lightning bolt, the microscopic space-time detonation blew out the back of his skull. His brain was still boiling during the autopsy.

After that, they intensified the augmentation procedures, injecting us with stimulants, neurotransmitters and brain peptides. By the time we hit forty, each of us could kill a squad of soldiers with a single thought.

The ambassador the UN sent out was a last-ditch attempt to prevent the inevitable. He reached the alien fleet ten years out but before he could broadcast his message of peace and cooperation; they reduced his vessel to quarks and leptons.

When the aliens achieved orbit, our vaunted space armada lasted all of six minutes. What they didn't destroy outright, burned up as it plunged into the atmosphere. Pinpoint laser strikes annihilated the rockets and satellites. None of our weapons even scratched the surface of their ships.

They bombed us from orbit for thirty days, destroying our cities and factories. They knocked our ICBM's out of the sky with contempt and annihilated our newest subs miles under the surface. Humanity took it on the chin but, then again, our bloody past had prepared us well. After millennia of warfare, we were nothing, if not tenacious. We crawled underground, licked our wounds, and waited.

They landed on six continents. Massive ships descended and disgorged seven-foot tall warriors in gleaming liquid metal suits. Heavy fighting vehicles, five stories high, sprouted a confluence of lasers and projectile weapons.

That's when we struck.

We threw our tanks, armored vehicles and soldiers at them in a wave of fury and defiance. For weeks we battered them with every chemical, biological and projectile weapon in our arsenal. When we surveyed the damage, we hauled away our dead and marveled at their abilities. A force field prevented our weapons from reaching their targets. Even our guarded nukes caused only a temporary halt in their assault. Once we exhausted our supply, the alien advance continued.

They were relentless and merciless. They did not take prisoners; they did not establish a dialogue. As the war raged, tidbits of information leaked. From confiscated technology, we learned how they conquered thousands of worlds in their march across the cosmos, enslaving populations or eliminating them. They resembled Earth's arthropods with the distinctive head, thorax, and abdominal segments. Enclosed in their biomechanical war suits they were invincible.

Until they met us.

We sacrificed our armies like fodder just to get us within striking range. Millions of men and women charged into a maelstrom of laser beams and exploding ordinance. My limited schooling didn't cover how evolution allowed the altruistic gene propagation, but I witnessed it every day in the deaths of my comrades.

Indian Dave disappeared in a chaotic melee outside the ruins of Moscow after his psionics attack wiped out two alien divisions. Even after he routed the arthropods, we found no trace of my good friend.

We pushed them out of the Americas in a two-month campaign that laid waste to everything east of the Appalachians. That's the last time I saw Katherine. She led the climactic charge that breached their inner defenses. Seconds away from capturing one of the alien ships, the vessel self-destructed, taking her and half of Long Island with it. I still remember the victorious grin on her face captured on the tri-vid, moments before the ship went nova.

A rush of cold air stirred the cave's dank interior and I shivered. Pulling the fleece jacket tighter around my gaunt frame, I took out a small picture from my pocket and shone my penlight on it. The edges are torn and the image faded, but it still brought a lump to my throat. The wind lifting off the waves had messed up Jamie's hair. Dave— acting his usual childish self— stood knee deep in the water casting a set of bunny ears above her head. Katherine laughed at some unheard joke, and I ... I had the only serious expression in the crowd. The forced smile was hollow; the hooded eyes too old for my young face as if staring into a dark future.

My friends are dead. I'm the last. The hunters will find me.

A tear ran down my cheek as I returned the picture to my pocket.

After New York, the war with the aliens continued for another six months. We lost billions. We almost lost our civilization and yet at no point did we consider surrender. Survival was inscribed deep within our genetic code. This wasn't a battle for freedom; this was a battle for our existence.

The final clash outside Beijing was nothing less than genocide. Both sides bled dry by the constant warfare, refused to relent. When we forced our way onto the mother ship, Jamie and I were on the front edge of the assault wave. My psionics bullet killed a trio of aliens before they could initiate the self-destruct mechanism. We needed that

226

technology.

I froze. In the dark, my augmented senses discerned a faint heartbeat.

"Who's there?" I whispered.

A flashlight clicked on, aimed upwards, and illuminated a young face.

"Are you going to kill me?" he asked.

I sensed something on his person. "No," I said.

He shrugged as if the answer was inconsequential. "So, you won't mind if I approach?"

I couldn't move. The moment seemed surreal. My pulse pounded in my ears, the heavy beat pumping not blood but fear through my body.

He took my silence for consent and stepped across the small stream. "You've been hard to find." He tried to make it sound like a compliment.

I aimed my light at him. He looked young, perhaps all of twenty, with thick lips and a broad nose. He reminded me of Indian Dave.

"How did you do it?" I managed, unsure how this would proceed.

"We have trained sensor units now," he said. "Like you psionics, we can detect body signatures, however, we do not have your ... offensive capabilities."

"I don't kill humans," I snapped.

Despite the light shining into his face, he leveled his gaze at me. "The others did."

"I'm not like the others." After all, I was the last of my kind.

"You can't turn it off," he continued, ignoring my protest. "It's part of you, as integral as the motion of your lungs. Eventually, you will use it."

"I fought for humanity—"

He held up his hand, forestalling that line of logic. No doubt he had heard it before. "And we thank you for your sacrifice."

A faint smile crossed his features and I understood at that moment he believed what they had sent here him to say. Like me, someone had trained him from a young age.

"We will remember all of you in the history texts. Proclaimed heroes. We will bestow endless accolades upon your names." He left the word posthumously unsaid. "But you can no longer live among us."

Panic threatened to invade my disciplined mind. "But you'll need my abilities when they return."

He shook his head. "We have your DNA. It will be enough.

Besides, we have captured alien technology to decipher and improve. Next time we will be doubly prepared."

I took a steadying breath. "There was a friend ... a girl, around Buffalo."

He paused. I knew he was gauging how much to tell me.

"One of my colleagues found her. She was hiding in the ruins of a church."

"Jamie," I moaned. She said we stood a better chance splitting up ... that we would meet in the Canadian north.

Something died inside me.

"I'm s ... sorry," the young man stammered, revealing his age. "I'm told she was ... formidable."

A moment of silence passed and his flashlight beam fell to the cavern floor, illuminating a bulky structure strapped to his leg.

"A bomb?" I asked, wiping my eyes.

He nodded. "Something we found on the alien ship. It's connected to my myocardium. The moment my heart muscle stops contracting, the explosive mixture goes critical." He tapped the flashlight gently against it. "It'll take the top off of this mountain."

"Of course," I murmured.

"You are the last," he confirmed, regaining his composure. "You have served your purpose with honor. But humanity must move on."

I watched as he reached into a pocket and pulled out a sidearm. "I am going to shoot you now. You may choose to kill me first thus setting off the bomb or you may simply acquiesce and allow it to happen. Would you like a moment to decide?"

I almost laughed at the irony. I could kill the messenger and prove to the survivors they were right, that I could not live among my fellow humans anymore. That I was no longer human. Or I could allow the man to walk away, unharmed, and show them just how wrong they were.

I pulled out the picture and stared at the raven-haired girl. The image soaked up my anguish, and I smiled. A sense of calmness descended, solidifying my resolve. Mankind didn't evolve from a race of quitters. Our species was stubborn and tenacious. We would fight to the last man, to the last breath ... to the end.

I sent the psionic bullet straight into his brain.

Daybook of the Dead

By Jennifer Bradpiece

The dead don't
get around much anymore.
Door-stop coffins,
button eyes,
no chores
maybe some easy gardening.
Useful in their rigor mortis
repose, maybe mannequins,
if you can stand the smell.
Taxidermy scarecrows,
androgynous monotone
dreams.
If you listen silently for
seven months you may
begin to decipher the didactic
sermons that sent them off.
Each popped like a pea out the sheath
of their leaf on the family tree.
Even post-mortem,
they grow and they grow
in the years populated
by the blood they left
or the skin they touched.
Bloated like drowning
victims, regardless of
how last breaths
were spent,
until they cannot hold the
soaked weight of their
own memory any longer.
Then, like a vacant overgrown
lot, they deflate—
once again flat and vegetative—
uncoiled DNA.
Still, holidays are
less stressful
for the dead.
Their day books linger

open in the middle of
an empty table:
to-do lists short
as winter days
and no use for
day coats.

The Flaming Phoenix
By K.A. Mielke

The human capacity to turn every job into a mundane routine astounds me. It's how I'm here—fingers interlaced with a monster's, biceps bulging as I try to tip this bipedal cow—thinking my job is totally normal.

I grapple with the bull-man. Veins bulge beneath my skin and my feet slip on pavement turned to gravel. Seriously, I have no concept of what this guy is or how he even exists. He's fluffy, has got horns sprouting and spiraling out of his skull, weighs about as much as a Boeing 747, and literally just crawled out of the middle of the road. I do know, however, I'm not getting home by dinner. I don't know what to tell my daughter when I see her devastated face over another botched Daddy-Daughter Night because, to a child, "Sorry, Daddy was out fighting a giant monster and saving the city," isn't some outrageous feat any more than it's a ridiculous excuse. The point is, I'm letting her down. That's all she'll care about.

It's all I care about.

On top of all this, beneath the mask, my dandruff is acting up and I just want a time out so I can scratch myself into scaly white oblivion. My spandex is too tight and hasn't been washed in a week, and it isn't monster-proof or even monster-resistant despite my constant requests for an upgrade. Oh, and those cute women screaming directly to my left—you know, the ones whose lives I'm saving? They can see the outline of my genitals.

I shove back at the bull-man, his claws gripped between my fingers, and I'm wondering whether they're impressed or disappointed. By my junk, that is. Obviously, they're impressed by my amazing strength. Even I'm still impressed by my amazing strength.

"I am The Minotaur!" the anthropomorphic bull screams, spitting foul juices into my face. "Bow to me!"

Oh, now I get it, with the horns and the cow thing. I appreciate his willingness to mine Greek mythology. Everybody loves the classics.

My muscles are working overtime, and I twist and drive The Minotaur into the ground. Debris shoots out as shrapnel and hits my body with sharp little flares of pain. The crowd cheers, claps, and hollers.

"We love you, Flamer!"

"Woo, Phoenix-Man!"

I stop to breathe, hands on my hips. "Seriously, you guys," I say in between breaths, "it's The Flaming Phoenix." I hold up my faux-feather tail and wiggle it around like a used tissue. "Not that hard. Now, get the hell out of here before somebody gets hurt."

I approach the crowd and start shooing them away, but they only close around me tighter.

"I require virgins!" The Minotaur bellows. "Bring me unsullied maidens!"

Underwhelming anger flushes over me as I turn to where I floored him.

"Hold up. Don't you know virginity is just an archaic and damaging social construct created by the patriarchy to shame wom—?"

The swat of a massive arm sends me through the wall of a TD Bank, and it's times like these I wish I had a sidekick or feminist villains to meet eye-to-eye.

"Remember when superheroes didn't shove politics down your throat?" I hear from some guy outside before everyone starts screaming and getting the hell out of here like I suggested so many times.

Chunks of stone wall dig into my back. My head spins like the ceiling fans rotating above me. It's possible I have a concussion.

"Can I get the time?" I say to nobody in particular.

A teller peeks out from behind the counter. "It's seven-thirty, Bird-Man."

Yup. Missed dinner. My sister's going to let me have it, and that's a thought much scarier than anything this Minotaur can do to me.

"Alright." I get to my feet. Dust and stone crumble off my immaculate pectorals like I'm some sort of cookie with immaculate pectorals. That was a bad simile, but I don't have the time or energy for poetry. I shake out my arms—all that wrestling has them feeling as flaccid and useless. "Let's finish this up."

The trick to gaining public trust as a super-powered person is to always sound in control of the situation. You can quote me on that.

The beast slurps and snorts while he's hunched over with his back to me. Everybody's screaming and running off like scurrying rats. I whistle to get this dude's attention, giving them time to escape.

His head whips around.

The Minotaur's face is stained red with blood and veined pink sacs are oozing out of his mouth. A teenage boy, probably in the middle of taking a selfie to remember his action-packed visit to downtown Toronto, lies in two at his feet.

I'm falling, I must be. No, that drop like I've tipped over the edge of a skyscraper is just my gut throwing itself around without a care in the world. My skin freezes despite overheating in a layer of spandex for the last hour. I look at the boy and I want to cry and scream and let my emotions get the better of me, even knowing that's the number one cause of superhero casualties. Right behind capes, obviously.

I hold it all back. I can't let him know. I have to be strong for those still watching from rooftops and windows. For the rest of the city.

For this kid.

"That doesn't look like a young maiden to me," I say, somehow summoning my snark. "Not like that would be much better."

"You have failed your city," The Minotaur mumbles through a mouthful of person. He swallows and my stomach churns, then says clearer, "That is enough for me."

"You act like we have a long-standing rivalry. Reveling in my failure isn't how you make new friends." I roll my shoulders, flex to get some feeling back. Biding my time.

"You've ruined everything, Bird!" he roars, nostrils flaring and eyes bloodshot. "Your fight with The Slime caused the traffic jam that made me lose my job. Without a job, my wife left me, and I lost my car, my house, my life!"

The Slime: a nasty bastard who covered the 401 with snot for hours. Nothing big—didn't even kill anybody—but irritating for everyone involved.

"So now you're a murderer? I feel like that string of events maybe isn't totally my fault. Are you crying?"

He wipes his eyes with a ferocity that can't be good for his vision. "NO, I AM NOT CRYING!"

"Hey, there's nothing wrong with a good cry. Feel free to express yourself however you need. Toxic masculinity has reigned for far too long and, ah shit—"

The Minotaur bounds toward me, flinging cars out of the way with his horns. Metal crushes in on itself. Buildings crumble. People stumble in the distance like the fragile meat-bags they are and are almost doomed by their inability to run fast or far enough away. I'm left with the responsibility of being more, having forced myself into this obligation to protect them.

Instead of my life flashing before my eyes, it's my public image I'm concerned with. I can see the headlines:

Phoenix's Career Up in Flames!

Or, the more blatantly damning:

The Flaming Phoenix Lets Kid Die: Parents Plan to Sue.

I step into position and cock my fist back. My palms and knuckles burn as if squeezing the embers of a campfire, and I scream as my arm is engulfed in flames. Every nerve urges me to stop, and I want to—really, I do—but, I can't.

Some things are more important than what I want.

Daughter of Phoenix-Man Speaks Out: "My Daddy Couldn't Protect Us!"

Death awaits in his eyes, but I no longer fear death. The sidewalk rumbles beneath my feet. The Minotaur leaps and flies through the air. The warmth of his putrid breath moistens the little exposed skin on my body that's not peeling and crisping like lit paper.

My fist hits his nose, crunching bone and cartilage. The flames from my fist spread, flowing from my arm and engulfing the creature in its entirety. My arm then turns to ash and scatters in the wind. The creature, the man, the *whatever*, blasts a guttural roar that reflexively sends my remaining arm to cover my ear. Soon his roar stops as he piles into a small hill of carbon.

Tears run out from under my mask and down my dirt-caked cheeks. I clutch my shoulder stump and grit my teeth, but I can't help but bawl. The streets are empty, so hopefully, nobody is watching their hero cry like a child with a skinned knee.

I stumble to the kid. He smells like iron and shit, but I kneel next to him—this boy, this son, this potential father. A sack of meat and dreams strewn across the pavement.

"I'm sorry." Grabbing his hand, I sit and try not to look at or think about the empty socket of my right shoulder, until I hear the sound of sirens.

His phone rings beside us and rumbles over the pavement. The kid's picture is saved as the backdrop, and the screen has a single long crack spread from corner to corner. I was right about the selfie. I can see me and The Minotaur brawling behind his thumbs-up.

I grab the phone and let it vibrate in my hand.

Once. I close the kid's eyelids over his lifeless eyes.

Twice. I set the phone on the ground, letting the vibration send loose stone into spasms.

A third time. I'm an idiot for not letting it go to voicemail.

"Hello?"

"Hi," the caller says tentatively. Her voice is soft and feminine, like the hollow, tinkly sound of wind chimes. "I'm looking for Peter. Who... are you his roommate, or...?"

"Yeah."

"Is he there?"

I swallow, saliva scraping down my parched throat like nails. My gums feel like rocks. "May I ask who's calling?"

"His sister."

Peter lies with his long black hair fanned out as if floating downstream. His flannel shirt is torn open and his insides are pouring out. Dirt covers his pale, graying skin.

"Is that a siren?" she asks. "Is everything okay?"

"He's, uh, he's actually not in at the moment. Forgot his phone. Can I take a message?"

The sound of sirens gets closer. A block away, if that.

"Can you tell him I'll be at Union Station before eight tomorrow? It's the earliest train I can catch."

"I'll tell him. When he gets back."

"Thank you so m—"

I hang up and place the phone on Peter's chest, above his exposed abdominal cavity. Red and blue lights flash in my periphery and sirens blare in my ear, but I keep staring at that phone—staring and sitting and breathing and thinking.

I grab it and put it in a pouch on my utility belt.

Officers get out and aim their guns at me, cowering behind the useless cover of open cruiser doors. The closest one shouts into his megaphone. "Remove your mask and put your hands on your head."

Struggling through fatigue to raise my hand, I shout wearily, "Only got one, officer." I force myself to stand up.

"Don't move!" the cop demands. "Get on the ground or we'll open fire."

I step over torn up pavement that ripples away from the hole in the earth like waves frozen in time. Smoke gushes out of a jagged split in the street. I wag my finger as I walk, pantomiming a geriatric man telling off his naughty grandchildren.

"Come on, guys, you know me. Do I look like the bad guy here?"

I realize that with the real bad guy gone, a witness dead, and the vigilante left alone in the aftermath, it does look very much like I'm the bad guy here. Plus, I'm not an officially licensed League member, so I am technically a criminal.

Doesn't matter. I'm dead anyway.

"I said," the officer booms into his megaphone, his authoritative voice out in full force, "DON'T! MOVE!"

Something catches on my foot, and I fly forward with my arm outstretched. I get it, Toronto Police Service. I'm a super-powered monstrosity, a wild card, a far cry from a normal dude in civilian clothes. I could very well have been leaping forward to attack you. When your bullets pierce my skin, muscle, and bone, I scream, sure, because being shot feels much like being on fire. But, I also forgive you. We do the same job.

You're just at a disadvantage.

The pavement is cool and refreshing, but not for long. Flames engulf my body, boiling the blood seeping from my open mouth and bubbling my skin. My own screams seem a long way away as if the police are screaming instead, though they might be. I can see only fire until I can't see anything as my eyeballs melt, dribble down my face, and evaporate.

Darkness takes me, but the heat stays, burning, always burning until I'm gone.

With a gust of wind, I scatter over the cityscape.

* * *

I gasp for breath.

I'm filled with a comforting warmth. The warmth of blood flowing through my body. The warmth of being alive. Plus, the warmth of the raging inferno behind me, emanating from the portal and casting my skin in the glow of an extradimensional bonfire. Steel door after steel door slams shut, cutting off the doorway between the world of fire and the world of earth. The incubator opens with a hiss, leaking gas and fluid, and I tumble out into the nest. The scratchy straw and twigs scrape my naked skin and it feels so good, so real, so here.

Dying hurts every damn time. And every damn time I wake up so grateful.

"How was it?"

"Oh, you know. Giant monster crawls out of fucking nowhere and kills people. It's all great fun, all the time," I say as my eyes adjust to the harsh glow of the darkened laboratory.

Brittle twigs are crunching and snapping beneath my weight as I sit up, and my bare ass is itchy atop the enormous bird's nest. I always mean to bring a blanket or something up here, but I never remember.

Several feet below my perch, John hunches over a monitor and marks something down on a clipboard. From up here, I can still see the ketchup stains in his gray beard and the mustard splotches on his lab coat.

The Roost is my home. At least, home to the half of me that runs out and stops crimes by cremating himself. Whenever I die I wake up back here, naked in a giant nest like a freshly-birthed, placenta-covered baby bird. It's not the most dignified rebirth.

"You know what I like about you?" John says. "The snark. I sat down one day and thought, I wasn't a snarky enough Phoenix. We need someone snarkier, who tells everyone his secret identity."

"Hey, my sister isn't everyone. And if you ask me—"

"I didn't."

"—you'd been waiting for the biggest ass-kisser." I step out of the nest and climb down the ladder, all too aware of my ass hanging out. "How surprised you must've been when I developed a personality beyond Rabid Fanboy."

John scoffs. "If it looks too good to be true…" he says, letting the platitude's implications finish itself.

"Did Zoey send me any angry voicemails?"

He shrugs. "I don't keep tabs on your familial problems, and I actively ignore you when you talk about them. Besides, I was busy. You know, working."

He says it like I'm not out there busting my ass in his good name. I grab my bundle of clothes off my desk and get dressed.

"Using cam sites and watching porn is not working."

He laughs until his laugh turns into a barking cough that steals his breath and drops him to his knees with a crack of ligaments. I rush to his side as he coughs hunched over for what feels like forever. I look up at the clock on our comm screen and watch the seconds tick by.

"Tap the floor if it's time for Emergency Protocol."

John waves his hand dismissively.

Eventually, he falls silent and shakes my hand off his back. I help him up.

"I'm fine, I'm fine," he says gruffly. He limps back to the computer and discretely wipes the blood off his hand and onto his black pants.

"Right."

He'll be fine until the day he's not, at which point he won't be able to say otherwise. Until then, we'll keep not talking about why he needed a replacement.

I slip on my jacket and check my phone. There aren't any missed calls and only one text message:

"I'll be charging $75 an hour and starting a GoFundMe to pay for all the damage The Flaming Phoenix causes. Or maybe I'll save up for a Ferrari!"

More fearsome than The Minotaur, stronger than The Giant, more irritating than The Slime, my greatest foe: The Baby Sister. Eating away at my savings account faster than a speeding locomotive— if I actually paid her, that is.

I'm kind of the worst.

"Watch this before you go," John says as I tie my shoelaces. I sigh in anticipation of my next lecture. I walk over, being careful not to trip over one of my still undone shoelaces.

He turns the monitor my way as a recording of me punches The Minotaur in the nose, and both it and my arm vanish. The video pauses.

"How did it get this far?" he asks.

My stomach churns as it digests his disappointment in me, long past its shelf-life. "I don't know."

"Don't 'I-don't-know,' me. Think critically, it could save your life one day."

"As if I can even die."

"There are ways to kill everything in this universe. Think. What could you have done better?"

I phone it in. It's always something obvious or self-deprecating. I just need to get home before Zoey tells our mom I'm neglecting my daughter. "I got cocky. I was too concerned with putting on a show. Snark is, regrettably, my strongest power."

John's hand stings the back of my head. "And because of that, this boy died."

"I know."

"Don't let it happen again. No jokes if the situation isn't under control. And remember, casualties are like car crashes: you drive long enough, you'll get in one. Got it?"

"Sure."

"Good. Now, get out. I've got 'work' to do."

He does the air quotes and everything. As gross as it is, I laugh. I throw my hood up to conceal my face and step out into the hallway.

The doors seal shut, and the lights illuminate the long prison corridor of costumed men and women with absurd powers sitting behind impenetrable glass walls. John built the prison as the main entrance and exit to remind himself of his victories and the reason he fought crime in the first place. He also must enjoy the daily berating the villains give him. I'm not a fan.

"I'm gonna slice off your balls, kid." Classic Knife-Man. I pull my hood down lower on my face and really, really wish these cells were made entirely out of one-way mirror material.

The Roost houses only the worst of my rogue's gallery of all the supervillains over which John or I have yelled, "Dibs!" before some other up-and-comer can claim them. These are the guys that would break out of a standard prison and I had to reduce to ash, making them burn alive before they wake up illegally imprisoned.

The Minotaur now occupies a cell that was empty this morning, sitting on his new narrow bed and twiddling his big furry thumbs.

"I suppose you don't like me any better now, huh?" I say, stopping in front of him.

He doesn't look up at me, which suits me just fine.

238

I lean against the glass. "An innocent boy died today. Real tragedy. He was supposed to be meeting his sister tomorrow. That'll break her heart, right? Finding out her brother was eaten alive by some asshole with a cow fetish. Nothing could prepare you for that level of fucked up."

"He tasted like pork," The Minotaur grumbles with his head hung.

I slam the glass with my fist. Through clenched teeth, I say, "Burn in Hell."

"Already have." He smiles.

Suddenly, they all think they're invincible because I made them burn to death one time and, to their surprise, the death part wasn't as advertised. Like they're fucking Jesus Christ. They don't stop to think that I could have done so much worse.

"I'll write your ex-wife," I say. "She'll be relieved to know you won't be bothering her ever again."

I walk away before he can respond. His roar follows me into the elevator.

The lobby is huge and empty at this time of night. The effect is pretty spooky. Almost post-apocalyptic. Every footstep and squeak of my shoes against the shining, spotless floor echoes back to me, sounding a lot like I'm not alone.

My bike is still chained to the streetlight where I left it. This should be a given, but you never know. The Flaming Phoenix has had to track down a few bike thieves.

I put my headphones on, play the radio on my phone, and bike home in the dark. The radio tells me all about the things I've done, including being suspiciously close to a mangled young man and being shot to death again. Bystanders looking for their fifteen minutes defend or condemn me, whatever it takes to push their agenda before their time is up. I pedal faster, pushing harder as my thighs burn from the effort, speeding alongside cars. Downtown turns into long strips of shopping plazas which turns into tucked-away suburbia.

Zoey is sitting on the porch with a cigarette in hand when I skid into the driveway. A white headband holds back her hair and puts her disdainful frown on full display. She's in her Grim Crusader pajamas, just to piss me off. (The guy's such a jerk; he's been seen screaming at fans until they cry.)

"That'll be an extra fifty for extreme overtime," she says, holding out her hand.

"Very funny."

I pull open the garage door and lean my bike against the wall. The garage door slams on the concrete.

"Sometimes I'm not your biggest fan."

"BUT I AM JUST YOUR BIGGEST FAN, FLAMING PHOENIX!"

"Jesus, shut up!" I say as I scan the empty street.

She stands and puts her smoke out in the ashtray on the porch banister. "Relax, it was just a joke. Rough day at the office?"

"Something like that."

My place is torn apart from one end to the other. Shoes, hats, and mismatched gloves that shouldn't be out of storage flatten underfoot in the hallway. Toys lie scattered about the living room floor and the coffee table and drape over the television. A ladder of small army men descending the electric fireplace and a mountain of undone dishes teeters dangerously close to the edge of the counter.

"Would it kill you to clean up?" I ask without thinking, which is just about the worst thing I could have done. If I had time travel in my list of superpowers...

"Are you fucking kidding?"

I keep walking towards the kitchen, not turning to look at her.

"I only picked up your daughter, cooked her dinner, did homework with her, consoled her when she cried for half an hour because Daddy wasn't home, and put her to bed. Oh, plus I have covered for your vigilante ass every day for, what, three years now? Is that how long she's been gone? So excuse me for not having the time to clean up after myself, how rude of me."

"You're right," I say meekly.

"Yeah? And?"

Sighing, I continue, "And I'm sorry."

"Damn right," Zoey says, stomping off to her bedroom. "Ain't no goddamn respect in this house," she mutters from the top of the stairs, sounding eerily like Mom.

I empty the sink of any remaining dishes and run the hot water. A small hand tugs on my jeans.

"Look at this sneaky kid, gettin' past Aunt Zoey," I say, smiling. I pick Kitty up and wet her cheek with a big, sloppy kiss. "Good evening, baby. How was your day?"

She avoids eye contact. Her bottom lip sticks out as if stung by a bee.

"You missed our date."

"I know. I'm sorry. How can I make it up to you?"

Steam rises from the sink and I plunge my hand beneath the suds and water.

"Daddy! Isn't that hot?"

"Mm? Oh, right. Ow!" I dramatically tear my hand free from

the water, shaking droplets of dishwater around the kitchen. "Why didn't you warn me?"

"It's not silly time, Daddy." Kitty slumps over my shoulder. "I'm upset with you."

"Can I make it up to you with... popcorn?"

She shakes her head.

"How about chocolate?"

"You can't buy my love, Daddy."

"What about with a pony?"

"We don't have anywhere to put a pony!" She pushes away and drops to the floor, dragging her feet out of the kitchen. I turn off the tap.

"What are you talking about?" I ask as I follow her to her bedroom. "We can give it your room."

"Then where will I sleep?" Kitty climbs into bed, and I lay down beside her. I brush curly strands of hair out of her eyes.

"In my room, of course."

"I can't sleep with you. I'm a big girl," she mimics.

"You can have it. I'll sleep in the living room. Does that sound like a good plan?"

She nods her head and her eyes close. We don't talk anymore, but I run my nails lightly along her back, doodling invisibly until I hear her breathing become deeper and more relaxed. I sneak out of her room and make some coffee.

The heavy cream swirls into the darkness, transforming my coffee into a battlefield. Body parts strewn down Yonge Street, cars overturned, the sky the red of the blood flowing down the gutter. One face, the face of a young boy so much like me, once, with a family to love him and mourn him, mouthing words.

"You let me down"?

No. That's not it. That's too subtle.

"You let me die."

Tears ripple onto the canvas, washing away the scene.

"Daddy?" Kitty whines from the hallway.

"Go back to bed, sweetie!" I cry. I'm shaking, heat coursing through me. My fingers press into the wooden table. It feels like oxygen isn't making the trip to my lungs, stopped halfway due to heavy traffic.

"But I'm hungry."

"I'm sure Aunt Zoey gave you dinner. Go back to bed, please, you have school tomorrow."

"I don't want to go to school! I want food."

"I SAID BACK TO BED!" The sound of my voice scares

even me. I can hear her start to cry, run back to her room, and slam the door.

　　She'll get over it.

　　She's used to it.

　　Zoey's door opens and she shuffles to Kitty's room, wordlessly but not without judgment, the way she does whenever I fuck up at parenting. I want to scream at her and drag her out of my daughter's room because I am the boss, and I am the parent, but I do nothing. I take my hands from the smoking table, their heat engraving black, finger-shaped burns into the waxed wood, and press their warmth to my sore eyes.

　　"I'm sorry. I'm so sorry."

* * *

　　Union Station is encased by the same endless construction bullshit that's surrounded it since I moved here: the scaffolding, fencing, torn up dirt, and cement that never seems to attract any construction workers. Granted, my own tearing up of city streets probably doesn't help propel city renewal projects, but this is the scathing self-criticism of The Flaming Phoenix, not a critical review of my heroics by the mayor.

　　The sun creeps into the sky as the hands of my watch creep closer to seven o'clock. Pallid colors mark the horizon with pinks and oranges that remind me of the colors of the spandex I'm not wearing. It always feels like I'm wearing the Phoenix though, especially when I'm not. I double-check inside my shirt, fiddle with the buttons of my coat, and pop up the collar.

　　I head downstairs to the vast maze connecting GO trains to subway trains to buses, and I grab a coffee and sit down. Without waiting for it to cool, I gulp mouthfuls of the scalding liquid while looking for someone lost, alone, confused. When enough time has passed, I move to a different vantage point, sitting at benches around the underground until I decide she mustn't be downstairs at all. I get a second coffee and head upstairs.

　　The Grand Hall is full of tourists. I sit down and keep my eyes on the backlit clock and the departure board in the center of the massive room. People flit in and out, scuttling across the reflective floor, furrowing brows at cell phones and maps. Everybody's varying degrees of lost, but no one stays for long.

　　I slouch over my knees and rub my tired eyes. This is a waste of time. What was I going to say if she had come? "Oh, sorry I couldn't save your brother. Yeah, I'm a superhero. Yeah, your brother's dead.

Enjoy Toronto!" I stand up and swill my coffee, tossing it in the trash before I go.

A rack of newspapers catches my eye. Splashed across the front page are The Flaming Phoenix and The Minotaur, like the cover of a comic book. The headline reads *One Dead, Multiple Injured in Superhero Scuffle*. Why wasn't I prepared for this? The news cycle was bound to cover my first casualty. I'm the worst kind of idiot. This girl's probably already read the story on every social media platform in existence.

A phone rings in my pocket, playing the theme song from an obscure eight-bit video game.

It's not my phone. Hurriedly, my hand fumbles with the outside of my pocket, desperately trying to silence Peter's cell phone. I look up.

I think I see her. A young woman of South East Asian descent, long black hair, lingering. She looks back at me, a curious expression on her face, and walks toward me. Blood pounds in my ears.

"Excuse me," she says, voice light, soft; tinny. She smiles nervously, dimples forming in her cheeks. "You've been here a while. Have you seen a young guy a bit taller than me? Long black hair. Dead brown eyes. Entrails like what you'd find on a butcher's floor. Soul fleeing the body. Been told he looks a bit like me, though I don't really see it. I swear, I've spent the last hour just finding my way back here. This place is huge."

She doesn't know yet.

Shaking my head, I have to pry my teeth apart from their clenched embrace to mutter, "N-no. No, I'm afraid I haven't."

"That's weird. Normally he'd be here early. He's very punctual. Not something I inherited." She laughs nervously.

"Family?" I ask, thumbing a Loonie in my pocket.

She pinches the tips of the hair sitting at her chest, twisting and untwisting the strands between her fingers. "My brother. He's supposed to show me around the city today. I don't get to come down much with school and everything. Are you visiting somebody?"

"I'm a resident. Just, uh, waiting for a friend."

We've started walking, meandering toward the doors. I'm thinking of ways to get her back on the train home without putting my identity at risk. Chasing her around like a crazy person as either myself or my alter ego wouldn't end well.

"Oh, cool!" she says, her face lighting up in excitement. "Have you ever seen The Flaming Phoenix? I'm a huge fan. My brother, Peter, he says he knows all the Phoenix's favorite hangouts. Figured one of these days he'd see him without his mask, or get his autograph or something. Maybe, snap a picture and send it my way."

"That's funny," I say, but I don't laugh. "I used to be his biggest fan."

"Used to be?"

Cars caved in and overturned. Blood pooling in gutters, leaking beneath the streets.

"I lost faith," I say coldly. "Realized he couldn't save everyone. You know."

"No, I heard about that," the girl says. "Somebody died yesterday, right? It's horrible. But, like, imagine being The Flaming Phoenix in that situation. Most people don't—can't—do anything about supervillains. I think what matters is that he tries even when he can't save everyone. He probably has a life of his own, you know? Family to meet at the train station and all that."

The tears come before I can stop them, careening down and staining my cheeks, dripping onto my shirt. She doesn't know. How the hell doesn't she know?

The woman frowns and puts her hand on my shoulder. "Are you okay?"

I want to thank her, but I just nod.

Standing beneath the electronic board listing transportation departure times, Peter's sister thanks me anyway, wishes me a good day, hopes I feel better, and gets back to looking for her deceased brother. My stomach knots as I think about her spending the day here waiting for a brother that will never come while the rest of the world reads a message meant for her.

Nausea worsens when I think about the inevitable: eventually, she'll find out he's dead and that it's my fault, and then she won't think trying hard is all that matters. It's a matter of time before she's called in to identify his body. The way she views the world will change into something darker, scarier.

I've changed this woman forever. All because two strangers had to go punching each other in the street and had to escalate things until someone died. The ripple effects of violence.

I watch her disappear into the labyrinth that is Union Station. I don't know what I expected. I don't even know what I wanted. But, if I leave now, maybe Kitty and Zoey and I can catch a movie. The Flaming Phoenix can take a break and live his life. Appreciate what he has before it's gone, you know?

Opening the door onto the blinding world outside, I take a deep breath.

"Nobody move!" screams a man behind me.

He stands purposefully in the center of the room and drops his trench coat, revealing a glass tube of black liquid on his back, attached to ten hoses.

He says, "This is a squick-up!" because he's The motherfucking Squid. He means 'stick-up' but he's The Squid, not The Pun Maker, who is an entirely different shade of crazy.

With a groan and a conspicuous change of outfit, I appear in front of him in a pillar of flame and punch his stupid face. His nose crunches between my knuckles and squirts blood onto my Kevlar beak.

I shake the pain from my hand. The "supervillain" squirms on his back, little more than a turtle, holding his face.

I turn to go.

"What, no snarky come back?" The Squid squeals in outrage. "No witty repartee? What's the deal?"

Ignoring him, I pull out my cell phone and call the police. Then I text Zoey about the movie.

"Come back here and banter like a real man!" The Squid cries.

And, like a real man, I leave so I can spend more time with my daughter.

I wonder what's playing.

Memory Box

By Lisa Fox

"To A Sweet Daughter"
A shimmering heart
adorns the yellowing cardstock.
"Love, Mommy," you signed
with teacher-perfect printing.

"Sweet Sixteen, A Mother's Pride"
A young girl's silhouette
stands framed in lace,
understated and elegant.
"Love always, Mom" inscribed within –
confident loops pressed with a firm hand.

"My Daughter, My Friend"
Two women hold hands
as they watch the sunset.
I trace my finger over your signature,
the shaky cursive scrawled over the matte parchment.

I lay the cards in a box
and close the lid.
No flowers this time,
no tears.
Just a smile
as I remember.

The Day Death Died
By Boris Glikman

It was widely known that Death had been ailing for some time. Its poor health made it slipshod in the execution of its duties. Whole generations were taken away in the flower of their youth, while others were living for an extraordinarily long time—over 400 years in certain cases.

For a while, Death hovered in a half-alive condition with one foot in the grave, and mankind held its breath, fearing Death would rally and make a complete recovery.

Then the day came when Death breathed its last.

Nobody believed their good fortune. It was hard to grasp that Death no longer dwelled in the world and that life would never be burdened with the ever-present spectre of extinction hovering nearby. No one would have to grapple with the problem of incorporating one's own demise into their lives.

The task of performing an autopsy on Death was assigned to the most eminent pathologists of the land. Their unanimous conclusion was that Death died of natural causes. Nobody had suspected that Death possessed a finite life span. Everyone assumed it would live forever, yet it too carried within itself the lethal seeds of mortality.

The burial of Death was humanity's next most pressing concern, for the world wanted to be sure Death was dead and would not rise again. Where should the funeral ceremony be held? According to which religion's rites should the memorial service be conducted? Who should give the eulogy? Where to entomb it?

The matter of whom to invite to the service proved to be the most intractable issue of all. A number of tickets were reserved for those most affected by Death's passing—morticians, grave diggers, psychotherapists, blues singers, goths and horror film directors. Otherwise, it was impossible to distinguish the genuinely grief-stricken from those who only wanted to attend to be a part of this historic occasion.

Eventually, all of these matters were resolved by the International Committee for the Interment of Death. After lengthy debates, the Committee announced that the ceremony will be held in Jerusalem's Church of the Holy Sepulchre, the site of Jesus Christ's crucifixion, for Death's death was seen as the ultimate fulfilment of Christ's promise of Eternal Life. The heated objections of atheists and adherents of other religions were appeased somewhat by granting them special dispensation to be present at the ceremony inside the church. The world's political leaders and its leading religious figures, philosophers and scientists all gave eulogies, each expressing their own views on the meaning of Death and the meaning of its demise. It was widely agreed that Death was given the exact send-off that it deserved.

Straight after the funeral, the world kicked up its heels and celebrated.

When the unbridled, hysterical wave of joy at being liberated from Death's tyrannical rule had abated, people sobered up and recounted the ways Death helped out in the past.

They recalled with fondness Death's unique ability to provide clear-cut and definitive solutions to any inextricable, inflexible or abstruse problem of existence; its unmatched faculty of erasing the pain, shame and misery of those affected, for example, by unbearable physical suffering or by severe mental anguish; the way it was always there, ready and obedient, offering a helping hand to anyone who asked for it; the way it brought equality to the world, and the way it granted perpetual rest to the weary.

Religions could no longer survive without Death, for their appeal and authority derived from the promise of ideal and everlasting existence in the next world and their expert knowledge of the Afterworld. New religions arose, prophesying that mortality will return to Earth and the virtuous will be rewarded with Eternal Death.

Mankind recognised how much it depended upon Death's existence for the preservation of social order and peaceful international relations. Given that capital punishment and armed conflicts ceased holding any threat to a person's life, nothing stood in the way of lawlessness and immorality in human affairs, and countries went to war on the slightest pretext.

Life lost its meaning, for Death provided the contrast that distinguished being from non-being. Without it, existence turned into a grey shadow of its former vibrant self, and being alive was now an unendurable, yet inescapable, fate worse than death.

Each human being was forced to search for the strength and courage needed to face a baffling future where the saving grace of demise no longer existed. Only then did they realise how inextricably Death had woven its fateful thread into every aspect of man's existence and how much they had irremediably lost the day Death died.

Resolution

By Ethan Jones

I dropped my equipment in the back and slammed the van's door, staring at the faded sign,

S. Mackle and D. Gerson Exterminating

If It Scurries – Never Worry!

Dave had insisted on that rhyme, but I hated it.
I touched his name for a second, closed my eyes, and breathed.

I got into the front seat and turned the key. It chugged, it protested, but it started. I worried about the old girl – she had nigh on 150,000 miles – but she was almost as reliable as the day Dave and I bought her. Just a little cranky.
Today's wet sky gave up its light without fanfare, flint to graphite to charcoal. Typical Portland January. I'd just killed a nest of rats—mom, dad, and baby—at a bungalow in Montavilla, one of the far-flung city neighborhoods that used to be affordable.
This year I'm going to…
I'd been trying to think of a good resolution for weeks. I was never good at them, but I always tried. Last year, it was the typical stuff: lose weight, save money, drink less. I'd done well on the first two, but then. . .
But then, October 21st.
I pulled the flask out of my jacket, took a swig—just a small one—put it away, and popped a mint.
The van's engine chugged, and I checked my phone for the address of the next job. It was far away in St. Johns. I wasn't looking forward to the rush hour traffic, and I was going to be late. I called the client's number.
"Hey, yes, this is Steve Mackle. Yes, the exterminator. Sorry to do this to you, but I'm going to be about twenty minutes late depending on traffic. My last job took longer than I thought it would. Ok. Thanks for your understanding. Bye."
I set up my navigation and hit the gas pedal.
This year I'm going to. . .
Maybe I'd do one of those "live life to the fullest" things. But, it wasn't like I could just sell the van and the business and jet off to

Tahiti. I mean, I *could*, but what would happen when the money ran out?

It would be disrespectful to Dave if I did anything too out of character right now. I wasn't the kind for impulsive decisions, anyway. Dave knew that. For me, everything had a plan.

This year I'm going to. . .

I'd had my mourning.

I had to find the colors again myself.

Up the winding road that skirted Mount Tabor, the volcano covered in pine and cedar, down Burnside past the mansions, right on Cesar Chavez, the street named after the farmer labor leader who could never afford to live in this city now, up the city's spine to its northernmost edge. St. Johns, the city's fifth quadrant, the small town within the big city.

This year I'm going to. . .

Should I take up a new hobby? Sewing always interested me, but the startup costs intimidated me. I'd actually shopped around for a machine, but the good ones cost hundreds of dollars. Then there was fabric, supplies, and I didn't have the foggiest clue where to even begin with any of it.

I could brew beer. Everyone in this city did that. But forgetting the competition, the startup costs, and the complication, there was also the fact that I might make poison instead of beer. And I didn't really have space for a brewing setup in our. . .*my* small garden duplex.

Although these days it seemed so much bigger.

I turned left where Siri told me to and looked for the house. Early 1900s craftsman bungalows oozing expensive charm filled the neighborhood. Small neat lawns straddled buckled sidewalks towered over by skeletons of trees and flanked by rose bushes. I pulled over, got out, slid open the side door and grabbed my equipment.

My customer's house was typical for the neighborhood. Wood stairs led to a big covered porch framed by wrought iron columns, friendly dormers and a low-pitched roof. I knocked on the door.

This year I'm going to. . .

What would Dave's resolution have been? Some wild scheme to write the great American novel, open a gourmet catering business or who the hell knew. Every year Dave dreamed big, and every year nothing came of it.

Except the exterminator business. That was his idea. His way for the two of us to quit the desk job grind and do something more interesting. Together. He talked me into it despite my arachnophobia, insisting that we'd focus more on rats and vermin than on bugs and skittering things. But the bug jobs came, and he and I had our fair share of arguments over accepting jobs like exterminating the nest of black widows under the porch. We always did, of course, and I gritted my teeth. Did my best.

The gray-haired woman who answered the door stared at me with brown eyes behind thick glasses and a tight bun. She wore an argyle sweater, mom jeans and fuzzy slippers on her feet.

"Hi, I'm Steve Mackle, the exterminator," I said.

"The rats are in the garage. Here's the key," she said, "Knock again when you're done." She handed me a small brass key and closed the door in my face.

I walked around to the detached garage, strapped on my headlamp and adjusted it to light the path in front of me.

The garage door slid open manually. I put the key in the center handle and hoisted the door upwards.

Inside, I fumbled and found a light switch. A bare bulb in the center flickered on.

The garage looked like it never had a car parked in it. Tools and supplies rested in labeled white drawers against the back wall. A lawnmower, assorted shovels and spades, and other yard equipment shared space in one corner. A box labeled "Christmas Decorations" sat next to another one labeled "Halloween Decorations" on a high shelf. It was a practical garage for a practical family. A neat slice of a tidy life. A family that had figured out all the big questions long ago, and now only needed to know where the hammer was.

I thought that Dave and I would get there someday. I could see him now, coming out to this garage to get the lawnmower. Fighting to mow the thicket of grass that had accumulated in the three weeks of near daily rainfall since the last dry day. Coming in for a glass of lemonade, smelling of grass, sweat and gasoline. Staying for a kiss.

Memories of things that could never happen didn't care if they were clichés.

I took the flask out, looked at it, and thought about another sip. Just a little one.

A scurrying from the corner near the lawn equipment brought me back. I put the flask away and adjusted my headlamp as I crouched down looking for the telltale signs.

I found the hole. The baseboard had rotted away some, likely due to rain intrusion, allowing the rats to get in from outside.

First order of business was to seal the hole so the rats couldn't chew it open again. I had to remember to tell the homeowner to get these baseboards repaired, and get someone out here to talk to her about water intrusion.

I looked carefully for any other holes, but that seemed to be the only one. I put out the glue traps.

That was that. On my way out, I turned off the light and locked the garage door behind me. When I knocked on the front door, the woman with the gray bun opened it and eyed me again through her glasses.

"I plugged the rat hole and put out some traps." I said, and handed her back the key. "I'll come back on Friday and check on them, ok? Be careful walking around out there not to step on the traps."

"Thanks," she said, and handed me a check.

"Make sure you get your baseboards fixed and have someone come out here to check the garage for water intrusion. Rats like to get in through weak spots, and water likes to make that easier for them."

"Ok thanks." She closed the door.

I sat in the van for a few minutes with my eyes closed and the engine running, glad that I had no more customers today. I needed a drink, a shower, and another drink.

This year I'm going to. . .

What kind of resolution did I need, anyway? A big, meaty project that would distract me and get me out of my own head? Or maybe just a few small, simple things that might give me trivial satisfaction.

My phone rang. It was AJ, a longtime friend who was always good for a warm night at a bar. Exactly the kind of night I needed right now.

"Hey AJ, what's up?"

"Haven't heard from you in a few weeks."

They'd come out as non-binary while we were in college together, and I'd been the first cis person they'd trusted to tell. A decade later, we were still close.

And since October 21st they'd been the hand hoisting me slowly upwards out of hell.

"Mick's? Like in an hour and a half? I have to get home and shower."

"Yeah no problem," said AJ.

I drove home on surface streets, taking shortcuts to avoid traffic. Our apartment. . .*my* apartment. . .was in far Southeast Portland, a cheaper part of town. Two duplexes framed a central courtyard on a street lined with small bungalows. Like everyone, I worried about my rent being raised.

I stepped inside, the air still wrong, the silence still empty. I shook it off.

I showered, lingering, breathing in the steam. I dressed in

simple clothes, warm and comfortable, slipped on my old sneakers, and checked myself in the mirror. The dark circles were starting to fade from under my eyes, but...was that *gray* in my beard? Plucking them made my eyes water, so I gave up.

Mick's, a neighborhood dive bar, was only a few minutes away. It served strong cocktails, good beer, the best onion rings I'd ever had, and almost never had blaring sports on the TV.

Most importantly, it wasn't anywhere Dave and I had gone together. No memories to get stuck in.

AJ sat at a booth with a martini. They'd cut their black hair short, but were dressed, as always, in their own modern interpretation of Annie Hall. We hugged. I sat opposite them.

"So? Nu?" AJ asked, using their favorite Yiddish expression.

"The usual."

The waitress came over. "Double Jack, neat," I said. "And some onion rings."

She nodded and left.

"Still?" asked AJ.

"What still? It's my drink."

AJ took a deep breath and leaned back. "All right. It's time."

"What?"

AJ gave me the look. I knew what it meant. I *wasn't ready*.

But something had already shifted in my mind. For the first time since I lost him, I *wanted* to be ready.

This year I'm going to...

I wanted a better resolution. Something to put my life into sharper focus. Something to help me see the colors again.

"I ... don't know, AJ. OK? I just. . ." I couldn't put it into words yet.

AJ nodded. "We've had this conversation. A lot."

"I know."

"And how does it always go?"

"You'll say, 'You two were together for a long time. It's going to be really hard.'"

AJ nodded. "And then *you'll* say..."

"I'm not ready."

"And then I nod and decide to give you some more time to grieve."

"And I appreciate it. I. . .need more time." I did. Although. . .

"Ok, so here's the next part of the conversation," AJ said. "The part I've been waiting to have with you."

"What?"

AJ paused, and then launched into it. "You're drinking too

much. Way too much. And you're falling into the pain instead of climbing out of it. It's time to start. . ."

AJ's voice faded as my drink arrived. I stared into the glass, thought about how it lit the dark places with warm amber. How it softened the sharp edges that just started to dull. How it kept me company in ways I thought I needed, but probably not as much anymore.

I turned my attention back to AJ, their kind eyes boring a hole in the barriers I'd put up.

"Steve..."

Dave appeared on the other side of the booth, a reflection lit by amber. I remembered him, all of him. His blond hair, before he lost it to the chemo. The warmth of his cheeks, before they went sallow. His sky blue eyes, before the light went out of them.

I saw his smile, felt the warmth of his hand on mine.

"Let go," he said.

I fought, sank deeper into the amber.

"Let go," he said again.

"No," I whispered. "I can't." The glass trembled at my lips and I dove in. Heat hit me as hard as the words this ghost of a memory was saying to me.

"Let. Go."

Something broke, shattered the amber. I glimpsed the colors again, blurry and far away.

I blinked, clearing my vision, and breathed hard. I pushed the glass away and looked up at AJ.

This year I'm going to...

Let go.

Letter from the Bereaved
By Sara Marchant

Dear Makers of the Final Rest, Velvet-Lined, Sliding Lid Teak Box,

 We are writing to lodge a small complaint about a feature of your product which our family purchased to contain the ashes of our departed ex-brother-in-law. We are not complaining about the price—although it was absolutely absurd—of a fancy box that was only used briefly to transport ashes from the crematorium to the spot where we illegally scattered them. The price is the price. It was our foolish sister's foolish decision to pay it, no doubt to assuage her guilt over abandoning her cancer-stricken husband of thirty years for another man. Not that we are casting judgment. Only our sister will ever know what being in her marriage was like, although we are beginning to get small clues about the man whose chemo-addled last request included instructions to be scattered in such a god-forsaken spot.

 We, the ex-wife, the children, the children's mates, the children's children, the ex-mother-in-law, and the ex-sister-in-law, are not accustomed to the dusty hinterlands of backwoods California on a hot August afternoon. Had we realized we'd be tromping through gopher-hole filled, drought denuded soil covered with tumbleweeds—did you know tumbleweeds are not natives of this land, dear Makers? Tumbleweed seeds came in the bedding of emigrants from the Russian Steppes—these rattlesnake sheltering, thorny skeletal remains of bushes no more belong here than we, in our city sandals and pastel-colored dresses, with our lacquered nails and gel-combed hair, do. But I digress from the issue at hand: the box in which we carried our loved one's ashes.

 We are not writing to complain about the crazy sliding lid with its hidden catch that left a group of teary-eyed, grieving people mad with frustration on the side of the road as they broke their fingernails and tempers trying to pry open the stupid goddamn box like it was one of those Chinese treasure puzzles evil grandparents gift to their least favorite grandchild. But instead of a twenty dollar bill, when we finally understood that the fucking lid slid open to the left—the left! like we were reading the Torah— all we found was a gallon-sized plastic baggy containing chalky dust and bone shards. Although we're not complaining about that either, that startling bag of once-human dust because what the hell else were we expecting? Pixy Stick powder without the stick? Clinking gold coins? Lucky Charm Cereal? A creepy clown doll in a polka dotted dress waving his plastic hands in glee? What the hell else were we expecting?

Waiting for the putative clown doll to burst out, studying those dry shards of humanity, we couldn't help but picture our Loved One looking down upon us as we stood in the hot, windy stink at the end of summer, trying to celebrate the life of a man we were beginning to realize that maybe we didn't know as well as we thought we did. Or maybe we all knew a different version of the same man, but we couldn't help but visualize him laughing his ass off at the silly mortals he'd left behind.

But you will not hear us complaining of how he, the departed, now views us. Laugh away, we say. Openly mock our ineptitude at bidding you adieu, we beg. You have the right to laugh, Beloved, we all realize in our own way. We all have it coming.

No, we are not complaining about a dead man's attitude towards us.

What we are complaining about is the hard plastic zip tie that was used to close off the bag of ashes and then clipped short. That thing was impossible to break or cut or loosen with any of the tools we had available, namely our nails and teeth. We ended up flipping the baggy over and ripping the bottom open along the seam.

It was a windy day, dear Makers of the Final Rest, Velvet-Lined, Sliding Lid Teak Box. The Santa Ana's were blowing and we were crying tears of grief, anger, and frustration. We were not prepared for a face full of ash. We were not satisfied with the resulting mask of a powdered former loved one. We could have lived without knowing how human dust grits between the teeth.

In conclusion, Dear Makers, please do not send us any Discounted Cremation Coupons in response to this letter as you did to our last. Insult to injury, we say.

Sincerely Yours,
The Bereaved

Shower

By Aaron Pasker

He hobbled behind the tour group, putting distance between himself and the pack.

If anyone had bothered to look back they may have thought his lagging was due to the pain in his old knees, or from the weight of his backpack. Both were true, but not his intention. He lagged with purpose, waiting for a chance to slip away.

As the group rounded one of the crumbling barracks he took the opportunity and shuffled up against its red brick wall. He listened as the footsteps tamped on and the tour guide's voice faded. After a minute of silence, he chanced a peak around the corner.

The gravel path was empty and he was finally alone.

He tightened the straps of his backpack one more time then started off, using his cane to maintain his balance under the weight. He hobbled along the route he had walked so many times.

The buildings had changed, wood and brick torn from most of them, leaving shells of what he remembered.

"I'm here," he whispered to them.

The breeze whistled threw the fences and dilapidated buildings.

"I'm here!"

His words echoed back.

"Are you? Still?"

Silence.

He continued trudging along. It wasn't long before he reached the single shower building that still stood.

He hobbled up to its steel door. Though worn and weathered by time, it was still the door he remembered. The door he had watched for months as the women and children went in, sniffing and crying. The door he locked behind them.

He took a last look around, checking for any witnesses. When he was sure he was still alone he pushed the door open. It wasn't locked—would never be locked again.

He lumbered inside, the weight of the backpack heavier with every step.

There wasn't much left. Not even the faux showerheads. It was just a brick-walled room with concrete pillars. That was it. All people these days would see.

He imagined the lines of tourists coming to visit, paying their somber respects, but never seeing what he had. Never truly knowing this place.

He took off the backpack, letting it fall to the concrete floor with a soft thump. He leaned against the nearest pillar and slid down to sit.

He pulled the backpack to him and unzipped it. From inside he pulled out his old black and gray uniform, his boots, a tin can, a bottle of sulfuric acid, and the cardboard box full of pellets that had taken so long to procure. He arranged the items in a neat row in front of him.

He undressed as so many others had been forced to do at gunpoint.

"I'm sorry. So sorry."

He pulled on the pants of his old uniform.

"I should have had the courage to walk through that door seventy years ago."

His voice echoed off the walls.

He put on the dress shirt of his old uniform and pulled up the same knee-high boots he had worn while guarding this place.

"I should have had the courage to try and stop it."

The walls didn't answer.

He twisted the cap from the bottle of acid and poured it into the tin can.

"I should have had the courage not to be a part of it."

He opened the cardboard box, poured the small black pellets into his hand, and tightened his fist around them.

"I have no excuse for you. Just cowardice."

He opened his fist and dropped the pellets into the acid. They boiled as they touched it, releasing an almond-scented cloud of white fumes.

"Judge as you will."

Schutzstaffel Trooper Otto Hoffman inhaled a deep breath.

Karyotype
By Deborah L. Staunton

I study the small, black
caterpillar-like marks
Their story
written in a solitary word:
abnormal.
An extra chromosome
on the thirteenth pair.
So thirteen really is an unlucky number.
I search
the unfamiliar image
for the intangible,
willing the black marks
to rearrange themselves
into something less foreign,
less removed from the son I will never know.

The Authors

Learn more about the authors at <u>Ourlossanthology.com</u>

Aaron Pasker, Alice Lam, Andrea Goyan, Bernadette Fah, Boris Glikman, Cari Greywolf Rowan, Chad V. Broughman, Christy Nicholas, Connor Edick, Deborah L. Staunton, Donald J. Bingle, Edward Ahern, Erica Marchant, Ethan D. N. Jones, Jennifer Bradpiece, Joanna Michal Hoyt, Joshua George, Judi Dettorre, KJ Hunter, K.A. Mielke, Leah George, Les Bernstein, Leslie Cushman, Lisa Fox, Liz Perry, Lynne Buchanan, Mark Towse, M. Kari Barr, Melissa Schell, Michael Riley, Michael Simon, Michelle Tang, Mika Doyle, Benjamin R. Barnes, Samantha Pilecki, Robert Stephenson, Robert Walton, Sara Marchant, Winston Plowes.

Made in the USA
San Bernardino, CA
23 July 2019